In Leicester Fields

Also by Ross Gilfillan:

In Leicester Fields

The Snake Oil Dickens Man

The Edge of the Crowd

Losing It

Crime and Punishment in Victorian London

Writing as J.R. Fillan:

The Capo's Daughter

In Leicester Fields

Ross Gilfillan

This edition published 2026

First published in Great Britain in 2025 by Ballingdon Books
ISBN: 978-1-9192184-2-7
First edition
A CIP record for this title is available from the British Library.)

BALLINGDON
BOOKS

In Leicester Fields

Ross Gilfillan

This edition published 2026

First published in Great Britain in 2025 by Ballingdon Books
ISBN: 978-1-9192184-2-7
First edition
A CIP record for this title is available from the British Library.)

BALLINGDON
BOOKS

For Lisa, Fae, Tom and Alice

With thanks to Leslie Gardiner, Jane Kearns, Mattie Sandys-Renton, Chris Scoggins and other encouraging voices.

Prologue

London, 1783

On the day before the catastrophe in Leicester Fields, another curious note is received by the editors of *The Enquirer*. While the first – slipped under the door a few days earlier – was a terse, nasty little scribble of dark but vague import, the second is sickeningly explicit. As it is addressed to *The Enquirer*, it is opened by Mouse at Molly's. The pot-man stands over him while he opens the letter and appears gratified to see Mouse's face blanche as he digests the warning it contains.

"Trouble, sir?" Dick Clik says, rubbing his hands. "Not bad news, I hope?"

"Nothing of the kind," Mouse says. "Just business, nothing more."

But if this is the business he has found himself in, he isn't sure he wants to continue in it. He tries to refold the repellent paper with inky fingers that he cannot keep steady. His stomach welling with chill nausea, Mouse slips from his stool and exits the coffee-house with as much dignity as he can preserve before briskly making his way eastwards.

For the first time in his life, he marks how many suspicious people there are on the streets of London. Idlers propping gin-shop doorways, sullen labourers awaiting hire, anyone who glances his way. Which of these is watching him, he wonders? But after scurrying through a maze of side-streets and narrow alleyways, colliding with a furious fish-seller on Great Wild Street and almost being run down by carts and cabs in order to avoid an ostler with a lazy eye on Drury Lane – he arrives safe and unmolested on Grub Street.

He closes the door behind him and noisily shoots the bolt before handing the note to *The Enquirer*'s editor – who is lodged in his fireside chair where he cons his latest edition. The slightly older, probably much taller man reads every word of the letter with a lawyer's attention. Then he smiles, shakes his head. Mouse is surprised, somehow dismayed, to see that rather than being duly terrified, Obadiah is gratified. Observing him spring to his feet and clap his hands, Mouse thinks to himself that a folded fifteen-pound note could hardly have pleased him more.

"At last," he says to Mouse's questioning face, "I had begun to entertain doubts, Morris, I had started to think we were going too far without solid proof."

"I have been thinking the same. We must desist."

"And lose our new readership? Not we, Mouse."

"Obadiah, you must see sense. This is a final warning."

He reads his friend's face for some sign of agreement, but Obadiah has begun to pace up and down the print room, which he does whenever his blood is up.

"This note tells us we were right all along. We are on the scent. Desist? Not when they think us close upon their heels. Let us go to work, my friend."

Mouse would rather throw away the note and violently upset the forme in which the type is already set to make its explosive revelations.

Once again, he finds himself longing to return to the quieter, safer life he had known such a little while ago.

One

Golden Square, Mayfair. From where he perches atop his hemp-bound tower of creaking, wooden scaffolding, he is lord of London. He lays down his trowel upon the newest-laid course of small, yellow bricks, pops a broken, clay pipe unlit between thick, brown lips, and surveys the city, "Made glorious," he loudly declaims across the tranquil square, "By this pink God's summer sunshine!" Golden Square is wonderfully quiet, he thinks, a continent apart from the crowded court where he sleeps, when God wills it, with his wife and four children. Fifty feet below, the sounds from the street, the chivying of shovel on stone as mortar is mixed, and the complaining of iron-bound cart wheels on new-laid road, are muted by altitude and his own happy distraction.

He arcs his south-easterly gaze from somewhere in the direction of the gardens of Burlington House, over a wilderness of brick and smoking chimney pots towards Covent Garden, that magical place where last night he surrendered himself and a full week's wage to the fragile embrace and juniper breath of a virgin child no more than eleven years old, they had assured him. It's not been a day since that happened, but already he feels better, so much improved. It is, as he said to Pissing Billy that very morning, like two full hods of Essex bricks had been lifted clean from his shoulders.

Now someone is calling from the street below. It's not Billy – he's off to find a place to piss again – but the pretty girl with the unmarked face who sells milk from the beast she drives before her with a switch. "Milk, milko, warm from the cow, milk a half-penny a pint," she's calling. She looks country-fresh and young, someone a man might spend a night with and not pay the awful price. And now there's the rattle of a bunch of keys and the scrape of a heavy door opening. A kitchen maid in a bright white bonnet, clutching a jug and hitching her skirts, pops up from down in the area of the house next door. The milkmaid unstraps her stool and gets to work, talking to her customer all the time, balls of shrill laughter bouncing across the empty square and one or two unfettered words rising to the rooftops.

Now, as if called on stage for his amusement, come the chairmen again, turning into Golden Square, as they have at this time for five Thursdays past, the big, ox-faced one at the front huffing and cursing and a damn to the fines and behind, the other one whose face is hidden by an oversized hat from which sprouts the cue of a grey wig. The big one offers a loud profanity as he sees not only the cow and two heedless women but three men who are unloading stacks of slates from a carrier's cart.

Like two flatirons with a box between them, the men in the dark hats snake and dog-leg around and between the obstacles in their way, the chair swinging wildly, the chairman cursing and whoever is inside holding on, no doubt, for sweet life. The builder chuckles and his broad, white smile follows them as they progress quickly down the road until they turn, a little too sharply, onto Brewers Street and are lost to sight.

Two

Leicester Fields. The room is as the master will have it, sunk once more into utter blackness. Beyond these walls is a bright July afternoon but in here, where the shutters are all closed and locked tight, it might be midnight in Hades. We await the master's word. I'm ready at my bench with my pots and bottles, wearing the oilcloth apron which protects my dress from the worst of the spills. Our guest sits on the high-backed chair I placed in the centre of the room and the master is once again reclusive behind his articulated screens. I can hear him breathing, that rasping, snuffling sound that reminds me of a Suffolk hog rooting for buried apples.

The sitter remains silent when he comes to us now. He's overcome the anxiousness of his initial visits, when his nerves provoked a womanly flow of senseless chatter, a vain attempt to fill the black void. When first he came to this house, in the sedan which the chairmen set down heavily in the hallway, he had stood upon the bright, chessboard Dutch floor-tiles and nodded at what he saw, the gleaming white walls lit by the lantern high above the great staircase, the polished silver candelabra on side tables and, of course, the gilt-framed pictures on the walls. "Just so," he had said, while the chairmen noisily swivelled their contraption and knocked wood from the doorframe as they made their exit.

And then, still dazzled by sunshine and bright paint, he was shown into a room so black he immediately barked his shin on the edge of a cabinet. As the master wished, the door had been closed behind us and while I thought I could discern the amorphous shapes of familiar things, a minute ago he had been carried through sunlit streets and was now as blind as the Beak of Bow Street. And this is how the master prefers his visitors. "What is this?" he demanded as I set him in an unfamiliar chair. "Let in the light, someone! It is monstrous that you keep me in the dark. Do not you know who I am?" It was no easy task to explain to him that this is how my master works and that it is this way, or not at all. We wait a little longer.

And now, from behind the screens comes the sharp ringing of a little bell and Mr Gretch, who has been standing stock-still by the tall, west-facing window, unbolts a single shutter, folds it back just enough to allow the ingress of a narrow stripe of brilliance. Sunlight engulfs the sitter on his chair. By whisper and gesture, Gretch turns the man on his seat and adjusts the long mirror at his side, so that a gentler diffusion softens the shadows on his other cheek. The sitter blinks and struggles to adjust his vision to the sudden influx of light.

The light is made brighter by the darkness beyond, chiaroscuro enhancing the colours in the silk of his coat and each detail of its embroidery, every fold of cloth, and it glints too on the rings on his fingers. But it is his skin which benefits the most. His mottled cheeks and shiny forehead are now like luminous parchment. To the trained eye, a dozen delicate hues and tones delineate the course of every vessel and inform the depiction of every pore. There is something in this trick, the darkness, the pouring of light, which appears to help the painter see his subject anew and bring him halfway towards creating that luminosity for which he is still renowned. Before he has begun to paint, the sitter himself is already improved; he is an altogether finer thing than was deposited on the tiles a full hour ago.

A little blinded by the light, he cannot easily discern my master, who scrutinises his subject through small apertures of gauze set in his screens. From the bench behind him, I watch closely as the artist takes his view. His crooked finger beckons me; he calls for yellow, ochre, lake and light red, colours he will mix himself on his palette and so keep privy the precise secret of his lustrous skin tones.

As the afternoon wears on, the sitter's patience wears thin. Earlier that afternoon, he was kept waiting, for whatever reason, by the chair we sent to Golden Square to fetch him. And then, when the chair brought him back, the Master was indisposed, leaving word that it would be an hour or more before he could possibly begin to paint. He was left with the choice of joining the servants in the kitchen, which is where, I think, his natural inclinations would have led him, or spending an hour in his own company in the painting room, which is what he felt obliged to do. And now someone must pay the reckoning.

"You're a rum fellow," he calls out. He has never before had the temerity to address the artist directly, despite his own new title and the land in Staffordshire that his brewery has bought him. "They warned me of that." He frowns as he peers into the darkness beyond. "Why do you hide yourself like that, man? Damme, is it equable that you gawp at my visage for hours at a time and I have yet to catch sight of your own?" But he might as well have been mute for the sum of attention my master returns him. I leave my bench and take up my position behind him, ready to hand him clean brushes, or his mahlstick, or to fetch him whatever colours he has in his mind today.

I watch him crane over the sunlit canvas, his wig pushed back on his head, the curve of his backbone showing clearly through the stretched linen of his shirt. After four or five visits by this sitter and hours of work between, the portrait is beginning to look something like complete. There he stands, the proud brewer in his recently-purchased coat and buttons, given stature by the artistry of a man I once heard him call a nobody with a brush as he boarded his chair. But no matter, because all of this is here in this portrait. I can clearly see a pentimento of irony in this study of a fat little man in new coat and breeches who buys his art only because it is quite the thing to do, and has heard, very likely, that one of London's greatest talents now paints for a much reduced fee.

My master has placed his subject before a fanciful background of rolling green slopes, scattered copses and little white temples. It is a rural idyll in which the brewer looks both awkward and incongruous, perhaps because this is not his estate in Staffordshire. I know this with some certainty, because I am regularly tasked to paint my master's backgrounds, running off vistas of Wiltshire, or Surrey or wherever, in great lengths. Anyone excepting the brewer himself will appreciate the satire of the juxtaposition to be seen in this picture. It is almost, but not quite, humorous. Peering over my master's shoulder at his portrait of the small man in the big coat, I think I hear his voice, whispering, You are not what you would pretend. You are someone come from nothing.

"You have risen above yourself," says the brewer at last, wagging a stubby finger. "You may have painted the great families in your better days, but mark me well, you are not one of them. You are an artisan, a jobbing tradesman." He lets the word hang in the air, waiting for a response which does not come. "Do you hear me?" he says. He leans forward, trying to peer into the darkness behind the screens. "I allow that you have your talents," he says, "And I'm paying you well to exercise them. But I know coach makers and carpenters who are skilled men and they give themselves no airs. They know their places, by God!"

He stands up. “Hiding yourself away like this. What is wrong with you? Are you ailing, or just damned unsightly? Whatever it is, I have had my fill.” I think he means to march out. But instead, before Gretch or I can do anything about it, he steps towards the screens. “Let us take a look at you.” His fingers grasp the edges of the partition. “Let us see why you lurk in the dark like a crab in its shell,” he says, and at the same moment he pulls aside the two screens with such violence that one of them collapses to the floor.

The brewer jumps back. This is plainly not what he expected. His head swivels on its fat neck as he looks to Gretch and then to me for some explanation. Whatever he expected is not what he sees. There before him sits the painter, his brush poised, his head cocked, as if there has been no disturbance but now he wishes to find how best to capture this interesting and unexpected moment. The brewer takes another step back, uncertain, perhaps, of what to say to a man whose expression is hidden, but whose eyes blaze forth through the apertures in a fine and beautifully worked, white and gold Venetian mask.

Three

North of London. At Hampstead, later this same day, French doors have been thrown open to allow heat from the assembly there to escape, but little relief is to be had from the sultry summer evening without. The storm had come, but now is almost passed. The last bolt of lightning crackles over the London skyline and makes briefly brilliant the statues on the parterre. The thunder, which hammered on the roof tiles like the fist of some furious old God, had smothered the mouths of the young ladies and put a stop to the playing of the musicians – to the obvious annoyance of the little Prodigy seated at the piano, who slammed shut the lid and glared heavenwards. The young ladies laugh nervously and talk about a Hampstead house struck by lightning, which had fallen down upon the heads of its inhabitants.

The Prodigy, not yet ten years old, or so it is advertised, expresses a much older person's sigh before he lifts the lid and begins to play once more. Little white hands stretch wide over the keys and a small brow furrows. The expressions on the faces gathered about the piano are just as intense, the ladies and one or two gentlemen quite rapt. Music fills the room, accompanied by the percussion of heavy rain bursting on the flags outside.

The prodigy plays and all eyes track the course of his little fingers up and down the black and white keys, every ear follows the intricate lacework of notes that this child should not be capable of conceiving or rendering so perfectly here. So complete is the attention of every soul in that large room that a new arrival goes unnoticed and few ears register the strange and discordant notes which start from somewhere in their midst.

No-one sees her come through the open French doors – with the exception of a footman, who sees "a small woman, old and bent and half-drowned," in such a state of dirt and dishevelment that "it would have been madness" to have risked clean linen and white glove while others less perfectly attired might deal with her.

From the corner of his eye, he watches the crone stumble through the opened windows and when she looks his way, he sees her wild and staring eyes. She shuffles past the tables laden with cups and bowls of punch and onto the floor, looking like "a veritable hag from the heath", as someone will recall. The sheeting rain appears to have passed straight through her witchy hair and her thin garments. She has brought in the waters with her, the drenched and torn dress leaving a trail as the assemblage, tutting and talking, parts and backs away from this foul-looking thing whose dress they now see, is ripped and whose face is scratched and bruised. They see too that this is no old woman, but a young girl.

"What is this horror?"

She might well ask, this gentlewoman who peers over her lorgnette at the alien creature which has penetrated her world of powdered wigs and polite conversation. Now, as they look more closely and a hundred best beeswax candles pick out small, dark pools on the floor, those who listen make out words in the incessant babbling. "What is it? What's that she's saying?" says one. "It's rebels," says another, "rebels, over and over." The word sends ripples through the assembly. "It's the Jacobites again," is heard from somewhere.

Mr Reubin, whose ear is applied to the child's pale lips, says they are all wrong. "The word she's repeating is devils," he says. "Now what can she mean by that, I wonder?" A physician called McCormick approaches the girl and makes a professional assessment. His face darkens as he begins to gauge the extent of the injuries to this child, who can be no more than thirteen years old. He asks her name and where she resides, but when he gets an answer, it is the same. "Devils," she murmurs. Mrs Reubin, against her better judgement, leads her towards the pristine satin of her best couch.

"Footpads, for certain" says Mr Holyfield, the art dealer, as they lie her under the chandelier and so reveal that her white face is covered with bloody scratches, the certain result, Holyfield says, of running blindly through woods in the dead of night. Everyone sees, but no-one comments on the bloody patches that stain her dress. Mr McCormick sees it all and shakes his head. He takes a limp wrist, looks at his watch and measures the pulse.

No-one except Mr Holyfield thinks that the young girl's injuries are the result of a robbery with violence, and this is proven when his wife discovers the girl's purse. "Three gold sovereigns," she says, showing the palmed coins, which add much to the puzzlement that has followed the shock of the girl's intrusion. One of the young ladies, a Miss Brakespeare, pushes through the crowd that rings the couch. "I think I know her," she says. "Isn't she the sextant's girl? Mr Brown, who lives in the cottage beyond the church?"

"Then fetch him immediately, someone," Mr McCormick says. "Her pulse is weak. Find her a bed and take off her wet clothes." He turns towards his charge. “My poor, poor girl,” he whispers, “What terrible thing has befallen you? Where have you been?”

The girl stops her fevered ramblings and her eyes roll up, looking at the faces that crowd upon her, or perhaps at some indefinite place far beyond. She swallows and coughs weakly, appearing entirely spent as she struggles to offer a coherent reply. “I have been in hell,” she murmurs.

Four

St Martins Lane. A little below a bow window past which two men with their sedan chair are labouring, sits the Mouse, at a table strewn with newspapers, his blackened forefinger tracing lines of fresh type across a page. Occasionally, the finger pauses upon a word, very often a name, and the Mouse takes up his pen. He dips the newly-sharpened nib into an ink pot and scratches something on a blotted page of his notebook. His finger moves steadily over reports of robberies and bodies of young women dragged from the Thames and flies over news from Parliament. He learns that a man has fallen into the foul Fleet ditch and drowned.

He reads of a gent in Hampstead village whose only daughter of twelve years has been abducted and driven to such distraction that she has been committed to a madhouse. He gleans something of developments in the field of electrical medicine and of a shop selling Italian hams and olive oils and Parmesan cheeses which has opened on the Strand. There are accounts of violent highwaymen at work on Hounslow Heath and of the final days and last words of felons recently dispatched at Tyburn.

But Mouse pays much closer attention to the news from Court and the theatres, reports of masques held in Soho and other such tittle-tattle. After a while, he leaves off his reading and his scratching, and looks about him. He rubs his nose and then a little condensation from the grimy little window panes behind him and peers into the street, above whose gables the sun is setting. He squints up one way and down the other. As always, the attention of the Mouse is divided between his newspapers and the comings and goings of gentlemen in the coffee house.

He is an odd little fellow – this is a remark that has been made of him more than once at Molly's. He comes here most days, pays his penny and sits with a bowl of coffee, his nose deep in the latest editions of the *London Evening Post*, *Tatler* and the *Gentleman's Magazine*, and he watches, and listens, it is said. His deep-set and heavy-lidded eyes gaze out from beneath a wig which is not of the best quality and very possibly, Molly has said, came from a penny dip. In moments of deep cogitation, he is given to removing the wig and burying his fingernails in the untended garden that sprouts from his scalp and giving it all a good scratch. He sits by himself, more often than not, and he looks, Molly once remarked, like someone's puppy which has been left out in the rain.

But in the evenings, Molly has other business to attend to, and does not see the Mouse when his expression is changed, his eyes alert, his hands slapping his thighs as he loudly appreciates a remark of his nearest neighbour. He sits at a table with people you would never have thought would consort with a Mouse like this. Dick Clik, who collects the pots and clears the tables, has his own ideas about the Mouse, but the gentlemen and lawyers and titled bigwigs have no other thought but that this is a funny little man who seems always among them, an ever-ready audience for their observations and opinions and an appreciator of their wit. But which of their number he came in with, they might not have been able to say.

Despite his attire, which is only just the right side of respectable, his coat wanting a button and its sleeves worn and greasy at the elbows, he is not unwelcome at the tables of people who are patently his betters, at least not here in the coffee houses, where normal rules of social interaction are, of course, suspended. In a coffee house, a baronet may meet with a banker and a marquis with a major. In places like this, the Mouse has (his journal attests) sat only two places away from Viscount Trelawney and vigorously agreed with him when he demanded that the Wilkes fellow be pilloried. He has caught the eye of Lord Felsham on three occasions, heard the Earl of Rothesay talk on the propriety of keeping slaves, nodding all the time but nodding more vigorously when Sir Aubrey Sykes proposed the opposing view. He has had the King's privy opinion on the state of the nation, directly from one who is known to have his ear.

He rubs grime and new condensation from the dusty glass. A lady's voluminous dress brushes the panes as he peers out. Across the street, the lamps have been lit in the windows of the artists' Academy, but he has seen no-one leave, as yet. In these topsy-turvy days, there are artists who are accepted by polite society, and whose names appear in the newspapers almost as often as those of people with titles. As such, he should like to see these odd fellows in the flesh and perhaps make their acquaintance.

He looks again at the page of newspaper. Sir Geo. McGregor, lately returned from a tour of the Netherlands and an excursion to Italy, is to host an exhibition of art and statuary acquired on his travels. A Bristol merchant is offering for sale an African boy of 'perhaps ten years of age in good health and of comely appearance' whose English is 'more than tolerable' and whose purchase 'will assuredly prove a copper-bottomed investment.' He passes over reports of nightly violence in unlit streets and the under-manning of ships of the line and reads instead of the rakish behaviour of a young duke and his friends, who have attended church in a state of intoxication, and have been reported as holding bacchanalian rites at the duke's country house. They are said to be irreligious to a dangerous degree.

And then the door beside him swings open again. A tall, well-fed man in an expensively-tailored suit, his wig tied back in the new fashion, enters and is greeted by men sitting in a niche which is furnished with bookshelves and books. The man removes his hat and hangs it with the others. Someone helps him take off his cloak. He calls for a cup of coffee and with much bustle and scraping of chairs and people shifting their places to make room for him at the head of the table, he sits down and accepts a fill of tobacco for his pipe. Mouse, who has been standing in his shadow, as if he has arrived with this man, finds a chair and drags it up to the table.

Well, what say you, says one to the other and have you seen how the new Somerset House is springing up and do you know who is moving in? And are the rumours true about Lady Charlotte you-know-who and she not married a month? This and the prices of stocks and the newest pictures ready for sale at the auction room, the latest decisions from the bench at the Old Bailey and the extraordinary goings on at the assembly at Hampstead which ruined the evening for a certain little Prodigy, form the penny university's curriculum for this evening.

The men around the table who refill their pipes and call for more coffee and cups of chocolate and one for a little brandy, are a mixed bunch, a lawyer from Lincoln's Inn who sometimes smiles at him, a master cabinet-maker, a once-renowned violinist now employed at Vauxhall Gardens, a right honourable of independent means, an importer of coffee and cocoa beans, and a justice of the peace. Molly's is not one of those coffee houses which attracts a specific crowd, like the lawyers at Alice's by Westminster Hall, the politicians at the Cocoa House and the artists at Old Slaughter's, just across the street. Mouse visits them all, with the singular exception of Garraway's. But Molly's has become a second home. People come to Molly's because it is multi-denominational and attended occasionally by habitués of many of these other establishments. It is fertile ground for a man such as Mouse.

The table to which he has attached himself this evening is entirely to his liking. From what he hears, collectively, the men sitting here are acquainted with many who matter in all sorts of fields. As the evening wears on, Mouse is treated to second-hand introductions to many of the august personages he has thus far only read about. He learns of duels fought in secret by members of parliament, that an actress of great celebrity is really a man, that the Prince of Wales is bringing the royal name into disrepute. The arrival in the coffee house of a small but noisy group of painters from the academy across the street spawns a conversation about another artist, whose moon appears to be on the wane.

"Although I have it on authority that he paints still," Mouse hears.

"But not well, I think?"

"Not as before, no. But what can you expect?' says someone else. "He is as poxed as a Covent Garden doxy. It's a miracle he can still hold a brush, is what I hear."

"There was some very dark talk about him at one time," offers a slight fellow to his coffee cup, but his soft tones are subsumed by the booming baritone of his neighbour, who says, "Pardon me, but this is the same Henry Grace who painted *Hero and Leander* for the Earl of Strathclyde?"

"Have you seen it?"

"I have and was much affected. He had an extraordinary talent, I thought."

"His *Judith and Holofernes* is Strathclyde's too, I'm told."

"And *The Betrayal of Desdemona* hangs at Carlton House. He was admired in his day."

"Indeed he was. Much was predicted for him."

"But did you not know him well, my lord?"

"That was all a while ago. Others knew him better than I. He moved in higher circles and dined at the best houses, where he was received as something more than an artisan, I can assure you. I never saw such sudden success. After he returned from his tour of the Continent, it was much as if he had climbed the ladder and vaulted some uppermost rungs."

"Sold his soul to the devil, was what I heard. Like that fellow, Faust. Ha ha!"

"Well, if he did, he made a good bargain. He was everywhere seen, you know. At Blenheim and Holkham, with ladies in theatre boxes, promenading at Ranelagh... "

"But then?"

"Who knows? He disappeared, or he withdrew from society, which is much the same thing. He let it be known that he needed time alone to work upon his masterpiece."

"Do we know this picture?"

"Nothing of that sort has yet appeared for sale, although the rumours persist. It hardly matters now. All we have seen from him since have been hackneyed likenesses of the sort of people who wouldn't normally be able to afford the luxury of a portrait to hang over the mantle. And they get what they pay for, as I hear it: second-rate paintings from a man who is long past his prime."

Pipes are puffed, more coffee is called for and Mouse looks longingly at the pen and ink pot on the table he has lately vacated.

"There is talk that all is not as it should be in Leicester Fields," someone says, with such an air of intrigue that several of his neighbours draw closer, the better to hear what he has to say. "From what I have been told by one of my servants, it's all show. Beyond the splendour of the entrance, the house is in the utmost state of disrepair."

"Well, well," says someone else, as if he had always thought so.

"It's true. At the back, there is sailcloth covering gaping holes in the roof. Half the upper chambers are unusable, the plaster is crumbling and I hear that the staff all sleep in the cellar with the rats."

"Surely not?"

"He hasn't paid his butcher in weeks, months, maybe."

But the man who came late lets it be known that he thinks this has gone far enough. The conversation is sinking to the level of fishwives' gossip, he says, and he tells them of a fine Arabian he narrowly missed buying at Tattersall's this very day.

Mouse stores away all he has heard. As people begin to leave, he smiles his farewells. It has been a good evening. He has been acknowledged by several of the party and perhaps he has even felt part of their society. He has added to their conversation, if only to the sum of "I agree most heartily." And so, as he jumps down from his chair and collects his hat from the seat of another, preparing to find his way through the great dark streets to the house of Obadiah Bone, he is quite a happy little man.

Five

Leicester Fields. When I return to the house in Leicester Fields, my morning's errands done, I hear a sharp exchange of words and something else, too. From the scullery comes the soft, rhythmic sobbing of Poll, our kitchen maid of three days. Another time, knowing what it is to be unhappy, I might have offered a smile or a gentle word, but not today. This morning, I am eager to be in the studio, the master being again indisposed. I wonder if I can cross the kitchen and reach the back stairs without attracting the attention of Gretch, or of our housekeeper, Mrs Harris, who is dabbing up the toast crumbs off her plate with a wetted finger. Gretch's crossed legs and smouldering pipe suggest a man in no hurry to be about his duties or to clean the spoons which have been put out for him. He sees me, of course, and takes the long and spittly stem of his pipe from between his yellow teeth and jabs it at me. Not a word, he's saying.

Because last night, I heard him taking the new girl up the narrow stairs to his room, all whispers and breathy promises. Behind the thin lathe and plaster wall dividing Gretch's chamber from my own cramped crib, I heard the cajoling, and the demurring, and then his harsh, insistent tones met by a note of alarm. A short, shrill, muffled cry and I could see his hand over her mouth as he forced himself onto and into her, the silly girl surrendering her maidenhood before she quite knew what it was. And now, between bursts of sobbing, she works furiously in the scullery, attacking her pots and pans like she might scrub away the indelible stain on her reputation. When I was new to this house he tried such games with me until I bit on his ear so hard that he squealed like a stuck pig.

"We shall be advertising for another maid before the week is out," Mrs Harris says, sharply. "If some persons could keep their breeches buttoned we should all be the better for it."

"You don't know what you're talking about," Gretch says. Then he sees me starting towards the kitchen door. "You stay where you are, Miss," he adds. "I would have words with you."

"In any case," Mrs Harris says, pushing brown curls under a matching cap, "We may have to do without a maid. The coffers are empty, as well you know."

"Are you going to wash the pots?" Gretch asks, with a tobacco-cured chuckle, "Because I should like to see that."

"I have a household to run," Mrs Harris says. And with a nod in my direction, "What about the girl there? She can do it, alongside whatever it is that tomboy does for you."

"Michel works for me, woman," Gretch says, with something like the growl I heard from his bedchamber last night. "And there's an end to it." He takes up his news-sheet and begins to read, thin, colourless lips silently forming the words on the page.

"I have to size a canvas and make the colours," I say.

"You stay," Gretch says.

"I don't think you know the position this household is in," Mrs Harris says, draining her teacup and wiping her mouth on her apron.

"I've nothing to pay the staff and precious little for any food this week. And I don't need to tell you that the house itself is going to rack and ruin. There's no money coming in, Mr Gretch, and I for one don't know what we must do if we are to keep this establishment afloat."

"We'll get by," Gretch says. "We have a couple of patrons who need to cough up for the portraits, but once they do, we'll be all right for a while. And I'll see they pay, one way or the other."

"It's not enough," Mrs Harris says. "That won't pay the bills on that spike, nor settle his debts. Your man will be taken off to the sponging house one of these days, you see if he isn't. And then where will we be? I didn't come over here to live on toasted cheese, Jamie. These portraits of nobodies won't answer. Not with the costs of a sizable establishment such as this."

Gretch looks about him, as if he is taking in the dark and dismal kitchen with its cracked and filthy windows for the first time. He shakes his head.

"Not like the high days, is it, old girl?" he concedes. "When him upstairs had his reputation and shopkeepers would gladly wait for their money. But some things aren't meant to be, it seems, and such as we must make the best of it."

"He wastes so much money, too," says Mrs Harris. "The treatments do him no good, whatever the cost. He worsens, isn't that the case?" Mrs Harris rises from the table and looks at me sharply, as if I am somehow to blame. She shakes her head, tells Gretch to see to his spoons and goes off to chivvy the girl in the scullery. Gretch yawns and stretches his arms before he gets up and walks over to the fire. He stands there for a moment, looking into the flames as a low rumbling rises from his chest. He summons up his phlegm and ejects it noisily into the fire, along with a morsel of food, which sizzles on the grate.

"And where have you been?" he says to me, suddenly. I had thought Gretch was about some business of his own this morning, as he usually is at this time on a Tuesday. But here he is, prodding me now with a hard, bony finger. "While you're here, while we all still have a roof over our heads, you'll do my bidding, do you understand?"

He raps me on the forehead with the spoon he should be cleaning, and he does it quite hard. It smarts, and will probably raise a lump, but I don't mind Gretch's little torments, not now. This is not the treatment he would have meted out to me before. When first I was taken into this establishment, Gretch would beat me on a whim. There were days when nothing I did and nothing I did not do would spare me his rod. Gretch was a monster, his tread on the stairs something I listened for with the uttermost dread. For a while, Gretch haunted my childish dreams and filled my waking days with fear. I swear that I never thought that he could ever be anything other than a terrible ogre that I would fear for the rest of my life.

Which makes the change in Gretch all the more difficult to understand. It has been almost impossible, in these last few weeks, not to detect a softening in his soul. At first I thought I might be mistaken and that he would no doubt want something in return when he allowed me a rare afternoon to myself one day. But other, seemingly insignificant occurrences have caused me to think otherwise. Is this mellowing a product of his advancing years, I wondered? After all, he must now be forty or fifty years old. I can't be more exact; there are times when his gaunt face is furrowed with lines and he seems as old as London, but at other times his smooth, mostly-bald head and hard, glinting eyes suggest he is still in his dangerous prime. It is a wholly unexpected turnaround I still cannot fathom. But however much reality there is in this softening I perceive, Jamie Gretch remains a thorn in my side.

"I'll ask you once more," he says, with another sharp tap of the spoon, "Where have you been?" But there it is again. I'm certain I see a softer light in those hard eyes and for a moment, I fancy he will add "You young scamp!" and the world will be turned on its head. But of course, he doesn't, and only raps me all the harder with his spoon. I answer him by holding up my basket of bottles filled with pigments and oils, which my master sent me to purchase from the colourist on St Martin's Lane. "Don't play me for a fool, girl," Gretch says. "You have had time to do more than that. If we are to keep our places here we must make the best use of every hour in God's day. Now, where were you?"

"I went to the auction room to see Mr Jackson and The Turner Family," I say. These are paintings which were commissioned by their sitters but for which, for one reason or another, no payment was made and we have had to put them up for sale.

"Was there much interest? Were folk looking at them?" Gretch asks.

I tell him that people had looked, as indeed they had, but I forebear telling him that those I saw examining the portraits were quite cutting about the standard of work they saw there. I had stood in that great room, no doubt mistaken for someone's servant, as buyers milled around the space, softly disparaging the paintings by nobodies and loudly admiring the grander stuff. The pictures we have there will not sell. Where is the market for second-rate likenesses of people that no-one knows?

But I keep such thoughts to myself and tell Gretch that I think we will sell both works at a respectable price. I don't tell him that I had been in the auction house just long enough to be able to convince him that I had been there at all. I certainly don’t tell him that in reality, I had instead found myself gazing once more through the gates of the Foundling Hospital, where my story had its start.

Six

Grub Street. Across town, in a tumbledown house near Moorfields, a youngish man named Obadiah Bone says, "I hope you have something worth my ink today." He dabs hefty leathern ink balls evenly over the forme of type, gives the polished wooden handles of the screw two half-turns and then turns them the other way. He moves long strands of dark hair from his face and opens the boards. As always, the page he holds up is a perfect surprise for Mouse. Though he knows that this page is composed entirely of words that he has written, it is only when the reversed page is printed and the type righted that Mouse properly sees what he has achieved.

There is his revelation of the estrangement of Lord Onslow and his wife Lady Susan and beneath, the whispers he has heard about Rabelaisian parties being enjoyed at the Prince of Wales's residence at Carlton House. Set beside this are the various doings of those whose names are always familiar to his readers. Here is Royalty and the bon ton, the politicians and the successful merchants, the celebrated actors and the better-known poets, artists and musicians. There, positioned further down the page, with less space and more discretion than he would like, is his exclusive account of how two members of the London Society for the Improvement of Morals were found without their clothes at a molly house near Covent Garden. The discovery of a young girl's body is given another small space. It is not an unusual occurrence, but murder is suspected and the girl is thought to be of modest but respectable stock.

Mouse tells Obadiah that he has material to fill more than the single page he is allotted. He needs more room for his observations, more space for the names people know. The public, he says, has an appetite for such things. He stops short of saying that they might actually prefer that to the needling of the government and the satirical sketches of its members which currently fills the pages of *The Enquirer*.

Obadiah sets the newly-printed pages on racks to dry and looks out of sooty window panes at ramshackle ancient houses whose upper stories almost abut his own and which are no longer the pride of the gentry, but the abodes of people very like Obadiah and Mouse. "Yes, yes," he says, testily, "and who on this street would not like to publish as the fancy took him?" He turns to Mouse and softens his tone. "Really, Morris, you think the hacks in this writers' rookery have no better dreams than to pen tittle-tattle? That they learned their craft for this?"

Mouse has no answer. He gives thanks daily that he's doing something for which he finds himself entirely suited. The thanks are due to Obadiah, who gave him a roof and an occupation more valuable to Mouse than the couple of coins he occasionally finds in his hand. It was a lucky day for Mouse when he met Obadiah Bone.

"Make no mistake, Mouse," Obadiah says, "Whatever dreams we have, here it's money we're about. Whatever pays our rent and puts meat on the table. And right now, there is money in dissatisfaction."

"I confess, I do not follow you," Mouse says. His voice is pitched higher than it might be, another quality in his friend which Obadiah finds pleasing.

"Look," Obadiah says, leading Mouse to a table on which printed pamphlets lie stacked in two big, untidy piles. "I have been busy these last few nights. Here, you see, in this pile, are disquisitions which castigate the French and demand the rearming and refitting of the navy. And then in this second pile are the same number of pamphlets, but these argue that the money would be better spent on improving drainage here in London and damn the writer of the first pile as a war-mongering leech upon the public purse."

But rather than offering his approbation, Mouse only frowns.

"My dear Morris," Obadiah says. "Don't you see? These we will sell to dependents of the shipyards along the River and perhaps send down to the Medway. The others we will distribute among people whose lives are marred by filthy streets and whose income isn't dependent on shipbuilding, or a war with France."

But Mouse appears no wiser. "But where do we stand on this?" he says, "Where will our newspaper stand?"

Obadiah looks at Mouse as if he really cannot remember what had thrown together two such different souls. "We stand on the side that reaps the most cash, of course," he says. "As will *The Enquirer*. We must know which way the wind will blow before the first gusts are felt. Perhaps one day we can start that blow. But for the moment, *The Enquirer* will faithfully reflect the views of its readers."

"We are critics of the government?"

"You may think so. But just because we have attacked government policy of late doesn't mean we cannot side with the government in the future, if that is what sells copies then. But for now, Morris, none of this need trouble you. Open your notebook and show me what new gossip you have brought."

Gossip, he calls it, tittle-tattle. But Obadiah has always professed a dim view of what Mouse does. He unties the boards and surrenders his notebook to Obadiah, who reads, shakes his head, laughs. Mouse is silent, knowing full well that Lady Edgeworth's unaccountable carriage ride with a leading player from Drury Lane will feed a growing appetite for such fare. He is aware that Obadiah, for all his head-shaking, knows it too. But Mouse will say nothing of this. He is too deeply grateful.

"Grateful for what?" Obadiah had said only the night before, as together they cleaned ink from the press. "Are we going to have all that out again?"

He had grinned, thrown a wet cloth at his friend.

"Must I repeat it?" Mouse barely dodges the inky missile. "Delivering me from the baying mob. Giving me a home. This glorious occupation. It is all so much more than I dared to hope of life. How can I repay you?"

Obadiah sighs and waves Mouse's notebook. "This is all the repayment I need," he says. "For heaven's sake, Morris, who would not have done the same? When you were set upon by those Bart's Fair bullies and chased like a ..."

"A rat before terriers," Mouse says. The apprentices most likely had been drinking since cock-crow and something in Mouse's appearance had ignited the Saturnalian spirit.

"Fox before hounds," says Obadiah. "I only wish I had caught up with the pack soon enough to save you from injury. Be more careful. You have missed a bit."

While Obadiah takes a pen and defaces tidy pages with broad slashes and scribbled annotations, Mouse recalls the generosity of a man who had taken an injured stranger into his house. The notebook now in Obadiah's inky hands had been responsible for another extended kindness, or so Mouse saw it.

"What is this?" he had asked, examining the large green book which had fallen from his injured guest's coat pocket. The guest himself had been placed on an ancient couch, where his head was sinking into a mass of escaping horsehair. "Are you a writer? And if you are, what kind of writing is this?"

"Those are my observations," Mouse had told him.

It was curious – and somehow, exciting – to see another's eyes alight with interest on what had been an entirely private thing. Obadiah turned a page and frowned, but quickly turned another.

"The people I see here... forgive me, but they cannot be your friends? These are all names known to me. To half of London, I should think."

"They are not my friends," Mouse said.

"Then this is the product of your fancy? Are you beginning a new type of novel? Something on the experimental side, like Mr Sterne?"

"No," Mouse said, reaching over and reclaiming his book. "I could not do that."

"Then what are these stories then? Are they true?"

"Oh, yes, every one. I always check."

"Even this one – the bull in the bawdy house?"

"That too."

"But why do you write such things? And who do you sell them to?"

"These are my observations," Mouse replied, "Of London life. I thought one day, a book perhaps.... there are such things, I think?"

“This is not the stuff of books,” Obadiah had said. “I was a bookseller on the Row. I know what makes books. What you produce is amusing, I grant you, but it is ephemeral. In a month your readers would have forgotten most of what you have here. By tomorrow, some of it. It is a shame, because you clearly have a talent for amassing such curious information. Or is it an ear?”

“I do not quite know what it is,” Mouse says. “Only that this is all I want to do. Perhaps I am fascinated by people with lives more interesting than my own.”

“So you make no money from this?”

“No, it is only something I do when I am working”

“And what do you do?”

“When I can get work – and that is not always easy for someone like me – I wait upon tables at the coffee houses. At Garraway's mostly. Until recently, anyway.”

“And this is where you hear these stories?”

“In the main part, yes.”

“And do Garraway's give you a bed?”

And Mouse had been obliged to confess that just then, he had no bed. Not all of Garraway's clientele, as Obadiah understood his awkward explanation, had thought it amusing to be waited on by a circus freak.

Obadiah had taken longer than he might to find a use for Mouse's talents. To begin with, his new tenant helped him set the pages on the press, distribute copies of the newspaper and run errands to the cook shop. But then had come days when the editor had taken sick and was obliged to keep to his bed, although the newspaper was only half set. With mounting debt, Obadiah could ill afford to miss publication. As his fever rose, his talk became delirious, though these oft-repeated words were always intelligible: “The paper must go out!”

Such was his manic insistence upon this and so alarming his attempts to rise from his bed and publish the journal himself that inevitably, there came an instance when Mouse found himself alone with an enormous tray of type, a great oaken printing press and a Herculean task to perform. He took stock of his assets. The main story was set and ready to print. This was something of Obadiah’s concerning overspending by a department of government and there was another page mostly filled with an editorial on proper governance, as *The Enquirer* saw the matter. There was a motley selection of advertisements for oncoming comedies at the Theatre Royal, bankrupts’ property auctions, sales of pictures, and one for 'The Women's Petition Against Coffee'. But that still left a gaping space which something of his own invention would have to fill.

Obadiah didn't discover just how it was filled and how the newspaper had been miraculously published and distributed until he had recovered, by which time several similar issues had been produced. The first one contained half a page of Mouse's ‘observations’, the next issue, a whole page of the same. The more substantial writing, the reports of parliamentary debates, the political sketches and comment, Mouse had commissioned cheaply from hungry Grub Street neighbours.

Recalling the fright Obadiah had given him when he opened that first issue, he winces. Obadiah recoiled. He had sat down with that newspaper and had not spoken for a full half-hour. Mouse, sickened himself, had expected to be thrown into the street at any moment. Better to remember Obadiah mollified when he discovered that rather than losing sales, his newspaper had added a substantial number. The aberration, Obadiah explained, was almost certainly attributable to his own leader on the failings of the new Board of Agriculture. Or possibly to his pointed critique of a self-serving report from Captain Nelson, currently basking in the Bay of Naples. Any connection with Mouse's page of titbits, gossip and scandal was unthinkable, and was a thought left unvoiced by both men. If he had thanked Mouse a little grudgingly for stepping into the breach, his gesture was gratefully received.

Still Obadiah had prevaricated about printing more, and talked of putting the genie back in its bottle. But the increase in revenue was not to be ignored and the genie remained at large. When future observations appeared under the banner 'City Gossip,' Mouse was joyous and began labouring hard to ensure that what he contributed was both exclusive to the paper and irresistible to his readers. He does not mind that Obadiah makes no official acknowledgement of his page's success. He is much too pleased to be making a small but significant contribution to the survival of his friend's business.

"You will have us in the gutter yet," Obadiah says as he settles the book by the press and begins to pick out type. But Mouse can see that he is smiling.

Later, when Mouse has departed to see what truth there is in the rumour of a strange disturbance outside the gardens at Marylebone (and how many closely-set paragraphs might be spun from it), Obadiah tidies the press, wipes ink from his hands and, removing his leather apron, takes down a sheaf of papers from a topmost shelf. He shuffles through pages filled with a neat, close hand. Holding one up to the failing window light, he begins to read aloud some lines of poetry. Obadiah has a strident, Londoner's voice and talks in a dialect bred not to please the ear but to arrest the attention and be heard over a crowded street.

Now, though, his tones are much softened by the words he selects and by the music of his metre. On occasion, laying the paper on his desk, he takes his pen and substitutes one word for another or scores out a line. He stops to collect his thoughts. His eyes close at the moment of composition and the young man seems just then far removed from the dinghy little room which smells of rancid milk and the jakes in the yard. Wherever his fancy has taken him, he is brought sharply back to Grub Street by the noisy rapping of knuckles on wood, and the immediate opening of the door.

"I've not had my money," the stranger announces, looking about the room as if he might see what he wants in a neat pile upon a shelf.

"Bless you, I've not had mine," Obadiah says, more to himself than to the newcomer.

The older, stouter man who wears a misshapen tricorn hat, a heavy topcoat and a shouldered leather satchel, says, "Yours is long overdue, Mr Bone. My masters will brook no more prevarication. Three month's rent, or you and your friend and everything here will be out in the street. And you'll consider yourself well served if that is all."

"Mr Spragg," Obadiah says, opening the book of accounts where spidery figures are obscured by small spillages of ink and the marks of somebody's fingers, "If you will look down these columns, you will see what I'm owed. I need grace to bring out the next edition and make some money. Once I am paid, your Shylock will have his money."

"You people in this street are all the same," Spragg says, "More debtors than in the Mint and that's where most of them will be, soon enough. I've no particular wish to see you there, Mr Bone."

"Please, Mr Spragg, I beg you..."

"It cannot be done, Mr Bone, not this time. I must have something to show for my visit here today. Or the bailiffs will come, I promise. Tomorrow. Today even. It ain't up to me."

Obadiah shakes his head and then he reaches above the door, pulls books from a shelf and extracts a broken pot which the dusty tomes have concealed. He empties a few silver coins, and many more of copper, into an opened palm. "There," he says. "Your master now has every penny I have in the world. Every mite. Let that serve him for the moment."

Spragg sighs and runs a hand through thinning black hair, which is tied behind him with a once-blue band. "In full next week then, Mr Bone," he says. "And be ready for what comes if you fall short. Every penny, Mr Bone." He takes his hat from the table and unlatches the door, leaving Obadiah to put away his sheaf of dreams. He picks up his pen and begins to scratch out a plan for the next issue of *The Enquirer*, knowing it may be the last.

Seven

For those in the house at Leicester Fields who are long accustomed to my master's appearance, it makes little difference whether he wears one of his plain or fancy masks, chooses the pewter or the silver nose to tie to his face with a bit of ribbon, or goes without anything. His dreadful deformities are no longer a cause of dread for anyone but newly-hired housemaids who have yet to become used to the sight. The last few months have seen his condition worsen. Before then, the raw and festering gummas had confined themselves to his neck, arms and chest, and for a long time left his face untouched. These lesions could be concealed with clothing and the worse they became, the better he dressed himself. Silk scarves, satin tunics and lace made any idea that such finery might be concealing horrors beneath, all but inconceivable.

But when his face became afflicted too, and the bridge of his nose collapsed and his upper lip withdrew to reveal bloody gums and rotting teeth, no amount of fine clothing could hide the truth from him or anyone else. Henry Grace had become as hideous as a church-tower gargoyle. In times gone by, his condition would have been viewed as a visitation, a punishment for some terrible crime.

One morning, I was at my bench, preparing a grey ground with a combination of flake white, chalk, and black and umber pigments. I remember the mixture because I had been spending more time than I liked painting a vast area of featureless dark sky behind the full-length portrait of a sea captain, who stood at a window, grasping his sextant and telescope while a great chart unfurled from a table. I was pouring in the linseed to bind the colours when I heard a sound I still cannot accurately describe.

The door was a little ajar and I saw that in the hall outside stood my master. It was immediately clear that I had heard a sob, his destroyed nasal passages rendering it as an unearthly sort of grunt. He did not see me and I withdrew a little into the shadows. Although it was full midday, he was wearing his old gown and a pair of slippers. I noted a nasty new abscess on his lower arm and tried not to look closely at the abhorrent profile he offered.

He was standing before one of his finest small works, which still hung in the hall because it was not for sale, being a self-portrait which the master had painted when he was some years younger and altogether different. Having attended the auction houses often enough to sell other examples, I know that the painting would raise a considerable sum if it were sold, and would pay off many of our creditors at a stroke. Gretch has suggested such a course. But the painting remains. It serves to show prospective sitters what fine work has been wrought by his hand and, I believe, it reminds the master of the handsome man he once was, which is sometimes a comfort, but on a day like this, must also be a source of untold misery.

I have stood before it myself, transfixed by a level of skill which I used to think was worlds beyond anything I myself could ever attain. The sitter wears the fashions of the day, every satin fold and embroidered buttonhole finely delineated and the linen at his neck so perfectly realised that you might expect to touch canvas yet feel the textures of soft cloth.

But it is his face that exercises a morbid fascination for all who know him now. I have seen both Mrs Harris and Jamie Gretch pause to ponder and they passed the frame on the wall between the painting room and the front door. It does not help that the master was so very handsome in his day, though a little deficient in height, being no taller than I am myself.

Above his neatly-buttoned and trim figure are the fine features of an unblemished face, bright, blue eyes sparkling from beneath a newly-purchased periwig. His nose was of the Grecian sort, his lips caught at the moment of forming a smile, I always think, and the whole impression given by this portrait is of a man who is very pleased with himself, as indeed he had reason to be at that time. He was then a painter revered by his peers, commissioned by the nobility, and he was painting what he loved to paint. It was said that no-one on this side of the Channel had completed better history paintings, the type of artistry then in such vogue.

All this I have read in the newspapers and journals the master keeps in an unlocked box in the library. There was, I read, a special and yet indefinable element to his work. Someone called it maturity while someone else termed it a darkness. It was conjectured that this original quality had some connection with, or was born out of, some extraordinary experience in the life history of the artist himself. But if that was so, no-one knew what that experience might have been. At the time when he painted himself so finely into this small frame, he was young, talented, very rich and entirely ignorant of the cruel hand which fate was about to play. If he had secrets then, his features kept them close.

His days are no longer spent in the salons of high society. He is not feted as an artist, not by those who know something about the subject.

The disease affects his balance, his sight, and at times, his ability even to hold a brush. There are days when it seems to retreat and allow him to advance his work and make us sufficient money to keep the duns from our door. But at other times it surges through him, and he spends half the day with the physician, lying naked on a bench while one quack after another applies a mercury balm or gives him some other physic which never seems to make him better and quite often renders him a great deal worse.

Obtaining a cure for his condition has become more than his goal, it obsesses his every waking hour. I have heard him tell someone that he has tried every remedy known to man, but still he goes on, questing for the one which will heal him. Physicians, surgeons and apothecaries troop through the house with their apparatus, their tonics, ointments, leeches and lozenges and leave with more of the coins we need to pay for our existence.

Day by day, we become poorer and the house less like the glorious address it was of old. We have sold what can be sold. When the master bought this enormous villa, he had it fitted out with the best furniture that money could buy. Mr Chippendale supplied chairs and tables and tea was served to our numerous and august visitors in the best Wedgwood china. Now these and many of the paintings we used to decorate the stairs and the upper hall are gone, the money raised pocketed by so-called medical men who have found a sure and regular source of income in the syphilitic master of this house in what some people are beginning to call Leicester Square.

This afternoon, he surprised me. "The attic, girl," he had snuffled. "Help me with my things." Indicating that I should take two of the longer brushes and the pair of steps, he began to climb the stairs, carrying a basket full of the colours he had told me to mix that morning, for which I had run a special errand to Mr Powell's on St Martin's Lane. Bent under the weight of the heavy ladders, I followed him into the big attic room where I recovered my breath. I have assisted him in here before. This is where he executes his larger works. *Judith and Holofernes* and *Gethsemane* were born in this cluttered room beneath the eaves. The attic provides him with the space he needs and offers him privacy and the light he craves like a flower.

Some while ago, perhaps at the time when we all detected some impairment of his vision, he made an alteration to the roof. Slates were sent crashing down into the yard as an enormous rent was made in the roof at the back of the house. A great sail cloth was purchased and Gretch, assisted by two hired hands, made an arrangement of line and pulley and block and tackle by which the hole could be covered up and reopened with reasonable ease, protecting the house from the worst of the weather and allowing the master's beloved Northern light to flood in.

Now he signalled me to open it once more. I pulled on the ropes, the sailcloth noisily folded itself back and the weak light of a grey autumnal day filled the space with an even and shadowless illumination. The room was still full of lumber, but the old chairs and tables and other useless things had been stacked against walls and in corners, leaving a clear central space, in which was propped the huge canvas I had prepared for him towards the end of last year, making the frame here in the attic and nailing and sizing it as it lay upon the boards. A tarpaulin protected the canvas from any failure of the apparatus above. This, we now removed.

I took a step back, and then one more. This was a great work to take in, both in size and conception, but very roughly done, was my first thought. My master was now standing close to its surface, employing a magnifying glass to examine some tiny detail. "Before you comment, young lady," he said, "Bear in mind that this is a work in progress. It is only a beginning. What you see here is merely a base for the edifice I will build upon it." There was some relief in that. We were not lost yet. The extraordinary thing I saw before me was not, after all, final evidence that the master had lost his talent and was letting slip his senses too.

My gaze roved over this huge expanse of muddy tones, which made brighter the explosion of fiery colour just off its centre. Slowly, I began to make more sense of what I was seeing and perceived the details which had at first escaped my notice. It was a conflagration, taking hold of some great city. Many small buildings were already burned, I saw, and others awaited imminent consumption by the flames, which appeared to be eating their way quickly towards the fire-shiny, snaking river.

Coming closer, I could see boats on the choppy water and tiny men and women crowding the banks as they tried to escape the flames, some falling, other leaping from bridges, some drowning. Walls of burning buildings crashed down upon a frightened mob crowding the streets of this infernal place.

I could make out people in their night shirts, clutching bags of possessions and terrified cart-horses rearing in their traces. A woman threw a baby from the uppermost window of a burning house.

Closer still, I could discern armies of rats, which scurried from houses, swarmed through crowds, weaving between people's legs, and poured off the ends of a jetty into the turbulent Thames. This was London aflame, but it was not the Great Fire of the last century, because there was our modern St Paul's, its dome alight and there the new villas beyond the City, seemingly as combustible as any of the older dwellings. The author of this catastrophe handed me his glass, and I was astonished to find that I could see people's faces.

How the artist in his enfeebled state had been able to achieve such fine work was a mystery. So taken was I with the myriad details of this strange but fascinating work that I was only half-listening to my master, who was talking all this while, describing and explaining his great vision. Now I heard him say, but in such a low voice that whether it was meant for himself or for me I could not be sure, "This is a new fire of London, it is the fire we all deserve. The first fire burned out the plague. Well, we are plagued again, this time with sin, and we must be punished and burned again."

Like a brimstone preacher prophesying eternal torment for those who gambled in the clubs, drank in the taverns, spoke profanities or took whores to their beds, he appeared to be damning the entire town. But as Grace let more of his idea slip, it occurred to me that the plague which had fired his vision was the pox which had afflicted him for so many years, casting him from society, destroying his body, and poisoning his outlook.

He must have spent every private moment upon this work. So many of those times when we had thought him in his bed or sequestered with his medical men, he must have been labouring in this attic room. We knew he retired here to paint and that he liked to do so privily, which had given rise to the fancy that he was working on his masterpiece, the painting that would redeem his reputation and save our household from ruin. The work itself was extraordinary and so unlike anything I had seen at the auction houses that I could not say whether it might indeed be our saving grace, but there was so much that remained to be done before it could be offered to the world that I doubted my master had the strength to finish it. Surely this, I thought, seized suddenly by hope, was why he had brought me to the attic this afternoon?

"I need you to assist me today," he said, as if he had read my thoughts.

I prepared myself. I could see that whole districts of the city had yet to be rescued from their mere outlines and filled with the same fine detailing. I admit that I baulked at what I thought might now be asked of me. I had practiced my miniatures, certainly, but without great success. Certainly, no miniature I had yet produced matched the intricate art of those faces I saw before me now or matched the standard of examples I had stared at in the lockets now displayed (and yet to be sold off) in the glass case in the painting room.

These were my thoughts as he turned towards me and took a long brush from my hand.

"Today," he said, "I must attend to the topmost parts of the picture."

The bottom part, then, where citizens escaping in the boats waited to be properly illuminated by the raging fire, this will be mine, I thought. I began to identify those areas most in need of improvement. He pointed towards the set of steps.

"But I fear I am unsteady on my feet today and do not trust the ladders. You must hold them quite secure while I mount them and see if I cannot bring something like an iridescent glow to my clouds. I can trust you to do this?"

Eight

It was at the Foundling Hospital in Bloomsbury that I first became aware that there was someone in this world called Henry Grace. I had caught his eye while I was trampling down beds of flowers as I fought tooth and nail with an older girl, over a trinket which she had snatched from my neck. Henry Grace the artist had come to admire the Hospital's fine paintings, I was told by a stern matron, not to see a pair of Kilkenny cats.

I was not born at the Foundling, of course. I had been brought thither by my mother, as I understand it, when I was an infant. My story no doubt mirrored those of the other so-called foundlings. We were the children of fallen women, seduced housemaids, and other victims of broken promises. So we were told. The mothers and the others who appeared at the gates with little baskets or swaddled bundles were a pathetic sight. Some looked about fifteen, others only a little older. There were ones who seemed to know too well the way things went here and they perhaps had appeared at these gates on other occasions, with other bundles.

I have thought too often on the circumstances which obliged our own mother to follow a similar course. I wonder constantly if she did it with my interests at heart and if I had sisters or brothers who suffered a similar fate? What became of my mother I never knew but I sometimes look out for a face like my own among the sweepings of the city.

Once admitted, and so long as we survived the ravages of diseases that now and then blew through the wards and sometimes carried off half the inmates, we Foundlings should have been assured a safe and secure upbringing. There were dangers even here, though, which I will describe in due course. Boys left the Hospital at 20, girls at 21, the boys having been trained to become seamen or gardeners, the girls schooled for service. I left the Foundling Hospital much younger than that, and by and by, when my duties allow it, I will relate why this came about and how I used my time at the orphans' hospital to singular advantage.

It is the Hospital's practice to place its charges with nursemaids outside the hospital until they are old enough to benefit from the regimented education provided by that institution. I had been placed with my country nurse so early in my life that when I was returned to the Hospital, the curve of the long brick walls and the big iron gates were unfamiliar to me. As I passed before the immense wings of this great and forbidding place, it occurred to me that it might be a prison. That was where people were sent when they had done terrible wrong, Emmie had said, adding after a moment's reflection, or done something only to save themselves from starving. I had done neither and yet I felt I must have done something, to be snatched away from the cottage, and Emmie, like this.

This building was bigger, yet plainer, than any I had seen in Suffolk. The fears that had plagued me ever since I learned that the widowed schoolteacher under whose roof I lived, was not, after all, my mother, and that I would be leaving her familiar, whitewashed cottage in the country to begin a new life in London, became a dread apprehension as we approached the Hospital. The main house looked grand enough in the evening light (and, as I later discovered, boasted an opulent interior quite in keeping with its facade), but no such attention had been lavished on the great wings where the children were boarded. Here, all was bare floors and plain walls, and rows of hard, little beds.

In short, the Foundling Hospital was no palace and I no princess. I was only another motherless child to be stripped of my country clothes, vigorously scrubbed and examined for signs of infectious disease. A nurse as stony-looking as the building itself issued me with the stiff and uncomfortable brown uniform that marked us out as Foundlings, and assigned me a place in a big and noisy ward which, on that bleak winter's day, was colder than Hell.

As I shivered beneath my blanket and listened to girls whispering and heard the rackety calls of the nurses, it hardly seemed possible that it had been early in the morning of that same day when Emmie had packed my box with such choice items of food as she could provide, cut a lock of my hair as a keepsake and walked with me to the turn in the road, where the carrier would be passing with his conveyance. In this manner, holding fast to my bonnet as I was bounced about for mile after mile on an un-sprung cart driven by a man who spoke no more than a half-dozen words throughout the entire journey, I made my return to the Foundling Hospital.

The Foundling is not a hospital like St Barthlomew's or Guy's, where they fill you with physic and can take off your leg faster than you can slice bread, but a new sort of orphanage. My first days there were the loneliest I have known and I fell prey to the depredations of older girls, who demanded food from my box and would have made me subject to them had I not one day made a fist of my hand and broken the nose of a red-haired girl two years my senior.

But though I had established myself as an independent spirit, I did not fit in and I knew it. Perhaps I had spent too much time in the company of an adult, Emmeline Whitelaw, who had taught me my numbers, to read and write, to speak a little French and also how to make careful drawings of all we saw upon our country walks. Now, many miles distant, I was able to find consolation in books, borrowing every kind of volume from the Hospital's library. I read indiscriminately and very often with too little understanding of the matter I consumed.

But the drawing which I had learned to do on my walks with Emmie would be another call on my time and attention. The pastimes of the other girls held no appeal for me, and in my free time I preferred to walk the grounds alone and observe the other Foundlings. In this way I discovered new ways of seeing. I saw how the figures of children at play momentarily might fall into a pleasing geometry.

I saw how in the late afternoon, the oblique rays of the setting sun lent the Hospital buildings a solidity they had lacked at midday. I watched how boys ran and how they jumped, saw what happened to the muscles in their necks and lower torsos when they stretched up high to catch a ball and I longed for paper and charcoal to capture what I saw. I watched the nurses watching the boys, and the boys watching the girls in their regulation serge frocks, aprons and tippets. I practised my drawing and I learned from my mistakes.

A year or two before I left the Foundlings, I befriended a little girl who occupied the bed next to mine. Some years my junior, Georgie was thin as paper and at first, she said very little and answered my questions with only a 'yes' or a 'no'. That she was not well was easily learned from her linen features and unnaturally bright eyes. We found common ground in our East Anglian childhoods. Georgie had spent her first years on a farm situated no more than ten miles from our cottage, but she had not been so lucky in her country nurse. If I had gone hungry, she had been half-starved, beaten daily and made to work from dawn's first light until everyone else was abed. Years of such treatment had left her weak and defenceless against the disease she developed shortly before she was returned to the Hospital.

Here, she should have found a refuge, but Georgie was denied even that. It was not only the sickness that tormented her and made her existence a misery. Before the illness had ravaged her face and she was still bright-eyed and uncommonly pretty, she was subject to a number of strange and frightening experiences, the nature of which I could not know at such a tender age, but can perhaps guess at now. When night had come and the children had ceased their whispers and fallen asleep, Georgie was sometimes awoken and spirited away by a silent figure. The first time it happened, I saw the dark shape bend over her bed and rouse her from her sleep. The man – for it moved like a man and not like any of our nurses – spoke in her ear and caused her to rise silently and follow him from the ward. I was young and quite terrified, but still I am ashamed to recall how I feigned sleep whenever I saw this stranger's silhouette in the moonlight.

At such times I would lie awake awaiting her return, which always happened before dawn, frightening myself with imaginings, speculating where she might have gone and wondering why she never protested. When finally she did slip quietly into her bed, I would join her and give her the comfort of my arms. She would never tell me what had happened. This occurred on several occasions and then there came a time when she was absent for three nights and two days. No-one would tell me where she was gone. I had begun to grieve for her, the most likely explanation being that she had succumbed to her illness, but one Sunday morning she appeared in the washroom looking as pale as glass and, saying nothing to me, she took to her bed.

As her malady progressed, the disappearances ceased. The physicians examined her daily and sometimes gave her physic. More often, they shook their heads and went on their way down the ward. One bleak winter's morning, I found her deaf to my urgent whispers that we should rise immediately, as everyone else was already up, and we should be in trouble if we were late at breakfast again. Her small white arm was hanging from her bed but when I shook it, entreating her one more time to rouse herself, I found her flesh was stone cold. They took her away while the others were still washing. I feel the shock even now.

I had not known grief until then, unless you count my parting from Emmie. Georgie's passing was a more personal introduction to death and added a new layer of complication to my existence. Bewildered, I blamed the illness and the sinister disappearances by turn. In my worst imaginings I saw that dark figure as Death himself, come to claim her as his own. And I feared that the next time it glided through the ward, it might be coming for me.

Nine

"And what do I find you doing here?"

I cannot help myself. I shriek.

Gretch is in the painting room. I wonder what he has seen me doing. I don't know how much he knows about my painting duties. Just possibly, he doesn't comprehend that they are usually confined to backgrounds and, just lately, any furniture, properties and sometimes pets which our sitter has elected to be pictured with. I am certainly not allowed to touch the figure itself and if ever I was, I imagine that the eyes, the skin and the hands might be the last things which my master would trust me with. I pray that Gretch knows none of this, nor why the master relies on me more than was ever his intention, I'm sure.

This is because of the recent deterioration of his health. Increasingly, we hear him curse with frustration, and noisily throw something down. The last time he applied himself to this particular canvas, his mahlstick could not steady his brush when the hand that held it was unsteady itself. And that is not all. When he paints now, he sits so much closer to the canvas, and the finer details are not always as crisply delineated as once they were. The smaller buttonholes, I have noticed, are atrocious and there are portraits in which the eyes have lost their magic and no longer engage with and fascinate my own. I can only surmise that the fine detail he has achieved on the great painting in the attic was done some time before this new deterioration set in. Whichever the case, the painting of the merchant captain will be left on our hands, I'm sure, if the captain's own left hand, which rests upon a globe, is not carefully corrected. I can detect the faintest traces of the master's earlier attempts at this, but the fingers are ugly and disproportionate.

This is something I am certain I can fix and so early this morning, I mixed my colours and set to work, knowing that my master, who was loudly suffering last night, would be unlikely to appear before the afternoon. In any case, I think, he surely will not trust himself to paint today. I clean the area carefully with spirit and when the canvas is dry, I apply my base colours. I should like to have the sitter before me. However, I have studied the hands in a dozen paintings we have around the house and have taken my cue from these. The hand I build becomes more lifelike with each added layer of paint, the knuckles and joints, the carefully-cut fingernails and the fine tracery of veins all convince me that I have created something which looks as real as possible. I'm adding a burnished shine to the ring on a finger when I realise that Gretch is behind me.

"I didn't see you, Mr Gretch," I say, when I have recovered myself. "Have you been here long?"

"Long enough to see what you've been up to," he says. "The master won't like this, not at all. Shall I go and tell him now or would you like to explain this to his face?"

"It needed doing," I say, quickly. "He was going to present it to the client as it was."

"I thought this one was unfinished," Gretch says. "Why would he present it now?"

"I don't know if he is blind to its imperfections or no longer has the ability to correct them," I say.

Gretch looks closely at the hand. He inspects it with the authority of a connoisseur, someone who has been around paintings a long time. Then he steps back to assess proportions and says, "This is well done, Michel. To tell you God's honest truth, I cannot detect what is the master's work and what yours."

Then, I think, you need a pair of spectacles. It must be as clear as well-water that the work I have completed today is superior. But Gretch's approval fills me with pride.

"I can do better work than this," I say. "But I had to match the hand to the rest of the painting. I hope I have not been too fine with it."

"It is as it should be," Gretch says. "The master need not know about this."

I am relieved, buoyed with recognition of my talents, but also somewhat confounded. Had Gretch discovered me in similar circumstances just a year or two ago, my skull would have known about it. I finish my work on the ring and stand back, allowing light to wash over the surface. The hand is good: it looks relaxed and natural as it sits upon the globe. The shine on the ring draws the eye to the fineness of the skin and also to the part of the globe on which it sits, an archipelago of islands which the captain claims to have discovered. I am assured that he will buy the work after all.

"I should not have believed a woman could do such work. And certainly not an untrained girl. You have learned well," Gretch says. "Had the master allowed you more leeway and a better knowledge of his secrets, who knows how far you might have gone. A pity. Because you cannot match him at his best, I suppose?"

I do not tell Gretch that I have been a better study of the master's work than he knows, watching him when he thinks I am sizing another canvas or preparing the pigments. I have seen and noted how he adjusts the colours I bring him, adding a little egg tempera or oil as it suits him and I have seen how he works in patches and adjusts them while they are still wet, adding sage green and yellow ochres and tints few would expect to be employed in the painting of human skin. I have also seen how real and lustrous is the finished effect.

I practiced his arts in the attic on days when he was indisposed, completing such small pieces in my room upstairs, Gretch complaining that I brought the smell of the painting room to his chamber. I painted faces from memory and faithfully copied old works by the master. I painted dozens of eyes, with their varicoloured pupils, fleshy lids and specks of dirt left unwiped from their corners. I painted noses of every shape and I painted ears. I had painted more hands than I could remember before I allowed myself to paint the hand in this picture.

Since seeing what is missing in the painting he intends as his masterpiece, I have also been practicing my miniatures, spending long hours reproducing Mr Grace's tiny faces on remnants of canvas of every size, trying always to attain or exceed the highest standards of my master at his best. Only recently, I much enjoyed reproducing a perfect likeness of a terrified minister who is fleeing from some stew with an unpaid harlot giving chase. It would be hard to distinguish some of my studied faces from the originals in the attic, I am sure.

"I think I can match him," I tell Gretch, with sudden decision. "Sometimes, I am sure of it."

"You're an arrogant sparrow, aren't you?" Gretch says. The tone of his voice says he's pleased with me. "But you can't make such extravagant claims to Jamie Gretch without backing them, up, Miss."

"What do you mean?"

"You will know, by and by," Gretch says. "Meanwhile, you learn what you can and if you see any more miscreations like this hand, you will put them right, do you hear?"

He has his hand on the door, when he stops and turns. "One more little thing," he says. "I would not have you going out on the streets unnecessarily just now. There is talk of a maniac at liberty preying on lassies of your age – and some a deal younger, or so I have read."

"Thank you for your concern," I say. "I have read this too, but London is large town, Mr Gretch."

"This house will need every one of its valuable commodities," he snorts, and indicates the picture with a black fingernail, "and perhaps that inventory now includes you."

Gretch goes off to the kitchen, where I hear him cajoling Poll, whom he took again to his bed last night – she cannot refuse him, although at eighteen years she should be old enough to know better. Left alone in the painting room, I look at the canvases stacked against walls and the ones unfinished and drying on the easels in a new and lucid light. These were not my works, I think, but they might so easily be. Very few of these recent paintings are beyond my powers and the more I look at the handful of fine works that we retain in the house, the more I entertain the idea that I might one day be as good – and yes, perhaps better – than the master in his prime. That is how overweeningly sure of myself I have become. I stand before a painting mounted upon an easel and then, taking a cloth and a little oil, I begin to erase one of the poorly-rendered eyes of the youngest Lady Burnham. Her pretty eyes were not, I remembered, the dull things painted here. I work quickly but with assurance and before the next hour has struck I have restored life and beauty to the young lady's face.

Ten

My newfound confidence in my abilities is my rightful reward for the hours I have laboured to learn and perfect my craft, I think. But this isn't entirely true. At the Foundling Hospital, Mr Gilpin, a young tutor with aspirations as an artist himself had shown us how to draw each other and how to see and render the world outside. To those who displayed an aptitude for such things, and I was one, he offered extra tuition. He was not like the others and spent his time and attention on boys and girls alike. His lessons were markedly different. Mr Gilpin did not stand at the front and wave a stick and make us chant our tables or the dates of famous battles. He sat with us, sometimes guiding our hands, and was as keen to teach us as we were to learn.

"Your hand is too stiff, Michel. Hold the porte-crayon so that it moves freely. There, you see? You have it already!"

He taught us proportions, explained perspective and demonstrated how to use light and shade. He showed me the shortcomings of drawings I had made in the school yard and how I might improve them. He introduced me to brushes and watercolour and then to the rudiments of oil painting. In the Hospital chapel, he tried very hard to teach me a simple tune on the organ Mr Handel had played. Mr Gilpin believed in sharing everything he himself knew and if that included firing a flintlock or setting a trap for a rabbit then he was as keen to inculcate that as he was Latin grammar.

Some of the Hospital governors did not agree with the liberality of his educational efforts, one remarking within my hearing that "the children should be confined to that practical learning which will be of real use to them in later life." Another had opined that it was an indulgence to teach girls such things. What was the point of a house servant who could draw? But Mr Gilpin believed that we girls had capabilities beyond the bounds that society had set us.

Though he was doubtlessly regarded as something of a renegade, Mr Gilpin was allowed to continue his lessons. This latitude probably owed much to the other governors being artists themselves, the tradition of the artist governor having been begun some forty years before, by William Hogarth himself. When Mr Gilpin relayed this same fact to us, a tiny hand was hoisted at the front of the class.

"Who is William Hogarth, sir?" said a small boy.

Mr Gilpin made a humorous face, his jaw dropping and his eyes bulging as if he could not believe what he had just heard. "Does anyone know?" he asked us. We did not.

Without another word, he swept out of the school room, beckoning us to follow him. Shoes clacking on the bare boards, we trooped down the empty wards – the other children were playing noisily outside – and then across the yard and through the front doors of the main house. I remember something of the wide staircase and the polished clock cases and the gentle giving of carpet beneath my feet. But these little hints of luxury could not prepare me for what I saw when we stopped at brass-handled doors, which Mr Gilpin threw open. In a great room corniced with plaster and hung with patterned paper, whose floor was covered with a beautifully-worked rug, were enormous paintings, great windows upon another world which struck me with wonder.

“This is the picture gallery,” Mr Gilpin said. “In here and in the Court Room, are works by the greatest painters working in England today.”

I stood gaping like a loon.

Someone said, “Why are they here?”

“A good question,” Mr Gilpin said. “We have Mr Hogarth to thank for that. You have all seen the grand coaches of the ladies and gentlemen turning in here on Sundays?”

Of course, we had seen the rich people strolling about the grounds, some of whom patronised us with smiles while others gawped at us like we were animals in the Tower.

“They come to see you because it is the fashionable thing to do,” Mr Gilpin told us, with audible distaste. “But they also come here to see the exhibition of pictures in these rooms. For a long time, this was the only place where people could see the works of English painters for themselves. Before then, paintings were hung on the walls of those who commissioned them, only to be admired by a privileged few. This place changed all that. Now, let me show you something which Mr Hogarth himself painted.”

The painting was not as big as the others but there was not a child there who was not immediately engaged by the teeming life that was packed into it. It was a picture of a crowd of people on a road somewhere, soldiers, drummers and drinkers at an inn on one side, and more crowded beneath what I can now distinguish as a brothel on the other, girls hanging out of each of its nine windows. Drunken, foolish, censorious and oblivious, they looked like they might escape the confines of their frame at any minute and spill out into the room. With some people shouting, beating a drum or playing a fife and others trying to make themselves heard, one above another, this was a painting as noisy as it was vivid.

I had seen younger prototypes of the people in that painting every day in the yard and had noted their flickering repertoires of expression and seen how they betrayed their wearer's innermost thoughts. I had never before thought that such animation could be captured by a steady hand and a perceptive eye. All sorts of new possibilities presented themselves to me.

If Hogarth could draw this, then surely I could draw Foundlings at play, working in the gardens, arguing and fighting. I might draw the ones who were more forward and vigorous in their actions but also the ones who sought the shadows, like me. I could draw the life I saw, the kitchen staff unloading the food wagons, the fashionable people in their carriages, even the night-soil man making his early morning collections. I took so much from one painting, little knowing then that Mr Gilpin had yet to show me examples of other styles which were to have an even greater impact upon my young and malleable mind.

I sneaked into the gallery at every opportunity and sat for hours in front of some of the finest paintings England had ever assembled. It was here that I was surprised, some twelve months after my first visit, by a group of ladies, the bustle of silk and their tutored tones alerting me to their approach. There was nowhere to hide, so I stood where I was, before *The March to Finchley,* as if I had the same right to admire these works as had they.

The ladies were talking and laughing as they entered, obviously enjoying their excursion to Bloomsbury to see the Foundlings and to be seen themselves by people of their acquaintance. I watched them out of the corner of my eye. Pale and pretty, they looked, in their expensive dresses, their hair elaborately dressed and piled high, or hidden beneath fine wigs. They were amused to see me looking so studiously at the picture and one said that I must be a young critic, while behind her fan, another asserted I had come to steal the painting.

It was not unusual for me to be found out in this room. It had come to the notice of the governors that I might sometimes be discovered trespassing here, but Mr Gilpin had a good opinion of the copies I had begun to make of the paintings. He had shown them my work, he told me one day, and had persuaded the artist-governors to allow me regular access. And so it was that I spent some of my most treasured times at the Hospital in that room, my pleasure sometimes augmented by celestial music emanating from the chapel, where Mr Handel had played his music not so many years before.

The stories I read, the music I heard, and the realisation that I might express myself through drawing and painting were slowly turning me into something very different from the awkward little girl who had arrived at the Hospital four or five years before. My previous ignorance of art, and techniques born of not knowing the correct way to do something, had already given me a style quite unlike anything else, Mr Gilpin allowed. Whether it was good or bad, he did not say.

Eleven

We have been in the attic room since sunrise, the master and I. Now that I am assisting him, if only by mixing his colours and passing up to him one or other of his finer brushes while I keep a steadying foot on his ladder, *The New Fire of London* as I call this great thing, goes on apace. The conflagration explodes from a coal-black night, casting a volcanic glow as far as the outlying hamlets where tiny pricks of paint denote families stumbling from their houses to find out what has turned night into sudden day. The more I examine the details of this canvas, the louder I hear the screams of the terrified and the wails of the newly homeless. I hear too the hooves of runaway horses and the mad plashing of oars as boatmen steer overladen craft across the river.

In its conception and narrative, it is a fantastic picture but a great part of it is recognisable as the London I know today. Men in rich clothes who are rich no longer, gaze about like senseless idiots. Fools carouse in taverns oblivious to their imminent destruction, while a riderless horse canters foaming towards the viewer as if he would leap from the frame. There is so much to admire in this gargantuan work, so much to take in.

But though many hours and much labour has been spent on it since Mr Grace first asked me to keep him safe upon his steps, it still shows no sign of approaching completion. Those faces, those burning buildings, theatres, churches and counting houses, the gilt-edged storm-clouds and the dark, distant hills of Hampstead and Highgate are well enough but something is not right in this picture. Something is needed to give cohesion to its many disparate elements, but what that something might be, I cannot think.

And though he would never say as much to his apprentice, as I am in all but name, Henry Grace seems to share my doubts. More than once, I have seen him throw down his brush and abruptly quit the room, with a curse upon his breath. At such times, I can feel his irritation, the frustration with his failing abilities. I do not know which of these is presently hampering this picture. He now observes the world through the thick lenses of a pair of spectacles, but still he struggles. The sun had yet to set today when he had me risking a blaze in our own house by holding the candlestick much too close to the canvas.

Then there is the trouble he sometimes has in controlling his muscles. Too often his hands will tremble and oblige him to rest his brush upon his mahlstick and make tentative dabs at some small part of the picture, working at a slug's pace until he thinks that he can improve it no further, or just gives up. I can see how much it vexes him to be reduced to this, but I can see too his fixed determination to arrive some day, somehow, at the point when the painting will at last be complete. I have wondered if the whole conception of this vast and ambitious scheme is not the product of his fevered mind, or his intense frustration with his declining abilities, and the burning anger he harbours for a world which cast him him off, believing his talents gone from him.

Sometimes he will refuse my offer of assistance and work alone, locked in the attic. We have heard him up there, his shoes clomping across the bare boards and the crash of something overturned by accident or, just as probable, in a flash of anger. This afternoon, Gretch and I were replacing candles in the niches on the stairs, when from above came the sounds of things breaking. We went up there and stood before the door to the attic room, but neither of us ventured to knock. For a while, there was a deep silence. Then, from within, came the plaintive sound of a man weeping.

In the kitchen, where Poll can be heard scolding the cat, and Mrs Harris is engaged in preparing another unappetising repast as money for food becomes ever more scarce, Gretch is silent, apparently lost in thought and oblivious to the griping of the housekeeper. "Well?" Mrs Harris is saying, putting a pot of murky liquid on a trivet to boil, "What's he about up there? I never heard such a noise! He's going mad, you mark what I say. Any more of that and they'll be carting him off to Bedlam and then where will we be? On the streets, that is where."

"Enough," Gretch snaps, "We will be there soon enough if something is not done. Only we might stay that time a little longer if you betake yourself somewhere you can do some good." Mrs Harris is "Not used to being talked to in that manner" but we all know that tone of Gretch's, and it doesn't do to stand in his way.

"Look at this," he says, when we are alone. "This ledger contains accounts of this household made just after Mr Grace bought the place. Look at what we were spending then. How we entertained. Whole geese, hams from Italy, champagne, French brandy, fine wines. Look at that figure there – that's how much he spent on my livery back then. That is how I dressed when we had money. I ate like a lord, in those days. We all did. No-one noticed when some some of the better things stayed below stairs, not then."

I can hardly conceive of such times, so broken is this house now.

"I had standing, too," Gretch goes on, "Not only among other footmen, but people in the world of art, as well. Mr Grace entrusted me with the sale of some of his greatest works and in this fashion I was introduced to important men. I didn't wear my livery on these days and I was treated as quite the gentleman. People knew me then, Michel. But look at what we have arrived at now. And I tell you this, it will get worse."

"How is that possible?" I ask. A fine display of ignorance, I think now.

"On the streets, that's where Mattie says we'll be and she's right. Look through these recent entries and you'll see that we have been living beyond our means. Some distance beyond them, despite the economies we all have made. And then there is the master himself, who continues to write notes of credit for treatments which do him no good and drag us deeper into our morass of debt." He pauses for a moment or two, appearing to shudder at some passing thought. "You have never lived on the streets of this city."

I admit that I have not.

"Let me tell you it is not a thing to be wished. A girl who has no experience of the streets will die on them. Unless she can find safe shelter on a freezing night and learns to pilfer carrots and cabbages from Covent Garden. And avoids getting her neck stretched for her trouble, of course. If she does not know such things, London will do for her quick. And there's people in those streets, Miggs, wicked people, who can make a young girl wish it had done for her, should she fall into their tender care".

"There's one such prowling about now," Mrs Harris says. "Murdering little girls or sending them raving mad, that's what I hear. My friend Mr P. at Highgate says the authorities know who is doing it, but they are powerless to stop him."

"What can we do?" I ask him, ignoring Mrs Harris who is expecting some return on her prattle. "What will you do?" I say. Gretch seems a survivor. I could do worse than follow him, perhaps.

"Do? I will remain here, one way or the other." And then he adds, shaking his head, "I am nothing without this house."

I picture Gretch filling the blunderbuss with tin tacks. He falls silent, brooding on his future, I think. Then he says, "When was the last time you saw that painting in the attic?"

"Two days past, Mr Gretch," I say.

"And how did it look? Was it much progressed?"

I shake my head. In these last sessions Grace has done nothing to improve the picture and in places has made it worse.

"That is unfortunate," Gretch says, "Because in that attic lies the key to our future."

"I do not understand you," I say.

"It is like this," he sighs, as if this is something I must of course know. "That picture, properly completed, might compare with anything Mr Grace did when he was at the height of his powers. Do you follow me? Sold at auction, such a work would return more than enough money to save this house. I know this as if it were already a fact."

"You are very certain of its promise, Mr Gretch," I say, doubtfully. Because my own opinion of this extraordinary, half-finished work is still divided, of course.

"I have not spent years as Grace's agent without gaining some little understanding of art and its market," Grace says, shortly. "Believe me, lassie, if that painting lives up to its promise, these last years will be painted over. Other works of his will be in demand too. Anything that appears with his name in the future will sell too. Money will flow, there will be food on the table, guests in the drawing room. The great days will come again. We will be safe."

I say nothing about this, fearing that Grace will not have the strength to complete the picture upstairs, let alone undertake future commissions. I doubt we can solve the problem of the missing element in the composition. How can we possibly help Grace to decide upon the central focus of his own masterwork? He would not tolerate the views of an assistant or a servant on such a matter, I know. And he would need to decide his course and begin the painting soon, too, before his power to complete the picture is gone.

Gretch voices my own doubts. "But of course, all that may never be, not with the man as he is now."

I wonder that he can say this yet sound no notes of despair.

He beckons me to follow him out the kitchen door and into the area, where the chill night air is a reminder of streets which await, should this house collapse.

"Is there no cure?" I say. "No doctor who could restore him long enough to finish the task?"

Gretch rolls his eyes about the starry heavens as is he might find the answer there.

"He has tried them all, every cure and all the quacks," Gretch says. "He has tried things, I think, that he tells no-one about."

"So Grace has a promising painting which will never be finished?"

He is silent as a falling star burns itself out over Greenwich.

Somewhere in the black square, drunks are shouting; glass shatters and a woman's scream splits the air. It passes my mind that I may be among these cast-offs soon enough if money fails us. I might despair did I not sense that Gretch himself remains hopeful.

“Do not be so glum, lassie,” he says at last. He sounds almost avuncular. Then he surprises me further by laying a gentle hand on my shoulder. “I have something in mind,” he whispers. “Be patient a little longer.”

Twelve

"I never saw such a thing."

Mouse looks at his friend as if he might have an answer for his bewilderment. Obadiah is smoking his pipe in the niche behind the fireplace, over which an old cutlass suspended from the chimney breast lends the newspaper a buccaneering character, in his opinion at least. Obadiah sometimes sees the newspaper in piratical terms, an unruly marauder sailing forth under the flag of truth. Or sometimes profit. The ship's captain tries not to roll his eyes. "Then you must walk through London with your eyes closed," he says.

"She was so very young. Lying there among the daffodils. Only a child, and quite dead, Obadiah."

"Young, old, it doesn't matter. It is dreadful, of course it is, but the truth is that the streets are full of such things."

"But what kind of a person…"

"Any kind. Vicious fools, opium eaters, some bagnio's drunken bully looking for new flesh. Disgruntled Scotsmen. It is all the same. Is this really so strange for a little man who is everywhere in London? Ah, but you keep your eyes where I want them, don't you? On the stars. Good old Mouse!"

"You should have seen her, Obadiah. No, I would not wish anyone to see such a thing. A more pitiful sight I cannot imagine. It has quite undone me."

"Oh, my dear friend! It is truly commendable that you care so, but really, have you not seen death on the streets of London? Not been out at night and seen the huddled bodies in their pitiful rags, lying one upon the other for warmth like stacked bones in an ossiary? Or a baby washed up by the Thames? Or hard-frozen beggars who fell asleep in doorways and never woke up? There is death enough on these streets, Mouse, more than people have tears to cry. Here is my handkerchief. Wipe your eyes."

"What can we do?"

"We can write about it, Mouse. We can alert those who have the power to change this world. What else is there to do? Now, tell me what has happened, but do not expect me to cry with you."

Mouse takes a moment to compose himself.

"Well," he says at last. "You will recall I heard of something amiss at Marylebone and as I had planned a jaunt to the windmill anyway, I thought I might find something to fill our pages at the same time."

"Good, Mouse, good."

"As you also know, it's not a long walk through the fields from Oxford Street, but when I got there she had already been loaded onto a carrier's dray. Someone had sent to Bow Street for a Runner and had given into his custody a fellow who had been apprehended at the scene.

The poor girl was found in a shady part of the gardens by a courting couple, who came upon her murderer in the very act of robbing her person. The gentleman was able to apprehend the villain quite easily, the witnesses said."

"Such savagery, eh, Mouse? And all for the sake of lust or a few pennies, I'll warrant."

"No, no, that is what is so strange. The man who was taken up had in his hand gold sovereigns, or so I heard."

"I agree it is sad, Mouse, but I do wonder what sort of girl would be walking there unescorted."

"There was a small crowd when I arrived. I pushed through, the better to see if there was hope for her. But she was white as marble, quite dead. There was blood, such a lot of blood, Obadiah, blood on her pretty little dress."

"Oh, my dear Mouse, do you not know why young girls are found in such places on their own? There is usually only one reason."

"No, I won't hear that. This was a child, Obadiah. As innocent as a freshly-born lamb. And did you not hear what I said about the dress? It was nice, Obadiah, respectable. She was no fledgeling street slattern, you may take that as a fact. This girl was of a poor but honest family."

"You can tell all that from a dress?"

"Of course not. This is what I have since found out."

"Clever little Mouse. So why would the child of such a family be roaming alone in Marylebone Gardens?"

"It is a mystery, I admit it."

"And in possession of gold sovereigns, you say? You are certain of it?

Now, that I find interesting."

"Why?"

"Let me see our recent editions. Do we still have the one from August 28?"

Mouse burrows into a mountain of old newspapers stacked loosely in a corner and somehow retrieves what he looks for.

"Your thoughts, Obadiah?"

Obadiah unfolds the newspaper and angles it to catch the fading window light.

"The little girl who appeared in a dreadful phrenzy at a performance of the German prodigy? In Hampstead?"

"The one who had been violated by devils?"

"I'm not sure we were quite exact in printing that. But yes, that one."

"But what of it?"

"It may be nothing, dear Mouse. The world is full of coincidence. But look at this: she too was found with sovereigns on her person. And both were girls who might not, in the normal way of things, see such a coin in all their lives. There is surely some connection here. But no matter, they have the culprit and there is nothing more to feed our press."

"If indeed he was the guilty party."

"What do you mean?"

"This man was taking money, Obadiah, not giving it. He looked in desperate need of it too. I think the authorities will quickly find this is not the man they seek."

Obadiah reads one more time what he had written two or more weeks before.

"Dead girls with gold coins. Did you ever hear of such a thing?"

Mouse removes his wig and scratches his scalp.

"Well, now that you put me in mind of it, I did hear of one other incident bearing similarities. This happened in the depths of winter, last year. A young girl had been wandering in falling snow on Hounslow Heath. She confessed to the traveller who found her that she had been used unspeakably and later, cast from a coach. Whoever did this dreadful thing had left her to find her own way home, or die in the attempt. The fellow could not say more about her, only that she had paid him a gold sovereign for guiding her to the shelter of the inn on the heath."

"Well, well." Obadiah stops his pacing and gives Mouse his full attention. "As you say, it may be nothing. And then again, who knows? It may be everything."

"You know, *The Sentinel* has been reporting similar outrages."

"Have they indeed? And with what result, I wonder?"

"People have been frightened. Its reports have been widely debated."

"Frightening readers is hardly the job of a responsible news-sheet? I am surprised that a newspaper of such standing would soil its hands with such stuff."

"I'm given to understand that those reports have done its circulation no harm. No harm at all."

Obadiah sits up. "A matter of coincidence, surely?"

"Sadly, I think not, Obadiah. Extraordinary to think it, but there may be an appetite for such things."

"Well, well, I must say that surprises me. But who knows? Perhaps a responsible newspaper should not quite overlook the predilections of those who keep its press working? We have long catered for readers of differing opinion ourselves."

"I think this it is not a path to be taken lightly," Mouse says.

"And nor will we. But has *The Sentinel* found a linking factor in these occurrences?"

"It seems not to have thought to look for one."

Obadiah stands, walks up the room as far as the door, turns about and comes to a stop by his printing press, on which he now rests his weight.

"Well, then. If they have succeeded with such poor stuff, imagine what this newspaper might do if we can prove such a connection. First thing tomorrow, set that inquisitive nose of yours to work, Mouse. I want to know all there is to know about these girls and where they had been before they were found. Who knows, but perhaps this will be the story to save *The Enquirer*."

Thirteen

I begin to pay close attention to my master's state of health. Though it fluctuates and some days he is able to do things which the day before he could not I believe that Gretch is right and that he worsens by the week. It would much aid our plans, such as they are, if we were to know his prognosis with a better degree of accuracy, but the opinions of quacks are not to be trusted. The respected physicians he began with departed long ago in a flutter of unpaid bills.

It would, of course, be a gross impertinence to ask Grace himself and useless in any case; he is too closed a book. He has kept so much to himself that even Jamie Gretch can only guess at how little money he has left and how near we are to ruin. He tells me he has broached the matter of being granted legal permissions to act as his financial agent. There will come a time, he says, when Grace will be unable to deal with such matters. Grace is indeed a mystery. No-one knows much about my master, beyond certain facts which are generally understood. That he went abroad as a young man and that when he came back, he very quickly became the celebrated artist that is still talked of today, despite Henry having, during these last several years, fallen from grace.

You would think that Gretch would know something more, as he was taken on by Mr Grace on his return from the Continent, years ago. He has been closer with the master than I have been, or ever will be, having played every part for him as his fortunes and those of the house have changed; butler, footman, valet, artist's agent. But difference in station would have prevented Gretch from playing the part of his confidant. His master remains an enigma to us all.

"He was a great man, so he was," says Mrs Harris when we sit down to a skinny fowl and a few boiled potatoes. Since the cook was let go, her duties have been shared between Mrs Harris and Poll, with varying and often unpalatable results. "He was the sort of young fellow," Mrs Harris retails her oft-heard story, "to make a supper of pheasants, guinea fowl and lobsters and to fill his cellar with wine and spirits from France."

Gretch puts down his knife and begins to enlarge on this, as I knew he would.

"We had a properly-staffed house then," he acknowledges, "capable of providing dinner for thirty, a thing we did on numerous occasions, mark you. When we entertained, that road out there would be choked with carriages as guests came and went, a dozen link boys on hand to see home the foot passengers. Great people visited this house. People who had position then and who have position yet. The name of Grace held sway in those days, let me tell you."

He boasts for Grace like he is boasting for himself, so tightly intertwined has been his life with that of his master. And yet for all his talk, I doubt he knows his master much better than we do. How much at odds such secrecy seems with the open face of the self-portrait in the hall.

Poll has taken the chair by the dresser, resting her legs unnoticed while we talk.

"I never thought we would come to this," Mrs Harris says. "I took him for a better man than he turned out to be."

“We none of us thought it would come to this,” Gretch allows, scraping back his chair and picking meat from between his teeth. “But I will not have him shoulder all the blame. We should have taken more notice of the signs. For signs there were.”

“What signs?” I ask.

“Sure, there was a change in the man,” Mrs Harris says. “We all saw it.”

“A change in him and a change in his work,” Gretch says. “Which became drab, lifeless. The spark had gone, as had his muse. I thought that we just had to wait for the hussy to return.”

“The disease had struck?” I say.

“No,” Gretch says, slowly. “The change began before that had taken hold. Something had happened to him. Something that stripped him of whatever it was that had made him brilliant.”

“We all saw it,” Mrs Harris says again. “He had been a good master before that. Now he had moods. One day it was 'Mrs Harris, be so kind as to.' And then the next he was using language to me that would make a coal-heaver blush. I thought he was gone staring mad.”

“That is your master you talk of,” Gretch says. “Take care, Mrs Harris.”

“I tell you that he did not act like a sane and sensible man. Stopping the entertainments and hiding himself away. Telling callers he was not at home”

“Enough of your prattle,” Gretch snaps. “You know nothing of this.”

“I know that man was frightened,” Mrs Harris says.

"Frightened?" thunders Gretch. "Frightened? What did a man like Henry Grace have to be frightened of? You're babbling again."

"Something was frightening him," Mrs Harris persisted. "He had that look about him. He had lost his certainties, something a man should never lose. I could see it in the way he walked, the way he spoke. He was not quite here. You know it as well as I do, Mr Gretch."

"There has never been anything wrong with his mind, woman," Gretch snapped. "You do not know what you are prattling about."

"There were some funny people about this house in those days. People I might not have invited, had I the charge of such. I saw things."

"Lord save us," says Gretch. "She presumes to tell me what I do and I do not know and then says that her master is mad. This is the day I thought I would never see, Mrs Harris. Such behaviour would not be tolerated at any other house."

"Any other house would pay its staff, Mr Gretch," Mrs Harris retorts.

The old order is breaking down as the money goes.

"Well, then, what did you see, woman?" Gretch says. "You would have been no more than a housemaid then. What could you have known about the people who came here?"

"I saw them closeted with him in dark corners. Him in particular, the one who wore the garnet ring, him you didn't take to, Mr Gretch. Death, I thought his name was and well it would have suited him. He was always whispering to Mr Grace. The master seemed to shrink from him. I do not know why he was ever invited here."

"How do you know all this?"

"A servant changing a pot or trimming a candle is rarely seen. I never heard the subject of their whispering but it was something not to the master's taste, I can tell you that."

"Get on with you," Gretch said. "This is all in your silly mind. When men talk business they do so privily. He had money and everyone wanted to invest it for him. And a pity he let them, the fortune he lost."

"I'm not gainsaying you, Mr Gretch," says Mrs Harris. "But I saw what I saw. And I remember how that man used to come here on his own sometimes and dine with Mr Grace. I took them for friends at first and perhaps they were. But not in the latter days, anyone could see that. And not meaning to be forward, but I remember how you and he were with each other, Mr Gretch."

Poll sits up. She has a nose for ripe tattle.

"That man," Gretch growls, "Was an impudent puppy who usurped my position. God help me if I would not whip him, gentleman as he is. Ordering my staff like they were his own and regulating the entertainments. What right had he?"

"What right indeed, Mr Gretch," Mrs Harris says.

"I had my differences with that fellow," Gretch says, "Lord knows I did. And Mr Grace no doubt had his. But that does not mean he was the root of Grace's troubles."

"I have heard things about him," Mrs Harris says. "Things I would not repeat in front of the children."

"Ah, the rumours, again," Gretch sighs. "Fools' chatter, every one of them. Mr Grace has ever been the subject of rumours. I have heard the damndest things bruited about that man upstairs. That he has become an opium eater, a slave to the pipe. That another man wears a mask to paint in his place. Rubbish, all of it, of course it is."

“Well, some rumours, Mrs Harris begins, “have a grain...”

No-one has noticed Poll stand up and approach the table. Dark curls escape from the thin girl's greying mob cap as she looks first at Gretch, then at Mrs Harris and then at me.

“I have heard,” she says, as hard eyes meet mine, “That Mr Grace killed someone.”

Fourteen

I thought that my master might ever remain the mystery he was to me at that time, little knowing how soon I would come to know very much more about him. This came about following an unexpected discovery in the library. When first I came to this house, the library was off-bounds to anyone but Mr Grace himself, as were his bedchamber, his dressing room and cabinet and the attic. These rooms Mr Grace regarded as his personal demesne. I might enter the library only on rare occasions, as when he asked me to fetch certain books or papers. I recall that when first I opened the door to this room (and this was not so long ago, Grace being extremely reluctant to have a child loose in here) I was met by a fragrance that was instantly familiar, and which transported me back to the library in the Foundling Hospital.

This was the aroma of old leather and vellum, of glue and decay, termites and dust. It was not only the smell that struck chords within me, but the look of the place too. Great oaken bookshelves lined every wall, except where tall, narrow windows cast trapezoids of bright sunlight over some boxes on the floor. Although the books themselves looked like they would all benefit from being taken out and given a thorough dusting, and there was the smell of slow rot in the air, no doubt they would remain much as they were, arranged beautifully, shelf upon shelf, for many years to come. So I thought, in those days..

I ran my eye over the titles, recognising not a few from the depredations I had made upon the Foundling's library. *Le Quattre Livre*

Stagione by Vitruvius, four volumes of architectural delights whose illustrations had assisted my drawing of buildings; Dante Alighieri's *Divine Comedy* (which had disturbed my sleep) and *The Lives of the Artists* by Georgio Vasari, from which I had drawn encouragement as I began my own journey into art. It was revealing that the owner of this library fuelled his imagination with the written word as well as the visual world. I thought that if I could catch the master in an amenable mood, I might ask to read these books again. They would surely make better sense now that I was nearly seventeen, than they had to a little girl of nine.

On the enormous and intricately-patterned rug and beneath the windows, the room bore a much more confused aspect. Here were boxes which had recently been opened or perhaps were about to be nailed shut, filled with straw and ornamental treasures such as the statuette of Aphrodite I picked up and admired, decorated vases and suchlike – that I surmised that Mr Grace had picked up on his travels abroad. Other boxes contained papers, yellowing documents, tied bundles of letters, stacks of old sale catalogues and pamphlets of every permutation. I saw that on the wall opposing the filled cases were empty shelves and on the floor before them, more boxes, some brimming with a chaos of brochures, periodicals and booklets, others neatly packed with catalogued books ready for sale. Seeing these brought to mind something Gretch had said some weeks ago about it now being the turn of Mr Grace's books and writings to go to the sale room.

That was some little time ago. On the day I make my great discovery, the whole place bears a very different aspect, one of great confusion and to my eternal shame, I am its cause. What has happened is this. Minutes before the library became this place of chaos, with books and papers strewn all about and furniture violently upturned, I had been hunting for sketches of Rome and other places that Mr Grace had made on his Grand Tour as a young man. Gretch had advised me that I might learn much from the mistakes Grace had made in the preparatory exercises that had laid the foundations for the great, finished works themselves. "It seems to me," he had said, shaking his bald head at something upon my easel, "That there is a sequence to be followed which you cannot overstep, stages in his development which you should understand if you are to paint like Henry Grace at his best. Yes, you would do well to see his old sketchbooks."

The largest bookcase occupied the best part of the back wall and commanded the remaining space like a hill fort. The cupboards at its base I found filled with bric-a-brac, trinkets, gee-gaws and other small mementoes of his travels. The shelves above were given over to beautifully-bound editions of modern novels with the authors' names – Fielding, Richardson, Wakefield, Swift, Walpole, Smollett – picked out in gold letters and arranged in alphabetical order. What caught my eye and excited my interest lay on the shelf above, a stacking of bound papers of a weight suitable for sketching and drawing. Certain I had found what I was looking for, I threw the library ladder against the bookcase, ascended the steps and pulled out my prize.

Opening one of these books confirmed that I had indeed found what I was questing. In the first sketch the artist had seemingly been trying to depict the vast interior space, quite as much as the beautiful carved stones that enclosed it, of some mighty Roman church. I had to admit that the young Grace's handling of light and shade was beyond anything I had yet achieved. The sketchbooks I had tucked under my arm would teach me much, I thought, but there was one more yet to be had, a larger book which lay atop the bookcase and just beyond my reach.

I mounted the last step and hitching my skirts, I took my next upon a high shelf. Standing upon this I would easily be able to reach the last sketchbook. The bookcase had looked sturdy enough to take my weight but I had no sooner transferred my other foot to the shelf and reached out towards the book than I felt the upper part of the casing, that appeared now to be mounted separately upon the cupboards below, come away from the wall. For a moment it rocked as if undecided whether to return to the wall or to come away entirely. Books sliding from their places and falling to the floor told me which way it was to go. There was a moment of strange calm in which I knew that the case would fall and I with it and its weight would probably kill me and there was nothing I could do about it. All this must have occurred within a fraction of a second because in the next I was falling backwards, the bookcase following.

The sound the bookcase made as it came down was not the crashing and splintering and breaking I had expected, but a heavy crump accompanied by the shuffling and sliding of a hundred or more heavy books. I remember the smell of those books, the taste of old paper and the swirling cloud of dust motes that engulfed me as I lay entombed in a triangular sanctuary created when the topmost shelves came heavily to rest upon the sole soft furnishing in the room, an eastern divan, thankfully of the sturdiest kind. Had the case not fallen here, I might not be writing this today. I thanked merciful Heaven that I was, after one or two moments, able to emerge from beneath the furniture with no worse harm than a filthy dress and a bloody nose.

As I hauled myself to my feet and surveyed the anarchy I had brought to this peaceful place, the scattered books, pamphlets and papers of all sorts, I heard a familiar clacking of shoes on floorboards. My heart stopped as the door swung open. I hung my head and waited for James Gretch to vent the violent fury of which I knew he was more than capable. I waited and then, when the silence remained unbroken, I looked up. His face was a carmine red but he appeared for the moment to be controlling his temper.

"Well?" The tone is one I have heard many times before, the presage to a storm about to burst. I am no longer the promising painter, only a naughty girl awaiting her doom.

"I was looking for Mr Grace's sketchbooks," I manage to cough out. "The ones you advised me to consult."

Gretch expels a pent breath, slowly. "So. I see. Then this is *my* fault?"

In my experience, this moment in which he appears to consider the justice of a situation is the most dangerous.

"No, of course not. I did not think to see that the case was affixed to the wall and I..."

Gretch takes another breath and holds it. He appears to be engaged in some internal struggle with himself. At last, he says, "You did not think. How very like you that was."

"The sketchbooks," I say, quickly. "You were right."

Gretch picks up one of these and browses its pages before handing it to me.

He expels another breath, loudly, this time.

"Of course I was. Take them and study them well. As for this pandemonium, I have no time for it, not today. I will help you to re-stand the bookcase and then you must set this room to rights yourself. It must appear as if none of this has happened, do you understand me?"

I nod, amazed at a restraint he could not possibly have displayed only a year ago, when I might have expected a stream of invective and the threat of violence at the very least. Today Gretch appears concerned with other matters and says nothing more as he takes hold of one end of the great casing. Now empty of its contents, setting the bookcase back against the wall is not quite the Herculean task I have foreseen. Harder, I think as Gretch closes the door behind him, will be replacing the books on the shelves in such order that nothing might be seen amiss. But those books, along with all sorts of papers, rolled documents tied with ribbon or sealed with wax, lie everywhere about. I set to work.

Restoring harmony to the shelves is in fact easier than I had feared. Recalling where I had seen some volumes before reveals to me the order in which others had been housed and I am able to replace the books on the lower shelves and stacks of prints on the higher ones. To all intents and purposes the job is done. I stand back to admire my work and then make one or two adjustments to placing of the books upon the shelves. To my mind at least, it is indeed as if nothing has happened. Whether Mr Grace himself would detect any anomalies in their disposition is another matter, but it has been some weeks since he last picked his way down the stairs. It only remains for me to pluck telling fragments of broken sealing wax from among the warp and weft of the rug and to restore some sort of order to the pamphlets, papers and small notebooks that have been dislodged from the lower cupboards. It is I am sorting through these things that I make my discovery.

At first I take this item for only a small, but expensively-bound book, another to be found a home for, somewhere on the shelves. But this one is different. Its spine lacks the gold lettering of most of the other books on the shelves and is instead quite blank, showing nothing except for the Roman numeral I. When I open the flyleaf I am surprised to find no author's name, nor a title for the book itself. Although later I find the name H.R. Grace inscribed on the following page, what I recognise as I turn over page after page is the close hand and constrained prose that I have seen on the strangely prolix notes which I have been entrusted to deliver variously to the colourist, the apothecary and the bank. It belongs, without doubt, to my master, Henry Grace. I have found his journal.

Fifteen

The Journal of Henry Grace

On the day of my nineteenth birthday, we arrive at Calais and I think I never was so glad to have solid ground beneath my feet. We barely had quit the harbour at Dover when the wind got up and began to toss us about with such violence that my sympathy for people who recall earthquakes in London increased a thousandfold. There are just the two of us in Calais, myself of course, and Dr Shepherd, my divinity tutor at Cambridge. No, there are three, if we are to count my recently-acquired manservant, Bennison. He deserves mention, I suppose, for the trouble we so often put him to. It was Bennison who got us through the douaniers virtually unscathed, despite our too-numerous boxes, and this night finds us comfortable lodgings in the centre of the town, and a fire to warm us, when at last we are ready to face a light repast.

The waiter brings us wine, to which Dr Shepherd helps himself quite liberally, but shakes his grey head when I try to follow suit.

"Let us be straight about the terms on which we embark this journey," he says, his ponderous manner returning me to the slumberous lecture halls of this past Michaelmas term. "Your father, Mr Richard Grace," he says, "Has entrusted the welfare and well-being of you, his youngest son, to my care. For the duration of this sojourn, I shall be in *loco parentis*. It will be my task to open your mind to the culture and customs of the lands through which we shall travel, while keeping you true to the faith." He pours himself another glass of wine and settles further down in his chair.

"I should like to take a walk about Calais," I say, "And clear my head after the voyage."

"That is out of the question," murmurs Dr Shepherd. "This is not England. There are all kinds of dangers. In this town there are low inns and girls who provide for sailors. And that may not be the worst of it. I fear that as we progress deeper into the hinterland of this troublesome country we may encounter all sorts of nefarious vagabonds only too ready to assault and rob you and turn you from your proper path. The wise are vigilant, Master Grace. Now get along to bed, for we shall have an early start on the morrow."

I need hardly tell you that this is not as I had envisaged celebrating my nineteenth birthday. Young and full of vigour, I am at last free of the encumbering chains of my English upbringing and with Dr Shepherd as my only fetter, am set to make the most of an interlude pregnant with opportunity. And so, no sooner do I hear Dr Shepherd close and bolt his door than I take up my satchel with its book of useful French phrases, open my own door and slip noiselessly down the stairs and out into the cobbled street. Relishing the freshness of the chill night air, I make my way back down to the harbour, where I can see lights flickering in windows. The sun has long set but the moon has risen. The silver shimmer it gives the sea beyond the harbour walls silhouettes the ships at anchor and shines also on the buckles of my shoes as I walk for the first time on foreign soil.

All sorts of possibilities are revealing themselves to me. I am picturing the adventures I might have, the experience I will gain, the brilliant sketches I will make and also, the manly figure I will cut on my return to England – when I hear the sound of footsteps behind me. I turn and look, but the moonlit road is empty, and the windows of the small houses that crowd it are all shut up. I go on, thinking that whoever it was, has turned up another of these narrow streets. But then I hear the footsteps again and when I stop, so do they.

My mind fills with awful possibilities. Why should not footpads, highwaymen and other desperate men be as common here as they are on Hounslow Heath? Very probably there are types of French villain of which I have never heard. My heart is thumping as I cast off propriety and run headlong down the winding street, all the time listening for sounds of my pursuer over my own laboured breathing. By the time I reach a cluster of buildings by the quay, I am exhausted of breath and have to steady myself against the harbour wall before I can begin to think of what to do next. I can no longer hear footsteps, but that does not mean that my pursuer has not taken cover in a doorway until he sees an opportune moment to make his assault.

Around me are several buildings, all low in every sense of the word. In two of these are lights and from one issues the scratching of a fiddle. I can see no inn sign but as this is what the place seems to be, I push open a rough door and find myself in an unlit passage. The fiddle-playing stops. I call out for the patron, and receiving no answer, I call again. French innkeepers, it seems, are less attentive than English ones, who would already have opened my account with a room, an order for food and a hot toddy, together with a promise of breakfast in the morning. I open the door on my right. A guttering candle faintly illuminates the corpulent figure of a big man asleep in a chair, whom I try, but fail to rouse.

And then, between loud Gallic snores, I hear the sounds of raised voices emanating from the back of the house. A door at the end of the passage opens into a small room that looks something like a taproom but more like a stable. Inferior candles, a single oil lamp and the dying embers of a fire faintly describe tables and chairs and the straw which litters an unswept floor. The voices I heard belong to a party in the corner, a young man and an older woman who are seated at a table on which, I notice, is an empty wine bottle and a violin. They appear to be arguing with the serving girl. Dropping my hat and cane upon a table, I seat myself and call for wine.

The girl, who is young, dark and I suppose pretty in her way, is engaged with the party in the corner and though I expend much patience in awaiting my turn, it is apparent that something is detaining her there. It is late, I am tired and would take refreshment before I find my way back to my bed. The girl ignores me, but before my irritation can give way to anger, I discern the reason for her heedlessness. The woman, a quite well-dressed and good-looking example somewhere about five and forty, is grasping the little girl's wrist and much too tightly, it seems. "Are you stupid or just being willful?" she is demanding. "Why cannot you understand the simplest of things?"

The girl tries to pull free and calls out "Jean Michel, aidez moi!" as loudly as she might. She will get no help from the unrousable person in the chair, I think. The young man appears to be relishing the moment. But whatever the cause of the altercation, it is standing between me and a long-desired draught of wine, and so I rise and approach their table and say something to the girl.

"Ah, at last," the young man says. "An Englishman who can talk the gibberish! You, sir, can you make sense of what this fool of a French girl is saying? Can she or can she not find us an alternative billet to the rat's nest that we have been assigned? That is all we want to know."

He is not much more than a boy, but he talks like a man of the world. I am intrigued.

“You wish to change your room?”

“What are you, an imbecile? Get on with it. Ask her, man.”

My command of the French language is imperfect, to say the least. Though my dancing master, M. Diderot, had taught me some fancy steps and what to do with my hands in every kind of social situation, he had impressed on me no more than the rudiments of what he claimed as his native tongue. Nor had he taught me how to refuse importunate requests such as this. However, the young man being most insistent, I pose his question to the girl in faltering French.

At first she does not appear to understand me. “C’est impossible,” she says, when she has untangled my words. The rooms had been filled. Les Anglais must stay where they were or find somewhere else. "That will not do at all," the young man says. "Tell her that Lady De'Ath and her son will be properly accommodated or the British consul will know of it." The girl's black eyes blaze when I press the point and she wrenches free her wrist.

I can glean only fragments of the tirade that follows. She will take no more from these English pigs, she says. How much longer will they remain here spitting on her food, shouting in their violent tongue and keeping people awake at night with that dreadful instrument? Why do they stay on? Have they nowhere else in Europe to go? When I settle the matter by the simple expedient of pressing two livre into the girl’s hand, I cannot say who is the more delighted, she or my new acquaintances at the table. A glass of wine, I remind the girl.

"You will take that glass with us," the boy says. "More vino!” he calls after the girl.

And then, quite clearly, I hear the woman say into her hand, "You are too hasty, Os. Prey ask him where he is from. Who are his people?”

I tell them my name and that I am newly arrived to take a tour of Europe.

The woman nods approvingly. "Very proper too. You must tell me about your family. The name of Grace is not familiar to me but I may know some branch of your tree, perhaps."

I do not much like being asked about my family. My fellows at the university fell into two camps. Those who saw my father as the flag-bearer of a coming age (this camp amounting to no more than two close friends, both of whom regularly came to me for money) and those who thought that the son of a common manufacturer had no business mixing with blue-blooded gentlemen. My family, I will say now, is as respectable as any, and you may call me a republican for it, but I do not see why we should be any the less regarded because our money comes from cotton. And so I tell the woman about my father, Richard Grace, and the mill in the West Riding which made our fortune.

“He speaks like a servant,” the young man says and earns an admonishing glance from his mother, who says, “Prey sit, sir, and forgive my son his manners. Let us share a bottle of wine and discover what a mill-owner's son will do in Europe. Why not? It may amuse, and certainly will inform us. Os, you may introduce me."

And so it is that I meet the De'Aths, Lady Jane and her son, a dark, handsomely-attired young man named Osiris. Both profess amazement that I am not familiar with the De’Aths of Steyne Hall. Surely I know it? Off Clerkenwell Green? But I lived at Clerkenwell when I was sent to spend a season in town and the only large house I saw of that description was a burned-out ruin where, it was said, the owner had gone stark mad and had set the place afire. Some in Clerkenwell said that he had staggered from the raging inferno dressed as a human candle before expiring on the lawn outside.

Osiris De'Ath drains off the last of his wine and changes his tack. "But divisions be damned," he says. "We are not in England here. Let us eat!"

The girl is summoned but seems reluctant to render any service until she sees that I have joined the table. A bottle of wine is brought and promptly sent back by Osiris. "Your best," he calls after the girl, "Not this cat's piss." Two further bottles appear and disappear before the fricasee of lamb is brought out. Having had, as I say, only a light repast after my tumultuous Channel crossing, I fall upon it, though the meat is tough and the cheese smells of old clothes. Despite their initial reserve, I now find the De'Aths quite eager to converse and they take a most polite interest in me and my doings.

I open my satchel and show them a selection of my sketches and speak about how I am resolved to become an artist. We talk of itineraries. I tell them that I intend to perfect my French and learn Italian and make sketches of the antiquities at Rome and Herculaneum. In short, I will complete my education. This provokes an unexpected reaction from Osiris.

"Education be fucked," he says. "I could show him an education, hey, mother?"

"You've had a glass too many, I think," Lady Jane says. "Do not upset the boat, Osiris."

"What rubbish, Mother. Hey, you, girl. Encore du vin, is it?"

"What do you think of the French, Mr Grace?" Lady Jane says, as if she would wrest the conversation from her son. "They are filthy dogs, are they not? I am ashamed that we find ourselves in such a place."

I confess I am surprised to see such an eminent family housed in a place like this.

"Do not think for one moment that we took this by choice," says Lady Jane. “We are the victims of a hideous twist of fate. Letters of credit arranged for our collection here failed to arrive. We left the matter in the hands of Mr Fishman, our agent in London, who normally is the most trustworthy of men but now he does this! I can only surmise he has fallen ill or been knocked down in the street. Nothing else can explain it. And so we find ourselves in Calais with only enough portable money to put up at this abominable place. We have dispatched a messenger to London to set things right but it may be days before we can lay claim to what is ours. Well, it is only a temporary inconvenience. Once we are restored we will spend a day or two refreshing ourselves at the Hotel d'Or before hiring a carriage and going on."

“He does not want to hear of our damned bad luck,” Osiris says, bringing out a pack of cards. “A man needs distraction after an arduous journey. We will have a little game before we say goodnight to our guest.”

“I shall partner Mr Grace,” says his mother. She moves up close to me, so she can see my cards and I am quite overpowered by the scents of rose water and juniper. We play and we drink and then Osiris proposes another game, the rules of which are never made clear to me but at which I seem to have a natural talent, winning the first few games and a handful of sous before my luck suddenly changes and Osiris begins to fill his pockets with my money.

Despite his luck changing for the better, Osiris’s mood is taking a turn for the worse, I notice, and the more he drinks the more provocative he becomes. His mother, I think, is only degrees better. She sits too close to me for my own comfort. “Let us be lucky this time, Henry,” she says as we are dealt another hand, and intertwines her little finger with mine in such a way that I think mine might break.

It is not only this which gives me cause to think I have found extraordinary company. While we are at cards, the serving girl brushes past with a plate of bread and cheese for someone who has recently arrived and is installed in the alcove behind us. As I say, the girl is very young but quite pretty. Osiris watches closely as she deftly uncorks another bottle. “Do you want her, Os?” His mother says. “If you do, you can take her to your bed tonight. Girls like that come cheap.” I see his eyes follow the girl across the floor. “She is filthy,” Osiris says. “Probably covered in lice. I will dip my wick in Paris, if it is all the same to you."

“You know best, of course,” says Lady Jane, as she rises from the table. “I will retire. Good night, Mr Grace.” And, then, to my astonishment and discomfiture, she bends down and kisses me on the tip of my nose. Her dress is not the most modest creation and so as she kisses me, I cannot help taking more notice than I should of her décolletage. But no sooner has she done this then she is away to bed, and Osiris is charging my glass one more time.

“So, Grace, you drink?” he says. “A man should. But there’s more to it than claret, you know. Try this. It is oil of wormwood.”

I swallow the bitter liquid and feel its warmth spread through my body. “Do you like it?” Osiris says. “Then have some more.”

We sit quietly for a moment, and although he appears to be gazing into the dying embers of the fire, I have the feeling that Osiris looks also at me and is sizing me up.

"Your first night abroad and already a new experience," he says. "That is excellent. Life is all about experience, Grace. Experience and success and damn the cost, yes? Damn form, too – I shall call you Henry. Do you gamble, Henry?"

"You have my money," I say, "You know I do."

"Not for pennies. Have you ever ridden to roulette and lost your horse?"

I have not, of course.

"Or discovered the beauty in opium? I'm not talking about a spoonful of laudanum to soothe a wakeful child, but sufficient to induce a trancelike state? You have not? Then I suggest you do so, Henry. You say you sketch and paint? Opium will transform your vision."

While the girl makes a show of sweeping the floor, patently wishing us gone or in our beds, Osiris says, "Henry, have you enjoyed a woman?"

I had managed to evade such questions at university, having then had no experience of women at all; now I feel myself put upon the spot. But Osiris, his boots upon the table and his pipe dangling from his mouth, seems lost in thought. He cannot be that much older than me yet he talks like a man who has lived whole lifetimes. "Have you ever bedded a mother and her daughter, Henry?" he says. "I have. It can be stimulating. But can you guess what I yearn for? Twins, Henry. I long to take twins to my bed. I have heard there is nothing on earth like it."

Life, Osiris tells me, is entirely a matter of acquiring experience. Whether it is eating insects to discover their taste or fasting for a week to induce a change in perception, experience is all, I learn. "There is so much in this world to be experienced before we are carried off by smallpox, typhoid or cholera, or we suffer whatever poor hand fate deals out to us. So much to experience, Henry, so much to win and yet we may have little time to do it. We must seize the moment while we are young. All it takes," he adds, seemingly as an afterthought, "Is having the courage – no, there is a much better word – is having the audacity to fulfil one's own potential."

"And the means to do it?" I suggest, perhaps because surprisingly little of such is evident here.

He drinks off the last of the absinthe and wipes his mouth on his sleeve.

"There is always money to be had, somewhere," he says.

This young man is a fascination, I think. He seems possessed of so many secrets that I am not. And, it appears, he is ever ready to surprise.

"What did you think of my mother?" he says as his red ring, a garnet I think, flashes in the candlelight. "She is a handsome woman is she not?"

I agree that she is. I think of the dark curl which falls over her eye and of the perfume which seems to linger here still. "She likes you, you know," he says. "Some women like an older man, someone who will guide them, provide for them and correct them with a rod when necessary. Others, like dear Maman, prefer a younger man. It is only a matter of taste. So there you are, Henry. Already you have taken the eye of a noble siren. But rest you there a while, I must go and piss before I fill my breeches."

I have plenty to think about while Osiris is absent. I sit alone in the darkness and think how fortunate I have been to make the acquaintance of this singular family. I had embarked on my tour with every intention of slipping my leash and acquiring the very quality Osiris possesses in abundance, experience. It is true, I concede, that some of his ideas are decidedly strange and others perhaps even dangerous but I allow that being only a little older than I am, he has likely done what I do too often and either invented his stories or inflated them beyond their true worth.

I envision myself telling rapt listeners about this singular family on my return. Lady De'Ath, I will say, was arrogant and beautiful but at the same time amiably condescending to one such as I. Perhaps by then I will understand enough about Osiris to be able to talk about him, too.

I survey the table of dirty plates and empty glasses and concede that whatever else it may be, this strange family is at least hospitable. Or so I am thinking until the serving girl appears again, and thrusts a scrap of paper at me.

“L'addition,” she says. I look about for Osiris but he is still not returned. It is clear even to my wine-addled mind that the girl sees me as the evening's host and expects no-one but me to settle the bill. I fish in my pockets but, of course, they are empty, the few livre I had having been lost to Osiris at cards. I try to explain my quandary, assuring her that all can be easily settled if she will allow me to return to my lodgings, where I will awaken Dr Shepherd and ask for money. "Jean," the little girl cries, "Jean-Marie!"

And now a man appears, the hulking fellow I had found asleep and who now seems not at all pleased at being awoken. “What is the matter with this man?” I construe. “Why will he not settle his account?” But before anyone takes the discussion further, he produces an axe handle and thrusts the end against my nose with such force I think it will break. “You will pay now, Monsieur, or you will very much wish you had.”

In an instant the whole adventure has become a nightmare and I see what a fool's part I have played this evening. I long to be back in my lodgings, no, I long to be safe in my bed at home in England. I wish I had never seen the De'Aths. I wish, more than anything, that the enormous French person before me would put away the cudgel and sit down. And just then, in what sounds to me like the most perfect French, a low voice says, "Let me see that bill. There has been a misunderstanding, I am sure."

The account is passed to someone who stands behind me, who checks off the listed items aloud. "Fricassee, cheese, brioche, five bottles of wine from Bordeaux, half a bottle of absinthe, a glass of geneva and some calvados. I understand your anxiety, that is a lot of money to lose. Here, I think this is enough to settle the account and provide something for your inconvenience?"

While the brute counts the money, I count my blessings. Never in all my life have I been so glad to see anyone as I am to see Bennison this night, who has surely been dogging my steps since I left the hotel. I make a mental note, one which I know I will forget, which is to review his wage or provide him with something extra for his Christmas box. How this night might have gone without him is not something I want to think upon.

"Come along, sir, he says, taking my arm and helping me to my feet. It's high time we were in our beds."

Sixteen

It has rained for almost two long days; men and flowers bow and wilt under such a remorseless assault. Occasionally, it stutters and splutters and halts long enough to spawn hopes that this will be the end of it, that soot-grey clouds will clear, that the sodden rags of those who repose under costermongers' carts and in doorways will dry out, and for others there will be nights unbroken by the trickling of water into iron buckets. Perhaps the weavers will be able to spread their cloths at the tentergrounds, feculent roads will be traversable and market gardeners will salvage some produce. But those who said it wasn't finished yet are proved right and it comes on again, as heavily as before.

In the squares of Mayfair, where the better streets are correctly cobbled and adequately drained, and new slate is proof against the elements, there is no cause for alarm. Hot buttered toast and tea before a well-banked fire diverts attention from what is happening beyond tall windows, and minds from considering the case for people whose slates are not so sound.

Eastwards, the kennel which runs down the middle of Grub Street overflows and waste that has been accumulating there for months comes bubbling over the sides, leaving cabbage leaves and potato peelings, offal and excrement where inhabitants and visitors must walk. In places this noxious effluent laps against the ancient doors of the street's rickety, tottering buildings. No-one has tried to sweep the filth back into the kennel, or to shovel it into a cart that it may be taken away. Most of the street's residents have shut themselves up in their houses, although one or two have betaken themselves to fire-lit taverns, trusting to Providence to set matters right before they return.

The little tenant of the tumble-down house built in the reign of Good Queen Bess is distressed. It is in Mouse's nature to sweep and clean and bring order but the shambles outside is beyond him and his dustpan. A dead cat, its fur sodden and matted and its belly opened by rats, lies on his threshold like a terrible doormat. The sight causes Mouse to yield to his advancing black mood and to retreat to his chamber, which is up two pair of stairs.

The small, dark room with a distinctly keeling floor is an oasis of order in a world that is given over to chaos. So thinks the Mouse as he casts a gloomy glance through leaded diamonds at the havoc below. Seating himself upon a hard chair before the swinging glass of his toilet table, he takes a bound ledger from a drawer with the intention of addressing the fluctuating fortunes of *The Enquirer*. Obadiah's head, its owner says often, was made for words, not for figures. But Mouse finds he has not the heart for such work today, and instead peers into the foxed glass, his gaze taking in the small bed with a clean coverlet whose colours are dusty with age, the two framed etchings of prim Dutch interiors and the pair of hard chairs, on which are some of his clothes. Here, neatly folded, are his coat with its missing button newly replaced but elbows still shiny, his threadbare wig and a yellowing white shirt.

The room may be bare but at least it is swept. What a contrast it presents with the squalor of every other space in the house. Armed with cloths and brushes and pails of water he has long struggled against dust and disorder, but no sooner has he restored some part of the house than a discarded crust of bread appears, or a single filthy boot and the tide of dirt and detritus flows back and undoes everything. Ah, thinks Mouse, if he were the only tenant, how different would it be. There would be no ink spills on tables, no dark smudges on walls, sills and door handles. Mice would decamp because food would be always locked away and crumbs no longer scattered across the floor. There would be no garments left where they were dropped, no dishes unwashed, no towering stacks of dog-eared newspapers always threatening to collapse and entomb a Mouse. But in such a case, there would be no Obadiah.

And that would never do.

He hears the door open as Obadiah himself enters the house, loudly cursing the rain. He can almost see him down there, dropping his old hat on the table, sloughing off his heavy, sodden coat and sitting down to eat as quickly as he can the viands he has brought home from the corner cook-shop, so that he can set the type for tomorrow's issue of *The Enquirer*. In normal circumstances he would join him in his meal and they would discuss what news Obadiah has found out that day and what gossip Mouse has heard. They would eagerly sift through correspondence from people who contribute more of the same and decide what this next issue will contain and what prominence will be given to which items.

But Mouse remains where he is, being under an even blacker cloud than that which shrouds Grub Street today. He looks again at the accounts open before him but the numbers might be so many ancient runes, and his gaze soon strays again to the glass. Idly, indulgently, he considers what he sees there. On another day, he might see the cheery little fellow who is a popular addition to tables in the coffee houses. He might see Good Old Mouse who makes Obadiah smile, or the mysterious City Gossip whose tales of London life are often paused over even by those who purchase the paper for its business news. He might see any of these, if he so chose. This would be typical of the Mouse, who is not by nature a despondent soul.

But today he sees a dwarf, a Lilliputian misfit, a freak more suited to the circus. How he can ever be of interest to anyone, he does not know. He is so wrapped up in himself that he fails to hear Obadiah's step on the stairs.

“So here you are,” he says, picking his teeth as he ducks his head to enter. “I called for you. I have left you some veal pie. Well, that is what it claims to be.”

Obadiah glances about him, unsure where to sit. Mouse seems awkward too; Obadiah has not visited him in his chamber before. With a look, he proffers the chair unencumbered by clothes and Obadiah sits. The chair creaks.

“Are you not hungry?” Obadiah asks.

Affecting to examine the accounts, Mouse regards his friend in the glass. He wears his two and thirty years well, Mouse thinks, and would indeed be quite a presentable fellow were it not for the negligent state of his dress. He has a defined jawline and long, dark hair (too often unkempt) and deep, grey eyes for which Mouse would forgive him every one of his sartorial misadventures.

“You are not yourself, I think,” Obadiah says, which in itself is enough to lighten Mouse's lowering mood. It is not often that Obadiah can spare mental process from thoughts of news and newsprint to ask after him. He glances at the small window, whose panes are rattled by raindrops. “This Biblical flood is enough to put anyone out of sorts. You could float an Ark out there.”

"It is not that," Mouse says, with decision.

"Then what is it, dear Mouse?" says his friend.

Mouse take a moment to consider his answer. Now he is asked, he realises that neither the rain and the chaos it has brought, nor the state of the house he lives in, have caused the mood which has sat upon him with increasing weight these last two days.

"It is the dead girl," Mouse says at last. "She has been in my dreams. I think of her when I wake. It was so horrible, Obadiah. And what has troubled me most is the knowledge that I shall have to relive it all at the trial."

In his eyes are tears and an unspoken plea for release, which Obadiah notes.

"I am not blind," Obadiah says. "You have not been yourself since you found the unfortunate thing. And I know the trial has loomed larger than it should for you."

"I have thought of nothing else."

"I could go in your stead," Obadiah says, gently. "And I would, if I thought it would help you. But seeing justice done will lift that weight from your shoulders, my friend. There will be no more dreams once you have witnessed twelve honest citizens seal that devil's fate. Believe me, Mouse, I know I am right."

"I pray that you are," Mouse says, uncertainly.

"Of course I am," Obadiah says.

"But if you are not right?" Mouse says suddenly. "If this man is proven innocent – he was with the murdered girl, but I could not in conscience swear to his guilt – if this happens, will we look into this and find the guilty party ourselves?"

"My friend," Obadiah says, surprised at this insurrection, "This is not work for a newspaper."

"But why is it not?" Mouse asks him. "How is it different from revealing the fraud of Oxaca?"

They sit in silence, listening to the fast-falling rain and the shouting of some men caught outside. Then Obadiah rises and takes Mouse's hand. His smile renders Mouse powerless to do anything but to respond in kind. "I will think about it," Obadiah says, gently pulling him to his feet. "I can promise that much. But now you will eat some pie before the rats feast on it. There is a lot of work to do tonight if London is to see a paper tomorrow."

Seventeen

I am keenly aware of occupying an ambiguous place in this household. Socially, I am positioned somewhere between a servant and something rather superior. I am the master's assistant but also, alas, Gretch's factotum. If I am not acknowledged by Grace as his apprentice it is only because he refuses to let himself believe that a female could ever paint with serious intent or real skill. That Mr Grace has had another use for me, one which he likely had in mind when he removed me from the Foundling Hospital, further confuses the issue.

My master occasionally employs me as a model in the history paintings which he still undertakes, his parlous state of health permitting, alongside his bread-and-butter portraiture. This avocation, I should quickly say, is not as romantic as it sounds. I am never Salome dancing before Herod or even a penitent Mary Magdalene. These roles he reserves for a flame-haired flibbertigibbet called Garcy Dunne who probably does more than just model for some of the artist clients with whom she is so improbably popular.

While this silly girl appears half-dressed in some tawdry, gauzy thing with one or both of her unexceptional breasts on show – and, I am certain, becomes the subject of low conversation in the grand houses where her image is hung – I am cast as a servant girl, a kitchen maid, a starving beggar. Garcy Dunne is illiterate, ignorant and has a tongue like a Billingsgate fishwife. When I first encountered her, it amused me to imagine what purchasers of her pictures would think if they could hear their Desdemona or their Persephone open her foul mouth.

Recently, I have had cause to slightly revise my opinions of Garcy Dunne. She claims to eat well and to live in great comfort somewhere, but this disagrees with the times I have seen her pocket food from our table or found her asleep under the kitchen table, when she had given every appearance of leaving the house the night before. It has come as a sad surprise to hear from Poll that like me, Garcy is an orphan, although not one with the good fortune to be taken in by the Foundling Hospital. She has clearly had and continues to lead, a difficult life.

Now that I know this, I sometimes put out food and hide a penny or two where she can find it and I also give her access to the kitchen where I leave a blanket for her use. Sharing the status of orphans does not mean that I am entirely sympathetic when Mr Grace continues to choose Garcy over me as the focus of his composition. I have thought long about this and concede that there may be something about my appearance that has not appealed to Mr Grace's schooled eye. Could it be that my hair is a little unruly or my mouth a measure too small? Or does he not care for my deep-set, some have said, sunken eyes? It is possible, I suppose, that he objects to my boyish physique or the dress which I wear high because, as Garcy once hissed, I have nothing below my neckline worth showing.

But though it is Garcy who parades in meretricious finery and stage jewels, let us remember that it was me whom the master chose to invite into his house and study his art. It is worth taking a moment to record how this extraordinary change in my prospects came about. Before his face became so sorely afflicted, Henry Grace was in the habit of visiting the Hospital in the company of other fashionable men and I saw him many times in the gallery, debating the merits or otherwise of works by his contemporaries. He was noticeable among the group even then, having a disfigurement that ran up his neck and settled under his left ear like a great pink caterpillar.

These men became used to finding me upon my chair assiduously copying the picture I had chosen to learn from. By this time my appreciation of art extended beyond the raucous comedy of Hogarth's *The March to Finchley* and I might be seen replicating the grand portrait of a Hospital governor, or one of the ambitious Biblical paintings. It was not unusual for one or other of these fashionable men to condescend to glance at my work and tell me I was a clever little girl. I was repeatedly assured that there would always be work for someone who could copy to a high standard.

The only one of these men to understand that for me, copying these paintings was not an end in itself and that I was as earnest a student as any in the Academy was the master himself. Perhaps he did not say that to me – he would not say as much to an aspirant of the other sex – but that was what I saw when he took up my art and held it close to his face, the better to examine the detail and to assay my technique. He nodded and sometimes looked at me in a way which I liked to think expressed his surprise that someone of my tender years might produce such work. I liked that there was someone else besides Mr Gilpin who thought I had talent. I didn't know, or have any reason to hope, that we would ever have a deeper connection than this until the evening when Mr Gilpin took me aside and asked if I could bear to quit the Hospital earlier than usual and begin a kind of apprenticeship?

I had always thought that no matter what my aspirations as an artist, the likeliest outcome of my years at the Foundling Hospital would be a life of service, as a ladies maid if I was lucky or in some lowlier position. But when Mr Gilpin told me that Henry Grace the painter, whose name I might recall from my studies, had expressed an interest in taking me as "not quite an apprentice, but something very like it," I was enraptured. What a thing it would be, I thought, to learn the trade of a master painter. I imagined a life in which the secrets of the master's art were daily revealed to me. I saw Henry Grace guiding my hand as I completed a magnificent painting such as I had admired in the gallery. To help create the fantastical scenes I had seen in beautiful frames and to enjoy the appreciation of my own talents was a gilded existence much to be desired.

Well, those were my fantasies, ones which of course, were quite unmatched by reality. I knew nothing then of the hours I would spend carrying out irksome and repetitive duties, the nailing of canvas to stretcher, the sizing of canvas, the grinding of colours and the endless cleaning of brushes and palette knives or that when I did take up a brush, it would only be to paint greenswards and cloudless skies or with luck, some folds of drapery. And it never occurred to me that a man who had spent his life acquiring such knowledge and skill would be reluctant to sell it cheaply and might keep his secrets close. But that was for the future. Mr Gilpin told me that this was an extraordinary opportunity which I must grasp right away. I told my tutor that I would work very hard to become a fine artist and that I would never forget him or the assistance he had rendered me. I did not know then that the Hospital had already told Mr Gilpin that it would dispense with his services. His innovatory methods had apparently proved too much for some.

If I had not foreseen the monotonous nature of the work I would do, neither had I imagined that the survival of the house might be predicated upon the see-sawing condition of its master. An example of this was provided this very morning when I made an unsettling discovery. Changes had been made to the picture. Faces had been altered and passengers added to the already overladen boats, which now look like they will founder at any moment. The work is inferior, hastily done, and will require some hours of careful correction. I was puzzling when the master might have done this – he has lately kept to his bed – when I recalled being awoken by some violent noise in the attic painting room, which adjoins our own accommodation in the eaves. It was dawn and the birds on the square were announcing the fact. I was then too drugged with sleep to consider what had roused me but later, in the attic, I saw that a heavy washstand had fallen over and the ceramic bowl in which Mr Grace cleanses paint from his hands, had smashed upon the floor. Was it possible that Grace had dragged himself to his palette as soon as there was light? These last few days he has survived in his room on a diet of thin soup, which is all he can digest just now. I would not have thought he had the power to rise from his bed, much less to paint.

But on days when he thinks himself well enough to continue, no carefully-worded warnings from Gretch or anyone else in the household, or admonitions from his quacks, will prevent him slowly ascending those stairs and mounting the steps set by the canvas. Before his most recent relapse he had been working feverishly, stretching himself to the very limits of his physical powers in order to take his conception further. Gretch and I have both marked this acceleration, which has been sudden and inexplicable. To see Grace using every hour of sunlight God sends is what we have prayed for and it is a poor joke that his precious energy is being expended uselessly. This morning I am distressed to see what has been accomplished. I look at this crazed canvas and I think that like its passengers on a fiery Thames, we too sail in a frail bark.

Eighteen

Just before noon, the heavy doors in the great stone walls swing open and the City Marshall's armed phalanx comes forward to clear a passage for the procession of carts. The man upon whom so many eyes are fixed, a tall but malnourished example of the species who wears what looks like his second-hand Sunday best, occupies the first cart. His hands tied, he stands with difficulty, blinking at the bright blue sky and only slowly comprehending the crowd, that amorphous, animated body which sways and swells as it surges forward to follow the vehicle westwards from the gates of Newgate.

Lincolnshire-born and new-come to London, such a multiplicity of faces whose every eye is upon him alone would ordinarily have petrified this man. Now, these loudly racketing Londoners, broken-nosed and toothless, hatted and hairless, bewigged and scarlet of face, are only shades infesting the waking nightmare which is filling his final hours. He looks into this mob, wildly, expectantly, as if help might come from within its midst. Momentarily, his dull gaze happens to light upon a dwarf, clutching his wig to his chest, as he squeezes through the front ranks to stare up at him.

Mouse sees the Newgate ordinary standing with the condemned man, a tall black raven who holds his prayerbook open and moves his lips, although the litany is lost in the angry baying of the enormous crowd. This presses upon the cart as if it would have justice two or more hours before it can be executed by law. Then cart, priest, prisoner and cheap, deal coffin, begin to bump slowly over the cobbles and make their way down Hart Row Street. Behind this cart follows another, conveying a middle-aged man, a woman of about the same age, and a boy of perhaps seventeen; but sex and youth are passed over by this discriminating crowd in favour of the man in the first, whom many have come here especially to see. As the wig-clutching journalist knows, the name of this man has been blasted from the newspapers, spat into fires, cursed in inns and carried upon coaches to distant parts. The dwarf is soon lost in the crowd again.

The cart stops on Snow Hill; a bullock has escaped the pens at Smithfield and is playing havoc with the interested parties which line the route. Mouse sees his opportunity and squeezes through a densely-planted copse of coarsely-covered thighs and struggles towards the front of the crowd. But close as he gets to the wheels of the cart, still he cannot see what is occurring above him and will not, he laments, be able to accurately describe the scene for readers of *The Enquirer*. "A first-hand report will be just the thing for us," Obadiah said. "Clark's conviction is selling our newspapers like nothing else has this year. My stars, we should have connected these outrages before! A pity that hanging day has come so soon after the trial; how much more might have been made of it!" Obadiah seemed not to see that witnessing justice being done had little eased his friend's mind. "Get along to Newgate and use those sharp eyes of yours," he said. "People will hunger for the last moments of such a monster."

But now Mouse finds himself not only unable to follow the proceedings, but in real danger of suffocation. Snared by beer-fed bellies and booted legs, gasping for air like a man on a rope, he turns around and tries to force his way back through the crowd to the street beyond. But withdrawing, he realises, is quite as impossible as going on. He tries to force an egress this way and that, but the crowd, the dreadful, noisy crowd, is starting to move again, the cart beginning to rumble over the stones.

Mouse is wedged deeper into the foetid mass of cloth and flesh. Just when he is starting to admit the impossibility of his position and is resigning himself to whatever might happen next, he feels an unexpected and violent constriction about his waist. Huge arms pluck him from the black mass of bodies and heft him into light and air, high above the heads of the crowd. Mouse fills his lungs. "My thanks, whoever you are!" he says at last to the thick tangle of coarse, sandy hair on which he places his hands. His rescuer, a huge, bearded fellow, it seems, with tools at his waist, now settles him on his shoulders as a father might a large child. "How's that, sir?" he shouts, "Is this more to your liking?"

On another day, Mouse will know his saviour as Adam Brewer, a blacksmith and farrier, who once had a forge by Romney Marsh. For now he is only a good samaritan, on whose great frame Mouse now follows the wagons, getting a better view than anyone, even the people who crane and call from windows above the street. When Adam Brewer wades through the crowds, few resist his advance. On they go, his huge hands tightly grasping Mouse's calves, until the fatal parade stops outside an inn. The crowds, as noisy here as at Newgate, are held back while the prisoners are helped off the carts and escorted past a knot of dignitaries who drain glasses by the door, and into the dark tavern.

"They stop to sup?" Adam Brewer calls to Mouse.

"It is a tradition," Mouse returns. "It is supposed to steel the prisoner."

From his elevated vantage, Mouse looks down through the tavern's small windows upon grey and wigged heads. He cannot see the prisoner. The ritual is soon complete and the guard troops out. Joseph Clark side-steps a deep puddle of recent rain and trying to avoid the stares and taunts of the crowd, looks to the sky where he meets the dwarf's stare. As he is once more dragged upon the cart, he summons ebbing strength and says, just loud enough for the giant and the dwarf to hear him, "It warn't me, maisters. I will swear to it. For the love of God, tell them it warn't me as killed them. I have children of my own." He crumbles and cries, but before before Mouse can reply, there is a sharp snap at the bridle and horse and cart go on.

Mouse and Adam Brewer follow the procession beyond the last face-filled windows of Oxford Street. A little ahead, the cart and its escort is enveloped by a human ocean. "This is as far as I will go, I think," Adam Brewer says. "Shall I put you down here?" Mouse looks about and sees people of every kind. Vendors of oranges, trading briskly, gangs of apprentices, mostly drunk, servants with baskets, ballad singers hawking their wares and women waving before him the printed last words of the man about to die, a man whose cart has yet to arrive beneath the dismal geometry of Tyburn's triple gallows.

The banks of tiered seating, advertised in Mouse's newspaper at a shilling a seat, are fully occupied. Below them he sees whole families come to enjoy the Monday hanging holiday. Mouse takes one last look at the man in the cart, the man with a face as white as paper, who has turned to peer into the crowd and seems to find his eyes only. He cannot return his gaze.

"If you are leaving this place now," Mouse says to the man who bears him, "I should consider it a merciful kindness if you would take me with you."

Nineteen

The last few weeks have seen my master's condition deteriorate at an alarming speed. When his physicians called for boiling water, I carried the kettle into the room and saw his bare torso, cadaverous on the table. It was barely recognisable as human. His back was covered in a great many scarlet, festering pustules and I saw such terrible lesions all over his body that I wondered that he still lived. His hands tremble and he struggles; bright light hurts his eyes. He has kept to his bed these last seven days and speaks only rarely. Do I need to say that he has progressed his masterpiece not a brushstroke further? But if he has not, then I have.

Pursued by creditors who dun us on the doorstep, we have become virtual prisoners in our own house. I have my own methods of ingress and egress – which sometimes mean blackening my dress in a coal chute – but Gretch, Mrs Harris and Poll mostly stay within the walls. The master of course, remains abed and knows nothing of this or much else, it has to be said. *The New Fire of London* – I called it such in the master's hearing one time and ever since then, he has done the same, without acknowledging my authorship – has been our hope of salvation, but it has been unquestionably clear to us all for many days now that these hopes are rootless. Henry Grace can no more paint that he can piss in his closet.

Gretch has had this moment in mind for a long while. His gentler attitude towards me, his encouraging remarks about my painting, his blind eye when I have corrected something my master has painted all make sense when he leads me once more into the attic and we throw off the protecting tarpaulin. "You have been making your mark again, I see," he says. I have yet to understand his intention and am immediately alarmed, thinking that this time I will at last have to pay for my meddling with the work of a master.

Gretch examines the portion I completed last night, after I had told him I was going to slip out and find us some cheap oysters for our supper. He looks at the faces of people drowning in the Thames. "This work is not bad," he says at last. Gretch examines a fine detail painted by the master, a man in a burning house filling his hands with money, the coins glowing gold as they spill from his hands upon a dark shape at his feet. He turns his attention to the upper window, in which a woman tears off a burning nightgown. He smiles as he sees the ginger cat I have added, scooting from the outhouse, its eyes shining like black opals, its tail brush-like in its terror. "No, that is unfair," Gretch says, not at all grudgingly, "This is fine work, lassie."

He now stands back and takes a view of the painting in its entirety. "You have done a lot, have you not? I can see which is your work and which the master's, but only because I followed his progress. I doubt anyone else would tell the difference."

"That is high praise indeed, Mr Gretch, I thank you for it."

Gretch laughs, but there is nothing jovial about it. "I'm not here to offer you criticism, good or otherwise, you little fool. Cannot you see what must be done? Surely you can guess what I am going to ask of you? For the salvation of all in this house?"

I need him to say it.

"You must finish this picture. You, on your own. You can do that, can you not? How much remains to be done, eh? Not just to complete it, but to bring it to that state of perfection where it might be judged alongside his greatest works? Answer me that, Michel Angelo."

I am still taking in the import of what he has just asked me to do. I have of course dreamed of such a thing, that Henry Grace would one day say, "I took you on here, Michel, because I recognised genius in you. I knew that you would be the one to help me in my hour of need. That hour has come. Take up my dropped brush." Or something like that. And now it has happened, if not in quite the way I imagined.

But the result is the same: I am babbling as I tell Gretch that work needs to be done in defining the jumble of charred houses; that the city needs to be a little more hellish, somehow, and the clouds more heavenly. And so on. To tell the truth, I am incapable of putting into words what needs doing to this picture, but I know that this work requires more than this and I am praying that once I have mixed my colours I will have found the missing element, the device which will draw together the many intricate threads in this great tapestry of a picture.

"Well, then," Gretch says, "While there's still light left in the sky, we'll have that troublesome cover off the roof and you can get about it."

Twenty

The Journal of Henry Grace

For everything those gay dogs say about it once they are safely back in England, touring the Continent can be a tedious business. Day after day, our hired coach has swayed from side to side like a ship in a gale as we negotiate pot-holed roads and risk being turned over by the weight of all the things that Dr Shepherd has strongly advised my father to equip us with, all of which have to be unstrapped and taken down when there is something that someone – commonly, Dr Shepherd – finds himself in need of.

Piled high above us we have such essentials as an inflatable bath complete with bellows; a mariner's compass and sextant (useful in the event of being lost at sea); some linen maps; a watch and (in case it breaks) a pocket sun-dial; three umbrellas; two pairs of eye-preservers (blue); a wide-brimmed hat for protection from the sun we haven't yet seen; enough handkerchiefs to last the year; some notebooks, pens and two pocket inkstands; a perspective glass; tea, sugar and brandy and every kind of condiment and spice; a tinder box and a portable close-stool.

There is also a brace of pistols and a sword, although I am by no means sure who is supposed to wield them, should we be attacked by brigands. Then there is the multiplicity of clothing that has been packed against every possible eventuality of weather and social situation that Dr Shepherd has been able to foresee. If you imagine all this and a deal more, then you will have a very fair idea of the weight the coach is struggling to bear and how slow our progress has been along the ill-kept roads of Northern France.

Bennison sits atop with the driver and sometimes manages a conversation with him in Norfolk-accented French. Dr Shepherd sits with his back to the horses, peeling Norman apples with his pocket knife and taking nips of Norman brandy from his pocket flask and when he remembers his duty, treating me to a dry discourse on the history, topography, customs and culture of the land through which we are traveling, usually parroted word for word from the little book he keeps about him and cons when he thinks I am dozing.

We sleep, as best we can, in damp and flea-ridden beds at inns which charge the earth for some old bread, rancid butter and soft cheese. I find this preferable, though, to the stale mackerel and the omelette made with raddled eggs which we were offered for breakfast at Calais.

I am hungry because I cannot eat and fatigued because I cannot sleep but more intolerable than either of those things is the ennui, as the Frenchies call it, the stupefying, stultifying bloody boredom that is my daily lot with only the good Dr Shepherd for company.

I had expected so much more, especially after my first night in Calais. I had imagined quite wrongly, it transpires, that my encounter with the interesting Osiris De'Ath and Lady Jane augured well for a truly educative tour. Yes, I am fully aware that he fleeced me at cards and that he left me with a bill I could not pay and said the most provoking things, and of course, that neither of these actions spoke well of him as a gentleman, but by God, I felt alive in his company. I truly think I would learn more in 24 hours with De'Ath than I might in half a year listening to the second-hand dronings of Dr Simeon Shepherd.

I confess that for all his faults, Osiris De'Ath has intrigued me. I am hopeful of meeting other stimulating company when we arrive at Paris but how I shall slip Dr Shepherd's leash, which has been tightened considerably since my escapade in Calais, I do not yet know.

Twenty One

Satire, Obadiah is thinking, as he pauses before a print-shop window where people of different walks have congregated to look in, is now the province of the caricaturist who – and he has said this in print – wastes the opportunities it affords him. It's his lurid displays in windows like this that draw the crow-headed crowds to caw and cackle. Where else can they see their King as a corpulent Colossus, bestriding the Channel with his enormous buttocks bared, filling the sails of little ships with a powerful blast from his anus? Here, in pane after windowpane, are politicians at stool and men of renown rendered ridiculous. But there is nothing reflective about this satire, nothing to stir more than a knowing nod among the politically sentient. Its targets are made to look foolish but that is all; this satire is not dangerous. So asserts the man who chooses words as his weapons.

This, Obadiah reminds himself, is why each of his own barbs in *The Enquirer* has to be that much sharper and his targets must be boils in obvious need of lancing. He has expended much effort and ingenuity in exposing poor governance and double dealings by men of trust. He is proud to have been instrumental in the public fall of one or two of these men; and that he has saved the fortunes of people who invested in their daring new schemes.

It was *The Enquirer*, remember, which revealed the gold-rich American island of Oxaca as a phantom, despite the thousands of pounds ploughed into expeditions to find it by credulous investors.

Provable fact and a dash of satire have been the foundations of his newspaper since he began it, some seven years ago. In his quest to right wrongs and expose hypocrisy, he has not been entirely altruistic; what man is? Obadiah sees in his newspaper his path to social acceptance and with this as his goal, he has sought to capture the attention of those who accept wit in lieu of breeding and money.

These men he would like to see picking up his newspaper as a matter of course. If he can make *The Enquirer* the essential accessory of every coffee-house going gentleman, success will come. Elevation too. In these modern times, the social membrane is permeable. He only has to glance at Mouse's page to see that a state of affairs once unthinkable has come to pass. These days, artists, musicians, poets and novel-writers attend the salons, where they hob-nob with nobility. And if them, why not the journalist and would-be poet, Obadiah Bone? The new man hired by Mouse, this Adam Brewer, is proving a tireless and effective distributor of his newspaper. The newspaper is everywhere available; he only has to encourage people to pick it up.

And now, quite suddenly, there are encouraging signs. After a year or more in which he feared the paper might fail at any moment, his creditors seize his press and the landlord his home, this latest issue has sold singularly well. So well, in fact, that Obadiah is starting to think not just in terms of survival, but of actual success.

At first he accepted this turnabout as due reward for his exposure of financial misdoings at the Admiralty and with very mixed feelings has come the discovery that his change of fortune is owed to something else entirely. It has not been hard to identify the item which has excited debate among his readers. When Obadiah needs to gauge how his work is being received by the reading public he heads for the coffee houses, where just like Mouse, he sits and he listens. In Garraway's in Exchange

Alley, at Will's in Covent Garden and at the Chapel Coffee House in Paternoster Row, he has overheard his paper discussed by booksellers and writers. He has sat with Tories at the Cocoa House and among Whigs at Arthur's but the conclusion he draws at all these establishments is the same.

What has so captured their attention has been an account of a hanging which might have been carried by any pamphlet or cheap broadside. But, Obadiah discovers, it's not the execution itself which has aroused interest but the man's last words. This is doubly interesting for Obadiah, because he knows that his reporter, Morris Malone, his Mouse, no more heard these words than he witnessed the execution itself.

"Half the town turned out for this execution and yet you saw nothing?" he said, when Mouse returned, looking pale and fatigued from London on a hanging day.

Obadiah bends, his grey-green eyes and sharp, unshaven chin too close for Mouse's comfort. A beetle in a bell jar, Mouse edges towards the fireplace and refuge. He can stand under the mantel without ducking his head, while Obadiah can not.

"Of the hanging itself? No, nothing at all, thank God."

Obadiah blinks and affects bug-eyed astonishment. "Surely," he says, "You jest with me, Mouse."

"No, it's true," Mouse says. "I followed the cart to Tyburn, but that was all."

"Let me try to understand this." The heels of Obadiah's buckled shoes clack as he paces the print room flags. "We reported the trial, I think?"

"Of course. You know we did."

More clacks and then: “And you attended that, I suppose? You didn't fabricate your report over a pot of coffee at Molly's?"

"No, of course not."

There is always the problem of knowing when Obadiah is being quite serious.

"Then why, in the names of all the saints, did you not report the hanging? That’s the story of John the Baptist without Salome, it's Gethsemane without Calvary. Our story must have an ending, Mouse, a first-hand account of the dying struggles of the wretch who has brought terror to the streets of London. The creature who caused honest men to lock up their daughters. And you are telling me you do not have that account?”

Mouse is too tired to be terrified and relinquishes the sanctuary of the hearth nook for the comfort of one of the two rickety chairs by the unlit fire. He stares into the pile of ashen faggots. “I could not witness the death of a man I knew to be innocent," he says at last. "That was all. I could not do it."

"Innocent?" Obadiah says, “What can you mean by that? Did you, or did you not, report his conviction yourself?" He has stopped his pacing and has taken a rag to clean fresh ink spots from the frame of his press.

“Of course I did. But what I could not report were my feelings about the way those proceedings were conducted. They were so terribly hasty, Obadiah, everyone was in such a hurry to do away with the man they thought had done those awful deeds."

“Well, of course they were. You spoke to the surgeon who examined the bodies. You know what he did to those girls."

“Dreadful things. But that is no excuse for capital proceedings to be rattled through like children reciting their catechism."

“Speed is neither here nor there if due process of law is observed. Besides, the outcome was really never in doubt. What was important was that this fellow was despatched quickly.”

“Why was it important, Obadiah?”

“This was something more than murder,” Obadiah says at long last.

"How can that be?” Mouse returns, “Murder is murder, surely?"

“Not always. The deaths of the girl you came across in Marylebone and those of other girls found in circumstances too similar to be coincidental, have ushered fear and uncertainty into the quiet places of London. We were not the only ones to connect him with the other fatalities. He was justly charged. The streets must be kept safe, Mouse. Good people cannot live their lives in terror.” Obadiah’s blackened fingertips fidget through a tray of type. “These girls weren't street urchins, who might be abused and disposed of without anyone raising a murmur. The child of a village churchman, a shopkeeper's daughter. And that one who was found by Limehouse stairs with her throat cut, what was she?”

“An unfortunate innocent. Her father was a schoolmaster.”

“All dead within the space of a year. Decent, respectable society cannot be threatened,” Obadiah says. “Not for a moment. If these families are unsafe, then who can consider themselves secure? It was in everyone's interest to get this Clark up to Tyburn with all expedition. People need to be shown the power of the law and how swift and certain its retribution."

“That is well enough but I tell you there was something about him, this Joseph Clark, which unsettled me deeply. Something was not right. At his trial, he did not sound like a guilty man."

Obadiah stands now at the big tin bowl, slopping water as he attacks blemished fingers with a scrubbing brush. He says with a quick smile, “And you know how a guilty man sounds, I suppose?"

“This man was confused and mortally frightened,” Mouse says. “His answers made little sense. However, I had the clear impression that he had not even heard of the other two murders, let alone committed them. And more importantly, on the day of the second murder, he claimed he was incarcerated in the lock-up at Bow, having been found drunk in the streets."

"But this was disproved?"

"No-one looked into the matter. He was guilty before they led him to the dock. But after I saw the condemned man in the cart today and he begged me to believe him innocent, I went directly from Tyburn to the police offices at Bow.”

He falters.

“And?” Obadiah prompts.

“And found that Clark had indeed spoken the truth. He did not commit that murder, just as I'm sure he was innocent of the others.”

“And what said the upholders of law?”

“They would not listen to a dwarf, or not to this one. A mistake in the ledger, they said. The constable who had locked him up had been dismissed for drink soon after, or so I was told. It troubles me, Obadiah, that if I had further acted on what Clark had told the court, I might have saved his life."

"My dear Mouse, this innocent man as you call him, was apprehended in the act of robbing money from a girl's corpse. From a corpse! He would have hanged for that anyway. He was guilty of something, so let's have no more of this. Our readers have been promised 'An authentic account of the shocking last words and the final moments and of the beast who has preyed on the young women of London.' And that is what we will give them."

And it is this hastily-concocted account, Obadiah thinks, as he shaves a paucity of whiskers a few days later, this thing that was got up between himself and Mouse over a pint of port in the early morning hours, which has brought *The Enquirer* more readers than ever before. Two additional print runs were made, necessitating late nights for Obadiah, Mouse and for young Will, a youth from the printer's shop across the way who would much sooner work as a newspaperman. Several drafts were made before Obadiah pronounced himself satisfied with the wording.

In the first, Mouse tells of how a reporter from *The Enquirer* had been the only newspaperman to put himself in such a position that he was able to exchange words with the prisoner before his execution. "I am innocent," Clark had told *The Enquirer*, "And may the Lord have mercy on my soul." Obadiah glances only briefly at what Mouse has written before he sharpens his pen and begins to amend the draft. "My innocence can easily be proved, although God knows it is too late for me now," Clark is reported as saying, in the next draft. "Only ask who was confined at Bow on the night Clarissa Beckham died."

The ink dries while Obadiah reads and rereads his text. "Something is missing still," he says, and the soles of Obadiah's shoes begin to clack again. And then: "I have it! Mouse, more ink, if you will!" He scribbles, crosses-out and rewrites, he reads again and finally, nods his approval.

Mouse takes up the sheet of paper and reads, "...And having established my innocence, look to protect your daughters. See you keep them safe, under lock and key if you will. This abominable fiend has an appetite for murder and will kill again, as surely as I will die today on Tyburn tree."

And then, while Obadiah composes an addendum promising further dreadful revelations in the very next issue, Mouse takes the cloth cover from a tray of Mr Baskerville's new type. He looks at his friend, who is already wiping ink from the press in preparation for a second run, which will take them until the morning to print, and expresses an imprecation which Obadiah is too preoccupied to notice.

More issues of *The Enquirer* have been printed and sold before an evening comes when Obadiah and his reporter address themselves to a dish of steak and onions at the Cheshire Cheese tavern, which huddles in a narrow passageway off Fleet Street. Obadiah says, "We now have half of Grub Street helping us turn out the paper. I am glad that I helped Latham at *The Messenger* when he was down on his luck. He has been particularly useful."

"They are grateful for the work," Mouse says. "Those that don't curse you for your luck, anyway."

"This isn't luck, it's our due reward. We are doing something different, Mouse. We are providing what people want."

Mouse concedes the truth of that. *The Enquirer* is indeed different. It is beginning to be written in a new fashion, one which Obadiah claims to have invented himself. Reporting the murders of children on London streets, he selects his words from a more emotive vocabulary. *Brutally slaughtered*, the dead children are *innocents*, *lambs* and *defenceless victims*; the killer is a *sadistic monster*, a *cold-hearted killer*, who is *still loose in our midst*. Some details of the incidents are withheld in order that they may provide further fodder for future issues.

Obadiah writes and rewrites until he is sure that he has addressed every anxiety and doubt that his earlier editions might have aroused in the minds of his readers, who already pen him letters full of their fears, suspicions and wild theories. He writes of children snatched from the streets, children who should be safe. He describes their known injuries and suggests the possible causes with forensic precision. He speculates and suggests that no-one but a rich and perhaps, therefore, powerful man could afford to lose three golden sovereigns and on more than one occasion, too.

The unnatural concept of a rich and brutal killer careless of money would have him rubbing his hands with glee were this not so serious a matter. He thinks that by bringing terror to the pages of *The Enquirer* he does the best job he can of alerting his readership to the danger among them and parries Mouse's comment that he is titillating his readers as much as warning them.

"What I have learned, Mouse," he says, "Is that there is much to be gained from addressing the various appetites of our readers."

"Even if some of those appetites are base? You would sooner frighten them than offer reassurance? That way lies chaos, surely? *The Sentinel* is no longer adding sales."

"If this is what they want" – Obadiah is no longer listening – "then why not give it to them? What right have we to supply anything else? It is no good purveying only the subjects and opinions which inform and amuse us and our sort. All kinds of people are learning to read these days. We must keep them curious. Feed them what they hunger for, titbit by titbit. The newspaper is becoming a powerful tool. A weapon, too. In the wrong hands, I think it could hang a man." Something about his friend's face causes him to pause and say, "But I see I have set you thinking?"

"I cannot help wondering," Mouse says, a little uncertainly, "What might be the response of a weak-minded malefactor on seeing his deeds written up like those of a character in a cheap storybook? Just suppose, Obadiah, that what we wrote encouraged him to commit further misdeeds? Would we share responsibility? But, of course, I am being ridiculous as usual."

Obadiah seems not to hear this, is momentarily adrift in thought.

"What we write may discover a murderer," he says at last.

Mouse leans over the table to whisper, rocking the settle in his agitation.

"Then you are coming around to my way of thinking? We will investigate the murders?"

Obadiah scrapes his teeth with his napkin.

"I do not think we will be allowed a choice," he says. "It seems that our readership expects it of us. I will need you to redeploy your skills, Mr City Gossip."

"Whatever is needed, I will happily supply," Mouse says and tries quite hard not to suspect his friend of any mixed motives.

Twenty Two

I have the Bible to thank for helping me to find the missing element of this composition – because I see that is what it undoubtedly was, now that the characters of Lot and his family foreground the picture, towering over all as they flee this scene of fiery retribution.

It has been a bold decision and not one I made without weighing many alternatives. Nor was Mr Gretch reluctant to voice his own opinions. To set Biblical figures in modern dress against a modern ground was audacious, we agreed upon that. That it was a step too far was also a possibility. But we agreed that the vacancy apparent to all must be filled and I have done that magnificently, I think. The new figures have been painted over a part of Southwark which included the horse which had leaped from the frame, and is now sacrificed to the grand design. I had looked for inspiration in the same place where Henry Grace had found his. This was in the pages of his great family bible, whose richly-coloured illustrations – including a rendering of Lot's flight from Sodom – he still likes to glance over in his bed, his eyes being now incapable of reading small text.

Garcy Dunne, who I employed more as an act of charity rather than for her supposed abilities, surprises me by making a credible tragic wife for Lot (otherwise Mr Riordan, a young Irish chairman whose sinewy physique is much in demand by artists in this town). Lot's daughters are two street urchins who were glad of a sixpence. Before I introduced these foreground figures, the subject of this picture might have been a conflagration, the only moral to be drawn being one for those careless of their candles. It must be now be luminous to all that today's London stands for Sodom and Gomorrah. We have rendered England's capital as a nest of sinners, as deserving of destruction as the Cities of the Plain. It is a bleak vision, informed, no doubt, by the canker which gnaws away at the artist's body. The new figures complete his conception and I almost wish that he were capable of scaling the stairs and seeing it for himself.

In order to convincingly counterfeit the style of Mr Grace I had found it necessary to see for myself the works on which his reputation was founded. I discover their purchasers and visit the places where these great works now hang. On one occasion, I have the impudence to gain entry to a fine house on Sackville Street on the pretense of carrying a message for the master of the house. I wait in the entrance hall, where I know the painting hangs, until he can see me, taking note of every brushstroke. On another occasion and at another house, I tell the footman that I am sent by Henry Grace himself to make a sketch for his records.

I discover I have a talent for dissimulation, and I am easily taken for a serving girl (though in general, this happens more often than I might wish) or some lowly assistant. The paintings I see are revealing. It is said that *The Death of Germanicus* and *Samson* are two of the finest works Henry Grace ever did but to me they do not appear to be the peaks of a painter's art. I can see the flaws; there is no longer a veil between me and his technique. I know how he brought life to the straining muscles of a man's back, I know how he managed to convey detail in even the darkest corners and, of course, I know how he achieved that trick for which he was famous, his lustrous skin tones. I know all of this and I can do all of this.

With a work on the scale of *The New Fire of London*, it is difficult to know when it is really finished. I stand back and assay the composition, its balance and proportions. And then I stand close enough to see the tints of eyes and the scorches on cheeks. I look at my painting in morning, noon and evening light. I add specks of colour, lightly wiping at places where tones appear too thickly applied. I call it my painting, you notice, because it has become my painting. I have brought order to Henry Grace's chaos, I have honed and smoothed and made new. With the addition of this family I have changed it, augmented it and come somewhere near to completing it. This painting, I am thinking, as a door opens and someone enters the attic room, is my masterpiece.

"It is not yours, you know," Gretch says, having successfully read my mind. "It never will be yours. You've done a fair job, Miss, but you must never think of this painting as your own. Never."

"I was not thinking that," I lie.

"This is Henry Grace's painting, his and his alone. Only his name will sell this canvas at the price it must return. Your contribution must never be known."

"But I have done as much as he. More, I think." I say.

"Listen to me," Gretch says, shortly. "This is the painting which will salvage his reputation, not make yours. If we do what must be done, it will launch the name of Henry Grace anew. It is his name which will change our fortunes. You must be painted out of this particular picture.

Do you understand me? Your part in this is to do what I tell you, and that is all."

He gazes at the picture, scans every part from top to bottom as if searching for areas in need of improvement. When he is done with that he grunts, sits astride a chair and waves a piece of paper at me. "Anyway," he says, "It is the picture I would talk to you about."

I wonder if he is about to offer criticism, which I will reject as I think this thing is as near perfect as a picture might be.

"Well? What do have to say?"

"Just this. It is high time that people saw it. The people on this list."

Twenty Three

While Adam Brewer gazes at the vast picture in silent awe – he has never seen such a thing in all his born days, he will say – Mouse is thinking about what he will tell Obadiah about the painting. That he feels dwarfed is his first thought. Obadiah thinks himself quite the wit when he says that Mouse is dwarfed by this or that. Obadiah should see him now, dwarfed by the figure of Lot, who appears to stride from the frame of this enormous and quite extraordinary creation. He hasn't realised he has laughed out loud until the man at his side, a merchant and the owner of two Wapping warehouses, whom Mouse happens to know by sight and reputation, says, "You find this amusing? Prey share the joke with us all, little man."

The merchant, Mouse, five other men and a woman stand before *The New Fire of London* in the attic room of the house in Leicester Fields which belongs to its author, Henry Grace. There is a great hole in the roof, through which gauzy grey daylight evenly illuminates the surface and shows up the strokes of the painter's brush. The girl who has shown them up to the room seems remarkably knowledgeable about the work they stand in awe of and speaks of hues and tints and the uses for egg-white and distemper. The men in this room are too important to be talked to by a girl, however knowledgeable she thinks herself, and begin to offer their own appraisals of the work.

Mr Soames the owner of racehorses slaps his gloves upon his thigh and pronounces the painting “Devilishly daring!” His friend the jeweller seems about to enlarge on this but apparently thinks better of himself, takes another pinch of snuff, and nods his head. The portly brewer in his fine new suit of brown clothes says he wouldn’t give it space on his wall, though he is almost certainly the only man there, he says, with enough space to hang it. He cannot believe that the same hand painted his own portrait, which seemed to him perfection in paint. “No wonder people are talking about it so,” he says, “It’s a damnable monstrosity.”

“And you think it is funny?” repeats the merchant.

“Not at all, Mouse says, “I was musing on something else. I think it is astonishing. I never saw its like.”

“Nor I, and I hope I never have to,” replies the merchant. “Who would want to gaze on this scene of infernal chaos? A painting in this day and age must be a reflection of tranquility. Cows, swains, milkmaids. Tumbledown cottages. Not this.”

“You cannot see what is before your eyes,” says an angry Scottish gentleman. “This will blast away all your silly glades and temples and all your nymphs and shepherd boys too. Finally, we have something which is bursting with life. And death, too – look at yon fellow drowning in the Thames. Him with a face like the Bishop of London. It’s quite magnificent.”

“But what is it trying to say?” asks a celebrated poet.

"That we are damned, laddie. Finished, if we dae'na change our ways."

"Damned, is it?" says the merchant. "Well, we all know he is ill. I believe the affliction has affected his mind."

"His mind seems sound enough to me. Strumpets in the streets and drunkards tumbling out of the alehouses. It is a warning, so it is."

"I have had my fill of this," the merchant says. "We can at least say we have seen it with our own eyes. Come along, Eleanor. We will see ourselves out."

They are joined by the brewer. "Be off with ye and good riddance," the Scotsman calls after them. "Yon fellows know no more of art than Jack Ketch."

News of the growing curiosity about this painting has reached *The Enquirer* and for some days now, Obadiah and Mouse have debated whether the paper will praise the painting or damn it. As the picture is currently a matter of public interest, the organ must have an opinion, "Or appear to, at least," Obadiah says, as he sits by the extinguished fire, leafing through *The London Messenger*.

"They know all about it at Molly's," Mouse says.

"They have seen it?" Obadiah looks up with surprise. "Does that painter fellow keep an open house?"

"Certain people have been invited to view it, I hear," Mouse says. "*The Enquirer* has received an invitation, as it happens."

"Has it? Then I suppose that one of us must go and see the thing. You shall go, Mouse, I am not one for such stuff. I have letters to write and some enquiries to make."

"I allow that I advocated this investigation," Mouse smiles archly – quite unlike him, his friend thinks – "but this newspaper cannot survive on murder alone, Obadiah."

Who sometimes wonders if his face really is so legible.

"True, Mouse, true," he says. "But I thought we had turned a corner. *The Enquirer* has never sold as it did in those two or three issues. And just as importantly, I thought that we were about to right the wrong that was done to Clark. Right it in his memory, if no more."

"We did what we could," Mouse says. "We aired the facts. We said that whatever Clark was guilty of, he was innocent of those murders. And people responded to that."

"We made them angry," Obadiah agrees, "And not with us, for a pleasant change. But where is that anger now? Today we have not received a single letter on the matter."

"I am aware of that," Mouse says. "Perhaps everything has its time. And unless the real perpetrator is found, or a similar murder is discovered, that time may be over for this affair. We have spent a long time getting nowhere with this."

"No," Obadiah says. "It cannot be allowed to rest there. You were right all along. It does fall to us to discover who has been committing these dreadful crimes. *The Messenger* here is content to do nothing, it seems. But for how long, I wonder?"

"Then of course I must remain here and further our investigations," Mouse says, unbuttoning his coat. "I cannot set us upon something then leave all the work to you."

"Your duty lies elsewhere today," Obadiah says. "People are interested in this picture. As is *The Messenger*. Go and see it, Mouse, I will further our work here. Take Adam with you – there are people in those streets who will not be happy with what we are about."

And so Mouse re-buttons his coat and hurries from the house, leaving Obadiah settled in his favoured seat behind the warm chimney breast, pondering on a murderer still at large and puzzling again over what sort of assailant could afford to leave such wealth on his victim's body. It really is quite extraordinary, he thinks. Was it possible for rich and presumably refined men to be murderous beasts?

The chatter by those who remain in the attic expands to one about Art in more general terms. Mouse is unobserved as he looks again at the picture. Being so much shorter that anyone else present, his view is necessarily of a lower portion of the composition, where people crowd at the river stairs, pursued by flames and desperately searching for the boats which will take them off to the safety of the Southwark shore.

Here is where the detail is finest. He wonders how on earth the artist has managed to render such small faces so completely and imagines strong lenses made in Switzerland and hair-fine brushes. He bends his back and looks closer. And is immediately arrested by one of the faces he sees.

It is the subject of a painting he admired in the entrance hall of this very building, the self-portrait of Henry Grace himself. Yes, there is the Grecian nose and there the small chin; it is indeed the artist. But why should Henry Grace include himself among a group of frightened people who are apparently damned? He is about to ask their young guide about this, when he spots another oddly familiar face.

"Great heavens!" he exclaims aloud. "How very extraordinary!" The girl follows his gaze and she too looks closely at two tiny figures that cower before the flames. "This," Mouse tells her, "is Augustus Hepplewhite, Master of the Rolls. I have seen him many times at Alice's on Bruton Street."

The name of this august personality has caught other ears.

"The little man is mistaken," someone says.

"If this is not him, then it is his twin."

"It cannot be him."

"And will you tell me that the man at his side is not Terence Shaw?" Mouse says. "You all will have seen him at the Covent Garden Theatre."

People gather to take a closer look. They are excited and scan the frame, pointing to this or that small figure. There is wild conjecture. Only Adam and the girl who lives in the house and had been thought knowledgable minutes before, fail to catch the mood. The dwarf is closely examining other parts of the enormous canvas and with evident enthusiasm. Mouse's familiarity with the faces of the famous has never proved so useful. He identifies a notable banker and thinks that the fellow tumbling from the stairs into the water may be Sir Josiah Vanbrugh, a painter who was once a rival of Henry Grace.

"There must be some mistake," the girl says. "The faces here are so small that any similarity is probably coincidental."

"I have seen miniatures made by your master," Mouse says, "Which were very good indeed."

"Even so," the girl says, doubtfully.

"See here," says the Scotsman, jabbing a finger at the canvas. "Yon fellow with the ears like tankard handles is Sir James Fenwick. The King's physician, no less!"

One or two more faces are identified and then three or four more. And then it seems that wherever they look is some physiognomy they have previously seen upon a stage, on the hustings, in the clubs, at the coffee houses, in Ranalagh Gardens or parading on the Mall or in Hyde Park. It is quite extraordinary.

There is a moment when all there take in the enormity of what they see before them.

"I say," says Soames at last, slapping his gloves with evident glee, "We will have much to say to them at White's this evening!"

"I should think so," his friend, the jeweller says. "Knock me down if this will not be all over town by the morrow!"

What a very strange thing to do, Mouse thinks as he scans the canvas for more faces. Why has the artist chosen to render these people as scourged sinners fleeing the wrath of God? And why, he ponders, has he included his own visage among them? There are many questions he would dearly like to pose about what he is beginning to see as a cypher in paint, but the girl has been called away and they are now in the hands of Grace's man, a gaunt, hatchet-faced fellow who smiles thinly and will brook no other observation but that this is the finest, most daring picture to have been executed by a British artist these last fifty years.

Twenty Four

The Journal of Henry Grace

When fate brings me together again with Osiris, he is walking with his mother in the Luxembourg gardens. Perhaps it is having only the dull Dr Shepherd for company or maybe I saw in Osiris something I hungered for, I really do not know. But for whatever reason, I am much too forward and greet him like a long-lost friend. Bennison, who had been walking at my side, mutters something about attending to Dr Shepherd, whom we have left at the apartment with an attack of gout, and disappears. Osiris watches him go.

I have not seen the De'Aths since Calais and I am not displeased to see them here, having wanted some such encounter to relieve the tedium which has settled upon me like a lowering cloud since we departed the coast. Lady Jane De'Ath, wearing her hair undressed and unpowdered, so that it falls quite naturally and most becomingly from under her wide-brimmed hat, looks quite captivating. She offers me her hand and says she is delighted to renew our acquaintance.

"At last, we are on our own," Osiris says, when Lady Jane has excused herself, pleading a sightseeing engagement at the Tuileries. "We have much to discuss." As we walk about the gardens, Osiris tells me about the adventures the family have enjoyed since Calais and about how a sum of their money has suddenly been restored to them. "But this is not what I want to talk with you about," he says.

"If it is only the matter of that business at Calais," I begin.

"No, no," he says, rather too dismissively, I think. "And besides, my poor mother insists upon repaying your generous hospitality at the first opportunity. No, what I have in my mind to discuss with you is the matter of your whole future."

"My future? Why would that concern you?"

"Well, perhaps because you have a talent, Henry. I have seen it in your drawings. It is a foetus just now, but it has the possibility, I believe, to become something unique, possibly even great. If it is not stillborn, that is. There lies the danger."

"You riddle with me," I say. "Stillborn? What can you mean?"

"I have seen something like this happen before," Osiris says. "A young man with obvious potential – you can see it in the way he handles some particular thing, the eyes, or the hands, as examples – is told he has talent. Usually by people whose idea of art is a pretty picture to hang above the card table. The young man takes notice of these compliments and paints more of the same. His pictures get a little prettier but become a little more insubstantial every time. He hardly notices the gap that is widening between his early intentions and his present production. Eventually, he finds that he is incapable of painting anything other than pretty pictures and besides, the public who buy his pictures will not allow him to paint anything else. He is Hawkins the pretty picture painter and that might as well be written upon his tombstone. The money and influence that could have been his is buried with him. A tragic waste, as I see it."

"But what has that to do with me? You cannot see that as my fate?"

Osiris raises an eyebrow and allows me to draw my own conclusions. I think of my sketches of woodland glades, my watercolours of rural idylls, and hesitate.

"No," I say. "I will not allow that to happen. I will take another course."

"But how, Henry? How will you find that course? How will you prevent your talent from being stillborn?"

"You confuse me, Osiris," I admit. "I do not know. Not as yet."

"Then you must find out, Henry. Before it is too late."

"But how?"

Osiris lies his hands upon my shoulders and peers into my eyes, as if he might find therein something of which I am completely unaware.

"You must do more than take in pretty sights while you are here, Henry. You must submerge yourself in the strange and the wonderful. I promise you this. If you fully exploit every possibility, if you experience every arcane and recondite thing that might be experienced in these colourful lands, then you will return to England a changed man and an infinitely better painter."

"I repeat, how?"

"I have just told you. You must seek out and try the new and the strange. Experience is everything. And you will not do that in the company of that dotard who calls himself your tutor. You must travel in the company of someone who can open your eyes and guide your brush."

"But who?" I ask.

As if the matter were not already settled.

Twenty Five

When I have persuaded Gretch of our need to purchase yet more colours – I have to take him into the painting room and show him how little remains of the ultramarine, carmine and cobalt blue – and he has prised open his purse and parted with the necessary coins, I make my customary scan of the square (ever alert for creditors or their agents) before setting out for the colourman's. St Martin's Lane is no great walk and I intend to enjoy the brief respite it often affords from the dismal mood that prevails in the house.

I walk northwards, passing the tree-shaded villa which Mr Hogarth rented twenty or more years ago and, progressing further up the road, I am in hope of seeing Mr Reynolds leaving his own smart abode. I skirt the top of the square, where conversational cabmen in greatcoats smoke pipes outside Leicester House as they await visitors to its museum of natural curiosities. Soon, I am traversing Bear and Castle Streets and, cutting through Cecil Court and passing the house where Mr Grace once executed a portrait of the young Herr Mozart, I find myself upon St Martins Lane. I have walked quickly, conscious that my time is precious. My foregrounding figures must be further refined before I will convince expert eyes that this is the work of Henry Grace and there are a number of the master's unsold works to be improved. Gretch is keen that I bring these to a standard where we will be able to sell them with ease, once Henry Grace's name has currency again.

Mr Powell's is situated in an ancient edifice across the road from Molly's coffee house, from where a dwarf is presently leaving with some papers under his arm. I think but cannot be sure – he hurries away much too quickly – that this is the same dwarf who has twice come to see the painting and has been so illuminating about the identities of the figures that Mr Grace has included in the composition. I had never assigned significance to these but it has since troubled my mind that Grace's extraordinary decision to depict the faces of powerful men may spell trouble for its artist. I decide to seek out the dwarf and take his opinion on the matter, as soon as I can spare the time.

Behind the dusty panes of *E. Powell, Colours & Artists' Supplies* is an easel supporting an indifferent oil painting of country life wherein a herdsman arcs his switch as he drives his cattle under shading trees. A distant windmill competes for attention. The brushwork is lazy, the foliage too much like the vegetables he probably used as modelling. Before the painting are sprays of artists' brushes in pots, some handwritten endorsements on cards, a stack of engravers' copper plates and a box of noted Swiss crayons offering a *compleat assortment of shades and colours*. A printed bill proclaims that the establishment retails *the very best prepared canvass, pannels, & oil colours and also superfine water colours universally approved by the most eminent artists*. These are all items of enormous interest and desirability to me.

Through the window I can see a composition of gentlemen engaged in desultory conversation, two of these languorously resting elbows of navy-blue and rose-coloured coats on the shop counter as they might rest them on a bar-top, while a third wearing shirtsleeves and waistcoat and splashes of vermilion paint sits upon a stool and tickles his chin with a paintbrush he perhaps intends to buy. Mr Powell attends them closely, occasionally leaning over the counter to interject some remark of his own. Two at least of these gentlemen are painters, men I saw recently at the sale room, where one was adding final touches to a seascape about to be sold. The fourth, an older man who has dressed in a close-fitting dark coat and a cream coloured waistcoat which matches his silk stockings, may follow some other calling. Unlike the others, whose hair is powdered and tied back, he wears a wig and is less like the artist for it.

They look up as I enter but seeing my brown drab, mistake me for a servant of course and I very quickly fade from their attention, becoming no more interesting than the furniture of the shop. I must be assumed to possess no better auditory powers for all the effort they take to be careful of their conversation. The men talk of fellow painters in much the same way that women gossip, weighing their merits and then disposing of them with a cutting thrust which raises a laugh from the others. Even Mr Powell laughs, though I know that some of these targets are his best customers. I pay little heed, wishing Mr Powell would do what he was put on Earth to do and sell me my colours. But then it is borne upon me that the youngish man in navy, the pockmarks of whose cheeks are disguised with powder, is talking of someone who has been angered by Henry Grace. Mr Powell, who knows me as a servant of the artist under discussion, now flashes a look in my direction.

"I have never seen a man so wrathful," Navy Coat says. "He had recently heard of the interesting turn he gives in Grace's so-called masterpiece and was apoplectic. He cursed and profaned and would have kicked his dog, if he had one to spare. And this performance not just for me – I was there to oversee the hanging of my *Sinking of the Sans Pareil*, you understand – but before his undersecretary and footman too, who have no doubt been spreading the tale like a dose of diphtheria!"

"Not the recommended behaviour for a man who is like to be prime minister in a matter of weeks."

"Or perhaps not, if this painting does not sell into safe hands."

"Is it really that bad?" asks Mr Powell.

"No, that is the trouble. It is very well done and the likeness is him to a nicety. But there he is, fleeing from a burning bawdy house in Blackfriars with his breeches at half-mast and an expression of the utmost terror on his face as he attempts to board a foundering boat. Hardly a man to lead the country."

I edge a little closer, hoping to hear something about the painting's execution, to hear what, in fact, they have made of my own work. But it is only the little figures which hold interest, it seems. Navy goes on: "Godolphin has heard of his own inclusion and is – you surmise correctly! – far from pleased. There he is, knocking women and children from his path so he can secure his place among the exodus across the river. And Edward Featherstonhaugh, mark you, has fared little better. He appears at the window of a Molly house, most improperly dressed. For a man, anyway."

"The spymaster?" says Vermillion. "I have heard the worst things said of that man."

Pink offers a low whistle. "Now there is someone I should not like to vex," he says. "Not if I preferred my ribcage to remain unpricked."

There is a pause, while this last observation is digested. Then, Vermilion says,

"But really, does any of this matter? People of position must expect to be ridiculed and to become the butt of the caricaturists. That in itself is a sign they have achieved some position. And if the king is lampooned, surely his ministers can expect small mercy."

"Print shop humour is ephemeral," says Pink. "Not so with the case in question. If this work restores Grace to the ranks of the British greats (and people who know about such things assure me that it will) then this painting will assume far greater importance than a mere print. Wherever its home after its sale – Chiswick House has been mooted, though I have it that the Prince of Wales has shown an interest – it will be visited by the greatest in the land and the victims of Grace's tomfoolery, viciousness, call it what you will, will be jeered at now and very likely for years to come. No wonder they are angered."

"No, no, that is not it," says Navy. "Jem here is right. People must expect raillery, whether it spills from the artist's brush or the scrivener's pen. It is all the same."

"So what do they fear?" asks Rose, opening Navy's snuff-tin which lies handy on the counter and helping himself to a liberal pinch.

"I think," says Navy, "I think it is not that they cannot bear being seen as such poltroons, but they fear being seen together. It is the association with each other that terrifies some of them. I imagine that is particularly the case with Collins and Featherstonhaugh, who will have much to lose if their advancements are approved."

"Well, you may have something there," says Vermilion. "Grace has assembled a motley crowd. A man destined to lead the country cannot be seen in the company of actors, whores and, God forbid, painters!"

He awaits his laugh, which duly comes.

"It is more than that, I think," says Navy.

"How so?" asks Pink.

"I have heard that the ones who have seen the painting at Grace's house, or have had it closely described to them, are angry, but none has confronted Grace about it. They do not talk about it. They do not make the fuss they might if they were only angry."

"I should have expected action from Featherstonhaugh at least."

"Grace is sick. Perhaps they await his recovery."

"Men like these would not give a fig were Grace at death's door."

"Some think he may be there now," offers Mr Powell.

"They have done nothing yet because they are fearful," Navy says. "Much more so than they might be if this were only a matter of their humiliation. That is what some people are saying. And the more I think about it, the more I think there is some dangerous connection here which we cannot see, but someone else might. And that is what they fear."

Twenty Six

I have talked to Gretch about the dangers we entertain, keeping that picture in the house. If what I overheard at Powell's is true, there are powerful men who would like nothing better than to see it destroyed. Gretch scorns my craven spirit and says this will only raise the price. It is even possible, he adds, that it may be bought to keep it from public view. And though I am aware now that we run risks by maintaining any connection with it, I have poured my life into that picture and no more want to see it harmed than does Grace.

In a moment of weakness I say that we might paint out any face that is recognisable, but who is to say which face will be known by someone and which not? I try to imagine the composition without those countenances frozen by fear, bloated by avarice or contorted by pain and I cannot. Is it the judgement of these cursed souls that endows this work with greatness? I tell myself that art should be the artist's first consideration, in which case once it is completed, not a brushstroke of that picture should be changed.

But today there has been something else to occupy my mind. A telling scene confronted us when Gretch and I went to see the picture again. Day had not broken an hour since and Mrs Harris was still battling coals in the grate when we mounted the stairs to decide what must be our next moves towards its completion. We will leave intact Grace's identifiable figures, but the Hogarthian crowds bringing up the rear cannot be left as an amorphous mob; some degree of detailing must be introduced. To this end I had thrown on my painter's garb and had barely passed a comb through my hair before I was arming myself with my finest brushes, intending to make the best use of the early morning light. We passed Grace's door as quietly as we might and went on up to the attic room.

There we found Henry Grace lying senseless on the floorboards before his masterpiece. A ladder had collapsed beside him. His face was bruised and his night-linen was soiled. Whatever energy he had gathered to propel his withered frame up the stairs to the attic had deserted him when he began to paint. A brush had rolled from his grasp. With great difficulty, we got him down the stairs, washed him and returned him to his bed, where his breathing soon became more regular and he seemed to slip into a normal sleep. His injuries, we were perhaps too eager to believe, looked worse than they were. I wondered, with a pang of guilt, if the shock of seeing his composition changed out of recognition by the addition of my huge new figures had caused his fall. He had not visited the attic since they were painted.

I wish we had the services of a reliable physician who might provide an accurate prognosis. The course of his disease is so hard to predict. There are times when he is so weak that life appears to have only faint tenure in that brittle shell. At others, his malady bares its fangs and shows itself with violence. Grace is then overpowered by his demons and appears to inhabit a waking nightmare, though what inspires his terrors I cannot say, although I have twice construed the words 'monstrous' and 'caverns' amid the prattle.

He seems not to know me when I bring his soup, or a bowl and sponge for his ablutions. Some things of which he talks are mysterious to me but others I can make a little sense of, now that I have read parts of his diary. There are periods of respite, too, when he can remain lucid for days together, suggesting a corner has been turned and at such times I wonder if he may, to some degree at least, recover his strength and abilities, if not his looks, which now are lost for ever.

On such a day, a cab stopped before the house and a gentleman got down. Taking me for a servant, he demanded to see Mr Grace. He wore a dark muffler and large hat, which meant I saw little of his face – and hardly had time to look closer, as I would show the gentleman immediately to Mr Grace, or my ears would know about it.

Mr Grace was awake when I opened his door and quite conscious of his surroundings, because a cloud crossed his face the moment he saw the gentleman. But he waved me away, murmuring that he was not to be disturbed. The stranger was closeted with him a long half-hour, after which I heard him ascending alone the steps to the attic room, no doubt to inspect the picture. When I had seen the stranger out, I went upstairs to ensure that was all was well with the invalid. I found him looking most careworn and more fatigued than I had seen him in days. In his open palm was a single gold coin which could only have been a gift from the strange gentleman.

My professional self, I will admit, sees no profit in Grace's eventual return to health. The painter in me is determined to complete this picture without any help from Henry Grace. The work is no longer his. But my humanity, I am thankful to say, still hopes every day to see some improvement. The painting itself is fast becoming the talk of the town. Some are saying it will be the salvation of Grace's reputation, others that it will prove what they have all along said, that Henry Grace is nothing more than a second-rate portrait-man with a run of luck.

People are intrigued by the rumours and want to judge the painting and its artist for themselves. Uninvited gentlemen come to the door and demand to see Henry Grace. Gretch tells them that regrettably, the master remains indisposed because of his illness but is improving every day, thanks to the efforts of his physicians. One visitor is admitted daily to make drawings of the painting which are skilful and exact.

The work itself is so nearly complete, I think (though I have thought this before and still found room for improvements) and while Grace awaits the most propitious time to sell in Grace's name, I go on with my own art, closeting myself in the painting room for days at a time as I turn drab, workmanlike portraits into bright and often imaginative renderings. It is sometimes the case that when I am finished, the subject looks a little less like the man who walked through our doors, but is very much improved. He would, I think, purchase the picture, were to be given the chance again.

Twenty Seven

Painting has always brought me peace and I feel the first intimations of that better state early one morning when I seat myself before a virgin canvas. Today I find myself with much need of that peace; I am angry with James Gretch, who has mistaken my reproductions of details from *The New Fire* as test pieces painted by Mr Grace and sent them to the saleroom along with more books and statuary. I suppose that in some way I ought to see this act as a testament to the excellence of my work. But it has drained my enthusiasm for creating more of the same and I am in a mood to forget about the painting in the attic and try something fresh. This day, I intend to address another necessary skill which I must acquire if ever I am to become a great artist. As I tie the paint-soiled apron over my dress, adjust the mirror at my side, peer into it and make my first brushstrokes, my mind is occupied by no worse thing than the self-portrait I will make today.

Now that I will reproduce my own likeness, I notice as if for the first time the clear signs of wear on the collar and sleeve-ends of my dun-coloured dress and see how it has faded through repeated washing. It is true that I might have bought myself a decent one with the pennies I earn as Grace's apprentice, nothing very new, but something on the right side of respectable. However, good paintbrushes command a high price. In any case, I argue, painting my everyday apparel will give my art veracity. Oh, but what a poor watercolour I am about to make. Self portraits are the necessary calling-cards of every great painter and this is not a card I would be happy to give out. But it is a skill I should master and nothing else calls on my time. There is no painting of Grace's that requires completion and we are leaving alone *The New Fire of London* in order to see it with fresher eyes. And so I listen to a voice in my head.

That portrait of Mr Grace in the hallway, it says.

What of it? I reply. *It is very finely done.*

Paint that.

I do not want to make a copy. I want to paint myself.

You can paint yourself and paint that picture, it says, adding, *And have a perfect way to measure how close you have come to Mr Grace's old standards. The clothes he wore for that portrait are still in the linen press adjoining his room.*

And in this manner I persuade myself into the same embroidered blue coat and white stock which Henry Grace had worn to make his own self portrait, years before. I prove proficient in dressing myself up as young man of fashion, or the fashions of some while past. I consult the portrait in the hall and make adjustments to my attire accordingly. I apply a little lead to my face and lighten its tone. I use the hundred and one tricks we have employed with our sitters to improve their looks, I dab with rouge, pluck eyebrows and cheek hairs with tweezers – a thing I have not done before – and make endless attempts to tame my hair into something resembling the style that Grace wore when he made his own self-portrait.

As a girl, I suppose I am what is termed plain. The face of the young man who stares back at me looks somewhat better. Fellow foundlings soon disabused me of any misplaced ideas I might have held about my looks and the idea of building my future upon them has always been foreign to me. Under Mr Gilpin's sway, I soon decided that a degree of wisdom and a little learning are more important things to have than a pretty face. And so I borrowed books from the Hospital's library and spent happy hours reading about the lives and works of painters, and architects too. In such ways I came not to concern myself with my own appearance and never think of how I must appear, of the shapeless old dress I wear daily.

I adjust the position of the mirror so that I fill its frame and make the first marks on the sky-grey wash I have already prepared. I work the morning long, holding in mind my master's accomplished self-portrait. But today is not one of my good days. The more I paint of the reflected image, the more the comely youth on the canvas falls short of my intentions. Perhaps this was a crazy idea after all. Neither new clothes nor a talent for painting can rescue the image that gapes back at me as I apply the last of the lead white to the Mars red and produce a tone which exactly matches the more rubicund patches of my cheeks.

Perhaps the fault lies with the subject and not the painter. Certainly, it is an image unworthy of the resplendent appellation which was bestowed upon my younger self by the governors of the Foundling Hospital, where infants are stripped of any name they may have had since birth and christened anew. Names of founders and benefactors have always been popular and I met not a few children named for our founder, Captain Coram. There were William and Jane Hogarths too, and namesakes of other artists who had supported the hospital, such as Francis Hayman and Joshua Reynolds. I had been at the hospital some five years before the origin of my own name was explained and I understood why I had been called Michel Angelo. Although people have at various times found in it a source of amusement – Michel is uncommon, usually bestowed on a male child and, I discovered, French to boot – I have seen sufficient sublime prints of Buonarroti's work and read enough about Michelangelo the artist himself, to be proud of the appellation and see it as an omen that augurs well for my future as a painter. So I am thinking, when I hear a familiar, sand-dry voice.

"We must talk, Michel. If what I see is still you."

Gretch is framed by the doorway, his bony chin supported by folded arms and a cupped palm as he regards me thoughtfully.

"It's about *The New Fire*," he says, coming into the room and looking at me dressed thus with some interest.

He peers into the mirror from different angles, his spectral head appearing over my left and then my right shoulder. He straightens my stock, pulls up the collar of the coat. "You have been reading my thoughts, I see," he says.

"What do you mean?"

"It will save for later. As will something else of rather more import. For the nonce, what I have to say now is this. The time is coming when we must sell that painting." He frowns. "Once we have borrowed ropes and tackle. The thing is much too big for the doors. It will have to be wrapped in sailcloth and sent out through the hole in the roof. I will enlist the help of John the footman from next door."

"That will be a sight for those who want to see the painting," I say. "But to my mind, it was as good as finished weeks ago. Why did we not sell it then?"

Gretch yawns, a Tower lion with tobacco-stained teeth.

"You can paint tolerably well, girl, but you know nothing of business. Grace's reputation as a yesterday's man would have overshadowed everything. The painting itself would not have been enough, whatever its merits."

"What else was needed?" I ask.

"People want a story to go with it," Gretch says. "We had to create a spark of interest in the work and fan that flame until a great fire roared. And now we have. Our painting has caught the public's imagination like no other that I can think of."

"But how can that be?" I say. "We have only shown it to a few dozen people."

"That can be enough, if those people have been carefully chosen. And especially when one of them happens to be a scrivener for the newspapers. Look at this." He stuffs a newspaper into my hands, indicating a column which is headed *On a Visit to see the Painting Lately Executed by Mr Henry Grace*. I expect to read something quite laudatory but instead, I see the following report, written by someone calling himself Jeffery Hudson.

No greater confirmation is needed that the once reputable artist Mr Henry Grace is losing his mind than the most cursory glance at the atrocity which is his newest and, if we are to give currency to reports about his current state of health, perhaps final painting. A more shocking demonstration of the decline of a man's senses and woeful absence of sensibility this writer has not had the misfortune to see. The painting itself purports to depict London aflame and appears to be a representation of the Great Fire of 1666. However, the artist has made not the smallest effort to bring to life the city of that time. Not only has he neglected to attire his fleeing crowds in the appropriate garb but many of the burning buildings were not even erected at the time of the Great Fire. What, too, are we to make of the strange figures who dominate the foreground? To this viewer they seem like nothing so much as representations of the Biblical Lot with his wife and daughter, fleeing the burning Cities of the Plain. This execrable painting is ill-conceived and poorly executed. If anything in London should be burned, it is surely this picture.

"This is monstrous," I cry, feeling my temples throb with mounting anger. "These ink-wasters know nothing about art. They are not painters. Yet they can ruin artists. They have ruined me. Ruined us. So much work, so many, many hours, wasted! Well, we cannot sell it after this. We will burn it. That will be fitting."

I get up, intending to quit the house and clear my head of this gross calumny.

"Wait, you conceited baggage," Gretch says, "there's more. Listen to this."

He reads from a paper of a later date in which the painting is this time the subject of one of its readers, who claims to be an artist himself, and he begs to differ with Jeffery Hudson. Indeed, the reports could hardly be more different. This correspondent, who writes as 'Gulliver', sees *The New Fire of London* as *a veritable burning beacon for British art*, and, displaying a wanton carelessness about such matters as mixed metaphors, as *a fingerpost pointing in a brave new direction.* There is much more in this vein and also two long paragraphs about technical matters which Gretch skips through. *Considerable skill...great leap of imagination...superb luminosity... not at all unlike the finer examples of the Flemish masters.*

"That is high praise," he says.

I concede that it is.

"Just a little more. This painting, our Gulliver says, *is quite the most extraordinary thing to appear in years. It will, he thinks, wake people's ideas*. There's something about Grace too. *The New Fire*, he says, *has rescued the reputation of this sadly neglected artist, whose earlier works must now be reappraised in the light of this astonishing achievement.*"

Gretch throws down the newspaper. "And so it goes," he says, "To and fro, one damning and the other lauding. It's the same in the coffee houses. Every man-jack has his opinion."

"How this can be," I say, "when next to no-one has seen the painting?"

"Everyone has seen it."

"But how?"

"You have not seen the prints? Everyone else in London has. What do you think of this?" He unrolls a large mezzotint print, a smaller version of the painting in the attic, skilfully etched in many shades of grey.

"Who did this?"

"An engraver I know, over in Covent Garden. The one who has been making the sketches. It's fine work, do you not think?"

The detail is indeed so fine that even smaller things can be made out, some of the larger faces quite clearly. Gretch says, "Those little folk you're looking at there have caused a stir, too."

"How is that?"

"This newspaper has hinted that one or two faces among them are recognisable. I know you did not paint those physogs, but did you know they were the likenesses of real people?"

"I did not. It was the dwarf who saw it first. I suppose that report emanates from *The Enquirer*?"

"Some of these people used to be very important. One or two still are, these writer fellows are suggesting. Now why Mr Henry Grace has gone and done a thing like that, I cannot think. Of course, this journalist is too clever to say who those faces are supposed to be. But it matters not a jot to us. All that matters is that everyone wants to see that painting, Michel, every man and his dog. You have seen me turning people away from our door. It happens daily."

Warmed by a sudden flow of pride, I say, "This is all good news. Surely it means the price will be high at auction?"

"Auctions are unreliable beasts," Gretch says. "But I am hopeful."

"So when will it be sold?"

By which, I do not mean when will we be able to leave the house without being dunned by creditors or when will this much discussed artwork carry its attendant dangers elsewhere. What I mean is, when will my work, that large part of the painting that was either conceived and painted or improved by me, go on show to the public at large? When will I be judged and, I hope, endorsed by my peers?

Gretch picks a strand of tobacco from his teeth and frowns. I can see that he thinks there is some impediment to our plans.

"What is it? Is there a problem?"

"There is indeed a problem," Gretch says.

I await Gretch's pleasure. I think he is deciding whether or not his interests will be best served by divulging the nature of the problem to me.

"Part of that problem," he says at last, "Lies in the fact that it is not just the painting they want to see, it is Henry Grace himself. They want to see him too."

"Why him?" I say, hotly. "What he did was only a beginning. I perfected and completed *The New Fire*. I made it what it now is. I'm the reason they want to see that painting."

"Cocksure, as I said you were. It's not a pretty trait for a young lady, but we may have use for it yet."

"I cannot see why Mr Grace is of any interest to them. He is a bedridden invalid and no more an artist now than is Poll."

"He is also the keeper of a mystery, Michel, and people do so like a mystery."

"What do you mean?"

"Even as indisposed as he has been these last few weeks, he has become an object of fascination. People are curious about great men who hide themselves away. They are curious about Henry Grace, whom they see as a treasury of unanswered questions. Why will he receive no visitors, they are asking? And is it true that on rare occasions when he does, he receives them with his face obscured by a mask? There is nothing like a mystery for fanning interest. People he knew or people he didn't know have written their memories of him, in the newspapers and in pamphlets too. Rumours and half-truths are flying about the coffee houses."

"If it is only a matter of presenting Grace to the public then I do not see a problem," I say, blithely. "He can attend the auction. People know about the mask now. They will not be shocked by it. If what you say is right, it may add a little excitement to the proceedings, which can only help the sale."

"Henry Grace is not going anywhere, Michel."

"He's very ill, I know that," I say, as my excitement mounts. "But when he knows that the painting is to be sold before a large and expectant crowd, he may find new strength. I have heard of something like that happening. We can borrow some contrivance, a bath chair..."

"No, Michel."

"All we need to do is satisfy the curious. Once they have seen him, dressed in his finery with the mask he bought in Venice, they will let him alone, I'm sure. With help, we could have him appear above them, on the gallery. What a spectacle he would make."

"We are not going to do that, Michel, not with Mr Grace."

"But why?"

I do not know whether Jamie Gretch is smiling or scowling. He coughs, has to hawk up a ball of phlegm, which he folds into his handkerchief, before he makes his reply,

"Because Henry Grace is dead, Michel."

"Dead?"

"This very morning. I took him something to wet his lips when I returned from the saleroom and found him gone. Cold as a side of beef."

For a moment I see the world stop. Henry Grace is dead. I am numbed by the news. I do not feel relief that his suffering is over. I do not think of the talent that is lost forevermore, because that expired weeks ago. I think, how will this affect me and my painting? And so I hardly hear Gretch when he asks, "Did you have occasion to look in on him while I was out?"

I do not tell Gretch that although I did not see Mr Grace that morning, someone else did. I do not tell him because Gretch had expressly instructed me to answer the door to no-one, in case we admitted the bothersome duns. But this man rapped his stick upon the door with an authority that I could not ignore and so, shortly after eleven, I let in the sharp-faced gentleman who sometimes calls upon Mr Grace. The visitor left after a quarter-hour or perhaps a little more and told me that my master needed rest and should be left in peace that morning. I do not like to think that this man's stony face was perhaps the last physiognomy that Henry Grace saw in this world and wonder idly if he was scared to death. But such reflections on mortality do not detain me long. For the sake of a propriety, I wait a moment before I say, perhaps a little coldly, "What happens to the painting now? What happens to me?"

Henry Grace had been good to me but all I can think of now is a future filling his shoes.

"If Henry Grace is dead, we have no authority to sell the work," Gretch says. "Others will sell the estate of Henry Grace and the money will go to Yorkshire relatives who never appreciated his talents."

"Then we are sunk," I say. "This has all been time misspent. The house will be sold and we will be cast upon the streets. I will paint no more. We will be lucky to eat."

"That all holds true," Gretch says, his flinty grey eyes flashing. "If Grace is dead."

"But you said he was dead," I exclaim angrily. "Did you not?"

“Henry Grace cannot die,” Gretch says. “Not just yet, anyway.”

“You are toying with me,” I say.

“Have you been listening to anything I have said?” says Gretch, closer now and peering over my shoulder again, “Or have I wasted my breath?”

Twenty Eight

Suddenly, we have money. *The New Fire of London* remains in the attic, as yet to be offered for sale and I know that we have sold nothing else of late. But now there are funds sufficient to pay off one or two of our more insistent creditors and to buy candles, fuel and food. This unlooked-for change of circumstance seems almost to have happened overnight. I am beside myself with curiosity, but Gretch has waved off every one of my questions and instead, gives me a purse and an interesting commission.

By the time I reach the Strand, I am so taken up by what Gretch has told me of my destination and how its contents put him in mind of better times in Leicester Fields, that I am no longer thinking of the late Mr Grace. At Mrs Holt's Italian Warehouse in the Strand, I drift spellbound through a lush repository of velvets and damasks and fans and parasols and past an artful display of Leghorn hats, before I come into a chamber at the back of the place rich with the appetizing smells of extraordinary food.

Closely watched by the proprietor, I touch and sniff and when it has been established that I carry a full purse of money, I taste too, such foodstuffs that only the rich must know. I read the labels aloud and savour the sounds of *Bolongnia sausidges* and vermicelli. I present my list and watch with great interest as she carves thin slices of Italian ham and cuts off a goodly portion of a hard cheese called Parmesan. I try capers and anchovy fish for the first time. I admire Italian wines with names I cannot pronounce and inspect flasks of olive oil and some cordials from Florence. The woman, who may be Mrs Holt herself, or perhaps her daughter, rolls a small piece of Parmesan cheese in her palm and holds it under my nose. "Now, you smell the pineapple?" she asks me, in an accent which I take to be Italian.

Though I have visited great houses as assistant to a commissioned artist and have seen how money might be spent on fine furnishings and gold leaf, the sensations aroused by my visit here are entirely novel. Overpowered by the aromas and tastes of new and piquant food, I resolve that the course my life takes will be one to bring me not only acknowledgement of my talent but riches at least sufficient to enjoy pleasures such as these. And now, catching sight of myself in a mirror placed for the use of ladies trying on hats and scarves, I think that perhaps I might allow a little improvement in my dress, too. All this might be possible, is almost within my grasp, I think, once my talents are widely and properly appreciated.

My pleasant meanderings are rudely interrupted by Mrs Holt.

"You should not be out on your own, cara mia," she says in the tones of a mother who is used to being obeyed. "You do not hear what they are saying, I think?"

"What do you mean?"

"This is dangerous place. Signor Holt did not tell me London was like this."

She takes a knife from a wooden board where it has lain with a fat Italian sausage and waves it across her throat.

"The murders," I say.

These outrages lately have disappeared from the newspapers and with the near-completion of the picture and Grace's death, I have had other matters to distract me.

"Yes, the murders. How quickly people forget. But still there is a very bad man out there, who takes little girls like you and" – she raises the knife and plunges it into the sausage – "kills them. Just like that. Be very careful, piccola," she calls after me as I leave quickly. "Stai attento!"

I don't know how much there is, or for how long the money will last but for the moment, the kitchen fire glows, I can light my way to bed and for once my belly does not feel painfully empty as it has these last few weeks. Mrs Harris gives Poll her share of the food with a show of reluctance. "Mr Grace kill a man indeed," she mutters as she slides a thin rasher of bacon onto her plate. Whether he did this or not seems of small consequence now that we are hungry no more. Candles, coal and food may not speak of a large windfall but whatever amount Gretch has suddenly acquired, he spends it well. This filling of Gretch's purse coincides with another piece of good fortune, which is the resolution of a dark problem which has been weighing on everyone's mind for above a week. No sooner has Gretch told me that Henry Grace is dead, than he quite shocks me with the news that we cannot bury him.

"Why? A pauper's grave will cost nothing, surely?"

"It's not a matter of expense." I can see his brain hard at work, the old veins in his temple pulsing as they always do when something perturbs him.

"Then what is it, for God's sake?"

"No-one must know he has died. That must be our secret. And to keep this secret I will let Poll go, tomorrow morning. We cannot have her finding him dead and blabbing it all over town. What I will have to promise Mattie Harris I hardly know."

"But why make a secret of it? People will find out, one way or the other."

"No. Not the way I plan this to go."

"But why?" I say again.

"Och, Michel, do wake up and consider our position." He draws a deep breath, perhaps to contain his rising temper. "The interest in our painting is largely dependent on the mystery surrounding its artist. It's not just the painting or whoever may be represented in it. It's Grace himself, the hermit of Leicester Fields."

And much as I would like to think that it is my own brushstrokes, the rendering of Job's awe in the face of God's retribution that draws our visitors, I know in my heart he is right. But I do not know how to express the right thing. And so I say, "Well, that is unfortunate. Because now they will have to settle for the painting alone. And me – don't forget how much of this has been my work."

Gretch holds his head in his hands as if he would stop it exploding. "You must never be associated with that painting," he flares. "How many times must I tell you? They don't want you. You are nobody. It's him they want."

"But it was my talent which rescued that painting," I persist. "They should be wanting to see me."

"Shut your mouth and listen, you foolish girl. And listen carefully. We will find a use for your talents soon enough. Do you want to hear more?"

I draw a breath which I manage somehow to release slowly and so become a little calmer. Sometimes I am granted a lucid moment in which I can see clearly how I must appear to others and I do not always like what I see. I am quiet.

"The newspapers are making quite the meal of our Henry," Gretch says. "Have you seen the things they are writing? That he once was an opium addict? That he frequented molly houses?"

"I have read some strange things," I admit.

"It does not matter one way or the other now. In fact it is all grist to our mill."

"Even the rumour that he killed a girl in Venice?"

"Even that."

"Did he? Kill a girl?"

"How should I know? That is not the sort of thing a gentleman tells his servant. But it will not hurt if people believe he did. It is all part of the making of his legend."

"In any case, our master is dead," I say, flatly, "And we can't change that."

Gretch rises from the table, takes his old coat from a chair, off upon some private business, I assume. Unbolting the door, he stops and turns.

"Dead?" he says. "Well, let us not be too sure about anything."

Henry Grace, who was at least accorded the dignity of being properly laid out by Mrs Harris, remained where he had died, in his bedroom on the second floor for some days after he passed away, quite suddenly.

Living with a corpse is not a thing I would recommend to you. Out of some misshapen respect for the dead, we talked in low voices and avoided the landing passage which terminates at that bedroom door. Always unasked, as we sat in the kitchen eating a scant meal, was the question of how we were to dispose of the body.

All sorts of grim possibilities presented themselves to my mind. Gretch and I armed with shovels and dark lanterns in a churchyard at midnight. A deep hole dug in the foundations beneath the cellar, the cadaver sprinkled with quicklime. I even saw Gretch dismembering his master on the kitchen table, before boxing him up small enough to be dropped into the Thames. I felt incriminated against my will. What right had we to deny this soul a Christian burial? That Gretch continued to deny him this ate away at me with every day that passed.

"A little longer and he will be gone," Gretch says to me one day.

"But how will he be gone?" I demand to know.

"You do not need to know, Michel. In point of fact, it's better for you that you do not know."

"But why are we doing this? What possible good can this serve?"

Gretch looks at me hard, perhaps searching for something in my eyes which will tell him that he can trust me with anything. He does not find it.

"Patience, Michel. Just a few more days and the old Mr Grace will be out of our lives."

"The old Mr Grace?" I say, "what can you mean by that?"

But Gretch is already upon the servants' staircase, the one which communicates with the passageway outside Henry Grace's bedroom.

Twenty Nine

Lured by Mouse's discovery of unlikely inclusions in Henry Grace's picture, Obadiah has seen the picture for himself. At Leicester Fields, he puzzles the girl who shows it to him by paying close attention to details she evidently considers insignificant. She watches his gaze explore the canvas before being abruptly arrested in one particular area. The visitor pores over this for minutes at a time, retreats from the picture, mutters something to himself and approaches it again. He asks for a magnifying glass and when she supplies one, spends another minute or more peering through the glass. "It starts to make sense," she hears him say, as he briskly quits the room and takes the stairs down to the street three at a time.

"This matter may go much deeper than we thought," Obadiah tells Mouse. "I pray that my darkest apprehensions are not true." He bites his lip, cogitating, forgetting Mouse for the moment. "And yet there is much in it for us if they are."

"You had better tell me," Mouse says, though he is far from sure that he wants to hear what Obadiah has to say.

"When you saw the painting," Obadiah begins, "Did you look much at the area North West of St Paul's?"

"I was obliged to concentrate on details at my eye level," Mouse says, flatly. "I did not want to ask for a pair of steps."

"Of course not. But that is where I found something that may be most germane to our enquiries. As I say, I almost hope it is not."

"Do not play with me, Obadiah. What is this detail?"

"Just this. There is a silhouetted person crouching before a crested coach who appears to be scattering small shiny objects on a figure who lies on the ground and may be dead."

"Well, what of it?" Mouse says, a little testily. "What is there in that to alarm anyone else featured in this painting?"

"Suppose that figure is a young girl. Which I think it is," Obadiah says. "And then suppose those shiny objects are gold coins. Which I think they are."

Mouse is silent for a moment. "It could mean anything," he says at last.

"It could. Perhaps I am looking for meaning where none is to be had. But, I tell you this. I have heard more than I want of gold coins and dead children of late."

"You would connect the painting and the murders?"

"Henry Grace has at least two known associates among those clearly depicted. Both are powerful men."

"A pity you could not make out the crest on the coach. Then we would know the family who owned the vehicle."

"It was too small and I think the painter did not want his mystery unlocked so easily."

"You are quite certain of what you saw, though? A dead girl, coins?"

"Yes. And the more I think about it, the more certain I am that there is an unwholesome relation between that image and the matter of these dead or deranged girls."

"Then there is a connection to Henry Grace too," Mouse says, "But what can we do about it? We cannot publish conjecture. Nor can we afford to make adversaries of men like these. Even the ones who are powerful no longer are likely to have friends who are."

"They may be counting upon that to deter us. It will not. My dearest friend, this will be a sensation."

"This is not wise, Obadiah. We must at least establish the artist's intention. We must be sure of our every move. Let us go again to Leicester Fields and speak with Henry Grace himself."

"He has relapsed," Obadiah says. "If what I have heard is true, he is presently too ill to answer questions."

"Then let me us ask the girl, Miss Angelo. She assisted the artist."

"The girl has gone somewhere with Grace's man. I have been enquiring after her. They were seen two days ago, boarding a conveyance at The Swan With Two Necks, where the Bath coaches go from."

"Then we must delay publication," Mouse says.

"And allow another paper to steal our glory? No, Mouse. We are rattling cages. Let us rattle some more."

Thirty

One of those whose cages are violently rattled is Sir Ranalegh Clayton, who sits in the back room of a tavern in Chiswick reflecting on life's vicissitudes. He has come up in the world but even so, he never can ride through the timber yards and tenter grounds of Bermondsey without being reminded of what his parents once had been. This, of course, was long before their eldest progeny – Dick they called him – took ship at Greenwich, bound for India as a cabin boy. This was the same Dick who would return twelve years later as a formerly successful dealer in commodities (mainly opium) for the East India Company. Dick's parents were in the rag and turd trade, his father collecting and trading in the rags, his mother wearing the black leather glove and carrying the lidded basket which marked her out as a pure finder, one of many women who scratched a living collecting up dog turds and selling them to Bermondsey's noisome tanners by the basketful.

Both his parents and his two younger brothers were dead of typhus when Dick came back from India under a cloud but with enough money to buy himself a seat in Parliament. The cloud was almost entirely compounded of rumours: it was rumoured that Clayton had a vicious temper which sometimes showed itself in drink and it was rumoured that he had killed a boy, very unfortunately the son of a local chief with strong ties to the Company. He had absolutely no idea what the boy had been doing in his room or who had opened his throat with a knife.

Rumours, Sir Ranelegh complained bitterly, he had been cashiered for blasted rumours.

Back on English soil, he had sufficient good sense to alter his name and settle at an address which was about as far removed from Bermondsey as the city allowed. But although he dressed in such a way that he appeared quite indistinguishable from others of his circle (he consorted now with the quality) something, he felt, was still not right. Not a day went by when he did not feel that he was a fraud and suspect that others saw him for what he really was, or at least, for what he once had been. His position as a prominent politician and friend to the powerful, member of Brooks's and long-term affiliate of a more exclusive, and certainly more secretive, club seemed sometimes to him like a parcel roughly-wrapped and tied with gossamer string. He felt this most keenly after a scheme in which he had invested substantially, went terribly wrong.

Sir Ranalegh was among hundreds who lost a great deal of money through the turpitude of others. For the people who had recommended this investment to him, their losses were insignificant. They might sell off a farm or two from the estate, or let their neighbour have the grouse moor they had wanted, and that would be that. For Sir Ranalegh, the matter was more serious. The disaster had moved him closer, he thought, to the edge of the abysmal pit into which he always expected to be plunged headlong, should circumstances ever be allowed to slide from his control.

And now it is looking very much as if they have. What had seemed unthinkable for so many years may yet come to pass. In recent days, Sir Ranalegh has learned to his profound perturbation that certain clandestine doings of his more secretive club have not been as deeply buried as he had been led to believe. Indeed, the talk is that they may yet come to light. This is an extraordinary and worrisome turn of events and one which threatens to bring down his carefully-built house of cards. They may yet be found out, they may be undone, all of them.

He finds small comfort in reminding himself that he had been against the whole damnable business from the start. It was others, not he, who had subscribed to the activities which ultimately had led to the disaster which now looms. Better men than he had advocated this step and back then, newly elected to the club, he had kept his own counsel and said nothing. And now it has fallen to him of all people to get everyone out of this damnable pickle. He has been approached by a leading light in this confraternity, who has shown him how the disaster he so fears might still be averted. He has been told that he is the very man for this job. He will do as this man says because he has been promised two things. One is that if he is successful, he will be handsomely rewarded. The other is that should he fail, it will seem to him that the earth has opened up beneath his feet.

Thirty One

"Not like that, Michel, not like that at all! What have I told you? Yes, he had the limp he got in a carriage accident, but it was hardly noticeable. It was perceptible to those who knew him but it would most likely have passed unnoticed by anyone else. Is that not plain enough for you?"

I try once more, walking across the kitchen floor with a 'barely perceptible limp.' Gretch stamps his foot. "No, no and thrice no!" he says.

Mrs Harris tuts too, before removing herself to the scullery, where she must wash the pots now that Poll has gone.

"We are getting nowhere with this," Gretch says. "Here, give me your shoe. The left one." Gretch holds out his hand while I slip off a man's buckled and high-heeled shoe. He reaches into the extinguished fire before handing the shoe back and asking me to repeat my walk. This time the small, cold ember he has put in the shoe is just enough to remind me to give the bias to my other foot and Gretch is grudgingly pleased with the resulting gait. "It will pass," he says.

The morning's lessons in which I am taught to impersonate my late master proceed in the same manner as the day before. I learn how to defer to my superiors and condescend to my inferiors.

"A duke, Michel," Gretch says. "Not that one is likely to cross your path, but you should know how to address the species anyway?"

"Your Grace?"

"Of course, and an Archbishop the same. What about, let me see, the children of viscounts and barons, the lower peers?"

"The Honourable?"

"We are getting somewhere at long last," Gretch says. "Here is another for you. The Lord Mayor of London and Judges of the King's Bench and Courts of Common Pleas. The answer is the same."

"Your worship."

"No, no, you dunderhead. Your worship is the term of address for a justice and one that is used only by his inferiors. I hope you will not consider yourself his inferior?"

"Then it is my lord?"

"My lord, yes, good Lord!"

After this, Gretch offers some hypothetical situations in which I might conceivably find myself. "Let me put another scene to you," he says. "Let us imagine you are Henry Grace. Now, there is a lady you have seen once or twice but to whom you have not yet been introduced. You see her approaching in a park. She is bearing down on you, Henry Grace, on the same path that you are using. What do you do?"

"I say good morning, or good day, I suppose. Mention the weather, perhaps?"

"Michel Angelo of the Foundling Hospital might do that," Gretch says, "But Henry Grace, never. You wait for her to acknowledge you with a slight bow and mark this, not until she has done that may you tip your hat and return the acknowledgement. And you do this not with the arm nearest her, where you stand a chance of knocking her eye out with your elbow, but with the arm which is furthest away from her. And under no circumstances will you speak to her until she has opened a conversation with you. Do you understand?"

I do not. We learned none of this at the Foundling Hospital, of course, and the house in Leicester Fields has long since ceased to be the hub of social intercourse that Gretch says it once was. I wonder how people of birth and standing manage to remember the hundred and one often quite incomprehensible rules they must abide by to live as gentlefolk.

"When should a lady never wear pearls or diamonds?"

"In the morning. But I don't need to know this, surely?"

"You need to know it all, Michel. Now, you are ascending a flight of stairs: who has precedence, you or the lady?"

"I do not know."

"You do."

"Is it me?"

"Of course it is. And descending?"

"The lady?"

"And do not forget it. Getting that wrong would have you marked as a rake. It could give you away."

I play cards, casino, whist, speculation, faro and quadrille with

Gretch, Mrs Harris and the chairman who posed as my Job, who is invited into our kitchen when we need to make up a four. We play until it is me who is taking the pennies from the table. I acquire other skills and graces. Awkwardly, comically, I learn how to dance. Gretch, who used to torment the catgut as a younger man, produces a dusty fiddle and strikes up a tune while I dance with Mrs Harris in accordance with his barked instructions. Mrs Harris has no more idea of how to dance than do I and it is a long time before either of us can move in any kind of harmony with the other.

I find it easier to learn about racecourses and horses and how to study form. I am encouraged to improve my rusty French and I am given access to the remnants of the house library. I will 'discover who is who' in *The New Peerage*, Gretch says and directs me towards books on etiquette, rhetoric and travel, all of which will improve my confidence and allow me to move with ease in whatever social situations I find myself. I am not so sure, but my faith in Gretch grows daily as I discover one more talent that has lain dormant these many years. Close contiguity with his social superiors has left its mark. Few of the guests at routs and dinners hosted by the fashionable artist Henry Grace would have known that their manners were often the subject of close study by one of his footmen. And none could have known that the fruits of this study would one day be frittered away upon a girl raised at the Foundling Hospital.

Lastly, I learn how to dress myself like a gentleman. Behind the screens in the painting room, I take off my painting clothes. Gretch has left my new clothes upon a chair. Some of these items are new and represent, I think, a considerable investment on Gretch's part while others are so foreign to me that I don't know which to put on first. But imbued with a little new-found confidence, I roll on the stockings and button up an elegant dark suit over pristine white linen. Gretch steps behind the screen to help me with my neckcloth. I take a moment to look at myself in the full-length mirror.

"Now, then," Gretch says, "Where did I put the wig?"

"I don't need a wig," I say. "A lot of people are going without these days. It is the fashion." Which angers Gretch.

"Fashion, you young monkey? I'm not dressing you so you can join the ton in Rotten Row. This is not about you. Now, the last time Henry Grace went out, he wore his wig. And so shall you. Put it on, the mask too. Then let us take a look at you."

Thirty Two

The Journal of Henry Grace

This morning we are joined by three others, a seaman, probably a Lascar, a Chinese and an old Frenchman who proclaims himself a poet. The Lascar and the Chinese man lie upon the floor, supporting their heads with their hands and say not a word. The Frenchman's tales of travels in China drift away and he too is silent. I have something I need to say, something which will somehow contain and express the voluptuousness of this experience and bond us all in brotherhood but the words are like enormous mushrooms which blossom in my mouth and die on my tongue. Osiris stands. "It is time," he says, and helps me to my feet.

I follow him into the adjoining room, which has been hired for our purpose. Light from a high window falls upon white ceramic bowls filled with colours, lush grass greens, mountain lake blues, flashing, warlike scarlet, Byzantine gold. I am fascinated by them all. On the lip of the easel on which stands a virgin canvas, are spatulas and palette knives, a jar full of brushes. I pick them up, one at a time, feel the smooth wood and soft bristle and test their balance. "Enough," Osiris says, "paint."

The difference that the drug makes to my painting is marked. It is like walls have been torn down and behind these walls are wondrous secrets which have been bricked up by convention and artistic dogma. Now when a subject sits for me – and very often these days that subject is Osiris – it is as if I can see beneath his skin. His entire musculature is revealed, the delicate spider work of veins, the solid frame of hard bone. Colours are not as I had previously thought them to be. I discover that the colour of human skin, for instance, is compounded of an infinite number of hues and shades. I cannot at first reproduce what I see when I have smoked a pipe of opium. It takes practise and experiment and the will of Osiris, who keeps me painting when I would much rather sleep. Sometimes I paint under the drug's influence and sometimes I do not.

A trader from the Levant came here last week and gave us hashish in return for a little of our opium and smoking this opened different doors. I dispense with what I know about making colours and experiment widely, using every kind of unusual substance and sometimes create a paint that looks new and behaves differently upon the canvas. I employ combinations of colours I have not before seen used in paintings. Slowly, I improve my technique and come closer to reproducing the visions I have seen through the smoke. I increase my dosage, knowing I should not but knowing too that one pipe no longer provides the same degree of enlightenment.

Opium becomes a nutritional need. I hunger for my pipe as once I had hungered for roast beef. I count the hours before Osiris and I will once again cross the bridge and we will make our way down these now familiar cobbled backstreets to the narrow house with the green shutters. Here I am free of Dr Shepherd and here I can become free of my peacock self, too. I leave more than my clothes on a peg by the door, to be reclaimed only when I am once more in what the world outside might call a fit state to be seen in.

I had not spent long in Paris before I saw that my skills were indeed fledgling and in need of something like Osiris's much-vaunted experience to grow them out. And so, with my new friend as my cicerone, I go to the Salon de Paris, in whose extraordinary rooms people gape and crane at pictures hung from floor to ceiling. Can I see my work exhibited alongside these paintings, Osiris asks? After I have wheeled about the room two or three times and seen examples which open wide my eyes, honesty obliges me to conclude that I cannot. Osiris takes me to places which hang the works of little-known painters, artists working with extraordinary techniques yet to gain acceptance in the world of art.

Wherever we go, I leave with more of my old certainties chipped away. At last, I look again at what I have achieved since I arrived in France, all the pretty sketches, the vapid watercolours and the indifferent small oils. Early one morning I haul them down to the Pont Neuf and pitch the whole lot into the river. Since that day, Osiris has been my mentor and my guide and presently, he is encouraging me to explore my powers of perception. Osiris does not smoke when I paint, preferring to remain sober and thus able to exercise his acute critical powers and tell me what I am doing right or where I am going wrong. I have already hit upon one thing, he tells me. Whether by design or by accident – my mind is so muddled I cannot say which – I have found a combination of colours which, when the subject is viewed in the right light, produces the most extraordinary and lustrous tones in skin. Osiris says he has never seen the like and I am only too eager to believe him.

I learn more. I find myself receptive to original and alternative ideas. I am happy to leave off my old ways and embrace the new. I begin to paint interpretations of the visions engendered by the opium, fantastic alchemies of colour and light whose subject I can only call pure emotion. I find new uses for my palette knives and my fingers, smudging and smearing trails of colour across troubled skies. Osiris laughs, he claps his hands and sings my praises but he says the world is not ready for me. What I am painting would be spurned at auction, and, he laughs, would probably have me carted off to Bedlam, too. Sometimes, when the effects of the opium have all but worn off and I am in my sorry morning state, I have to agree. But this has not been wasted time, Osiris says. I must condense what I have learned painting these vivid fantasies and bring my newly-acquired knowledge to bear on more acceptable subjects. I must measure out my skills like an apothecary, he says, and employ neither too little nor too much.

Between my periods of painting, I smoke my pipes of opium, burning larger pieces but becoming no more intoxicated, it seems. I think I am spending longer with my pipe than I am with my brushes. If it were not for Osiris, I doubt that very much would have been achieved. But we go on. And then there comes the day when Osiris takes up my newest work and slowly examines it with the eye of a watchmaker. "It is done," he says at last.

"What do you mean?"

"We are finished here," he says. "Finally, you have done what I wanted you to do. You have unlocked the secret place where your talent has been hidden away all these years. The talent I told you was there, if only you could reach it. The evidence of that talent is here for anyone to see. And mark this, Henry, they will want to see it, you may be assured of that."

"And now?"

"Now you can do all this without a pipe to help you."

"Even if that were true," I say, "I do not intend to give up such a pleasure."

Osiris snatches the pipe from my hand and breaks it.

“We have no time for such distractions,” he says, handing me my coat and hat. “Let us go. It is time to start making your name.”

Thirty Three

I wish Mr Gilpin knew of my progress. I have grown into my skills and become the artist I wanted to be. To say I am now the painter of the most-talked about picture in London would not be a lie. Henry Grace may have conceived *The New Fire of London* in its earliest incarnation but anyone who comprehends even the barest rudiments of art will immediately see that he was really only sizing the canvas for the thing that I have created. Jamie Gretch calls me a conceited puppy but it is not he who has brought this huge and magnificent work to completion, nor his inspiration which has added Job and his children to the frame and made this picture what it is today. The credit for that belongs to a woman. It belongs to me.

Who now would connect me with the Hospital foundling, or – you may as well know this – the little savage who once appeared before a beak in Bow St charged with common assault? Believe me when I tell you that the drunken young gentleman whom I bloodied some two years ago got no more than he deserved. It was printed that the judge said he never had seen such a vicious assault by a young woman, but that is the newspapers for you. I acknowledge my debt to Mr Grace for speaking up for me but I cannot repay him by allowing his memory more credit than it is due for this masterpiece. I go up to the attic room, I look at that canvas and I glow with pride. I did this. Michel from the Foundling did this.

I can hardly describe how it chafes that I cannot show myself to the world. When I dream, I see myself recognised as a rising star in the world of art, rich, admired and sought after by patrons of taste. Such are my thoughts when Gretch noisily hawks up something from his lungs which he expectorates upon the boards before saying to me, “No-one must ever suspect that he is dead. What I have taught you must be used to convince them that Henry Grace lives.”

“Can we really do that?” I am far from sure that we can.

"It will not be such a hard a thing to do,” Gretch says. “When you dress the part you almost convince me you are him. It helps that you were never the most womanly of your species. Let me see that limp one more time.”

He nods approvingly as I oblige him. “Add the fancy mask and the reek of decay and we will enhance the mystery surrounding him tenfold. And what will be the result of our efforts, eh, Michel? Have you thought about that?”

“More people will talk about the painting. More buyers will desire it.”

“Of course! They will be buying not just a painting but a legend. A painting with a story is doubly attractive, Michel. That painting may or may not be worthy of the attention it is receiving now and I do not care either way. I truly expect it will be more famous for the sum it raises at auction.”

“It may sell for hundreds, you think?”

"Possibly more."

"What will happen to the money?" I ask.

"It will be paid into the account of Henry Grace. Thankfully, I finally obtained some limited power over Grace's affairs. I could not have gone on running the house without this, not with Grace in the condition he was. Not that it has done us much good – his account holds barely more money than I have in my pocket. Such is life, Michel. But it will be a vastly different matter when we sell the painting, oh, yes."

"But we have some money now, do we not? We have eaten well of late."

Gretch smiles, thinly.

"You could, I suppose, thank Mr Grace for that."

"I thought his account was empty?"

"It very nearly is. Selling a picture can be costly, I have found. There has been your new clothes."

"But why then should I thank Mr Grace?"

"Because, Miss Curious," he says, after appearing to chew on the information for some little time, "I sold his corpse to the resurrectionists. He will have been anatomised by now. Do not look so dumbfounded, girl. I respected Mr Grace the man but this was only his shell. Which has rid us of our problem and bought us dinner."

Gretch laughs until he all but chokes.

We eat together this evening, as we have done quite often of late. Our positions in the house are changing. Gretch does not see me as his equal – I am a long way from that, in his opinion, not the least reason being my sex – but he clearly feels it would be politic to have me think we are working together. When we have finished our ham and potatoes he pushes aside the plates and explains just how we will be collaborating in the days to come. He begins with a rare compliment.

"When you dress up as Henry Grace," he says, "I almost think it is him. You are quite the David Garrick."

I savour this because I too am pleased with my aping of the older man.

"In order to appear so much older and convince others that I am a man," I explain, "the trick lies in suppressing my natural femininity" – Gretch coughs loudly – "and doing everything a little more slowly and with a deal more consideration."

"I suppose that knee breeches and a little hair powder help too," Gretch says, dryly. "I do not need a lesson in acting, Miss."

"I think I can convince people that I am he," I say. "People who did not know him, I mean."

"I shall endeavour to ensure you never come into contact with any who did," Gretch says.

"But what am I actually to do as Grace?" I ask. "Is it not time that you told me?" I imagine myself moving in lofty circles, appearing at assemblies and routs attended by the first people of the nation. Being followed by a flock of devoted admirers as I take the air in the pleasure gardens. Being celebrated.

"As Henry Grace," he interrupts, "You will make no more than one or two fleeting appearances in London. Too many people knew him, years ago and you never know what little thing may give you away. Besides, he is thought to be an ailing recluse. We will let it be known that though you are very ill, you have felt it incumbent on yourself to fall in with the wishes of the many interested people who want to see you. After this you will travel to Bath, where you have been advised to take the waters. And on your return you will retire once more to your house and the ministrations of your physicians."

"I am to go to Bath?"

"We will follow the fortunes. Half the old families of the country will be there at this time of year. With little to do and money to spend."

"Is there not the same risk of recognition there?"

"There will be some risk, yes. But we will be sparing with the times you appear in the character of Henry Grace. And when we return, we will continue to send out for the things Henry Grace always sent out for, his pills and his potions, the food he ate. I will dispute the accounts of his quacks and pack them off. This way, though Grace is dead, we can continue to live at Leicester Fields *ad infinitum*. In effect, the house becomes our own. Henry Grace will continue to exist as the anchorite of the art world, turning out much-improved works which fetch good prices at sale. We will no longer face being cast out upon the streets."

"What if someone wants to commission Grace to paint his portrait?"

Gretch coughs. "That is rather more than possible," he says as he re-pockets his greying handkerchief. "I have been meaning to tell you that Henry Grace is scheduled to paint a Mr Bembridge on Tuesday next. You, Michel, must be ready to carry this out in the style of Henry Grace at his best."

I start. This all so unexpected. It is all too soon!

"Pshaw!" Gretch says, through a yellow-toothed grin. "In the dark, with your screens and your mask, who is to know you are not the Hermit of Leicester Fields?"

Who is to know I am not the Hermit of Leicester Fields? Perhaps it is the garrulous gent before me today, faintly silhouetted as an angular shape perched upon the sitter's chair. The painting room is dark once again, but not as the master would have it. It is I who have ordered the closing of the shutters and I who will see them opened – only one to begin with, so that the stripe of light falls first upon the left side of this fellow's gaunt blue face, lighting his sharp nose, his feathery wig and the sheen of black satin on his shoulder.

I have had to experiment with this method, using irritable, impatient, fidgeting Gretch as my sitter. Henry Grace was right about admitting that one light. After accustoming the eyes to darkness, a shaft of even quite dull illumination will cause muted colours to burst forth, and skin to surrender its myriad secret tones. Most of the works Henry Grace completed in this fashion were essays in chiaroscuro, though by the time of the later portraits they were not good ones. The dramatic effect created by extremes of light, colour and shade was cruelly mitigated by the lack of care with which he completed his work. Portraits had become for him only a source of easy money and a chance to practise technique.

My exhalations rasp against the inner surface of the Venetian mask. Grace made similar susurrations. I feel him in the clothes I wear and smell him in the sleeves of his painting shirt. Nervous about this debut, I tell myself that I am him. I am Henry Grace. And must act like him. My subject is visible through an aperture in the articulated screens about me: a skinny, birdlike man with a beak for a nose. He would have us believe that the mystery of our procedures here at Leicester Fields amuses him vastly. "How delightfully diverting!" he giggles, upon finding himself in utter darkness. And then, like the majority of sitters who have found themselves in such alien surroundings, he fills the silence with prattle. This is bothersome but it provides me with all I need to reflect the character of this man whose portrait I am about to paint.

"I say, I say, are you there?"

He addresses himself to parakeets printed upon the screens. Gretch ushered him into the room and I have no intention of extending a further welcome. "I will tell you what I rather want from this," he chirrups. "You must make me look like a man of means. Let people know that I am not short of coal, yes? Hello? You hear me in there?"

I am not yet ready to try out my vocal impression of a dying painter of the opposite sex and so I remain silent.

"Dear me," he says again, "Quite the conundrum, you are! To repeat myself, you are to make me look rich, but something else too. I must appear the sort of cove you might trust. Benign, philanthropical. Good with children, kind to dogs. That sort of game."

I assay an interrogatory grunt.

"Oh, you must know, the sort of fellow you would not hesitate to accommodate with an investment. Or a loan. Someone you could believe in. You have the idea, I am sure."

I do, and have decided he is probably one of these people who are inspired to create schemes which will make their investors rich overnight, or so they assure these dupes. They live by their appearance and know that the right clothes, the right rented premises and a decent portrait of themselves over the mantle will offer the illusion of solidity.

"I paid well over the odds for a dreadful daub only last month," he tells the parakeets. "Some of these artist fellows are Dick Turpins with paint-brushes. “You must know that cabal at the Academy has admitted a woman? Ha! I can only suppose she got in wearing knee-breeches and a tricorn hat. You would as soon give a brush to a monkey.”

I try a little cough, a low clearing of mucas which might just conceivably have been born in the throat of a man. He takes this as my full agreement and babbles on about women in general, how they so often seem in danger of forgetting their place. How is the household to run itself and servants to be kept from the silver if the woman of the house is gallivanting about Town or trying to pass herself off as a painter? I am not listening. Rather, I am dashing off a likeness which I think does him full justice.

When I have done – because I am not giving this blockhead a second sitting – I stand back and compare the image with the original. I think I have caught the avian quality I noted when he first stepped in the room and was briefly lighted by the hallway windows. I have made his eyes small, black and sharp, his wig that much more feathery, his jet satin coat that bit glossier. I have turned this bird into a perfect jackdaw. If I judge him rightly, he will fall in love with his self-image immediately and only he will not see that I have caught the very likeness of a thief.

Thirty Four

The Journal of Henry Grace

Paris is a hive of gossip and before long I learn that the family De'ath has fled to France to evade its creditors. I suspected something of the sort, but to a mind unforged by experience (as Osiris has called mine), it only adds to their colour. This knowledge acquired, I am able to view Lady Jane's interest in me and my family in an interesting new light.

"Is your poor father very elderly?" she asks me on one occasion. "The old gentleman is in good health. I trust?" She has a great liking for young men of talent, she tells me, no matter what their background. She confides this to me with her ringed fingers resting upon my thigh. She is, I have noted, like this with any rich man who crosses her path. For a while at least, Lady De'Ath sees in me the answer to her prayers. My father, she quickly establishes, is old and infirm and his fortune, she reckons, makes me a good prospect. She does not know that Richard Grace thinks a man should make his own way in life and has warned me against expecting riches. I think that had she not quite recently caught the eye of a certain French count while she played at roulette, I might have found it hard to escape her snares.

I do not escape them all. Although she has finally desisted in seeing me as a matrimonial prize and a solution to the family's financial crises, this has not meant that her interest in me as a young man is at an end. She continues to tease and to flirt and make me think I am more of a man than perhaps I am. I must concede that once I see the way the wind is blowing and that she is no longer a threat to my single status, she becomes more interesting to me, too. One evening, as we are sitting together on a chaise at the Paris house of the Count (who has gone out for an evening at the tables) she tells me of how she worries for her son and how terribly dismayed she is that he will not abide with her in France. I can do nothing but offer my arms as she begins to cry on my shoulder.

Drugged by her perfume and excited by her warm proximity, I let myself be drawn into her embrace, closer and closer, until I feel her warm breath on my cheek and her lips upon mine. It would of course be ungentlemanly in the extreme to retail what ensues and nor shall I describe the extraordinary paintings on the ceiling of the count's bedroom. All I will say is that I leave the house at dawn, just as the count's coach is heard turning onto the gravel of the short driveway. Half-dressed, I drop from a window at the back of the house and run pell-mell down cobbled streets, towards the rising sun, a song on my lips and goodwill in my heart. I want to tell everyone what has occurred – and not just once, I might add. For my first assays at this new pastime I have had the best teacher in the world, a pedant for perfection. I leave that house not only a man but one who has, I know, received more lessons in the art of love than some men receive in a lifetime.

Thirty Five

My first foray into the world as Henry Grace is not a notable success. I wear the dark suit and white linen provided by Gretch, a new wig and the white and gold mask which Henry Grace brought back from Venice many years ago. With Gretch in the guise of my footman, I appear at the theatre in Drury Lane. At the entrance, we are stopped by someone apparently known to Gretch, who smiles, looks me over and says "It is very good." He discomfits Gretch, who hurries me inside. I forget this puzzling encounter when we enter our box. I see fingers point me out, ladies whisper behind their fans, there are turned faces all over the theatre. People in a box across the auditorium are more familiar: they acknowledge me with nods and a young man standing amidst them makes a short bow. I wonder if they have been known to Henry Grace? Gretch whispers that we may have to abandon the evening if it looks like they are preparing to pay us a visit.

But I am becoming accustomed to this attention and thinking how pleasing it is to be the subject of so much notice. In my old brown dress, I was practically invisible to people in the street and being an apprentice was little better. Here in this theatre, settled upon comfortable chairs and enjoying some light thing by Mr Goldsmith, I feel gratified and happy. I acknowledge my public's interest with a barely perceptible nod of my head and return my gaze to the players, whose impersonations of other people are almost as skilled as my own.

All that mars the experience is the realisation that these people are paying homage to Henry Grace and not to Michel Angelo. I am thinking that the day will come when I will have completed sufficient great paintings to cast off my mask and show the world what Michel Angelo has done. But no sooner have I entertained these pleasing thoughts than dark ones follow in their wake and distract me from the action below. I think how difficult it may be to explain the disappearance of Grace's body and why we kept his death a secret. It would be all too easy, in fact, for someone to think we had murdered the poor man.

I am thinking it may be safer to remain as I am, forever masked as Henry Grace, when a voice from the stalls interrupts my thoughts, calling out. "This an't a masquerade is it? I'd have bought my own mask if it was." It's one of the footmen who have taken the first few rows of seats down there. There is a wave of laughter around the theatre and faces crane upwards or swivel in my direction. Damn the footmen! Footmen have spoiled so many of the performances I have attended. Like me, they usually show up for the last acts of the play, when admission is much reduced but having then only a poor idea of what is in progress, their attention often wonders. Loosed from the restraints of their positions, they look for distraction off the stage as well as on it. Tonight, it seems, I am providing their amusement.

"This is not good," Gretch whispers. He scans the crowd, watching for any movements being made in our direction. I hear "A penny for the guy, anybody?" and "Mind your manners, that's the hangman up there!" The laughter is in danger of spreading beyond the stalls. On stage and used to such sideshows, the actors battle on. I am as angry as I am unnerved. How dare these people be so impertinent, I am thinking; do they not know who I am? But now Gretch's hand is upon my shoulder and he is hurrying me from the box, down the stairs and into the street, where we quickly find chairmen and I am carried – Gretch walking briskly beside – the short distance back to the haven of Leicester Fields.

Although the incident is reported in one or two newspapers, it does not seem to dull the interest people have in Henry Grace. Now that I have been seen in public, letters are received requesting my appearance at this or that social function. Being a better hand with a pen than Gretch is, I reply to these as he directs, usually excusing myself on the grounds of my failing health which has dictated that my excursions from the house must be strictly limited. When I am seen abroad in London after this it is either in a hired coach, from which I acknowledge greetings from others with the merest of waves, or so briefly at social occasions that people have time to do little more than shake my gloved hand.

At Bath, wearing the stiff, all-but-new dress that Gretch has procured for me, I promenade the streets of this resplendent new city of honey-toned limestone and marvel at its difference. While much of London crams all together, prince and pie-man cheek-by-jowl, so that a new villa of Portland stone might be abutted by crumbling edifices thrown up after the Great Fire, the rebuilt city of Bath shows off its finery with little contamination from the dwellings of those who built it. Its crescents and by-ways are thronged with well-dressed and prosperous London men accompanied by their wives or paramours. I am unsurprised to recognise several faces from my own perambulations in the metropolis but I *am* surprised and left unsettled when, walking by the Avon one day with Gretch, a passer-by inspects me too closely.

"He recognised me," I whisper.

"Impossible," Gretch says, "Men like him do not see girls of your station unless they are very pretty and free with their affections."

"Perhaps he came to see the painting."

"No," Gretch says, but I see that his eyes follow the man until he is lost to sight.

It is at Bath that I become two people, neither of which is Michel Angelo. For the main part of my time here, I leave Grace's clothes and wig in our rented rooms and cast myself as a young lady accompanying her ailing father, who is here to take the waters. As such, we range about fashionable places, lingering in coffee and chocolate houses, visiting the assembly rooms or walking upon Pulteney Bridge. To lessen the chances of discovery my appearances as the artist, Henry Grace will be strictly rationed.

We hear mention of our work at assemblies and in the streets. The name of Henry Grace, for whatever reason, is never far from people's lips. Outside a place of popular resort, we encounter a street preacher ranting to people who affect not to hear him. "That graven image is a warning from God," he is barking, "Those that sin must mend their ways, or be consumed by fire." Opinions are divided. I hear self-proclaimed experts in art debating its merits, some claiming that it is inspirational, others that it is hideous and vastly over-praised. London newspapers sold here keep Henry Grace and his painting in the minds of everyone. These include the one contending that the *The New Fire of London* conceals a code of some sort. I snort when I read this but I agree with Gretch when he says that this is a fire which needs fanning; the interest it breeds will surely help us to sell a talked-up picture at an extravagant price.

It is soon time for me to change my sex again and become the ailing artist himself, exhausted from his artistic efforts in the capital and paying a brief visit to Bath to obtain some blessed relief from his painful condition. It takes an hour for me to dress as Henry Grace and for Gretch to adjust every detail, carefully positioning the Venetian mask so that I can breath properly and also can see where I am going. He makes me walk up and down, ensuring no femininity remains in my gait and that I remember to affect the small limp that not one person in a hundred will know belonged to Henry Grace.

We visit the Pump Room, where we are immediately the centre of much attention and conversation. Every eye follows my masked face when we walk as slowly as we dare through the crowds, nodding to this person or to that little group. I am glad they cannot see the beads of perspiration which trickle freely from my brow and gather in the folds of my silk stock. My heart quickens its beat when we are approached and my health is asked after. Gretch replies that although the waters have alleviated his master's condition to a welcome degree, I am just now too weary to speak. People smile and nod and pass on. It is a relief to quit the throng for the open air.

As Henry Grace, I receive numerous cards inviting me to attend homes and salons, some from people of considerable position. It is decided that we will accept the two most important ones. We appear at a musical evening at the summer residence of the Home Secretary, who condescends sufficiently to say that I will hear from him shortly about an important commission. Thus bolstered, we also visit the house of Lord Addlestone, a prominent patron of the arts, who nods to Gretch and settles a lot of doubt in artistic circles by bestowing his blessing on my work.

He says that as Mr Gretch will remember, he had the pleasure of viewing *The New Fire* in Leicester Fields and proclaims it one of the most interesting pieces he has seen. Another man, known to neither of us but also proclaiming himself a patron of the arts in this town, is strangely disappointed when we refuse his insistent invitation that we stay one more day in order to inspect his own collection. Gretch has his reasons for taking our appointed coach.

These days in Bath burn in my memory for another reason, too. Even now, long after the event, after so much more has happened, this incident continues to occupy more of my mind than perhaps it should. It is something which happens on a day when Gretch and I are promenading in manicured gardens before the newly-built villas of the London rich who spend the season here. I am incarnated as Henry Grace, complete with suffocating mask and forever being reminded in hissing whispers that Henry Grace has a limp. It is as we are leaving the gardens and entering upon the street where a line of crested carriages stand that we almost collide with another couple. They are a small crablike thing of middling age, certainly a chaperone and her charge, a young woman who meets my eyes as I nearly run into hers.

"I am so sorry!" she says. "That was so careless of me."

It is the eyes which I remember almost daily. They are big, lustrous and sparkle blue or green depending on how she holds herself. She has a fine white neck from which depends an emerald pendant. The effect is quite captivating. "The fault was mine," I say, suddenly disarmed.

"You are Mr Grace, the painter?"

I nod. I have never seen eyes like these. Or such lips. I think of how I would paint them, the colours I would prepare. I think of the hours she would sit before me.

"Everyone is talking about you, sir," she says.

"Cicily," the chaperone says. "We must be upon our way."

"Have you been painted?" I say without thinking. "Your portrait?"

She laughs, so becomingly. Chestnut curls cascade from her tiny pink bonnet as she shakes her head. I have never before been so taken with a prospective subject.

"Cicily!" the old hag snaps. She gives me a curt nod and slips her arm under Cicily's. "We will be late," she says, as she propels the girl before her.

"Goodbye, Mr Grace," the girl calls. "I am so happy to have met you."

"Let me paint you," I call after her, as Gretch begins to squeeze my own arm. "Write to me at Leicester Fields." I little think then of the confusion which would ensue if an intimacy sprang up and she discovered me a woman. Gretch walks me away and begins to deliver a tedious harangue of the dangers of talking to strangers. Just now, he said, I forgot all he had taught me and sounded less like a sick man than a silly schoolgirl. What was I thinking of? I cannot recall another word. At that moment, all I can think of, all I can see, are those eyes, that neck and those lips.

And then, after three long days in which my nerves are tested with more public appearances, days in which I see nothing of Cicily, no matter how hard I look, we take coach for London, leaving the people of Bath chattering about the masked invalid whose paintings absolutely must be seen by anyone with taste. Gretch tells me we have interested one or two very important collectors of art and he now expects furious bidding when the painting comes up for sale. He has been pleasantly surprised by the number of people who have made enquiries about having themselves, their houses, their horses, their pets or their mistresses painted by a master.

As we trundle eastwards along the Great West Road, he confidently predicts that once *The Great Fire* is sold, the cash will roll in. He will visit the saleroom, he says, and sign the papers for its disposal two or three weeks hence. This will be long enough for us to arrange the physical removal by rope and tackle of the great painting from the building, which will provide spectacle and attract interest as we hoist it through the gap in the roof and lower it slowly to a waiting wagon. It will also allow sufficient time for all interested parties to view the work at the saleroom before it comes up for auction. Gretch now thinks in grander terms than simply keeping hold of the house in Leicester Fields. With the fever of interest which has been created by *The Great Fire*, he says, there is no knowing how much wealth we may go on to accumulate.

"But we cannot do that forever," I say. "Everyone knows that Grace's health is failing."

"They do not know the half of it, do they?" Gretch laughs. "But we can keep up the charade for long enough to make a goodly deal of money, I am certain of that."

"And then what?"

"Then your apprenticeship ends, Michel. I will be plain with you. I have been much impressed with what you have painted lately and especially with your work on *The New Fire*. By the time we are obliged to leave off this lay and allow Grace to die in both body and public persona, I am now certain that you will be mature enough in your style to be launched into the world in your own right," he says and then smiles at me. "A new Micheleangelo."

Nothing I have heard before has ever thrilled me like these few words. So the future I have dreamed of is within my grasp after all. I can and I will be recognised for the artist that I am, Gretch must see ways to overcome the obstacles I foresaw. All we have to do is await the sale of *The New Fire of London* and build my career on the back of it. I doze in the company of happy dreams, in which Cicily makes more than one appearance. I pray she will write to me, requesting a portrait.

A little while later later, awoken by the wheels clattering over cobbles, I open my eyes and see the distant spires and smoke of London. As we pass Tyburn, the sun has set but there is light enough to make out familiar landmarks. At last, after all the torment of bad roads and grasping toll keepers and poor meals in expensive coaching inns, we are almost home. I long for my bed. I wonder if Mrs Harris will make toasted cheese and a pot of coffee to welcome our return?

From here, we should be able to see Leicester House, in the last gleaming of the setting sun. I pull down the window to peer out – and in the same instant, my life changes. My sudden exclamation is loud enough to rouse Gretch. "Wake me when we arrive, I told you, not before," he growls, from under the cover of his enormous great-coat.

"Look!" I cry, "pray God this is not what I fear it is."

"No rest…" Gretch begins to grumble. Then he sees what I can see and throwing off the coat, he seizes my cane, smashing its glass end on the roof of the carriage as he cries out, "More speed, coachman, fly, damn you!"

As we rattle towards the corner of Lisle and Leicester Streets, the ominous glow which had defined the silhouetted roofscape becomes an incandescent explosion of brightness against the black heavens. The coach slows to negotiate the sharp corner and is immediately caught up in a mob of people. We see clearly now that the house in Leicester Fields, our house, is fiercely ablaze.

Thirty Six

The crowd gathered about the conflagration is immense. My first wild thought is for Mrs Harris. Pol has gone, Gretch and I were at Bath, only she had remained. I bawl her name as loudly as I can, threading as quickly as I might through the gawping onlookers, searching for a small figure with angry eyebrows, pursued by the hellish thought that she may be trapped inside this blazing house. It is only now that I appreciate her part in my life these last years; no-one else has seen to it that I am fed, my clothes laundered and my stockings darned. I think, the door to her room sticks – is she even now rattling the handle as she cries unheard for help? Did she sleep while the house burned, leaving no time for escape? I scream her name, competing with the awful cacophony of burning and breaking that issues from within the building, then scan the crowd madly for some glimpse of her. I listen for Galway tones. There is little sound from the attendant multitude, the scene is too grimly fascinating.

A wheezy voice – the old woman who sells combs and ribbons in the square – repeats itself in my ear until I understand that the 'colleen' who lived there was seen leaving the house early that day 'and getting herself into a carriage with her bag' and then someone else in the crowd assures me that she went off on foot, carrying no bag. And now, another voice intrudes, a manservant from the neighbouring house who has given trouble to our household on several occasions. "Off she flits the very day of the fire," he cries into nearby ears, "I say, she set it. A slow fire that would take hold soon as she was gone."

I search again in a crowd which has swelled to twice its size. It is the time of night when the theatres are turning out and their patrons stand now at a respectful distance from the loudly crackling and crumping inferno which roars from its apparent base in the painting room at the front of the house and has eaten its way into the rooms above. Even if Mattie Harris somehow found money to hire this reported carriage or, more likely, a cab, why is she not here now? She knew we were returning this night. And now, something is happening. I turn and see people point towards the entrance. A shout goes up. I cannot see the cause of the excitement. The steps to the porch and the door have yet to burn, but black smoke boils from the portico. A rumour filters back to me that some mad fool has run into the house – but this cannot be so.

Mesmerised by this unfolding disaster, I think of what was within. So many paintings, mine, Henry Grace's and those of his I had improved to such a degree that they had become mine by right, all stacked against walls or hanging upon them, my old clothes, my favourite brushes. And, of course, *The New Fire of London*, my hopes and my future, in the attic room. All is now fodder for the flames. For those standing by me, a clutch of drunken, shrieking whores, one or two notably well-dressed and imposing gentlemen and even for the old watchman who failed to raise the alarm in time, this grim scene is only an unexpected source of diversion.

I try to push my way through the milling, uncaring mob towards the house, to see if there is anything at all that might be done. The heat radiating from within is intense. The house bears no insurance mark, so no-one has attended with pumps and water. Only now do I hear calls for an engine to be summoned and this is from the people who rent the adjoining edifice, which is now threatened. I look around for Gretch, and can see no sign of him. But it is too late for pumps and water, the flames are beyond anyone's control. Servants of people from the neighbouring villa are lugging furniture into the space at the front of the building, where footmen stand guard over a growing pile of expensive tables and chairs.

I scream with the young whores as the panes of glass in the windows of the second-floor front rooms are suddenly blown out. Mr Grace's room is consumed and above it Gretch's, my own tiny closet and with that, my paltry possessions. I look again for Gretch but see only Riordan the chairman and the dwarf from the newspaper, who returns me a helpless look. There is now a great, angry gusting from inside the house, perhaps the fire accessing the hall with Mr Grace's portrait and funneling up the staircase, scorching the likenesses of the merchants and nobles who neglected to collect their imperfect pictures. The fire will be drawn quickly upwards by the great hole in the roof, which is insecurely covered with the tarpaulin. All about the house there was paint and flammable spirit in abundance and this will have accelerated the fire's progress.

I think of rooms in which I played and those where I painted, or modelled for Mr Grace. I think of Gretch and poor Pol and Mrs Harris who might be dying, now, in that house. I shout to anyone who can hear me, has anyone seen the housekeeper? There may be a woman in there! But enormous tongues of golden flame are now uncurling through the hole in the roof, leaping steeple-high, as if they might lick the stars. I think of Mattie Harris, burning, shrivelling, disappearing.

Such appalling thoughts are chased away by the ringing of a bell and beyond the square I see a fire-engine pulled by four horses making speed to attend. The other house has an insurance mark but if that house is to be saved, this fire must be extinguished first. Before the engine has reached the corner of the square, there are more screams, louder, more hysterical, and fingertips jab towards the top of the house. I follow their gaze. At the dormer window of the attic and wreathed in flames is the unmistakable figure of a man. He stands at the glass, a silhouette against the bright flames behind him. I recognise that angular shape and bony head immediately.

It is Gretch, though whether he has gone into the burning house to save Mrs Harris, to make some futile attempt to save the painting or has entered Hell for some other, more poetic reason, I do not know. Perhaps it is only for a moment that I see him standing there and perhaps he is not, as I think then, looking at me. Then he is gone, the glass too and there are only an enormous flame, which flicks and spits from the window like a dragon's tongue.

Thirty Seven

The Journal of Henry Grace

While Osiris disputes with the fisherman and Francesca bites upon his ear, my eyes are ensnared by the vibrancy of the blindingly colourful fruit in the boat that bobs against the quay. Each of the craft by the canal steps is piled high with produce from across the sea, or from further down the coast. Colours that smoulder with a quivering intensity will always arrest a painter's eye, but more especially, I'm learning, the eyes of one who has lately been smoking hashish. Melons and pomegranates, oranges, grapes and figs sing with colour; shrill soprano lemons and basso profondo aubergines.

Hearing Francesca shouting for me, I stand up and dust off my once-white breeches. Tomorrow I will bring paint and brushes to this spot. I will sit under the dusty pink canvas awning which springs from this elegantly faded house, whose shutters are the turquoise green of the water below, and I will paint. But now, early in the morning of another day in Venice, we will return to the rooftop of the palazzo and cook Osiris's fish in olive oil on a stove made of bricks. We will smoke a pipe and then Osiris and Francesca will retire for a while. The rest of the morning, I predict we will spend wandering the city once more, where Osiris will haggle with street traders over some silly bauble for Francesca and I will buy some overpriced little icon painted on wood which will be nothing like as ancient as the vendor pretends, but will be worth its money for the strength of purpose I see in such things (this, I know, is something that is still lacking in my own painting, so very much improved as it is).

When the heat becomes unbearable for Northern skins, and shadows shrink from the noonday sun, we will drift into some church and find relief in its cool stone spaces. Francesca, who quickly bores of this, missing the bustle of the streets and the catcalls of traders and gondoliers, will chatter loudly and complain until Osiris silences her with a look or a sharp pinch of her arm. And then he and I will stop before some mighty fresco and Osiris's analytical eye will coolly decode its composition and uncover the secrets of the artist's technique – while I stand beside him like a donkey, speechless, spellbound and awestruck.

In this heat we lead idle and languorous lives and one day varies little from the next. Put aside now are the London satins and the Parisian finery. While Venetians promenade in their own high fashions, we idle in sweat-soaked shirt-sleeves and straw hats. We spend our evenings – and some of our dawns too – upon the roof terrace of our run-down palazzo, which is as little like the palace it must once have been as it is possible to conceive. Osiris is without funds just now and I am loathe to lay out money on a fine apartment.

Sometimes, Osiris sits upon the roof edge, a pot of ink at his side and writes poetry, dark stuff that is unfit for publication but for all I know reflects some personal turmoil of his soul. At other times he disturbs the afternoon peace by scratching away with his violin while I set up my easel and try repeatedly to capture some sense of my own experience of living here just now. The canal below teems with life, boats and gondolas, people and goods, while the skyline crowds with picturesque domes and tall campaniles.

At this time, we are innocent, with no precognition of the terrible thing which has yet to happen.

It is just we three now: in Florence, Dr Shepherd had succumbed to his gout, he said, although it was difficult to comprehend what he was saying, by then he was so broken by drink. He could do no more to guide me, that was clear, and did not demur at Osiris's suggestion that he should return home in the company of Bennison. Lady De'Ath has remained at Paris, where she makes the best of her chances with the French count and hopes to call herself mistress of a large chateau quite soon. Osiris insisted that he and I go on; the illumination I had come for, he said, was still there for me in Venice. I would have an infinitely better chance of a thorough education, he added, now that I was no longer hamstrung by the doubtful stewardship of Dr Shepherd.

"We must go, Henry," Osiris calls, "Before these fish fry themselves."

I catch up with Osiris and Francesca and we walk through narrow streets and cross creaking bridges over foetid canals. We weave through crowded campielli to claim the shaded edges of the campo where we lie. Making a corner of the campo is our palazzo, whose towering stone walls look more like the keep of an ancient fortification than the domestic residence of two gentlemen and one of these gentlemen's concubine. At the top of countless stone steps is our spacious reception room, a sparsely-furnished chamber lit by tall, glassless windows – which look out over a quiet canal – and the light which falls from the doorway to the roof terrace.

Osiris kicks off the Moorish sandals he has bought and addresses himself to gutting the fish on a simple table. We have no servants. The small, lithe figure of Francesca drifts about the room trailing her fingers on the tops of chairs, the half-finished canvas sitting on my easel, the ornate head of the unmade bed which occupies centre stage, and then I feel her sharp fingernails reach up to walk across my own shoulders.

"What is it, Henry?" she says, in the unpolished dialect of ordinary Venetians, "Do you not like me doing that?" Osiris looks up from his task and grins. His dark-eyed beauty runs her fingers through my hair and traces the line of my unshaven chin before slipping the end of her index finger into my mouth. I move away, awkwardly. I find her painfully alluring. She has lived with us in our two big rooms these last ten days, perhaps one or two more. I don't know where Osiris found her. I came back from a painting expedition one day to find her in this bed, quite naked, Osiris the same. She has a firm young body with hips like Peter Paul Rubens might have painted, a mane of jet-black hair and bright eyes of an azure blue. She wears few clothes, as many bangles as Osiris will buy her and the age-old look of a temptress. She fills my thoughts day and night. Whenever I see her with Osiris or hear them together at night, I lose a little more of my composure. She is well aware of my feelings and so is Osiris, who likes to see her teasing me.

On the roof a little later, Osiris sprinkles the slowly-cooking fish with a handful of herbs. "If your friends in Rome could see you now," he says. "Dressed like a gypsy and behaving like one, too. I think they would have a very different opinion of you. I wonder if they would honour those handsome commissions then?"

"I thought you were proud of your creation and his acceptance by society?"

"You are indeed my creation and I expect you never to forget it. That callow boy I met in Calais could not have been appointed to paint the portraits of men such as they. He would have lacked the nerve to converse with them."

"Men such as they?"

Osiris leaves the fish to braise, straightens his back, and throws back the hair which has grown long in this time of indolence and turpitude. Behind his smile I sense his anger is quickening.

"Who on this earth did you think you were talking to? My dear Henry, all polite society is acquainted with Edward Villiers and Lord Godolphin. Or if they are not, they certainly know of them. Godolphin is the Earl of Chichester's heir. Villiers is cousin to the prime minister. They are both already marked for high office. You could not have made a luckier connection. This will serve us well in the future, you mark what I say."

I had set up my easel outside Rome in the shade of a great and ancient arch, before which lay huge tumbled columns and enormous stones from once-great buildings of the classical age. Osiris had recommended the place, having some familiarity with it, he said, from a previous visit. It was in my mind to convey something of the effects of the passage of time, a pictorial *memento mori* of how it will always bring down the greatest of civilisations and the grandest of people.

The blinding sunlight and Cimmerian shadows of the huge stone blocks created striking drama, I thought. I was standing back from the thing, looking at what I had done, and thinking it might turn out quite well if I made the most of the contrasts in light and shade, and also those that existed between the mighty ancient ruins and the dwarfed figures of the young English travellers I had introduced, when I found that I had company.

"That little fellow in the hat there," said a voice. "That is me, I suppose?"

"It is the most damnable likeness," said another.

"Do I really look like that?"

"Ha! It is you to perfection. Do not blame the artist."

I turned to find that the figures I had painted an hour ago were now beside me. Both carried swords and one, I saw, fingered an ornate dagger in his belt. "I have not meant to offend," I said.

But it quickly became plain that I had not offended. Instead, I had impressed. They took up the sketch book that lay with my water jug and paint bottles and finding shade, leafed through it quickly, but with all the attention of connoisseurs. They conferred in whispers much of the time and every so often they cast a glance at me, as if making some mysterious equation between the image on the page and the artist standing before them. They stayed no longer than they had to but before they quit the place, these men made me an extraordinary offer. I returned to Osiris like an excited schoolboy, breathlessly breaking the news that I was commissioned at last, and not for a single work only.

"And I was not in the least surprised," Osiris says, as he turns the fish, wafting fragrant smoke in my direction. "You are leagues better than anyone else who was peddling his talents in Rome that month. You have a depth and freedom in your work which they want."

He signals to Francesca, more wine. I watch her with inexpressible desire as she floats towards us, luminescent against the sun.

"Henry," he says, while Francesca fills one of the pretty glass goblets we picked up on our peregrinations in Murano today, "You have been close about what you talked about and have given me no details of these commissions. Very proper, given the standing of the people you are dealing with. But would I be far from the mark if I guessed that these gentlemen desire a number of three-quarters length portraits? Of themselves and some associates?"

"How in heaven's name do you know that?" I say. "I was asked to treat the matter in confidence."

"I have connections," Osiris laughs. "So, portraits. Good, there will be money in that. And what else?"

"I am not sure that I should tell you," I say.

"But you will," Osiris says as he charges my own glass.

That confidence is well placed, unlike my own. "I can never keep a secret from you," I say.

"Then what is your secret commission?"

"I am to paint an interior," I say. "Murals, I think, but of a particular nature. They were not explicit."

Osiris brushes off Francesca and looks hard at me.

"Listen to me," he says. "You have a peculiar talent and can provide the services they require. Whatever it is they want you to do, make sure you do it. Do you hear me, Henry? This is a connection you would do very well to maintain."

Of course, I have become dreadfully jealous of Osiris. He seems not to care for Francesca, or not in the way that I would, were our positions reversed. He fails to appreciate what a great and rare treasure he has in her. There are times when he treats her with complete disregard and there have been other occasions when he has been quite cruel to her. At times such as these, when he calls her a common slut, when he spurns or even throws down the food she has prepared for him, I am quite downcast and slide from the room, unable to witness such things. And worse, he beats her. This has occurred on more than one occasion, and once while I have been present.

At such times I am brought to such a state of frustration and rage that I think I might quite easily do violence myself. It is as if he knows just what he is doing when he makes love to her in front of me. He seems to taunt me, daring me to carry out my darkest impulses. I sometimes think he wants me to hurt him. Our relationship has changed. We are no longer a trinity. I spend more time on my own, on the roof terrace or by the canal, brooding about what is not, but should have been. I think I hate him and his family, too. I despise myself for my inaction and my impotence.

Slowly, I see a change in my attitude to Francesca, too. She is the prize that can never be mine. There are times when I think that if this is true, then who else has a right to her? I smoke more hashish and occasionally a little opium and I drink too much wine and I sketch like a madman, but even this is failing to bring me the peace I need and the resolution I want.

We live like this until the winter. I play along when Osiris tells me we are to attend a grand carnival masquerade. It is no surprise to me. My new friends in Rome have given me an introduction to Signor Caruselli who is, or so they told me, the master of revels in this city. Osiris has employed it to secure us invitations. He tells me that this will be the primo night of the carnival season that we must attend: if we are to make a good impression in Venice and meet the patrons who make the great commissions, then this is the place to do it.

Osiris is a clever man; he almost convinces me that he still cares that I succeed. We must dress as well as the Venetians, he says, and to arrange this, he will need money. This I readily supply, having long passed the point of caring about such irrelevancies. And then I forget about all of this until the very night of the ridotto, when Osiris and Francesca enter my room and interrupt my poisonous dreams. Osiris wears a scarlet frock coat, a lace-trimmed hat and a hook-nosed white mask. I can see no stray locks of raven hair, which had previously grown so long. Francesca is attired in the most beautiful and presumably expensive blue gown. She wears a small, black mask. The effect is dramatic and a little unsettling.

Osiris turns towards me the crazed mirror with which I used to dress myself, when I cared about such things, and demands that I peer into it. With reluctance, I do. There I sit, knees pulled up, in my dusty old seaman's britches and a shirt which I have somehow caused to be torn around the neck. My face is unshaven and my unwashed hair is matted and filthy. The contrast between myself and this pair of peacocks could not be greater. "Come along old fellow," Osiris says, giving me his hand, "Let us put you right."

Thirty Eight

Unusually, it is not the crow of the cockerel or the rumbling of laden wagons, or the squealing of pigs bound for market which rouses Obadiah very early one morning. Two floors below the garret in which he keeps his bed, there is a terrific hammering and crashing and the sounds of breaking in the print room. The hammering, Obadiah quickly discovers, is Mouse rapping very hard upon his bedroom door. Obadiah struggles to throw back the heavy coverlet. Mouse says, "They are breaking the press."

"Who?" Obadiah splutters, but he knows who. Mouse slips into the room and takes cover behind his friend as the sounds of violence below announce the breaking of more furniture. Something very heavy topples over. "Not my press," Obadiah says and would push past his friend towards the stairs, but Mouse clutches tightly to his nightshirt.

"For God's sake, do not go down those stairs," he says. "There will be violence."

With a sudden, impassioned effort, Obadiah shakes Mouse off, snatches an iron candlestick from the table beside his bed and begins to drop down the stairs, six at a time. "They shall have my blood before my press," he calls to Mouse and to whoever is another floor below. At the same moment, the noises cease and there is no more crashing to be heard. Mouse peers over the newel post at the top of the stairs and listens. Obadiah must now be in the print shop. Mouse calls to him but gets no answer. Slowly, stealthily, he creeps down the stairs, avoiding the boards he knows to creak underfoot. On the bottom step, he stops and holds his breath. He can hear nothing.

He waits another moment and listens. Someone is breathing heavily just inside the door. Then he hears a familiar curse and he opens to door to find Obadiah, alone amid a scene of destruction. He is kneeling by the fallen printing press. Several of the leaded windows have been broken; fragments of dirty glass lie everywhere. Trays of type have been scattered all about; upturned and broken chairs, tables, the press itself and bundles of newspapers drip with black ink. The cups and plates they used for dinner the night before are smashed.

Obadiah traverses the room like a man exploring new territory, his eyes full of wonder. Mouse regards his friend closely, ready to comfort him in his time of woe. There are other things they can do, he will say. Safer things. They will not starve. But before he can begin to speak, he sees that Obadiah has finished his examination of the upturned press. He stands up, dusts his hands. And smiles.

"They can break all this, but they can never destroy the press," he says. "Look here, Mouse. The damage is not as great as it looks. Adam Brewer will repair that and this hinge is easily replaced. I will have this working again by nightfall. We shall still print the edition London waits for."

"But look at this," Mouse says, miserably surveying the chaotic room. "Is it worth doing if this is the result? And if they can do this, they can do worse. That dreadful note warned of consequences if we continued to discuss that picture. And here we are."

But Obadiah has already begun to scoop up spilled type. "Our work is now more important than ever," he tells Mouse. "We have a commission from the people of London and I will not let them down. We will not let them them down."

His certainty is unmatched in the look which crosses his friend's face.

It takes all morning and the best part of the afternoon for Mouse to find and sort the jumble of type and for Obadiah, ably assisted by Adam Brewer, to repair the press. But before sunset, the stories which he had prepared the night before and had set in the formes ready for the morning, have been reset. There is only one story which matters in this edition and that, of course, is the disclosure of the identities of the men in the picture. The article is now augmented with a brief account of the destruction wreaked in the offices of *The Enquirer*, by men fearful of its power.

Obadiah makes one more change. Goaded by the attack upon his premises, he goes a step further. After he has identified a cabinet minister, a famous actor, a judge, a notable banker and the hero of a famous naval incident, assured by Mouse that these are indeed the people, but warned too against publishing their names, he draws his readers' attentions to the dark figure and urges them to seek him out in one of the innumerable prints now in circulation.

"What is happening here?" he teases. "Why is a dead girl showered with gold coins? Whose is the purse, whose the crested coach? *The Enquirer* thinks that golden coins and dead girls are quite topical these days."

This will be sufficient for one issue. He sets the type and promises that *The Enquirer* will discover this man's name before long and make it known to the world, when justice can take its course. And when it does, he thinks, people will be queuing down the street to buy copies. He sets the last pieces of type and turns to Mouse, who is drumming his fingers on the table, as he peers through the window, keeping watch.

"Word will have already have got out about the break-in," Obadiah says. "Some will think we are now unable to print a newspaper, others that we have been frightened off. Go into the streets, Mouse, go to the coffee houses and the theatres. Spread the word that though we print a day late, they will find it has been worth the wait!"

Mouse slips off his bench and is unbolting the door when he sees Obadiah's hand upon his shoulder. "Dear Mouse," he says, "it has been a long day and I am sorry I must make it longer for you. What a friend I am! I know this business is difficult for you but I promise I will not let you come to harm. We are on the verge of something decisive here. We can use this victory for the power of good. This newspaper will become the people's champion. And do stop worrying about me, Morris. I have never been so happy."

Thirty Nine

The Journal of Henry Grace

I awaken: not lying in my bed in the smaller, adjoining room with the faded frescoes of unknown figures, but draped somehow across that of Osiris and Francesca. I lie there, accepting this singularity while the sun creeps across the rooftops of the houses across the way. I cannot have slept long; I recall the moon shimmering on the water below and Osiris telling Francesca they would see in the dawn. But I must have slept, because I dreamed, and now, still drunk and befuddled, I am incapable of deciding which of the scenes that float before my eyes are real memories of this last night and which are little bits of dreams, cast adrift.

Osiris is standing by the tall, open window, staring down at the waters of the canal, which I can hear gently lapping against the stones of this building. His hands are outstretched as he holds fast to each side of the window's frame. His long white shirt is transparent in the early morning light; he looks like a man crucified. I watch him, with a vague unease. Then he mumbles something in a voice so low, so faint that I cannot construe its meaning. I dismiss the outlandish idea that I hear him sob. "What a thing you have done," he says, much clearer now. "What a very terrible thing."

Perhaps if I were sober I would ask him to explain himself. But just now, I am busy sifting dreams and memories. I clearly remember traveling to the ball in a fantastically decorated gondola, a great, golden boat, one of those which I have seen ply the waters at regattas, filled with men of rank. I was not myself when I arrived at the masquerade. Too much wine taken with whatever else and too little sleep had left me in a poor way for making merry. I discharged a large glass of punch but my next, Osiris wrested from my hands. "We are here to make new friends," he whispered. "Friends who can make you and I very rich. Stay silent. I will tell them you are English and do not speak their language."

He pulled down the fantastic white and gold mask I had raised upon my head in order to drink and leaving Francesca by the doors, guided me towards the great windows which gave onto the Grand Canal, where a group of gentlemen had gathered. These I recall because of the luminous colours of their raiment, the gold of their rings and also for the disdain they communicated, even while masked. After this, I cannot trust my memories, which appear like freshly-printed pages for a story book which have yet to be assembled in the correct order.

I see masked eyes peering into my own. I see Francesca here and then there, and then I see her everywhere. I catch her and kiss her but the girl in my arms is not Francesca. She wants to dance and follows me and I am unkind to her. Francesca again and a giddy whirl of candlelight as we dance. The dance ended, I take her arm and begin to speak to her, too close to where the musicians saw away at their violins and cellos. I choose this moment to tell her how I long for her and how her disregard is destroying me.

Her lips move, she makes her reply. I cannot hear what I so need to hear, and so I tear off her mask. This is not Francesca; another girl's laughter rings in my ears. More masked faces and people pointing at me. Osiris speaking sternly and without humour. And then I see Francesca, the real Francesca and I know it is her because her face is unmasked. She is livid with anger, because of something I have done, some error I have made. I see her, I feel her, pushing me away. A crowd encircles us. Osiris is trying to drag me away from all this but I will not have it. I will stay with Francesca, I say, and we will dance.

But these are all the impressions I have of this night. I have no memories of how we got ourselves home, can recall no returning gondola, or climbing the stairs of the palazzo, or anything which may have occurred after this. I have the vaguest of notions that voices may have been raised and some harsh words exchanged, but that is all. I know only that two bottles which were full of wine when we left now lie empty by the bed and that a torn sleeve of Francesca's blue gown lies at Osiris's feet.

"Are you even aware of what you have done?" Osiris demands. He steps away from the window and surveys the room before beginning to pick up scattered items of clothing. "Get up, you unconscionable dog, get up and collect your things. We must be away before Venice awakes."

"What are you talking about?" I say.

"There will be time for talk once we are gone from the Republic."

"Leave Venice?" I say. "I cannot go now. Not while I paint so well."

"You talk of painting?" Osiris says, stuffing things in bags and throwing my traveling clothes at me. "I did not take you for a callous monster. There is no time to talk about this now." He looks at me as if he cannot decide what I am and shakes his head. "Everything can wait while we clear out of this city."

"I do not understand," I say as Osiris pulls me bodily to my feet. And it is true; nothing makes any sense to me.

His face is in mine, all teeth and wine breath. "Do you not? You cannot remember what happened here? What you did? You must!"

"No," I say. "Where is Francesca?"

"Oh, great Lucifer, you really do not d remember, do you?"

"Remember what? What is it, Osiris?"

"You recall nothing of last night? When we returned from the ball?"

"Not a thing. I must have slept."

"Slept? How could you have slept, after what you did?"

"What can you mean? I did nothing, I slept. Tell me what has happened. You are frightening me."

He peers again into my eyes as if searching for some truth that is hiding there.

"You cannot remember how you threw yourself upon me? How we struggled by the window here? How you accused me over and over again of being unfit for her? Do you remember how she shrank from you? And then, Henry, when she told you she had never loved you and that you were a damned fool to think so, do you not remember what you did?"

"No," I say. But nor do I want to know. I have a strong presentiment of evil.

Osiris raises his fist. "You struck her, Henry. And I swear I never saw a woman struck so hard. She cried out and then she lost balance and toppled backwards. We were all too near the open window. One moment she was there, but the next…"

"For God's sake, what happened? Where is she? Is she hurt?"

"She fell into the blackness," Osiris says. His voice is flat, void of feeling. "There was a dull noise, like that of a bowling ball striking another and then a splash. I looked out but could see nothing in the dark and so I ran down the stairs to the canal. I called her name and I hunted the banks. I slipped on something wet by the steps, I thought it might be blood. Very likely she struck her head when she fell into the canal and was unable to swim. There was not a boat to be had at that time. I hunted along the banks. I called for her. There was nothing I could do. There is nothing either of us can do now. Francesca has drowned, Henry. Her body may have caught a current and have been carried away from here or even out to sea but may just as well be under a jetty somewhere, awaiting discovery in the light of morning. And when she is found and her wound is seen, the authorities will be looking for the two Englishmen who were always seen in her company."

I sink to the floor, unable to take in anything more or to think for myself. Later I will mourn for her and later I will be visited by guilt and despair and later still I will fear for my reputation, but for the moment I am like a beast stunned by the slaughter-man. Helpless, hapless, I allow Osiris to dress me and then I sit alone on the bed staring out into the heedless bright day while Osiris goes out to find a carman who is prepared to drive two *inglesi* with their bags and their brushes and paintings far beyond the borders of the Republic of Venice.

Part Two

When he has tapped the last brick into place and has smoothed away the mortar and one more chimney is added to London's crenellated skyline, he takes a seat upon the top of the false wall which hides the sloping roof from the view of people on the pavement, four storeys below where he now slowly swings his legs. He is not the same man who stood upon a similar roof only weeks ago and declaimed about a city made glorious by a pink God's sunshine. His brown skin is marked, his eyes are dimmed and he no longer has the energy to bound up the ladders with a hodful of bricks when Billy has gone off to find a place to piss once again. He looks upon the city below, his eyes slowly traveling from the West, where Tyburn and St George's Hospital mark the end of town, to the East, where a prickle of mast-tops give away East Indiamen at anchor. In one of the huddled hovels down there, up three pair of stairs and sleeping on rags in an unfurnished room, is his family.

This is his last chimney. The builder has liked his work and often has commended him for his speed, but the extraordinarily rapid progression of this latest bout of illness has impeded his abilities and now he is the slowest of the workers, at a time when new houses must be built quickly and cheaply. "Finish your shift and go home," his overseer told him. He looks again in the direction of that home and thinks of his wife, who now is ill too, and of his half-starved children who must complete their starving once he is without work.

In that direction too lies Covent Garden where, duped by false hope and desperation, he had taken the cure that was spoken of only in whispers but which, he had been repeatedly assured, was an infallible remedy for his affliction. The house he was taken to was filthy, a room in a tenement on Drury Lane which normally was shared by a couple of prostitutes. The girl they brought him was frightened and hungry. She was so young that his stomach turned and his mind revolted from what he had to do. She was indeed very young, they admitted, but only a virgin would do. They assured him that this was the way to be cured once and for all. At only a week's wages, he was told, she was cheap at the price. Also, he might look at it this way: she was starving and what she would get for this night's work would feed her and her family for a month. He would be performing a kindness.

He looked at the fresh, frightened face with its wide eyes and turned away. His heart pounding, he knew that whatever decision he made would be a final one and one which would decide the future course of his life. He found a way of viewing his dilemma which made him feel less awkward. For a long time he had lived with the certainty that no cure would be found and that all he had to look forward to in the years to come was penury and decay. And now, a chance to live. Was it so bad after all? She was starving, just like his own children would starve if he wasn't cured very soon. And now, he could keep them all from starving by doing something with this girl which would be second nature to her in a few short years anyway. His mind was made up. He laid her on the bed and covered her thin little body with his own. She screamed.

The scream still rings in his ears and rings louder whenever he allows himself to think that it has all been for nothing anyway, that the cure did not work. The disease returned within weeks of his union with the child and this time it was worse. He was angry and went looking for those who had brought him low. The people who had arranged this thing were not to be found. There would be no refund anyway. There is no way he can reverse the evil that has been done. The evil that *he* has done. He wishes he had never paid the money and had never hurt the child.

He remembers the frightened eyes he tried not to look at and how she shook with terror. He remembers that when it was over, she tried to hide herself away in a corner of the room. She was wet with blood. He has sinned and sinned mortally, he knows. He has gained nothing himself and has lost everything, the money that would have fed his family and his own self-respect. He has ruined an innocent little girl. And all for nothing. Nothing is what life holds for him now.

The pleasures and distractions of only a few months ago, when he would walk with his family to see the ships at Wapping and tell them that such a vessel was like the one that brought their father from Jamaica to Bristol where, jumping ship, he had found himself a free man. His family like his tales and think he was a jolly seaman. He would not walk to Wapping again and he would see no more third acts at the theatre, either, when the prices tumbled and anyone could afford an hour's respite from the cares and woes of life in London. Third acts have left him with the view that life is either finally tragic or relentlessly joyous. Few of the heroes he applauded or booed were left at the end to follow some middle course. There was always resolution.

But there is no resolution for him. The girl, wherever she had gone, has been ruined for life. Illness and starvation will blight his own family. He will perish himself, but after how many long years of suffering he does not know. He will be forever burdened with guilt for failing his family and for what he did to the girl, whose screams will ring in his ears for ever. He turns his gaze towards a heaven he knows will not receive him now. “Eyes, look your last,” he mumbles and then with a gentle push with his big black hands, he launches himself into the eternal void.

Forty One

A squabble over some little thing has broken out. Men get up from where they have been lounging and shamble over to watch two rake-thin boys engage in a brief flurry of violence. The fighting dies as quickly as it flared up. Behind gathered knees in a corner made by high stone walls sits a man who appears not to see any of this. With a quick movement of his hand, he brushes away a renegade tear; it doesn't do to show weakness here. Sitting under the smoke-sullied sky in the press yard, he is puzzling over the unaccountable miracle that has saved him from the misery he endured on the prison's common side. He now has a tiny room up three pair of stairs with a bed and a small supply of candles and coals. It is all very different from the desperate straits he found himself in when he was committed here some five weeks ago. The shock of his first encounter with Newgate will stay with him forever.

For the first two weeks or more, he shares one of the awful common wards with perhaps twenty other inmates. They are not the fearful monsters the turnkeys warned him of. There are no matricides or patricides, there is a self-proclaimed regicide but he should be in Bedlam and not here. There is only one prisoner in this room who has been accused of murder. Instead there are thieves by choice and thieves by necessity. There are common pickpockets and boys who steal from shops. Few admit to their crimes but there are whispers. All struggle to live in this dark, damp and overcrowded room with a foul sewer running through the middle of it like a kennel down a street, which fills the atmosphere with the most noisome stink imaginable. The chains chafe at his wrists and at first he is too green to secure his share of the filthy straw, without which the sweet relief of sleep is all but impossible.

At night, there is only blackness and the stink, moaning and cursing and the skirmishing for space and straw. This newly-rebuilt prison is quite as hellish as its designer intended. Inmates exist on a thin diet of bread and water with a tiny portion of beef once a week. They develop sores from sleeping against rough stone and such poor fare leaves the weak unable to ward off disease. Two people have died in this room while he has been incarcerated here, an old man who had been caught stealing a penny loaf and a Welsh coiner, who has denied the hangman his pay. There is pain and acute discomfort in trying to survive in this terrible place. There is the worry and looming dread of court ordeals and fatal pronouncements. And for some, there is the strange admixture of shock and shame to have become, overnight almost, just another piece of London's refuse, swept behind the towering walls of Newgate prison. Though he can hear familiar church bells and sometimes the cries of street vendors, he might as well be in Van Diemen's Land. All he can do is give himself up to the squalor and the suffering and await his awful fate.

What he does find himself pondering – and this with numbing continuity – are the events which preceded his arrest. That night in Leicester Fields, he remains by the burning house until those who came first to see the conflagration have gone to their beds – such a tragedy in such a house provides fodder for a curious newspaperman. A few tired and drunken whores and workers going to bakeries and early-morning markets stop now and stare at the smouldering remains. They talk in low voices as they watch people with poles hooking salvageable items from the still-hot and smoking ruins. Sometimes they turn and whisper about the funny little man who scratches his head, pulls on his chin and sometimes mutters to no-one but himself.

They cannot know that this is an editor of a famous newspaper, whose mind even now is upon how the *Enquirer* will present this calamity. After all he has heard about this contentious painting and the hornets' nest it has disturbed, he wonders if the acrid stench in the morning air contains a whiff of evil? He hopes that Obadiah prints nothing of the sort before they have sifted all the chatter and rumour to find nuggets of evidence, but doubtless there will be a certain flavour to the reporting of this suspicious incident. It is a terrible, terrible thing, he muses, the painter and his servants lost in the flames. That is the worst. There is also the destruction of that great work, the livelihoods gone. But now the tolling of a bell in the nearby French Church reminds him of what o'clock this must be and that there is a press to be fed and a blacksmith who will be quick to tell him how worried he has been. Absorbed in his thoughts, he does not see the painter's girl who stands beyond the small crowd with glowing coals reflecting in wet eyes, does not think that she now has no home and for all he knows, nowhere to go that day or sleep that night. With one last look at this place of destruction, he turns his shoes eastwards.

Entering Grub street he passes by familiar tumbledown houses with faded signs that creak and complain whenever the wind gets up and sees the newspaper's own sign not far ahead, a goose quill and ink-pot on a blue ground. When they have made enough money, Obadiah says, they will vacate this tall and narrow house with its patched roof and windows stuffed with rags and move to a better district and have premises more fitting for a successful newspaper. Mouse stops at the door and ferrets in his pockets. He has come out without his heavy key again. From further down the street he can hear the squeaking of cartwheels, someone whistling and dogs barking, but inside the house there is only silence. He yanks hard upon the pull, setting the bells inside jangling. Receiving no answer from Adam or Obadiah, Mouse pulls again and then knocks some more. The unbolted door begins to swing inwards. He crosses the threshold.

He calls but there is no reply. It is most singular. Obadiah should already be setting the type, Adam making the fires and setting pots to boil on the trivets. His heart beginning to quicken its beat, he proceeds deeper into the house. At the end of a screened passage he calls up the staircase which leads off from here; still no-one responds to his appeal. He enters the main hall, which has a great fireplace at one end and heavy oaken beams above his head. The printing press stands upright in the middle of the room, unused today.

The surviving lead-latticed windows cast their diamond shapes upon the floor and because of this he does not at first see the ink which is scattered everywhere. It is as if someone had taken a pot of the stuff and cast it liberally around the room. Something is not right. Then he sees that some of these pools of ink are still wet. He cannot avoid stepping in some, which is when he notices that the floorboards are viscous underfoot. Even this does not prepare him for the terrible truth.

He makes his way across the room, past man-high bundles of newly-printed newspapers all tied up and ready for distribution, around the great press itself to the alcove behind the fireplace. He has retraced these few steps over and over ever since. It is here that he sees a man's shoes and stockinged legs showing. No doubt their owner has fallen asleep and has not heard his knocking and ringing. What else is he to think?

Before he see him, he sees the blood. There is no mistaking it now. It is thrown upon the wall of the alcove and puddled all about the floor. He steels himself to peer into the alcove. He looks. It takes me him dreadful moment to recognise his friend, Obadiah. He lolls crumpled in a fireside chair, his face, his neck and his body fearfully mutilated by great and ghastly lacerations. His clothes have been slashed, a carving knife or something with a bigger blade has been used and he has been hacked about like a piece of meat, before falling lifeless into this chair.

For a moment more he can do no nothing but stare open-mouthed at this awful tableau. He does not think about what sort of a monster might have caused such a thing. He does not think of poor Obadiah and his harrowing last moments. He does not think at all. He does not know what to do. He tries to maintain some useful shred of composure, but his stomach has frozen and he is fighting for his every breath.

He tells himself to think, think! The first thing is to ensure that life is indeed extinct, yes that is it! But even as he takes up Obadiah's cold wrists, he can see how pointless this is. All he succeeds in doing is covering his clothes and his hands with blood. Only now does it occur to him with a cold stab of terror that whoever did this may still lurk in the house. He can almost hear his heart pounding as he backs away from the body. Then he see the weapon the murderer used. Obadiah's old sword lies under the printing press. He snatches it up and stands ready to defend himself should the murderer approach.

He remembers this dreadful scene like a memory of long ago. The action plays out with hideous variations in frightful dreams which haunt him nightly. Seeing himself enter those premises is like watching some other person, someone so much more easily gulled, someone who still had his innocence. He thinks, how could he have been so cotton-brained? Now that he has had little else to think of except of how a jury will view the facts of his case, he sees how parlously foolish he had been to touch the body and then to pick up the weapon with which the poor man had been so brutally slain. Should he have been surprised when the door of the printer's house burst open and men rushed in and he was thrown to the floor, the cutlass still firmly gripped? All he can say is that just then, he knew little of the powerful mechanism which was setting in motion this particular sequence of events.

It is a small consolation that he awaits his doom in better accommodation. The room is not large, but there is a bed, a table, some paper, pen and ink and enough coals to keep out the chill of autumnal evenings. There is a pale of water for washing and a dog-eared, broken-spined copy of the Bible. When he thinks of the foul and life-sucking conditions which are endured, or are not endured, over in the common side, he thanks God for such deliverance.

He has visitors, the turnkey says one afternoon as he unlocks and swings open one great, heavy door after another. He refuses to say more, so the prisoner has only wild conjectures as to who might retain some vestige of interest in Morris Malone, one-time reporter of *The Enquirer* newspaper and now an inmate of Newgate Gaol accused of the most terrible murder. Some cruel soul with a fascination for those cast low, perhaps, or someone come to remind him that a body such as he has no right to wield power over his betters. He does not expect to see the faces he recognises within the small, bare room used for visitors. At the plain table beneath the grilled window sits the girl from the artist's house in Leicester Fields. Beside her and looking as uncomfortable with these surroundings as he is pleased to see Mouse, stands the blacksmith, Adam Brewer.

Forty Two

Shortly before the murder, its fated victim and his assistant are preparing to distribute what Obadiah maintains will be *The Enquirer* to eclipse all previous editions. He has laboured long into the night, writing and rewriting, honing and sharpening the paper's message to the world. But now it is done and despite little sleep, he has risen galvanised by thoughts of what he will do this day. Accepting a slice of buttered bread proffered by Mouse, whose lined and worried face he fails to note, Obadiah snatches up a sheet of his newspaper still a little wet from the press and closely cons his work.

He nods and allows himself a smile as he re-reads his leading article in which he ladles scorn upon that cohort of power which, he asserts, harbours a vile murderer in its midst. People who judge *your* doings and order *your* existence, he tells his readers, people who are said to provide a pattern for your lives, are – for some unthinkable reason – sheltering the murderer of your daughters. His readers and their loved ones remain in danger, he warns; this Godless monster will strike again if a stop is not put to this business now.

Other newspapers, he adds, have lacked the courage of *The Enquirer*; have even said that *The Enquirer* is mistaken. But recent attacks upon his person in print and the destruction wrought upon upon the offices of *The Enquirer* itself have confirmed that his newspaper has been right from the start. He adds that the painting that some say holds vital clues to this affair will soon be put up for sale, when people can see it at the saleroom and draw their own conclusions.

The debate between Obadiah and his reporter about how much to reveal in this issue has gone on right up to the moment the screw is turned and the first impression is made. To reveal all and suffer the consequences, both legal and otherwise, is the way Obadiah favours. This is our moment. We publish! he says. His reporter argues differently. “We should await the return of Grace's girl from Bath,” he says, “What we do may have consequences for her, too.” Mouse is becoming increasingly cautious. The recent mayhem at Grub Street has shaken him, and he now tiptoes fearfully about the streets of Moorfields and only turns into Grub Street itself when he is sure that the way is clear of anyone who looks in the least part suspicious.

“You cannot list these names as those of murderers,” he says. “They are the pillars of the kingdom, lords, ministers. And the others…I don’t like to speak their names out loud, let along set them in print. We will be fighting the establishment and it will destroy us.”

“No,” Obadiah says, firmly. “People must learn that the same law that applies to us, applies to them too. All people must learn that.”

“Then God willing, the law will be applied to our adversaries too, in due course. But only if we are circumspect. We must credit our readers with intelligence, Obadiah. For this once, let me turn the tables and show you how we can use guile to give our readers just sufficient guidance to come to the same conclusions without drawing down destruction upon ourselves.”

Obadiah listens, though not without misgiving.

In Newgate gaol, Mr Malone's face betrays his surprise but I think I see something new written there too, which might be suspicion. Greetings are cordial but no more. Why, he says, would I visit someone accused of this terrible, foul murder and why is his own man, Adam

Brewer here with me? And so I tell him of how I had stood alone by the smoking ruins of my home until all the other onlookers had gone about their business and only I was left, staring into the last small flames. I stood there because there was nowhere else for me to go. I was hungry and had no food. I was tired and had nowhere to sleep. I had not the smallest hope in anything. I confess that after an hour I was entertaining the most terrible thoughts. Sleeping on the streets, begging for bread and then I thought of much worse. I asked myself how much the girls on the Haymarket might be paid for their company? I thought about London Bridge and heavy rocks in deep pockets.

Such desperate and contemptible thinking was interrupted by a weighty hand landing gently upon my shoulder. Adam Brewer had been walking all night, sorting out his thoughts he said, when he saw the great boiling of smoke above the rooftops and would hear nothing except that I would allow him to take me to the house in Grub Street where I must stay until I was set right."

"You have done well, Adam," Mr Malone says. Turning to me, he says, "And you do not mind sleeping under the roof of a murderer?"

"I was shocked beyond telling when I entered the place. Adam too, of course. But Mr Malone, I no more think you Mr Bone's murderer than I do Adam, here. From what I already know about the painting and the anger it has aroused I am certain that the blame for this atrocious act lies with those who feared the exposing of truths concealed within that picture."

"I thank God for that. But who else thinks like we do? The mood in town is against me, of course?"

I judge he is a man who prefers plain speaking but it pains me to confirm his suspicions. Only the *Messenger* newspaper has held back from calling him a murderer. I tell him of coffee-house gossip that claims his arrest and inditement were likely planned by certain powerful people who would like to see him hanged. I do not tell him that outside Garraway's, I overheard him dismissed as 'a loose end that must be tied up.'

We talk of the painting which had occupied so much of my thoughts. Already it looks less like the masterpiece I saw before. And I see the irony of it all: I had been so taken up by my masterstroke, the introduction of foreground interest and in aping Grace's grand style, that I did not see properly what lay at its edges. Though I had assiduously copied so many of those little faces, I failed to see their significance and dismissed them as secondary to the main composition, which I had now rescued, or so I thought. How many vital clues, I ask myself, did I destroy as I painted in the enormous figures of Lot and his family?

In breaking tones, Mouse – as he insists that I call him – tells me about his life with his friend Obadiah Bone, the victim of this so callous and brutal murder. I listen as patiently as I can but what I hear does not make me comfortable. It is quite plain that he blames himself for the death of the man he loved. "I was living in a constant state of unease and fear for my own safety," he says. "If I had not been so very long in returning to Grub Street that day – I had taken a circuitous route in order to throw off imaginary followers and would-be assailants –if I had been less craven and had gone directly home, Obadiah might be alive today."

His face is a picture of misery and I can think of nothing to lessen his load. I do not say how little I think a fellow of his proportions might have achieved against the madman who had butchered his friend in what must have been a frenzy of bloodletting. "I am not a brave man," he adds. "I have survived on my wits, nothing more. And this is what it has done for my friend."

“Let me help you,” I say.

“But how? I mean no slur, but you are a painter's apprentice.”

“I watched that painting come into being,” I say. “I remember its composition and what it contained better than anyone. And there is this: I have overheard a conversation between other artists who were saying that this picture threatens certain very powerful people. Some of these people were named. Does this help?”

“This is indeed a start,” Mouse allows.

“I know too how they feared and hated your newspaper's championing of it. Whoever is responsible for the death of Mr Bone has done everything in their power to destroy that work and anyone connected to it.”

“That has been my own thinking,” Mouse says, “but really, what can one girl do?”

“I will need help. To begin with, we must discover who remain your friends and go to them. If we can discover who are these people he painted in the picture we may get at the truth of this matter and God willing, discover Obadiah's killer and save your life.”

Mouse's smile is a faint one. “Time is against us. My trial will be upon me before I know it. I think you may achieve your goal and discover this animal, but I fear I may not be here to see it.”

"If time is short,” I tell him, “let us begin. You must tell me all you know about this business before visitors are shown out.”

“I will tell you all,” Mouse says, “If only to ensure ensure he hurts no-one else. It happened this way. Obadiah suspected that important men were implicated somehow in the fates of the little girls you will have read all about," he says, "Men who have done us both great ill and may not be done with us yet."

"But why would such men despoil and murder innocents? And then slay Obadiah?"

"We have yet to answer that," he says. "One of their number, it seems, was your late master, Henry Grace. It annoys me that we might have discovered the depth of his involvement had he not been consumed by the fire, as is commonly supposed."

"He did not die in the fire," I tell him. "But he passed some weeks ago. His death was disguised in order to sell the painting."

"An extraordinary thing to do. But no matter. Will you tell me about him anyway? You lived under his roof for several years?"

I shrug. "I was a child for many of those years. He was my master. I accepted him as that and knew little more about him until recently, when I discovered his journal."

"His journal?" Mouse says. His lips are quivering as his eyes brighten. "You have his diaries?"

"Not any more. They will have burned along with everything else in the house."

"But you read them?"

"Some part, yes."

"And what do you recall?"

"Something of his tour of the Continent, some acquaintances he made…"

"You must remember more. Think, Michel."

"I have forgotten most of it," I say. "I was not expecting to recount what I read."

"There may be some little thing in those writings that will serve our cause. So, please, think."

"There was a strange man he encountered in France. He seemed to possess a dark charisma and had considerable influence over Mr Grace. His name had been fiercely scored out, suggesting to me that Grace bore a virulent hatred for its owner."

"Go on, please."

"Mr Grace's talent was quite mediocre until this meeting. But under this man's tutelage, my master began to see the world anew and to paint the world as he now saw it. His technique became revolutionised."

"Did Grace win patrons while he was abroad?"

"Yes, he did. He was commissioned in Rome by men who held prime positions in the British establishment."

"Their names?"

"I'm sorry, that has gone."

"What more was there in that journal?"

"He wrote of decorating caverns with renderings of monsters. Before I could discover the purpose of these caves and their abysmal decorations, I was summoned by my master."

"A pity," the dwarf says. He thinks for a moment, scratching his bare scalp.

"So," he says at last, "Grace came to the notice of men of influence. Their commissions were no doubt the source of his sudden wealth. Once men of high standing had allowed themselves to be painted by him, society will have followed suit. I am wondering if these clients were the men he painted into *The New Fire of London.*"

"But why would he ridicule them and himself into the bargain?"

"That is something you will have to find out," Mouse says. "You recall our friend in the picture, the one who drops gold coins upon a corpse?"

"I saw it at close quarters when I was working on the upper areas of The New Fire," I say. "I thought it strange at the time but so much of that picture was beyond strange to me."

"That figure is key to this puzzle, I am sure of it."

"That and whatever chains the other faces in the composition," I say, hearing locks rattle and iron doors slam. "Please finish your tale quickly, Mr Malone. The turnkeys are starting to show out the visitors."

"I will be quick. Now, of these men – our adversaries – Henry Grace, it seems to me, was the keeper of their conscience. Whether or not he participated in the crimes we think they committed, which I believe are the despoliation and sometimes the deaths of these children, I do not know. My own theory – and I admit this is based on very little – is that he was so horrified by what he had done that he withdrew into his world of art and used his disease as an excuse to avoid further involvement. Does that agree with what you knew of him?"

"He withdrew into a single, dark room and from there, behind some screens and a mask. He could not have done more towards withdrawing from the world short of taking his own life."

"He could not go to the authorities, some of those men *were* the authorities. And besides, if I am right, he was implicated himself. All he could do by way of appeasing his own conscience and making some small restitution was to reveal as much as he could of what had been done and who had been responsible for it through his masterpiece, *The New Fire of London*."

"But his crime would have been discovered as soon as the picture was shown," I say.

"There is no doubt in my mind that his intention was that the painting would be unseen by anyone – excepting himself and an apprentice who would not understand it – until after his death. This is the act of a man wanting to lighten a cumbrous burden of guilt before he dies. But thanks to this man Gretch showing the picture prematurely, his actions too were coming to light before he intended them to. The people in his painting were now threatened on two fronts. Firstly, there was the painting itself. Secondly, there was Obadiah, who understood what the picture was about and did as much as he dared to enlighten our readers, too."

"And this is why he was killed?"

"That is why he was killed and your house with the picture in it was burned to the ground. The newspaper received a warning. No doubt someone visited Henry Grace to warn him, too."

"There was a visitor, who left a single golden sovereign."

"Once again, the coins. Obadiah saw those gold sovereigns as a cruel joke on the part of the perpetrators," Mouse says. "But I think Grace himself was behind this act. Perhaps he intended them as compensation. Was he the sort of man to have insisted upon such a decency?"

"Three gold sovereigns is no compensation for a dead or bedlammed child," I say.

"Of course not. Perhaps they were tokens from a troubled

conscience. But whatever the case, this business could not, under any circumstances, come to light. It would ruin reputations, perhaps even bring down a government. Obadiah let it be known that he would print the names of each and every figure who could be identified in the painting. And we know where that got him"

The downcast look he wore when I entered the room has returned, his shoulders drop. I try to cheer him.

"I say again, I will help you, if I can."

"I am lucky to have such a friend," he says, "But the evidence is piled against me like faggots around the stake."

"There is time before your trial. I will do everything that might be done. And there is something you might do to help me."

"But what can I possibly do? In here?"

"It would be extremely useful if you would tell me everything you know about editing a newspaper."

Mouse laughs bitterly and shakes his head. "It would be extremely useful," he says, "If you could bring to mind more of Henry Grace's journal."

"You have heard all that I read. There were further volumes but these would have been lost in the fire. But about your newspaper..."

"A tragic loss, as I think those journals might have helped our cause immeasurably. So, it is all over."

Adam speaks at last. "Mr Mouse, do you hear my voice?"

"Yes."

"Well, then. You are not yet dead."

Forty Three

The Journal of Henry Grace

Now that I consider it, here in my comfortable villa in Leicester Fields, I suppose I have all that I have wanted from life. I have fulfilled my destiny, although it has come at a price. I am the artist I always dreamed of being and something more than that, too. Osiris was right. The experience I accumulated on my Grand Tour proved more than enough to mature my style. It was, he has said, the unspeakable experience of that final night in Venice which completed my education and gave whatever I painted afterwards 'an unholy knowingness'.

It is this terrible thing, he says, which separates me from, or perhaps elevates me above, most of the artists painting in London today. I do not know if this is true or if it is only Osiris validating his own predictions. But what I do acknowledge is that success came quickly, suddenly, you might say. Upon my return to England. I received commissions, lots of them.

The most important ones came about through introductions supplied by the gentlemen I had met in Rome. Others followed as word of my style, which was sufficiently unusual as to be controversial, spread about town. I became a curiosity and then I became quite well known and then I became famous. In fact, I became very famous. Before I knew it, I was the toast of the salons and all London society, it seemed, was at home to me. Money filled my coffers. I bought the house I had rented in Leicester Fields and decorated it magnificently. It became the place to go and be seen to go.

For a while I spent far too much time entertaining the doyens of this or that in London society. I hosted lords, ladies, fellow artists and even two royal personages. My work was in demand, my name on everyone's lips. I had lovers, too, the pretty daughters and sometimes the bored wives of those men I courted in my own little salon. Osiris was ever present, to claim his share of the fruits of my labour.

But this fat and rosy apple, I soon discovered, was full of worms. Firstly, there was and will ever be, my poisoned memory of Francesca, whose fate at my hands sullies my every happy thought and brings a cold, hard edge to my pen which critics profess to admire but really is only a graphic expression of my disgust with myself. How often has my mind gone over and over the events of that night? Despite that, I remember no more of what happened than I did the following morning when Osiris told me that in a fit of drunkenness, I had struck Francesca and sent her plummeting to her death in the canal beneath the window.

We were safely out of Venice before any alarm was raised. Whether we were pursued I do not know. I never heard any more of the matter and the only reminders of that dreadful night have come from my own troubled conscience and from Osiris, who has never quite let me forget about it. In a way, though, Francesca lives on, appearing frequently as a detail or even a principal subject in so many of my paintings that the closely-kept secret of her identity has become part of the allure of the works of Henry Grace.

The other worm which eats away at my happiness is my involvement with the men who professed themselves admirers of my work and promised me commissions. In the beginning the association seems hopeful enough. Good to their word, I am indeed commissioned to paint three-quarters length portraits of the gentlemen I met in Rome and a few of their close associates. Some of the sitters come to me and others ask that I travel to their town house or country estate to have their likenesses preserved in oil paint.

Sir Geffrye Quicke makes a stern and imposing figure in his judges' robes and it is not difficult to picture him on the bench under a square of black silk, dispatching some poor wretch to a lingering death. When the pose is dropped, though, he giggles like a schoolboy at some little joke made by his valet.

Gareth Siddall chooses a human skull as his prop and a proscenium arch as his frame. He entertains me, to begin with at least, by declaiming from Shakespeare and Marlowe. His Grace the newly-appointed Archbishop of York and Viscount Binder are both condescending gentlemen, who take pride in showing me their gardens, while Vice Admiral Cockburn belies his status as a national hero by posing shakily for his portrait, three parts drunk on French brandy.

Not one of these men corresponds in my mind with the images I have built of them from the newspapers and journals and coffee house gossip. The more I come to know them, the less statuesque and unworldly they become. By the time I have spent several long hours in their company, most of these public figures, with their weak bowels and their carbuncles and their loud professions to understand more about some things than clearly they do, appear to be no more superhuman than myself.

In return for these lucrative commissions, I agree to complete a job of a very different nature. To this end, I am driven for some hours down the Great West Road, to the place where Lord Albemarle has his pile.

Set in newly-improved parkland, Mylnehurst Abbey, once an Elizabethan country house abutting an abbey, has been extended and remodelled in the latest fashion to such an extent that not a trace of its earlier existence remains. However, it is not his neo-Palladian mansion or the uninterrupted vistas he has created by having an entire village levelled and rebuilt beyond the eye-line of anyone in the house, which has brought me here. I have come here to see a network of caves which lies beneath the ruins of the old abbey.

I note that the wiry gentleman who meets me at the park gates favours a vivid palette – the elderly Lord Albemarle is dandified in a coruscating golden waistcoat underlying a similarly braided turquoise coat and flax-coloured stockings. He enthuses about his own travels in Italy and in France, where he has spent a goodly portion of his adult life, as we walk towards the elevation on which stands his house and the old abbey ruins. It occurs to me that I have already heard whisperings about this old roué and the decadent life he led in his Paris apartments.

At the base of the elevation, we pass through a dense copse of firs and then through a concealed fissure in a face of rock. It is a minute or more before my eyes become accustomed to the gloom beyond and I make slow progress down a succession of barely-lighted tunnels towards the caverns where I am to paint. Stopping by an oaken table, he takes a great and ancient tome from one of the twelve chairs, opens it upon the table and explains my task.

All that is wanted, he says, is that a chosen selection of the drawings in the book should be reproduced as grandly and as vividly as possible, upon the walls of the cave. This unusual scheme of decoration, he tells me, will make an amusing backdrop for certain rituals and observances performed by members of his circle, some of whom I may have encountered on my travels.

I leaf through the drawings, frankly amazed and quite often appalled at what I see. Had this book been shown to me when I was a little younger, before I had met Osiris De'Ath, I would perhaps have slammed shut its covers and walked away. But now, armoured by experience and tragedy, I do not. I look closely at page after page of satyrs raping, devils vomiting, monks murdering and at all kinds of beasts and monsters which I can only hope are the works of someone's fevered imagination and not in actual existence somewhere on this earth. "Make your choice," I am told, "The selection must be your own."

Forty Four

The date that has been set for the trial of the dwarf, Morris Malone comes ever closer and there is nothing in prospect to persuade jurors that he might in fact be innocent of the charge and that this trial will result in anything but a guilty verdict and a sentence of death. He spends his days walking about the press yard and sometimes talking to prisoners who know more than he about the workings of the Old Bailey and can tell him what to expect. He find no morsels of comfort there.

Michel Angelo visits him regularly and is the sole sustainer of his spirits. He wonders why she should be so good to him – it is she and Adam who have raised the cash to have him transferred from the common side and installed in his own room on the masters' side. But he understands that she is convinced of his innocence and that is a great comfort to him, especially at a time when all London has been thinking him guilty as Judas.

But perhaps not quite all of London condemns him. Michel to her great credit, has taken on the mantle of editor of *The Enquirer* and produces the newspaper herself, with help from Mouse's friends on Grub Street and Adam Brewer, who operates the press and organises distribution of the bundles of newspapers. Visiting him again, the girl shows him two issues of the newspaper which she has produced.

The first of these makes his heart leap with excitement and fills it with hope. In her editorial, the inexperienced editor makes no bones about protesting his incarceration and rails against the charges that have been made against him. He is unfortunate, but innocent, she writes. His great misfortune, she says, lies not in stumbling upon the body and picking up the weapon which had been used to murder his friend and protector Obadiah Bone. His misfortune has been to be the victim of evil men who not only committed the murder but saw that he took the blame.

He is, she says, the unluckiest body in London, but also as innocent as its newest-born citizen. His hands shake as he reads her kind words, his heart warming to this young woman who is probably risking much to come to his aid. Another editorial is written in a similar vein and the newspaper also carries two short letters which speak up in his defence. Their sentiments cheer him beyond words, until he considers the possibility that they too may be the work of Michel Angelo. After more mature reflection, he decides that Michel is fighting a one-handed battle against enormous odds and that little she publishes is likely to save him from the hangman's noose.

At his trial, Michel is to give him a good character. Another person who has promised to speak for him is Mrs Matilda Harris, someone Michel was evidently much relieved to discover had survived the fire. Cheering him with a rare smile, Michel tells him that Mrs Harris had been using Gretch's absence in Bath to see a gentleman friend in Highgate, about whom neither she nor Gretch, she is sure, knew a thing. At Highgate, Michel had told the woman of the false accusations against her innocent friend. Mrs Harris has a good heart and is untroubled by the awkward fact that she has yet to meet Mr Morris Malone.

There will be no counsel for the defence, of course. As is the case with the law in these enlightened times, he will be assumed to be guilty unless he can prove otherwise. Had he fifty pounds to pay for a good lawyer, it is possible that a better case might be made for him. But he has not got fifty pounds and given the weight of circumstantial evidence loaded against him, he cannot see that it would make any difference to the verdict or the sentence.

Going again to Newgate Prison, Michel shows Mouse a list of people she thinks may be caught up in this business, even if they are not directly responsible for the death of Obadiah Bone. "As you can see," she says, as if she were talking to some disinterested party and not to someone whose life might depend on her every word, "Every name on this list is a person of standing and reputation in the establishment of a while ago, and not a few of whom retain high places today. And every one of these names has his face reproduced in miniature on the canvas of *The New Fire of London*. What we must discover is what ties such disparate names together."

"You do not know that yet?"

Michel is gathering up a sheaf of papers, preparing to leave him to another night in Newgate.

"No. But I feel that with every day I look into their affairs I get to know them a little better and that at some point I will understand what all this is about."

He remain silent. The trial is almost upon them and all she can offer is that their adversaries appear to be some of the most powerful or celebrated men in England. He feels the knot tightening about his neck.

Forty Five

There is that in Michel's nature which cannot bear an injustice and that which she sees unfolding before her new friend Mouse is an unbearable example. Mouse's case is terribly, cruelly unjust. In some future time, she muses, there will be no injustice. She takes another printed page from the press and holds it towards the light and feels she holds in her hand the way to achieve this new, equable world. Newspapers like this, she thinks, which have started to speak to ordinary people in their own language and to address their concerns, will surely become crusaders for a better, juster world.

She visits Mouse in gaol to offer crumbs of hope and to speak a few kind words, but each visit to Newgate brings her pain. Arriving at the stout black door one day she finds that she cannot properly breathe. Her chest is tight and her heart misses beats; she feels nauseous and giddy. She says little throughout her visit as she tries to bring her body under control. A similar thing occurs on her next visit, when she becomes so ill that she turns back and asks to be let out of that foetid and airless place before she has even seen Mouse. Ashamed of herself, she returns home, leaving Mouse unconsoled.

In Grub Street, she is able to take more positive action. It has occurred to her that she might be able to use *The Enquirer* – which, with its apparently irresistible mix of insinuation and scandal and society titbits, it is now outselling every other newspaper – to swing public opinion in Mouse's favour. And so, while she investigates and baits the men he believes are somehow responsible for both the deaths of the little girls and of Mouse's dearest friend, she prints up a petition which proclaims Mouse's innocence. As soon as sufficient signatures are obtained from the readers of *The Enquirer*, each of whom will receive a copy of the petition with his paper, she will present it to the Home Secretary, who has the power to grant a reprieve or at least a stay of execution. The minister must be made to see that not only the mob but the franchised electorate believes in Michel's innocence.

Filling the petition will not be easy. In fact, she thinks in gloomy moments, it may be impossible. Too many Londoners see Mouse as the cold-blooded murderer of the champion of their rights and avowed guardian of their safety. Others simply will not care either way about one more morsel of gallows fodder. Changing these people's opinions will be like turning a beached 72-gun leviathan with two mules and old rope, but to do nothing would be unthinkable. And so, beginning in the weeks before Mouse's trial, Michel sets to work on this Herculean labour. As the trial date comes nearer, she wonders now how successful she has been in changing the mind of the British public.

She attends the trial at the Old Bailey, where she is allowed to speak briefly on Mouse's behalf, endorsing what she already perceives as his good character. The trial itself is a travesty, she thinks. The evidence against the accused is enough to hang a dozen men, she can see that, and Mouse's own stumbling account of how he was duped and lured to the house on Grub St is given no credence. Mouse appears overawed by the proceedings; his voice becomes lost among the fits of coughing and cries of "murderer!" from people in the gallery. He attempts to relate the theory that great men have conspired against him, but becomes confused, and when his voice trails away, he is loudly derided by the court. Sadly, Michel rises from her seat and quietly leaves the court, hearing only later that Mouse has been condemned. She could not have stayed to hear that doom pronounced.

Forty Six

The Journal of Henry Grace

Years have passed since first I witnessed the brothers' depraved rituals. Well. I do not see them that way at first, of course. Blinded by sudden social elevation, I feel honoured to be invited to become a novitiate of such a select circle. For my initiation I am taken to the Grand Cavern, stripped of my clothes and bathed in an underground pool so cold it nearly stops my heart. Baptised into my new religion, I am given my own robes and the name of Brother Thomas.

Becoming a brother is not an easy thing. Because I have earned my right to membership thanks only to my talents as an artist and have not the good name, nor the immense fortunes of others, I have ground to make up. Some of the brothers are keen that I should understand how singular an occurrence my enrolment is. I have to earn their acceptance and this I do by offering my services. I work tirelessly upon ever more ambitious creations, some that cover entire ceilings at great houses belonging to our members.

This work is long and hard. I paint upon scaffolds under high ceilings, necessarily adopting positions which are torturous and which will leave me with painful reminders of this time for years to come. However, the more I work, the more accomplished an artist I become. With Osiris managing my business and ensuring the work I do never sells beneath the price that he assigns it, my coffers fill and my reputation as an artist climbs. Osiris is making himself very useful as a procurer of my best commissions, as the guardian of my reputation and also as someone who can keep at bay the many time-wasters and other distractions. He gets my food, arranges accommodation when we travel and makes my life so easy that I have only my painting to think about.

I hardly know when Osiris becomes indispensable to me but slowly the relationship between us changes and I find myself at first agreeing with almost all he says and not much later, pandering to his every suggestion. He offers aid and friendship on one hand but on the other, something altogether less pleasing. This side I have yet to test. Though I read into every sharp glance his knowledge of the unspeakable thing I did in Venice, he has rarely been angry with me and has never directly threatened me. That said, he has let me see how violent in tongue and arm he can be with others who provoke him or get in his way – lazy ostlers and importunate beggars, to give examples.

He has barely avoided coming to blows with my servant Gretch on a number of occasions. Both men see themselves as being strongly invested in my future. Gretch will only grumble but Osiris, I am now finding out, is a dangerous compound of charm and violence and as combustible as gunpowder. He has begun to frighten me.

Qualities which I see he had subdued while he moulded me into a reliable source of money and access to influence come now to the fore. Such is the force of Osiris's character and his insidious ability to make himself indispensable that people of reputation listen to this scion of a doubtful family. They wonder aloud where they might be without the services he provides for them. He sets in motion all of their activities, just as he did for me. He persuades members of the club that they, like me, need to broaden their range of experience and in this way become more perfect, better tried and superior beings.

To this end, he introduces all kinds of new rituals and practices which previously might have been beyond the pale even for the members of this extraordinary club. Osiris may be the general factotum to whom they turn when they need to get things done, but he never looks less than the man who is running the show. If I had spent an evening with the club as a stranger and was afterwards asked who had charge of it, I would have said, "Why, it is that Osiris De'Ath, of course."

I come to think nothing of having sexual intercourse before an audience with some young strumpet whom Osiris has paid well to leave her London clients for a night. But one hussy is much like the next and I, like some of the others, begin to tire of the whole thing. Perhaps Osiris notes this and acts upon it; we welcome the refinements which he introduces. We enjoy twin sisters from Bow, a pair of identical girls with flaxen hair and brown eyes and an equal desire to please. Is the blind woman next? The nubian girls? Or is it the three boys recruited in the hop fields of Kent? I cannot recall.

A sense of excitement is introduced and the rituals are performed with renewed energy and the enthusiasm of old. Anticipating what Osiris might arrange next becomes a source of some excitement. These and other particular pleasures, a few of which I hesitate to record, are all enacted in the caverns beneath the abbey and after each of these, we disrobe and retire to the hearth of the great house above and become riotously drunk.

I have a full staff at this house, which is overseen by the capable

Jamie Gretch, whom I took on despite my housekeeper's oft-voiced views about the troublesome Scots. It is he who now orders my meals and sees to it that my clothes are washed and pressed. The house has been repaired and better furnished; it is now the sort of place where a sitter of some importance will feel at home. Osiris dines here on occasion but it cannot be comfortable to eat when a footman is always glowering at you and in any case, he generally finds his own amusements in the evenings, very likely at the gaming tables and almost certainly at my expense. It matters not to me. For several years past, I have been everything I have ever wanted to be, rich, successful and happy. People who were once only names from the columns of newspapers, I now count as my friends.

Forty Seven

The fetters that that the small prisoner has been wearing since he was sentenced to death are about to be struck off in the press room. He waits his turn. Various officials involved in today's piece of theatre look at him as they might a creature in a Tower cage. In front of him, dressed like he is about to be married and not going this day to his death, stands one Dermot McNally, who has been condemned for highway robbery. Everyone in Newgate knows something about McNally, his exploits, real and concocted, having been disseminated to an interested public through broadsides, ballad sheets and street gossip. McNally held up the Bristol Mail, McNally was always a gentlemen with the lady passengers and so on.

The highwayman has priority today, of course, and will take his place in the first cart. A highwayman is always first in these grim processions. It is intended that all should see him and understand what desserts highway robbery brings. In practice, though, such prominence only adds to their lustre. Highwaymen are popular, at least with those who have not faced the hollow end of a pistol on a bleak and lonely heath.

What makes them the subject of such senseless adoration Mouse cannot imagine. People are stupid, he thinks as he stands, still shackled, awaiting his turn at the anvil. This McNally has been convicted of two murders and yet people have written songs about him – and here am I, the dwarf thinks, who will be missed only by a blacksmith. This grievance aside, although his heart beats like the hammer which is striking now at McNally's manacles, his throat is dry and there is a cold, sickly sensation in his stomach, he is in fact a little calmer than he predicted.

Following his sentencing, he has had long weeks in which to contemplate this moment and to abandon any phantom hope he might once have harboured. Hope had made everything that much harder to bear. Quite when he gave up hoping for a reprieve, he does not know. Perhaps it was when the girl stopped visiting him. She had ever been hopeful and had made it her mission to keep his spirits buoyed and this she did by telling him about the articles she had published in what is now his own newspaper, Mouse having been willed the business by Obadiah. He finds some comfort that there is some published sentiment in his favour and that he will not die misunderstood by everyone.

For some days after the trial, Michel Angelo had come to his new, temporary place of incarceration – a plain space with a board to sleep on – bringing him sweetmeats, something to drink and balm for his wrists, which chafe against the shackles. She brings news, too. The remains of James Gretch, she says, have been found and given a Christian burial in St Martin's churchyard. Questions are being asked about Henry Grace, she says. There has of course been no sign of his corpse among the charred remains of the house on Leicester Fields. Some are saying he lives still; others that there is something more to his non-appearance than meets the eye.

He hears from the keeper of the prison that there will be no reprieve; he is to die on the next of London's seven hanging days. He sees no more of Michel after this. Indeed he has not seen her in a while and wonders what might be the cause of her abandonment of him. He surmises that she no longer entertains hopes for his survival. It would be hard for the girl to see her friend go to his death. She may continue to argue his cause in his newspaper and in the coffee houses but that will be all, he thinks.

He resolves to allow her to go her own way and turns his thoughts towards his end and the life beyond. A Bible has been left for his use and he finds some little comfort in the New Testament. He reads for hours at a time, interrupted only by the turnkeys who have been assigned his care until it is no longer needed.

The first time the one called Mr Thomas brings him his food (cheese and some vegetables now, in addition to the bread, water and occasional meat of the common side) he casts him a queer look. "You don't look that interesting to me," he tells his prisoner. "I don't know what the fuss is about." The turnkey Mr Nathan sees to it that he doesn't escape or cheat the hangman by opening his wrists in the later parts of the day. He too seems strangely disappointed by Mouse, or by his demeanour. But while the turnkeys distract him now and then, for the most part he is left alone with his thoughts and the rattling of keys, the slamming of doors and the cries in the night.

He is surprised at how quickly he gives up running over the grim sequence of events he anticipates experiencing on that fatal day. But there are only so many times you can picture the dreadful moment when the cart arrives under the tree and you feel the rough hemp of the halter as it is placed around your neck and only so many variances on the extreme sort of pain you expect next. The mind refuses to take too much of this; in the end there is a sort of dull-edged acceptance of it all. It will come, you will go, and that is all there is to it. And so he reads the Bible, he prays and he remembers happier times.

His fetters struck off, his hands are bound and he stands in the yard awaiting the carts and hearing the bells tolling at nearby St Sepulchre's. The day is cold and the clouds threaten rain. The City Marshall's men are mounted and ready to escort the line of carts to Tyburn. Today there is McNally, himself and five others to be hanged, his companions being three pickpockets, a rough fellow who assaulted and killed a Bow Street Runner and a bone-thin young mother convicted of her child's murder.

The carts stand before them but there is some delay while the Ordinary of Newgate can be found. At last, they see his short, squat figure hurrying from the direction of the jakes, with his Bible in his hand. Those about to die are helped upon the carts, in each of which is a rough coffin. The young girl is wailing piteously and one of the pickpockets has lost the swagger with which he entered the press yard and his face is now white as milk. Mouse fights the urge to vomit as he is told to turn about so his view will be of where they have come and not of the triple tree of Tyburn ahead of them.

When all is ready, a horn sounds and the doors of Newgate swing open. He turns his face to see the first cart leaving the prison grounds, with Dermot McNally trying to wave his bound hands to the great crowd outside the gates. The Ordinary travels with him and is making some attempt to read him the scriptures before he dies. Behind the cart carrying Mouse, he sees the other carts, the young mother in the one behind, the pickpockets following and the stocky figure of the hangman sitting on the coffin of the rough fellow while he takes a pinch of snuff.

The carts jolt over the cobbles and it is all he can do to prevent himself from being thrown over his own wooden box. He hangs on to the cart's side and though he looks, he sees nothing. His mind is too full of everything – his imminent demise and the pain he will suffer, where his soul is bound, his wasted life, his mistakes and lost chances, days when he had a future – to properly see the teeming crowds which line the streets several bodies thick and hang out of windows two and three storeys high, some standing upon the flat roofs above the line of carts.

He never expected this. So much noise, people shouting, some cheering loudly. He has the fleeting impression of a public holiday. Close by there is caterwauling and screeching from a band of street musicians. The cheering will be for the highwayman; it always is. The crowd surges towards the carts, held back only by the City Marshall's men. He thinks they are coming for him and almost would will the cart on – better the rope than being torn apart by the mob, which must loathe him for killing the man who promised to make them safe.

He can see the other carts following on. And then the mother collapses and the cart stops. There is confusion for a moment while the Ordinary hurries towards the cart and mounts it, and helps the girl to her feet. He stands at the cart end, clutching her small frame. She looks too slight a figure to hang and she will take her time to die, he thinks. As the cart turns onto Holborn Hill he thinks for a moment it is snowing: flakes begin to land at his feet. Then he sees they are not flakes, but rose petals, dropped by admirers of the highwayman, he supposes, from the windows of buildings, which freak gusts have robbed him of.

There is a stop at a church and another at an inn, where he is given a bowl of ale and becomes the subject of everyone's interest and conversation. Then on they go again, slowly progressing down High Holborn with its shops and taverns and coffee houses, and then through the crumbling rookeries of Broad St Giles. There are some among the crowds here, he thinks, who will take this same ride. He could wish they would be good enough to take it now in his place.

As the carts come onto Oxford Street, a woman runs alongside and tries to touch him. She has it wrong. People with warts and other maladies will often fight to touch the hand of a man once he is hanged, believing that it brings a cure. He tries to tell her to be patient, but no sound escapes his lips. Where Marylebone Lane meets Oxford Street, the thoroughfare becomes Tyburn Road and he knows his time is running out.

The procession slows now, perhaps so all can be made ready for their arrival at the gallows. And then, just when he is part-prepared to meet his doom, it stops outside another tavern. He is handed inside and chained to a bracket on the wall and given his last drink. Hauled up upon the cart once more, he feels something warm trickling down his leg and enough self-respect remains for him to hope it goes unseen by anyone.

As Marylebone Lane recedes into the distance and he knows they have almost completed their journey, he can hear the clamour of Tyburn's crowds. He is now among that crowd, a multitude surrounding him such as he never saw. People are jostling, fighting for a place with a good view of the proceedings to come. A shilling for a place on the tiered seating of Mother Proctor's Pews will seem money well spent to see McNally the highwayman dangle today.

The whole world has turned out see him, or McNally at least. People are making money here, too. He can see vendors of oranges and fried fish, and broadsheet sellers. One of these is held up for him to see and he reads its headline, *The True Last Words of Morris Malone*. The men on horseback are having difficulty in restraining the crowds, some of whom are getting dangerously close to the carts, provoking its escort, which fears attempts at McNally's rescue. People break through the cordon and the riders react. A young man is felled by a cudgel's blow, a woman with a baby at her breast is ridden down. There is a pause to proceedings while order is restored. The crowds are forced back, the cordon made secure.

Turning his head he sees the towering uprights; high above, men sit astride the crossbeams, fixing and adjusting the ropes. His ears ring with the noise of the crowd and nearby, someone calls for silence. McNally stands under the gallows, the noose already around his neck. He is attempting to make the dying speech he had spent his last days composing. He smiles weakly; he wants to die game, for the sake of the crowd.

People in the seats are waving their hands, calling for silence but there are other calls that he cannot make sense of but which grow louder and louder. Whatever they are shouting – and surely it could not be his own name? – prevents anyone but the Ordinary, perhaps, from hearing the words and wisdom with which the Highwayman wishes to leave the world. He wants to turn his head as the cart moves off, but instead he sees McNally drop, jerk and swing heavily from the beam. His polished riding boots kick at empty space as his big body turns.

Silence has fallen and Mouse distinctly hears his rasping struggles for breath. Round he goes, propelled by his own kicking. Then some ally of his, a brave accomplice perhaps, breaks through the crowd and grabs at the legs which still kick vainly at the air. The man gives three sharp tugs and then tries again. After two or more attempts, the body is still, the fancy breeches McNally had been proud to wear now dark with his own piss.

"Do you have anything to say?" someone asks in his ear. A raven flies high above the trees in Hyde Park. He shakes his head and gazes into the crowd before him, barely seeing the faces in it or hearing the noise they are making. Malone, Morris Malone is what he still thinks he hears, such is the hallucinatory nature of this experience. He feel the rope drop over his head and rest heavily upon his shoulders before the hangman pulls it tight.

The voice of the Ordinary drones on. He thinks that if he is not hanged immediately, his legs may give way and that he will hang himself upon the cart. He wants it all to be over, as soon as that may be, no matter how and no matter what comes next. There is a moment of awful stillness and quiet. Then the floor beneath his feet rumbles and shakes, the cart moves from beneath him and he plummets into the darkness.

Part Three

The Journal of Henry Grace

It occurs to me on occasion that perhaps my good fortune is too extraordinary to last. But it does, until high living and indolence take their toll on both my character and my painting. There comes a time when I no longer paint as I did when I was hungry for everything I now have. I rarely attempt anything which requires much effort and imagination, settling instead for the reliable source of income brought in by painting the portraits of rich men and their dogs. With a need for ready cash, I sell off two of my finest history paintings to His Royal Highness the Prince of Wales and accept his commission for a portrait of the actress, Mary Robinson. For a little while, I feel restored. But these paintings are no sooner sold to the Prince than I slip into my old ways and return to easier sources of revenue. I turn away the troublesome commissions offered by those who follow the tastes of the Court.

After years of living in this way, perhaps fashions in portraiture change, or my skills wane, but demand for my work all but disappears. Quite suddenly, it seems to me, I am neither fashionable nor rich. I have not noticed how the money has seeped away or know where it went. I suspect that Osiris continues to gamble and has found access to money that is mine. In any case, I see less and less of De'Ath, leaving me to wonder if he has found a new patron to bleed dry. Gretch tells me that cash is getting tight and we must make economies.

Staff are let go, the entertainments cease. The house becomes a *trompe d'oeil* of its former self, the polished wood and guilt-framed paintings left hanging in the entrance reassuring sitters that they have come to a place that is still sufficiently respectable to receive them, no matter what others whisper. The rest of the house slowly goes to rack and ruin. But still we go on, my painting earning just enough money for us to keep most of the duns from the door. Sometimes I attend a meeting of the old circle but with my cash draining and my reputation failing, I no longer feel comfortable among these rich, complaisant men and often feel resentful of them. I cannot but think that their regard for me is waning too.

And then comes the thing that changes everything. I hardly know how to approach this dreadful, most damnable business. Let me begin by saying that with the possible exception of the archbishop, members of the association of which I am a member are hardly religious in the accepted sense of the word, never mind that our liturgies ape those of the Christian church. Like me, most of the club's members live at least six days of the week guided by the principles of rationality or empirical enquiry.

But something happens and the ways in which we respond causes me for one to question my faith in reason. I become ill. We all become ill. Brother Andrew is the first to admit to harbouring the disease and others quickly follow. I examine myself as soon as I feel discomfort and find my genitals speckled with small, ulcerated pimples around which grow ridges of hard skin. At first we deny the virulence of this disease even to ourselves. It is only the pox, we say. Which gentleman has not had that? But then the symptoms speedily progress and we are visited by spasms of the most excruciating pain and each of us finds our lives changing because of this affliction.

It is hard not to think that the malady which has infected myself and my brothers and spread until every one of us bares its marks to some degree, is punishment for enjoying a life far beyond the bounds of Christian teaching.

There is disagreement about how and when the infection came among us. For a while we abstain from sexual contact, those who have yet to present with signs of the disease hoping to prevent their own infection. They hope in vain, because before very long all are reporting the symptoms of the French disease that are known only too well. To contract syphilis is hardly unusual, with armies of whores patrolling the streets and offering their services for next to nothing. This, though, seems a particularly violent strain and its visible symptoms more damaging than anything I have seen before. I am frightened. We all worry, not least those in high position, for whom the marks of the disease will be highly injurious and perhaps even calamitous to their public lives.

Of course, we want to know from whence it has come and whom to blame for our confusion and fear. But so many girls have made the journey from London to lie with us that the source might have been with any of them. Two or three girls' names are bandied about and in that impotent way men have when no other resort presents itself, there has been talk among some of doing something about these girls, that the infection is passed no further. Whether it is indeed one of these girls who is to blame, or some other, or whether it was one of the boys, or is simply a recurrence of a disease already contracted by one of our circle is very much a moot point.

There has been much of this useless talk. It only distracts us from the matter we must take quickly in hand. This, of course, is the finding of an effective remedy before we all look like lepers and are treated accordingly. Some members have already been taking cures. Sweat baths and mercury inunctions taken in heated rooms have been tried and holy wood tested. Every cure that I have ever heard of has been given its chance but none has proved in the least effective. Still the lesions and abscesses appear, still some part of the body has to be hidden.

Some brothers are becoming quite unnerved and do not act as men should. Others have retired to their houses and live secluded lives behind shuttered windows. Doctors and apothecaries come and go from our houses, receipts for medicines are passed around privily, like love notes. We convene on rare occasions to hear the best and most trusted medical men talk to us. The King's surgeon is consulted, to no better avail.

At last there comes the point where anything untried will be tried. Old wives' tales are tested and prove to be just that. All sorts of hocus-pocus is resorted to, as are remedies from beyond these shores. We amass an enormous library of knowledge about the disease, but still we suffer. Then Brother John, whose roof was lately mended by a fellow whom he swears had the disease just as we have – but miraculously was cured – tells us what we must do. The cure will shock us, we are told. To the civilised mind this cure will seem alien and terrible. But, we hear, he has seen with his own eyes how this remedy was strikingly effective with his builder. Even the visible signs of the disease disappeared.

This panacea is in fact commonplace among the denizens of St Giles and the region of the city called Alsatia too, he says, and what do we know of the people who live in places like those? They are as foreign to polite society as the natives of Africa or America. Why, who is to say that this disease is not as commonly cured there as a broken leg is set with splints and bandages? The builder, we hear, swore he had never felt healthier in his life. When last Brother John saw him, he was quite hale and his skin, which was terribly pitted before, had healed quickly. So who will try this cure, he asks? Those who have attended this meeting, seven of our twelve, shout their approbation. But, says someone, are we not to know the method? What is this remedy which will seem to us so strange?

Brother John looks at us each in turn, as if gauging our readiness to hear what he has to impart.

"To be cured of the disease," he says at last, "it is required that the infected person has sexual congress with a virgin."

"Is that all?" someone cries. "Then let us begin."

There is laughter, a perceptible sense of relief.

Brother John holds up his hand and his face makes it clear that he will brook no further levity.

"Listen to me now," he says. "For this is important. You should know that this virgin will not be of an age with some of the young ladies with whom we have liaised already. It has been stressed to me that for the cure to be efficacious, this virgin must be a child."

Forty Nine

A little while before the case of the Crown versus Morris Malone comes on at the Old Bailey, at the sign of the dipped quill in Grub Street, Adam Brewer is counting his blessings and thanking the lucky stars that gave him the chance to do a good turn for a dwarf in a crowd. After his own business in Kent burned down, he had taken himself to London, where there was work aplenty, or so he was told, for a jobbing farrier and blacksmith. A pity they did not tell him where this work was hiding itself, he had thought, after six days in London and not a sign of it.

Sleeping where he could, Adam had spent his dwindling supply of money on food and his last penny on a loaf which surely contained more plaster of paris and sawdust than it did wheat. That Mouse and Mr Bone had hired him on the spot, without demanding references and had also supplied him with a place to sleep seemed to Adam nothing short of a miracle and he included them both in his prayers the next time he sank to his knees by his truckle bed, which was stored under the counter in the print shop.

Mr Mouse was as plain in his dealings as anyone Adam had known on Romney Marsh. Mr Bone, though he was a complicated one and would see-saw in his moods, was as kind as he could be. Adam was only too pleased to be able to repay the generosity of these two men by working all night with them to print up and bundle and then to distribute the extra copies of *The Enquirer*.

And then had come the troubles. First there was the people who had come to break up the place and smash the press, though they had failed to do that. Adam had cursed himself for not being at home when that had happened, but Mouse had done his best to reassure him that it was not his fault. "They know your habits," he said. "They know you like to go walking across the town or by the river in the mornings. No, they waited until they saw you go out. They would hardly have wanted to break in the door and find a fellow of your size waiting for them, would they, now?" But Adam was unconvinced, and the impression that he had failed his friends remained strong upon him.

Ah, but if only that had been the worst of it. He had been out turning his thoughts over on the day the really awful, terrible thing happened. The last thing Mr Bone had said to him before he went out was to take good care of himself. "Not everyone is as keen on this newspaper and what is inside it as we are, Adam," he had warned. The blacksmith had nodded. Mr Bone was making some money now and when he came to buy a horse, Adam would see it was properly shod for him. He took up the last bundle of newspapers and as he closed the door behind him, he heard Obadiah beginning to whistle a popular tune.

He watches Michel sorting out the letters that she will arrange in some special order which will make sense to the readers of this newspaper. There are others here, too, people who remember Mouse's kindnesses and protest his present predicament. There is Will Templeton, the clear-eyed boy with unruly raven curls from the print-shop across the way who has been helping him to assemble a second press in another room and is now folding pages of newspaper, there is the old man wearing small, blue-coloured eye-glasses who is checking and correcting what Miss Michel has written and now, there is another young fellow standing in the doorway, who is asking to see the editor about assisting with her campaign to free poor Mr Mouse.

To Adam, it might as well all be magic. People who can do all this must be terrible clever. Admittedly, they might be hard-put to shoe a nag or to work the bellows of a forge so that the coals glow like the floor of Hell, and Miss Michel for certain would not have the power to beat a bar of red-hot iron into shape, but the skills of such people are special and far superior. They have the power to make people think and change the way they see the world, so he has heard.

What was said in that paper before Mr Bone was killed and Mr Mouse was imprisoned he cannot imagine. For a moment he sees the room awash with blood, and more blood, red drying to brown on the whitewashed walls. He screws shut his eyes, blinks once and puts it all from his mind. He would prefer not to think of that most terrible scene again. Instead, he turns his mind to the job in hand.

"What is all this?" he says, running his fingers over the tray of upturned type. "What does it say today?"

"It says it is time to smoke our devils from hiding," the girl says. "I am telling our readers as much I dare about the men in the picture. I cannot name them, because if nothing worse, I will be sued and Mouse could lose his newspaper, which must flourish as a force for good. But there are clues in what I have written, sufficient for intelligent minds to supply the names themselves. These are the men who are sending Mouse to the gallows, Adam, and I want the world to know that."

"If you put all that in the paper they will come again, like they did for Mr Obadiah," Adam says and then he adds, quickly, "But we must be steadfast. I will do anything to save the man who saved me. And if they do come, I will break them like they tried to break the press. Only, I will be more successful, I reckon."

Fifty

In Hell's name he has done all that was asked of him and a damnable deal more but where is his rightful reward, where the gratitude to which he is most certainly entitled? Sir Ranalegh Clayton dabs a lacerated cheek with a bloody handkerchief before upending a generous measure of cognac and slamming down his glass upon the tavern table. Though his colourless eyes appear to follow the collier now furling its sails in the lea of the bridge, in fact he sees nothing but the faces of the ingrates who have brought him so low. The whelp De'Ath had promised him everything, elevation, riches and the security he had sought for so long. In return he, Sir Ranalegh, had fulfilled his commission, only to be repaid not with coin or ennoblement, but with a whipping in the stable yard.

Did you intend to damn us all, you pox-brained half-wit?

De'Ath had pushed him down the steps into the yard and erupted so violently it had made his ears ring.

You were to close down the paper, not butcher its editor with a sword!

Taking up a horsewhip, his tormentor had begun to beat him, spitting foul imprecations, accusing him of incompetence, of having jeopardised everything, of deserving to be hanged like a varlet and only desisting when the ruckus had brought ostlers and servants running from their quarters to see what was going on. His back ached and his face stung like he had been lapping honey from the hive but the deepest injury had been done to his pride.

Damn them all. As if the fault had been his! They had not warned him that the newspaper wallah might be so fatally stubborn. After the dolts he had sent had been unable to disable the press and the next edition had appeared on time, they had told him to take no more half-measures, that on no account must *The Enquirer* publish another word about whose faces had appeared in that infernal picture.

He had gone to see this Obadiah Bone, to make him see sense. He would reason, bribe and then threaten. With powerful elements of the British establishment at his back, he was confident of success. Bone would see he was beaten and go back to pamphleteering, or whatever he had done before he got this bit between his teeth. In the event, his encounter with the editor did not go at all as he had anticipated. He sees Bone before him, raven hair flying, raging eyes glinting, feels rough hands on his person, the wretched man smearing his fine clothes with black ink as he tries to manhandle his visitor towards the door.

He sees himself lashing out, a blow aimed at Bone's thin face misses its target. There is a flash and sudden, blinding pain as the man uses his head, splitting his lip and breaking his nose. He had not anticipated such strength and passion from this wiry fellow who ducks a punch and delivers a second blow which knocks the wind out of him. He summons all his strength and hurls the man against the chimney wall.

He does not remember snatching for the old sword which had hung upon the wall, recalls only that he had it now in his hand and that to prevent Bone backing away and perhaps escaping, he had used it. He meant to inflict no major wound, not at first anyway. A small lesion would be enough for Bone to understand how serious his visitor was. But when Bone had wrestled for the sword until it seemed he might have to relinquish it, he, Clayton, had no choice but to raise the thing and bring it down hard and fast, slicing into the man's upper arm and causing gouts of blood to fly. He heard the man cry out, but his startled eyes and contorted face only drove him on.

He remembers striking at him again, catching his other side, letting more blood and then the blade came down one more time. By now, he had removed himself from the scene. He was back among the Bermondsey bullies scrapping for pennies, he was in India dealing with the natives in the only language they understood. He chopped again through a red mist of arterial discharge, venting frustration and hatred, swinging away as if he might clear away a forest of ignominy and insult with just a few more bloody strokes.

He kept on chopping long after the lump of meat had fallen against and then into the chair by the chimney and had stopped its murmurs and bleats. It wasn't until he had chopped it all out of his system and he stood upon those inky boards fighting for breath and stricken like a man with the shaking palsy that he surveyed the scene and wondered if this was quite the best thing he might have done.

But though he had gone through very hell and had risked his life to accomplish his mission and that stupid man would print no more lies, his masters had not recompensed him for his zeal or his valour. Instead, they had treated him like a dog and turned him out. They would deny all connection with him, they said, and have him arrested should he approach them in future times.

He was aware of drifting freely, of having become disengaged from lifelines that had kept him afloat. His money had gone, his seat in Parliament lost. Ruin or worse awaited and there was nothing he could do about it. Becoming aware that other patrons of the tavern were regarding him strangely, he emptied the bottle and drained his glass before getting unsteadily to his feet and pushing his way through them towards the door, beyond which he could see the river swelling against the great stone piers of the bridge, beckoning him to step closer.

Fifty One

The Journal of Henry Grace

I could not have imagined how easy it is to fall in with a plan of evil intention. You dress the deed in its finest clothes; you believe those who would convince you that ends justify means and that it is all done in the service of that nebulous thing, the greater good. Brother John proposes and others second his proposal. What he forwards is couched in the language of reason and good sense. "Let us remind ourselves," he says, "that we have exhausted all the alternatives. We have tried every remedy there is to be tried and still this pernicious disease eats away at us all. Its progress is more nimble with some than others, but all will arrive some day at the same state of decrepitude and decay unless something is done and that very quickly. The country cannot and will not be guided and governed by monstrous freaks."

In a graver register he adds, "That said, it is of the utmost importance that all here fully appreciate the gravity of that which we think to undertake. We must understand the harm we will do to innocents and also, the risks and the consequences to ourselves and our reputations if we are found out. We must decide what is our duty. For myself, I say the new way must be tried. We must put aside our qualms and our quibbles. We are all good men at heart, I hope. But needs must when the devil drives and he is upon the box at this very moment, lashing on his horses. Gentlemen, I say we would be failing ourselves and the country if we leave this avenue unexplored."

Brother Luke explains that the subjects will be treated with all due care, and that he will be on hand in his calling as a physician. A vote is taken. We all drop our coloured balls into a wooden box, green for a vote in favour, red for a vote against. The votes are counted and we find that despite two brothers loudly professing that they could not in all conscience support such a thing, when it comes to a secret vote, everyone is found to be in favour.

Following the vote, there is among most brothers a palpable sense of relief that our course in this matter is at least decided. Now attention turns to the mechanics of such a course. It is asked where we might find the participants. The terms virgin and child are avoided now by all. The obvious place to look, it is suggested, is among the anonymous masses of London's poor, where the spoiling of a child must surely mean less than elsewhere. Alsatia, Seven Dials, St Giles and Southwark are suggested as likely hunting grounds.

Brother Matthew, whose reputation has been made through his experiments in medical science, protests this most vehemently. The squalid tenements of Jacob's Island in Bermondsey and suchlike places are the breeding places of disease, he says. Nothing is likelier than we will exacerbate rather than relieve our symptoms by fishing there. And obtaining an actual cure from the sort of people who exist in these places would be nothing shy of a miracle.

No, he says, we must look elsewhere and poach from a safer place and that will mean looking one or two rungs up the social ladder. A participant from, let us say, the household of a schoolteacher or a piano tuner would be much less likely to have been exposed to disease and its parents will not be sufficiently connected to cause us problems. One among us says that he knows someone with nightly access to the wards of the Foundling Hospital and perhaps we might find what we require there? This is considered and finally agreed and as always, Osiris takes it upon himself to supply the needs of the club.

I do not intend to say more than is necessary about what we did. I estimate the ages of our first victims as between nine and thirteen years. No-one asks where they have been taken from or whether they are from halfway respectable families and unlikely to harbour disease. The state of their clothing supplies all we need to know. Nor does anyone enquire their names. They are things to be used and as such, best not to be looked at in the same way as another human being.

I do not know what they have been told by Osiris De'Ath but some tale has no doubt been spun: they have not seemed alarmed to be taken into a cavern where the light of countless candles is magnified by many mirrors. Has an adventure been promised? Baubles, toys or trinkets? I don't know, but unlike some of the girls who will follow, these sacrificial lambs do not arrive in a half-drugged state.

I cannot say that I have reconciled myself to what we are gathered here to do. I have battled with my conscience. In my heart I know that it is not right and that it is certainly not good. But this dreadful disease eats away a little more of me and my scruples every day. If something is not done soon, I will have lost my looks and be put on the road to decrepitude and vileness. And as a full member of The Albion Club I am sworn to support my brothers in all they do. I am obliged to believe what they say, that the good ship England may suffer if men such as we are not fit to take its helm.

And so I remain silent as the first girl, who has now realised that something is terribly amiss, is led to the table where hooded men await. One of my brothers recites a cod liturgy, which adds some specious legitimacy to the proceedings. We are encouraged to sing, as we do at meetings less pregnant with import. The singing falters and only resumes when the girl begins to scream as she is lifted upon the table and her garments removed. Our band of brothers sings louder now, to smother her screams, and louder still when she is entered for the first time.

And so it goes on with other innocents. There are those who clearly do not think as I do and take their turns with an enthusiasm which does them no credit. They laugh beforehand and they laugh afterwards and clearly give no thought to the harm they are doing. They act with impunity, certain that their deeds will not become known to anyone beyond our secret circle and that they will never be called to account for them. Their callousness towards the girls enrages me.

I tell myself that one day I will find a way to unmask them to the world. Perhaps I will unmask myself, too, for I am no less guilty. We participate in turn, in order that each has the chance to take a maidenhood and perhaps with it, a cure. When my turn comes, I close my eyes and pray that good may come of this evil, that I will be cured and that England will remain stable in troubled times.

I lie to myself. The cure is surely an old wives' tale, no more likely to be efficacious than any of the other so-called remedies which have failed us. England will survive without the help of any of these self-important men who stand around this table. And the girls? These we have defiled are girls with half an education, the daughters of skilled artisans and tradesmen, some of whom can speak well and describe what has happened and for whom three sovereigns will never be enough to recompense them for the loss of their maidenhoods and their reputations.

Whatever I try to tell myself, I know that the best that awaits any of our victims is a life of prostitution. I still see their terrified faces and when I do, I close my eyes tightly as I did when I played my own part in these terrible episodes. I think of what I did to Francesca and what I have done to those girls and I wonder if ever there was a guiltier man?

Fifty Two

He stands noosed and blindfolded, flashing blind panic. The cart jolts and moves off. His legs scrape briefly on the boards, pulling him in one direction while the noose around his neck drags him in another. His toes kiss the lip of the last board – and then he drops, heavily, like a sack of flour through a warehouse trap, into a pit of pain. His neck and shoulders take the sudden brunt of the impact as his weight stretches the rope and he bounces upon its end, the noose slipping tight at the same time. He kicks crazily, feet vainly searching for some solid purchase which will relieve the deadly stress upon his throat. He fights for breath, but the noose is too tight and the more he struggles, the tighter it becomes. The need to find a breath becomes a thousand times more urgent. He is a great drum beaten, he is his own name cried, he is a fizzing keg of gunpowder. Consciousness clings as long as it can and it is agonising moments before the keg explodes and brilliant stars burst and flash all around him. And then. Warm, welcoming waves of peace wash over him, white light envelops all and he knows no more….

…until the peace is shattered by a raucous squabble of wildly discordant voices. There is something hard and cold beneath his back; human hands are exploring his body as a river of pure pain surges through every vein and fills every capillary. For however long, he is pain made flesh and can think of nothing but this agony. Then at last he swims up through a soup of jumbled emotions, spiralling images and long-forgotten memories. There are hands on his bare chest and fingers upon his throat. Anatomists! is his first thought. His body was to be dissected at Surgeons Hall following his execution and it seems he has survived the gallows only to expire under the surgeon's knife. The lancing spears of pain tell him they are already starting to cut and probe and flay his skin. He tries desperately to speak, to tell them that he is ...

"Alive!" someone cries.

"Only barely," says someone else. "He won't live long…"

"I'm a physician. Let me see him."

"Malone! Morris Malone!" he hears.

"Stand away, all of you. Let him breathe. Throw open that casement and move these people back."

"Innkeeper, your brandy," commands another voice.

Each new breath is drawn at the expense of another internal torment. If the departure of the soul is painful, then its restoration is doubly so. He can feel the blood pulsing through him, a breached dam which expands his arteries, returning spiky new life and shooting sharp pains behind his eyes, under his ears, around his shoulders, up and down his back and into his groin. His thighs and calves don't escape and his toes, curiously cold a moment ago, now burn like hot embers. There are moments in all of this when he would happily die if only the pain were to die with him.

He gags and chokes. Someone has administered brandy. He is unable to swallow and the fiery liquid courses down into his lungs, provoking a fit of violent coughing which racks his whole frame with new suffering. But some respite follows: he is allowed to lie unmolested, but still racked with pain, for some minutes, while the physician consults a book. Slowly, much too slowly, the worst of the pain ebbs away. He can feel organs beginning to function again. He can breathe, but his attempts to ask where he is – this seems not to be an anatomist's surgery – results only in a grating noise that brings forth looks of incomprehension from the motley assemblage around him and tortures his throat.

"How long did he hang?"

"No time at all. They had him down before he had swung thrice."

This cannot be true. He cannot have suffered such intense pain and terror for a period measured in seconds.

"He is a lucky man. I've seen felons dead before the cart has stopped."

"Aye, and I've seen others struggle half an hour before they gave up."

"Thank God he had no friends. No one to weight his legs."

"Aye, the Lord save us from friends."

"This man had friends," a voice says. "He had many friends, we saw them all out there."

"That's true," says someone else, "Everyone who shouted the name of Morris Malone was his friend."

"Aye, well, you may have the point there."

"I never heard such a hullabaloo got up for just one."

"'*Morris Malone, you are not alone*,' they were shouting, every man-jack of them."

"Such a mob was raising in his favour as threatened the whole proceedings."

"The soldiers tried to restore order but the crowd was too strong."

He emits an interrogatory croak.

"Your reprieve arrived while you was still on the cart. But could they get to the hangman and tell him that in time? With that crowd? Of course they could not. And so you swung. Howsoever, they managed to cut you down in good time and that's what counts. A lucky thing you are not heavier."

"How…?" He does not recognise his own voice.

"The newspapers. The readers. I say they are the ones who saved you."

"Them and all the people of London out there."

He opens his eyes wider and sees a crazy dance of faces, rubicund drunks, a soldier on crutches, bewigged officials of some kind, a toothless old woman and a gaggle of curious and excitable young girls, all anxious, no doubt, to say they saw the man who survived his hanging. From beyond the window of the inn, the grim business of the day proceeds without him. He can clearly hear the Tyburn crowd, the voice of London, with its caustic, witty catcalls and damning boos, its wild laughter and its boisterous applause. His head is throbbing and the brandy which he can now swallow is taking its effect. He experiences euphoria, gratitude, bewilderment and also a lingering fear as he slides slowly into a deep sleep which is troubled by the most terrible of nightmares.

When he wakes he is no longer at the inn to which he was removed immediately after his near-execution. He can breathe without obstruction and his heart beats at somewhere near its usual rate. He understands that by some fantastical miracle he is in his home. His condition tells him this was no ghastly dream, though. He has an unreasonable fear that this may all be a cruel chimera of some sort, and he may find the door locked from without and discover he is in some well-appointed room at –

Newgate! He cries cry aloud, or thinks that that he does.

"I thought you might never awaken."

He tries to turn in his bed, but cannot.

"There is no need to say anything now. Time for talk when you are well."

He wants to ask so many things but the words will not form, seeming instead to stick to the roof of his mouth.

"*You do remember me, I hope? Your friend Adam carried you here, all the way from Tyburn. He is quite the Hercul*es."

He looks at Michel Angelo and at Adam Brewer who stand either side of his familiar bed.

"Do not fret yourself. We will take care of you," the girl says. "I hope you will not mind too much but I have been obliged to sleep in your friend's bedchamber."

"He is trying to ask questions," Adam says, "but he cannot."

"How was your life saved? Is that it?" Michel says. "You can thank the power of the press."

Mouse tries but fails to sit up, hungry to know more.

"I will tell you all," Michel says, "but this must wait until you are healed in mind and body. But now you must sleep."

Fifty Three

A while before this scene was enacted on Grub Street, in the cold, high-ceilinged drawing room of a great country house built upon a hill to the West of London, a well-groomed man who might still be called young despite the flecks of silver in his black hair had stood before a tall window and surveyed his kingdom. Beyond the polished glass, the greensward swept gracefully away, the vista leading the eye over ha-ha and water towards a distant hill where it passed through copses of trees to arrive at a cylindrical stone column on the skyline. The placid, bowed lake and curious little buildings combined to offer the impression that this was a perfect English landscape, albeit one with Greek and Roman statuary and other touches which could only have been provided by a gentleman of taste and fashion who has been abroad. It was the creation of someone who knew what to include and what to leave out, if the gardens were to approximate the idyll of a landscape by Poussin or Claude-Lorraine.

The man sipped from a cup of chocolate as he watched workers on the hillside, planting more trees. He smiled complaisantly as he surveyed all that was his. He looked across the grounds to where the tree-line hid the bluffs which descended to a small grassy knoll and one of two entrances to a labyrinthine system of caves. Lines furrowed his brow as his thoughts drifted back to another time. The grand scheme which started off all those years ago in such a promising fashion has been returning to trouble him.

In the beginning, the coming of the disease seemed pregnant with possibility. Until then he had been a general factotum, a liberally-paid one, but a factotum all the same. Taking this position has suited his wider aims. It provided money for his expensive way of living – especially useful after Henry Grace began to pauper himself through indolence, illness and poor work – but more importantly, it afforded him access to position and power. As time went on, the members of the club relied upon Osiris De'Ath to organise more and more of their lives and entertainments and like Henry Grace, they hardly noticed the power they were devolving to him.

After the infection became general it fell to him, as circus-master, to arrange the so-called healing sessions. He loudly advised against this course, saying to each that he performed this service very much against his own will and only as a favour to those he esteemed so highly. And they were grateful for it; these occasions offering the chance of a cure for the desperate and, he knew, a keener depravity for others. They did not much care how he sourced the young girls or what would happen to them after they were done with them. They thanked God they had found someone to deal with all of that. But, he recalled with a smile, how they came to regret allowing Osiris De'Ath such close admittance to their affairs!

One by one, he had taken them aside and had given them to understand what a very deplorable and dangerous thing they had done. The children they had asked him to find were not ragamuffins who might have disappeared without notice, he reminded them. Their parents may not have had rank but they were still capable of making an almighty noise if their children disappeared, or turned up alive in an unexplained state of disorder. You will hear from some of them yet, he warned.

Henry Grace had not needed to be reminded of any of this. Such is his tendency towards guilt anyway, that Osiris only had to make the vaguest allusion to Francesca and what happened to her in Venice, for Grace to produce money he protested he did not possess. Anything to have Osiris and his poisoned memories gone from the house. But other listeners trembled as he described the terrible fate which may lie in store for them.

Some of the men he talked with privately protested a degree of innocence. Yes, of course they had taken this cure, which was bound to be controversial, but these were singular circumstances, he must see that, they said. They swore they had nothing to do with the sort of thing that some newspapers seemed to take a delight in describing so graphically. The girls who were left bawling and shaking upon the table in the cave were distressed and bloody, there was no denying it, but that was nothing which would not heal in a few days, surely?

Osiris listened until they had no more to say. *Now*, he said to each and every member of the Albion Club, now, *you listen to me*. You have gone too far. The mark has been overstepped. People will not understand and they will not forgive. It would be most unfortunate if your name were to be in any way connected with these dreadful crimes (because let there be no mistake about this, that is what they undoubtedly are). And, of course, it would be catastrophic, perhaps even deadly, if you were to be accused of being complicit in any of this.

"But who would inform on us?" bleated the ones with small experience of the wider world. You never can tell, Osiris said to these. But in groups of this size, word has a way of getting out. It always will, sooner or later. What can we do to prevent this, they said. Nothing, Osiris replied, you can do nothing. I, on the other hand, can do everything. It will be costly, but settle with me now and I can guarantee your security. To others he was more blunt. They saw the game immediately and paid handsomely, wishing at the same time that they had never set eyes on this parvenu from a dubious family. Money was soon filling Osiris's coffers. But this was not the extent of his ambition. With veiled threats, and by dividing those who combined against him, he brought to heel Brothers Mathew, Luke and John and all the other disciples. Influence had flown into Osiris's cupped hands just as surely as the cash, the promissory notes and the deeds to property arrived in wax-sealed bundles at his bank.

Sometimes he squandered this influence on his own entertainment. Osiris was welcomed in green rooms and was seen on the town with leading ladies and one or two of the stage's better-looking men. But usually he spent his influence with more consideration and tangible result. There had been one or two troublesome bills progressing through Parliament, one which could impinge upon his right as landowner to certain tithes and another which threatened to curtail his running of foxhounds through nearby villages. It took only a few carefully-chosen words in the right ears to see both bills thrown out. What power he had then, Osiris reflects, when they all lived in fear that the disease might kill them at any time and could not know how slow its progress would be or how long they would have to suffer from its debilitating effects, both physical and social.

Osiris had occasion to test his power when he was in London, where he spoke with effect to the elderly Sir Geffrye Quicke and told him of a case coming on at the Old Bailey in which he took an interest. Sir Geffrye must preside, Osiris said. It would never do for this dwarf to be transported. He would know too much about that damned painting of Grace's. His conviction would prevent anyone mistakenly connecting us with the death of that troublesome newspaperman. He must hang, if the safety of the club and its members is to be preserved.

Hanging the dwarf, Osiris thought, would be the last of the leaks plugged. He had come back from London with the complacency of an artisan who had completed a job of work to his satisfaction. He would, until it fatigued him once again, resume the life of the country squire and set his mind to work on further improvements to a landscape that had remained little changed since God had created it. And then had come the news. The dwarf, against all possibilities, lived. For a short while he entertained hopes that a lesson had been learned and that the cursed organ would print no more of its febrile nonsense. And then Towse had entered bearing a silver platter on which lay a copy of *The Enquirer*.

Fifty Four

And so, only hours after his ordeal and against every single hope or calculation, the condemned man finds himself not only alive but beyond the dreadful walls of Newgate prison. Tormented by the darkest thoughts, he remains in bed for several more days, attended sometimes by an old, yet capable physician but more usually by Adam or by Michel. Despite his lingering pain, Mouse quickly becomes restless with his confinement and frantically desirous of doing something towards finding answers to questions that must be resolved before he can begin to think about how he is to go on, now that his world has been turned upside down.

On a day when he appears fit enough for converse, Michel sits on the chair at his bedside and tells him that she has been thinking about the fire in Leicester Fields.

"As have I," he says, slowly, hearing the rasp of his own voice. He takes a sip from a beaker of water before saying more.

"You think it was set?"

"I do. And I think whoever did that meant to destroy not only the painting but those who knew its secrets and retailed them to the public. These men will not be done with me. They will know you assisted in its completion and may see you as a threat, too. We must be on our guard."

"We cannot live like that, always afraid of who might be watching us?"

"I do not intend that we do, Michel," he croaks, "But this business will be over only when those who harmed these girls and butchered Obadiah are justly served."

"But how in the Lord's name can we possibly achieve that?"

Michel is surprised that Mouse seems unafraid and quite undaunted by what lies ahead. The miserable death of his great friend and his knocks in Newgate Prison appear to have chipped off soft edges and stiffened his resolve.

"The picture may be destroyed but *The Enquirer* lives on and we will give chase harder than before, you may put your trust in that," he manages to say. "This newspaper has built the most intricate spider's web of valuable contacts all over this great city and I promise you, we will make use of them all. We will smoke them out."

Speaking this much has tired him and he sinks back into his pillow, where it is not long before his eyelids droop and drop.

Michel and Adam sit vigils at his bedside and rouse him gently when he is tormented by spectral visions of Tyburn. Nightly, he tells them, he stands haltered and hopeless before a surging, baying crowd and it is with the sweetest relief that he awakes to find himself delivered from all that, safe in his own soft bed beneath his own patched roof. Hourly, it seems, he is brought cups of hot tea or warm broth, which he can swallow with more ease than the dishes of beef and potatoes which he craves.

From Michel he learns something of what has been occurring since he was confined behind Newgate's walls. She tells him all about the campaign that has been waged on his behalf and of how the case for Morris Malone was made. With some little pride, she shows him the following, which is from Mouse's own newspaper:

Will you honest Londoners suffer this helpless innocent to be made a scapegoat by the very people who keep you down, enclose your land and send agricultural workers streaming into the capital to steal your work? You will not? Then sign the petition. Those of you who can read, tell those who cannot to make their mark. Your champion, Morris Malone, depends on it. London depends on it!

"We printed handbills trumpeting your innocence and damning the law's injustice," she tells him, "Others on the street did the same."

"With what result, I wonder?"

"We struck a chord. The word was spread by people of every station, from men in coffeeshops to porters in fish markets, I hear"

"And the petition?" Mouse asks.

"You would not credit the response it provoked. It became quite the thing to sign it and everyone did. And then one wet morning Adam and I walked to Westminster with the thing kept dry under Adam's coat and we gave it to a footman who said he would present it to the Home Secretary."

"And so I owe my life and my freedom to the signatures on that petition?" he says, when finally his throat allows him to swallow meat and to speak like a human being. Michel permits herself a little chuckle.

"Well, no. It was not that which saved you. And to be honest, I doubted that raising such a petition would do more than fire up the people in your favour. But it had to be tested. In my opinion, the Home Secretary did not even look at it. I think the petition would have remained in whichever deep drawer it was consigned to, had not the hullabaloo of public opinion made itself heard beyond his windows. Just then, you could smell the unrest that was in the air, and of course, there is nothing this government fears more. Stability is everything for them, with that madman Gordon and his riots still fresh in the memory. In the end, the Home Secretary was encouraged to review his decision and grant a last-minute reprieve."

"I wish news had reached the hangman in that last minute," he says and tries a smile.

"I am sorry it did not," Michel says. "Early on the morning of your hanging, Adam and I were with a huge body of like-minded souls who stood nightly outside the Home Secretary's residence, calling for your reprieve. When that reprieve was at last granted, we took a conveyance and followed the Sheriff's men all the way to Tyburn but there were delays all along the way, families intent on securing good vantage, workmen mending drains, whatever an ill-tempered fate could place in our way, she placed in our way. To be quite honest, I feared that you would already be cold by the time we reached the gallows."

"Then why am I alive?"

"By then, the Tyburn mob had taken matters into its own hands. It was a quite extraordinary scene. You could hear them chanting *Morris, Morris, Morris Malone!* from one end of Oxford Street to the other. I suppose you were too distressed to make sense of this?"

He nods, no doubt recalling the great noise, hearing his own name but dismissing it as an hallucination borne of his terror.

"The hangman saw what was afoot and decided to turn you off as soon as he could. He had yet to hear of your reprieve. But no sooner had he done this than the angry crowd, which was already breaking cordons and pressing down upon the gallows, set up such a terrible roar that the officer in charge of the soldiers drew his sword and cut you down."

"All I recall is that my first breath was knocked out of me as the ground met my face." He stops, he has talked too much. Then adds with some effort, " I doubt I can ever sufficiently thank you, Miss Angelo."

"Your speedy recovery will be thanks enough," Michel says quickly.

He nods, half-way to sleep already.

Taking her candle, Michel slips out of the little room, closing the door softly behind her.

Fifty Five

Where medieval miners delved in search of mythical gold, there is a chamber where Osiris now walks on wet flags between long lines of racked barrels. The cave is long and high and the number of barrels must run into the hundreds. Finding the one he wants, he uses a mallet to deftly drive in a tap. Dusting a small glass with his handkerchief, he fills it half-full. The Cognac is warm upon his palette and releases a fiery finish as it slides down his throat. Undoubtedly, this is the finest French brandy he has yet acquired and it will fetch the best price too. In normal circumstances, beating the revenue men and making a goodly profit would have afforded him a deal of satisfaction. The business of smuggling is much like gambling and the stakes could not be higher – although such illicit goings-on are more easily facilitated when the authority in charge of putting them down is yourself.

Now, though, he takes a seat on one of the benches he uses when he entertains prospective buyers of tax-free liquor and allows himself a rare sigh. Was it only weeks ago that he was living the life he had long desired and to which he felt justly entitled? If there was then a cloud in his sky, it was only the realisation that he had no-one with whom to share his pleasure and to applaud his success. Osiris has never married; he could not give away so much of himself. Until recently, he never had reason to doubt his course. Could it be, he has surprised himself by thinking, that he is possessed of more sensibility than he thought? But the lack of a companion is not something which lies heavy upon his mind. With a fine house, admired grounds and a healthy bank balance, he calculates that he must, in fact, be very happy.

And then had come the letter, unsigned and plain-sealed, but unmistakably penned by Edward Villiers, prime minister-in-waiting, but once a pillar of the Albion club. The letter which was to change everything.

My dear Cyrus, Villiers had written. *There was a time, as well you know, when our little games went unremarked. How could we have foreseen that what we did would return to haunt us? You yourself will have perceived the injustice. Need I reiterate that these acts were not wrong, not when they are seen in the proper, larger context? We acted in the best of faith and we acted for England. I was as keen to participate as any – I could not know then that though the disease would take its dreadful course with so many of our number, it would spare me as it has spared my good friend, G. At that time we were all in this together and not one of us thought we would escape its ravages. Oh, for the gift of foresight! Armed with such precognition I would never have risked my name, most certainly not if I had known the prize which lay in store for me. As you will readily appreciate, in my present position, I can never be associated with the least part of this business. You may imagine what the Opposition would make of it and these infernal newspapers, too. This brings me to my point.*

Without becoming too specific, Villiers had told him what action needed to be taken to remedy the situation and so avert disaster. Specifically, he had told Osiris what would happen should he fail to act effectively.

If this painting is shown in public, then that may be the end for me and very possibly, for the government too. It will be the end for you, do not doubt that for a moment. How galling it would be to see everything you have worked for burn to ashes, your reputation blasted, your financial affairs investigated and your games with the revenue exposed. However, just as you always found a solution for whatever problem confronted us then, so we surviving Albions have the utmost confidence in your powers to find a neat solution now.

Osiris puts down his glass and takes a candle to light his way through damp tunnels and then up the narrow, winding stairs which eventually deliver him into the cellar beneath Mylnehurst Abbey. From there he walks quickly down cold passages, his polished shoes resounding on uncovered floors. He opens a door in a wall of books to enter his library, where he pulls on a silken rope. "Towse," he says, as a sharp face appears around another door. "We will require more of that last consignment. Thirty six casks, if you can arrange it."

Towse nods and closes the door. Watched by a youthful Antigone in a long, gold frame, Osiris takes up his accustomed position by the tall window and uses his sleeve to wipe away condensation, the better to survey his kingdom. What could be done about that matter had been done. It had not been done as he envisaged, nor at all as he liked, but it had been done; the painting and the newspaperman are no more.

His cares should have gone with them, but they have not. Like the many-headed hydra, this accursed newspaper goes on, continuing to print its poisonous nonsense, pointing fingers at men who should be above all suspicion. Villiers, he has heard, is furious. He too is raging. Which factions of this teetering administration allowed the dwarf to live? A pardon, indeed! Formidable forces beyond his influence seem to be aligning themselves against him as friends and allies drop away. If the truth comes out, Villiers will not hesitate to offer him up as the scapegoat, he knows that. It is maddening, intolerable, unnerving. For a moment he considers throwing in his cards and fleeing to France, where his mother is no longer with her count but is living in surprising comfort at an address in the Paris suburbs, where there will always be a place for him and his brother, she writes. But Osiris does not see himself living in France, not while a certain ripe chance remains for him in England, once his present obstacles are finally overcome.

Fifty Six

Slowly, I see his wounds mend. The terrible dreams which wracked his sleep come less frequently, he says. He looks much improved too and the once-livid marking around his neck has at last faded. When he can converse without constraint, he talks of Obadiah, of good times and bad, of his finer qualities and those that would test him to distraction. As his strength returns Mouse asks about how my investigation of Obadiah's murder is progressing, what new things have I uncovered and have I been able to identify more faces that were painted into Henry Grace's picture? He returns to this over and over again, certain he says, that the key to it all lies in that infernal image. He cannot hide his disappointment at the small progress I make. I want to tell him that I have been busy running his newspaper and looking after him but I am dreadfully aware that it is his own painful memories which cause him to become so fractious.

Quite soon he is able to quit his bed and now he spends much of his day in town, in his old way, making enquiries. Of course, these enquiries no longer concern which servants of the government have set the country's needs secondary to their own, or which members of the bon-ton have been behaving disgracefully (such *City Gossip* fodder is now supplied by Mouse's protege, Will Templeton) but about puzzles of weightier import whose resolution means the earth and everything upon it to my grieving friend. This morning, though, he has spent here, buried among the papers that pile up and spread across the table at which Obadiah wrote his poetry.

"You know of Sir Geffrye Quicke?" he asks me.

"Was he not your judge?"

Mouse shudders, doubtless seeing again the man's eyes peering out from under a square of black felt. Recalling himself, he says, "Sir Geffrye is not seen abroad these days. He is rarely in court. In your case he appears to have gone out of his way to preside. He retired early because, it seems, his health was failing. But before he retired he had been a very active member of the bar and a somewhat draconian judge. Death is mandatory in so many cases, of course, but even where there has been some arbitrary leeway, Sir Geffrye never shied from keeping the hangman employed."

"You are saying that your fate was sealed before you entered the court?"

"I am sure of it. Whoever persuaded Sir Geffrye to preside could count on a capital sentence."

"But not upon the verdict?" I say. "The jury might have gone the other way."

"Public sympathy may have been with me but the evidence was not. If anyone was ever caught red handed..."

"So Quicke has powerful friends."

"I know it," Mouse says. "I have been looking into his history, a disappointing labour at first as I could find nothing in his professional life to arrest the interest."

"But?"

"So I turned my attention to his private life and I think I have found something."

"Well?"

"It is just this. Quicke was often seen in the company of the present Chancellor of the Exchequer, Edward Villiers and the new First Secretary to the Admiralty, Lord Godolphin, at entertainments organised by that old rake Lord Albemarle. You may possibly have heard of him. His routs and masquerades at Mylnehurst Abbey and the caverns beneath it were still talked about long after he decamped to France."

"Is this connection important?"

"It certainly is interesting."

"Why?"

"Because the likenesses of all three of these gentlemen were discernible in *The New Fire of London*. As its artist, I do think you might have noticed that."

"I painted my share of that picture, but it was Grace who painted the New Citizens," I say, using Mouse's own appellation for the little figures.

"I know he did. I apologise. But do you not think that strange? Or is it only an odd coincidence?"

"I put no faith in coincidence," I say.

“No more do I. And so I looked further.”

He hands me a scrap of paper.

“This is a list of people I have identified in the painting, together with a few names who might also be depicted. I could not be certain of these faces because the smaller ones are not so sharply defined on the print.”

“You looked for something connecting them all?”

“I did. I considered this matter from every angle and was near to giving it all up when at last I came across something I found telling.”

“Which is?”

“I discovered that it wasn't only Quicke, Villiers and Godolphin who were well acquainted with one another. I visited an old friend of mine, Narcissus Pyke, an archivist who has collected journals and news-sheets these thirty years. He was very happy to see his industry put to good use. Together, we trawled through his papers and one by one, we came across the names of almost all the people on this list. The telling thing is that these names are very often mentioned in conjunction with one another.”

“What of it?” I ask.

“Do you not see?” he asks, surprised at my slowness. “I am convinced that there exists some curious spider's web which connects them all.”

I look down the list of mostly recognisable names. “But these are Ministers of His Majesty's government, merchants, physicians, painters, poets and actors, men separated by the cordons of breeding and vocation,” I say. “What could possibly bring them together?”

Mouse jumps down from my bed and replaces the wig which had

slipped off during his cogitations.

"I was thinking that a coffee-house might do that," he says, "Or, more likely, some sort of a club."

"What sort of a club?" I say, doubtfully.

"A secretive one," Mouse says.

"Everything points to some sort of association," I agree, "But where would such a club convene if it wanted to remain secret?"

"I have been giving some thought to exactly that," Mouse says and then turns his attention to another sheaf of papers.

I repay Mouse's great kindnesses to me by making myself as useful as I can. I clean and I sweep, cook fowls over the fire and stir pottage on the trivet, producing meals which are at least more palatable than anything Mrs Harris ever prepared. I scrub once more the floorboards where Mouse shed tears as he dipped his mop in his friend's spilt blood. I proof-read galleys and correct errors on the press, so that Adam I and I can produce newspapers while Mouse goes out to ferret news. He is sometimes accompanied by young Will Templeton, who Mouse says has the makings of an able journalist.

Yesterday, they made a discovery while engaged in examining the doings and associations of Lord Albermarle. It seems that the caves under the abbey at Mylnehurst are decorated in precisely the manner described by Mr Grace in his journal. I am confounded that Mouse is not already making plans to visit this place directly. No-one paints such hellish devices to preside over innocent pastimes.

But Mouse says that once again, I am being needlessly impetuous, we must not rush these things, we must accumulate evidence and visit this vipers' nest only when we are in possession of official permissions.

Besides, he thinks our foes may have become complacent now that the picture is no more. "They know we cannot name and charge them in print without incontrovertible evidence," he says, "So let us not be hasty, everything must be in its proper place before we take further action."

Though I love him dearly, there are times when Mouse Malone sorely tests my forbearance. Surely he must know better than anyone that we seek the verminous creatures who not only preyed on children, butchered his dearest friend and had his own self hanged at Tyburn? But he will listen to none of this, talking instead about the need for patience and being sure of our every step. As I lie atop my coverlet this night, I make a decision. If Mouse is not yet ready to act, then I must.

Fifty Seven

A light rain dries up and afternoon sun emerges from cloud as I pass through the gates of Mylnehurst Abbey, unchallenged by the gatekeeper, whose window frames him dozing by his fire. No-one questions a servant girl bearing a message or running an errand. Early this morning, I slipped unnoticed from the house in Grub Street and made my way to the coach office with a borrowed half-crown in my pocket. I travel alone – if Mouse knew what I was about he would doubtless try to stop me or if he failed in that, at least insist on coming with me. But if I am to discover anything of value it will be alone and by stealth.

And so I have arrived at this remote house set on the brow of a hill above the Great West Road with no other friend than Mouse's voice in my head which tells me I have not planned wisely. My long journey has given me more than enough time to imagine every kind of evil men might commit out of sight and underground and it has taken no great leap of the imagination to see abducted children taken there and most foully abused. Somewhere under these hills I hope to find answers to questions and with good fortune, the evidence we need to see justice done.

The great house I saw from the road is more distant than I imagined, appearing and disappearing among the elms and evergreens as I wend my way up the gently curving driveway. I choose a path leading into the woods which may provide a quicker route. All becomes dark, the canopy of autumn leaves producing an ambience uncanny at this time of day. I can no longer see the house, only the path on whose gravel I break the silence with the crunching of my footsteps. For a London girl, such quiet is unsettling.

Frequently, I peer over my shoulder, assuring myself that no-one follows. I am a trespasser here and having strayed from the drive, may be taken for a poacher or worse. I look about continually, searching for an entry to the caves which are said to underlie this place and as I do so, other surprising vistas slowly reveal themselves even in this untimely, crepuscular light. An avenue of horse-chestnuts draws my attention to a distant obelisk, another to the white statue of a naked man crowned with a wreath of laurel.

There is a tantalising familiarity about this place – it is as if I have been here before, not once, but many times. And then I recognise small buildings in the landscape as the temples in some of Mr Grace's bread-and-butter landscape paintings. I begin to feel more hopeful about my expedition. I peer into a coach-house and investigate an ice-house, without success. The house itself, I now see, is settled upon a high promontory above a placid lake whose narrow waist is spanned by a yellow stone bridge. I can see no-one at the windows, which are now flashing gold in the setting sun.

I circumnavigate the entire building, looking for anything that might conceal an entrance to the caverns below and wondering now if perhaps these are accessed from within the edifice itself? The cellars would seem a likely place to look for a door. Now, the difficulty of the mission I have set myself becomes apparent. I approach the building warily, expecting any moment to hear shouting or to see men and dogs bearing down on me. I am allowed to reach the sandstone walls of the house. None of the tall windows is open. I try the handles of the doors on the parterre. Shading my eyes, I peer through the glass, but can see no-one within. Apart from some workmen who are planting saplings on a distant hillside, the estate seems deserted. Heartened by this, I walk around the side of the house and into the stable yard.

There I stop dead. A stout laundress is lumbering across the yard with a great basket of bedlinen, muttering to herself as she disappears into what must be the wash-house. She doesn't see the strange girl who peeps around the door she has left ajar. I slip quietly inside the house and creep along a dark and narrow passage where greatcoats and stable jackets crowd on pegs and enter an empty kitchen, much larger than the one at Leicester Fields.

On the table, amid the detritus of a finished meal, is a half-eaten game pie, a wedge of yellow cheese and the end of a loaf. Impelled by my suspicions, I had left London quite precipitately without a mouthful to eat. Suddenly aware of my hunger, I seize the cheese and scoop up a mouthful of the pie, dispatching it as quickly as I can. My ears strain to hear the sounds of people in the house. The door latch loudly rattles and I hear the muttering of the laundress. "Who closed that door?" I hear. "I'll swear it wasn't I." Snatching up the slice of pie I have just now cut, I flee from the room, knocking a cup and a saucer from a sideboard, which skitters across the surface and smashes noisily on the flagged floor.

"What's that? Who's there?"

I hurry down a passage and through an opened door and find myself in a great room, grander than anything I have ever seen. The walls are lined with great cases in which are more books than I knew the world held. I see a huge woven hanging and furniture fit for a king. I quicken my pace. I hear the laundress, breathless in pursuit but still demanding to know who is here and threatening to loose the dogs. Finding myself in a splendid hall with a staircase as wide as a Stepney dwelling I fly up these stairs, the words of the laundress ringing in my ears. "He's had the pie," she cries.

I pick up my skirts and flee quickly down a panelled passageway decorated with gold-framed pictures, hung at equal distances. I am aware of a landscape which surely is the twin of a picture which hangs in the hall at Leicester Fields, but I have no time to consider that now. I can hear firmer, louder footsteps on the boards outside and men's voices. I try a door and enter a bedroom furnished with an enormous oak-posted bed. There is a dressing room beyond. Slipping into the dressing room, I hide behind a cushioned chair draped with fine clothes and hold my breath.

I hear approaching footsteps and expect discovery at any moment. Still I hold my breath, thinking my lungs will burst at any moment. But then I hear something being opened, a tin perhaps, followed by a sneeze stifled as someone takes snuff. A floorboard creaks, there is some muttering I cannot quite hear and then the footsteps recede. Slowly releasing my breath, I peer under the door's hinges and see two footmen searching the adjoining bedroom, looking under the bed and behind the curtains. "Come out, you varmint," calls the one who swings a stout stick with a knobbed end. "Or it will go worse for you." The laundress screeches up the stairs, she will send for the constable.

The footmen leave the bedroom. I wait until I can hear them busying themselves elsewhere before slipping off my shoes, picking them up and creeping out into a hallway. I hurry on, searching for servants' stairs. I try a door at the end of a long passageway but this opens into a sumptuous bedchamber, presumably that of the master of the house. Its interior tells me little about its occupant, except that he owns a gold pocket-watch, a small pistol, a garnet ring of a type familiar to me and a fine miniature of a plump-faced young man recognisable from print-shop windows as the Prince of Wales.

I hear the footmen ransacking a room nearby and have no other recourse but to ascend when I would sooner descend. I open the first door on this upper landing as quietly as I can, but the un-oiled hinges screech and I am startled to hear a sharp exclamation from within. A yellow-faced old man wearing a grey nightcap springs up in his bed and demands to know who would rouse a butler who is ill? Before I can conjure an answer, he sees something behind me and I have time to do no more than spin about before I am caught in the firm grasp of my pursuers.

Fifty Eight

"Anything might have befallen you," Mouse grumbles, when at last the coach has set me down beside The Swan With Two Necks on Cheapside. My head full of what I have seen, I have scuttled through early evening streets where costers are crying off the last of their wares and shopkeepers are bolting their shutters, cutting through filthy courts and narrow alleyways to speed my passage. Breathlessly, I have tried to deliver myself of news before I am properly over the threshold. I am exasperated that he does not immediately grasp the import of what I tell him and reach for his coat. But Mouse will not listen, not yet. "Sit down," he says firmly, wrapping my fingers around a warming glass. "First, you will take something to eat while you properly recover yourself. Only then will I hear your explanation of what you have been about while Adam and I have been wasting time and breath enquiring for you all over Moorfields and beyond. And let us all hope that your explanation is a good one."

I take a restorative draught of the negus and bolt a mouthful of bread and cold mutton and deliver myself of all. I tell him of the picture I saw which was a match for one at Leicester Fields and of the bedchamber I saw. He nods, raises an eyebrow, removes and restores his wig. I have not yet told him of my arrest but the journalist is quick to detect an unfinished story.

"A fly does not escape such a sticky web easily," he says. "You must finish your story."

And so, somewhat abashed, I tell him the manner of my escape.

I am held by two strong footmen, sickened by the realisation that being taken for a housebreaker will mean the rope for me. The old butler has risen from his bed and now stands before me in his ancient saffron nightgown, peering at me like I am a problem to be solved. "Strangers loose in the house?" he shrills. "The master won't like this one bit. How did she get in? Was it through the tunnels? Who are you, chit?"

"Say something, you trollop," says the ginger-haired man on my right. He gives me a savage shake as if he thinks he can spill the words out of me. The other footman is bigger, younger but nervous.

"Has she taken anything?" the butler demands to know. I am outraged to feel the ginger man's hands fumbling deep in the pockets of my dress.

The butler steps up, stands too close; there is an acrid stench of decay on his breath as he accuses me of being a housebreaker, a poacher, a gypsy. "So tell me," he spits, "What brings a young wanton like you to Mylnehurst Abbey?"

"Answer Mr Chadwick," The ginger man says. I experience a flash of pain as he treats my hair like a bell-rope, giving it a vicious tug like he would separate it from my scalp. Still I say nothing. I become more angry than fearful – angry at myself, mostly, for being caught by these doltish bumpkins. The ginger man gives my hair another sharp yank. My rage is rising like lava in a volcano – I do not know what I might do if he does not stop. But Chadwick, perhaps desirous of reclaiming his sickbed, restrains the man's arm.

"This is getting us nowhere, Thomas. Send news of this incursion to our master. Now, where can we securely confine this shrew?"

"Why not the caverns?" Robert says.

The one called Thomas says, “That place is haunted. I have heard screams. No-one goes in there.”

“I was lighting candles down there not an hour since,” the man called Robert says, scornfully. He turns to the butler. “I have been cleaning up after the master's last guest, Mr Chadwick, and the chamber is ready for your inspection. There is still work to be done in the Grand Cavern.”

“Good. The hoyden will be secure enough in there. Escort her to the caves, Robert. The master will decide what to do with her on his return from London, though the Devil knows when that may be. And Robert?”

“Yes, Mr Chadwick?”

“See she has food and candles. She may be there a considerable while.”

Outside, the light is failing as the man takes a burning torch and pushes me out into the yard. He marches me behind the stable block where a narrow track wends down the hill on which stands the house. In silence, we descend the path until we come to a fissure in a face of exposed rock, the black mouth of a cave. He pushes me into a cold, dark space and sets light to the first of a chain of torches bracketed along the walls of a low, wet tunnel. We begin to tramp, the path descending deep into the hillside, stone surroundings amplifying the man's voice whenever he exhorts me to make haste. Deeper we go, the fall of my steps sometimes returned to me as a faint echo. I tell Mouse I am more curious than frightened, I have found myself now in the place I have come to see. This is not true.

We stumble down one black passageway after another and then, as we navigate a sharp corner, I am astonished to see a blaze of light. Entering a great space lit by countless candles, I see movement and think we are not alone. I look again and see the reflections of the ginger-haired man and myself multiplied an hundredfold. It is the most extraordinary sight. I am surrounded by our reflections; countless facsimiles of a girl in a dowdy dress and a rough-looking man bearing a flaming torch disappear into nothingness, claimed by the dusty glass of a dozen opposing mirrors. No less strange is a great oaken table set with spider-webbed plates and attended by chairs as if for some weird banquet. I see now what I have hoped to see. Above, spanning this vast cavern and lighted by our torches, I see Mr Grace's devils, satyrs, fallen angels and ghastly monsters engrossed in the foulest of doings just as he described in his journal. Knowing their history, they do not frighten me. What I am convinced happened below these ghastly images is another matter.

We go on, walking again in darkness and then, just when I am thinking that the Stygian gloom can get no blacker and we must be at the very gates of Hell itself, there is a weak glimmer of light. We follow the curve of the walls and slowly, the light strengthens. Now, my nostrils are tickled by the sweet smell of smoke; somewhere a fire is burning. Light catches on quartz embedded in a rock wall as we approach what I take to be the entrance to another cavern but is in fact a chamber hewn out for some long-forgotten purpose. Robert waves his torch and I see a cupboard, a chair and a table on which are snuffed candles and a jug of water. A fireplace has been hacked from the rock and presumably, vents somewhere above ground.

My eyes are drawn by the straw palliasse on whose rumpled bedclothes lie leathern straps which I take to be restraints for hands or feet. I am starting to ask him the meaning of this, thinking some lunatic may have been confined here, when he gives me one last push, hard enough to topple me onto the bed and before I understand what is happening, I feel a rough hand seizing at my skirts. He holds me down while he whispers something urgent and abhorrent in my ear, something which positively blinds me with anger.

The volcano erupts; I hardly think I could have stopped myself from doing what I did. I offer my lips as if to kiss him but instead, I fasten my teeth upon his nose, biting him far harder than ever I bit the apprentice, which action saw me in court. I hold him close as he brays like an injured donkey and flails wildly, but the more he struggles, the harder do I bite. Warm blood fills my mouth as my ears ring with his awful screams. I am thinking I will have the end of his nose clean off when he releases his hold of me and rolls off the bed, screaming that I am a devil-bitch, a savage strumpet and I don't know what else. Before he has stopped cursing and crying with pain, I have snatched up his torch and plunged deep into the tunnels.

Mouse is gaping at me as he might at some fantastical beast from New Guinea. I have clearly shocked him. I have shocked myself. I thought I had outgrown such behaviour but it seems the 'little savage' in me is not yet tamed. When at last he is calmer and I have washed my face, changed my soiled dress and had something more to eat, Mouse begins to pace the floorboards, picking up things from tables and depositing them in places they should not be. Just now he has plucked a candlestick from the oak mantle.

"There were restraints on the bed," I say again. "It was the most terrible, perfect place to commit such unspeakable acts."

"So you have found the scene of the crimes," Mouse says.

"What will do now?"

I have counted on Mouse for answers before now. This time, he disappoints by shaking his head and showing me his inky palms.

"What indeed?" he says. "The brutes who used this place will not be returning to it now. A pity you did not retrieve some solid piece of evidence or discover at least who is the master of this house. Now we shall have to fritter time on a second journey to Mylnehurst Abbey."

"That may not be necessary," I say.

"Because...?"

"Beside the master's bed I saw a beautifully worked ring whose garnet was coiled about with a golden snake which showed its fangs. You will not have seen its like in this country. A man who was sometimes with Mr Grace wore just such a ring."

"You think this is the same man?"

"There cannot be another ring like that."

"Then who is he?"

"Alas, I cannot recall Mr Grace ever mentioning him by name. Jamie Gretch would only refer to him as 'that man' or sometimes, as something worse."

"So, after all that, we have travelled no further?"

"I have not finished. The housekeeper, Mrs Harris, thought his name was Death. But there is surely no such name as Death."

Mouse settles the candlestick on a stack of newspapers.

"The name was not De'Ath, I hope?"

"Do you know him?"

"By reputation, I do. According to Narcissus Pyke, Osiris De'Ath had some sort of association with Lord Albermarle and his coterie. But you saw this man at Leicester Fields, Michel. What more can you say about him?"

I tell Mouse that he was angular as an easel and wore dark clothes that accentuated the fashionable paleness of his skin and the whites of his sharp eyes.

"Yes, yes," Mouse says, "But what of the man himself?"

"I thought that he might hold some special power over Mr Grace. I once was mixing colours for the master, who was painting one of his histories while that man lurked somewhere about. It seemed to me that painter and models were merely this man's marionettes. He had the temerity to advise the master on his composition and was instructing Garcy Dunne how she must pose. It was like he were the master and not Mr Grace."

Mouse sits down and removing his wig, holds it in his lap and begins to unravel it with his fingers, quite unconscious of what he is doing. "De'Ath's name came up repeatedly in my searchings with Pyke," he says at last. "I thought little of it as he appeared to be some sort of functionary and not a leading player."

"But you think his role was something more than that?" I ask.

"What you have told me puts it beyond doubt, Michel. I will go to see Pyke again and find out what I can about this man. But you may take this as a certainty: the name of our adversary is Osiris De'Ath."

Fifty Nine

The father of this adversary, one Tobias De'Ath, was a reckless man, an habitual drunkard and a friend to excess. By the time his only son Oswald was nine years old, he had amassed debts all over town, gaming too freely and committing himself to a series of ill-advised investments. Now his numerous chickens were coming home to roost. The household was in ruins.

Oswald's mother Jane De'Ath had formerly been Jane Simpson, the clever, winsome lady's maid of Toby's late wife, Clarissa. She produced a single male heir who had no sooner drawn breath than he was hurried off to the confines of the nursery, there to be cared for by a wet nurse and then by a Mrs Leeds, who drank gin – and when he was bothersome, made sure that he did too. Oswald saw his parents briefly, or not at all.

Come dinner time, his father, mind already beginning to slip its gears, might be out at the tables and his wife noisily occupied upstairs with one of her visitors. School was a refuge for the child and he sucked hungrily on its teat until the money began to dwindle, after which the bright boy educated himself using books from the old library. He had been in the summer-house on the night his father expired in flames outside his burning home and when he finally lost interest in this spectacle, he made three resolutions.

One. He would be as unlike his father as it was possible to be (at fifteen he could not have known what a task he had set himself).

Two. He would be master of his own destiny and would bow to no-one.

Three. He would no longer suffer himself to be known as Oswald.

Osiris curses fate as he realises that adopting a new name is the only resolution he has quite kept. Permitting himself a second generous glass of his own French brandy, he broods upon the lost certainties of his youth. When he was young and all was before him, he did not doubt himself for a minute. Now, not a moment passes when he does not wonder what his future holds. He castigates himself daily for letting so much slip from his hands.

And yet he is not at fault. Like the Biblical Egyptians he had admired in books, he is hardly deserving of the plagues that have been sent against him. And such plagues! Foremost among them is that pestilential newspaper suggesting that the men in that accursed picture share membership of a hell-fire club and going as far as it dares in intimating that they are responsible for the fates of the girls that every damn fool remains so exercised about. With principal members of the present administration suspected of involvement the paper is, in effect, accusing the establishment of murder. As a result, his connection cannot be afforded and powerful friends refuse his letters at their doors or are no longer at home to him. And now has come a twist in events worthy of Satan's cunning.

Word has reached him that the picture, Henry Grace's cursed, abominable cause of all calamity has survived the fire. His man, Towse heard the tale from an innkeeper in the village below the Abbey who had it from a passenger breaking a journey from London to Bristol. He experienced an involuntary shudder when Towse delivered this ridiculous concoction, before his mind's workings began to whirr and purr again and he smiled at himself for his moment of weakness. The fire he had set at Leicester Fields was utter, the paints and spirits creating an inferno that only something born in hell could have survived.

It is one of those stories that are passed about in taverns and fish-markets, he tells himself, fodder for unprincipled pamphleteers or newspaper editors. He recalls one such story he heard recently, of a woman in Derbyshire who had given birth to rabbits. But in London not long afterwards, his attention had been directed to the following titbit printed in *The London Globe*:

A small picture has been drawing crowds of the curious to the window of a little shop called Gilpin's on Paternoster Row. This finely-detailed artwork depicts numbers of people fleeing a fiery disaster. It has been asserted by more than one viewer of Henry Grace's much-talked up masterpiece that this is a fragment of the same, rescued from the fire at his villa in Leicester Fields. If this is true, we wonder how it survived and how many other fragments also survive? Or was the picture in fact spirited away before the catastrophe and cut up into pieces for reasons and by persons presently unknown? And if the painting survived the fire, is it too fantastical to consider the possibility that its creator, Henry Grace might also have survived? Let us recall that only his valet's corpse was retrieved from the ashes! Of course, we ask this purely in a spirit of play and to provide highly seasoned food for thought. To return to matters more certain, we can say in all seriousness that there will be people in this city who will take a very keen interest in future developments.

Osiris is at Gilpins's that same afternoon, examining the picture under a lens. His hope had been that this is the work of someone passing off a piece as Henry Grace's, or that it is something 'in the school of.' But this looks very much like the work of Henry Grace. If it were possible, he would say the brushwork is in fact better than he has seen in many of Grace's works. But it is the figures in the painting which have drawn him here and at which he now peers most intently.

These are finely finished and closely resemble those he has seen less clearly in the prints. He looks again and picks out among the panicking crowd faces he knows well. There is Thomas Tilbury the banker leading the charge to the river stairs. The painter has included even the pock marks on his neck. And with him are Collins and Shepherdson, men he knows from the Albion. He curses his luck that the two people whose visages he would most like to see among the crowds are not present in the scene. What a powerful, pivotal lever that would have given him.

"Who brought this to you?" he demands of Gilpin, a man of about his own age who has been amazed at the interest in his shop, which is usually deserted.

"I picked it up at Christie's for a song," Gilpin says. "I thought it well-enough executed to buy for half a guinea. It was a deal better than some of its companions."

Osiris glares at him, so that Gilpin has to find somewhere else to rest his gaze. "There are others?" Osiris asks him, "Like this?"

"Just like that and undoubtedly by the same artist. It is a style I should recognise anywhere."

"Then why buy just this one?"

"As I have said, the composition in this is superior." He frowns before adding, "To be completely plain with you, one was all I could afford."

“These other pictures. Who has them now?'

“I cannot say.”

“You will take a guinea for this one?”

“It is not for sale. I show it because I like it.”

“Then take this, you babbling fool,” Osiris says, snatching up the painting as three bright coins clatter on the counter.

Sixty

“How is this possible?” Mouse says. “Where were our people?”

Mouse is furious that news of Mr Gilpin's curious acquisition has reached him not through one of the myriad tentacles of *The Enquirer* but through the medium of the *The London Globe*, a new paper whose mounting sales are costing him sleep. He kicks out at the iron base of the press and complains loudly.

“We would not have reported it anyway,” he says at last. “A salvaged portion of *The New Fire of London?* On public display in a shop window? More of their ridiculous lies!”

“*The Globe* would not send its readers to view an empty window,” Michel says.

“I am not so sure about that,” Mouse grunts.

“It is most likely a daub copied from the print,” Michel says, “Made in haste by someone seeking to profit from Henry Grace's notoriety.”

“I do wish *The Globe* would not print such piffle. This sort of thing drags the whole profession into the gutter and breaks our trust with readers. Young Will can run down to the Row to see what is what.”

Michel finishes rereading the piece and says, “But what if there is something to this story? What if fragments of the picture were indeed saved from the fire?"

Mouse snorts loudly. "You described to me a holocaust. How can this possibly be true?"

"But wait. The night the house burned I saw poor Jamie Gretch at the upper window. Suppose he tried to save the picture? Did he cut up the canvas, hoping it could be restored at some later date?"

"Might he have done this?" Mouse asks.

"It would not be unlike him. He pinned all his future hopes on that picture and its sale."

"How he thought he could cut up that enormous painting and escape the house before it became a cauldron of fire I cannot think. In any case as he did not himself survive the blaze, how could any piece he cut be from that picture?"

"I do not know," Michel says, "Unless such scraps were blown through the rent in the roof?"

Mouse drops from his stool and looks about for his weathered coat.

"I will know no more sitting here," Mouse says. "Now, I am not for one moment saying that I give credence to something printed in *The Globe,* but I will be the one to run down to the Row and I will see this wonder for myself."

For some time now, Osiris has heard nothing from Edward Villiers. This vacancy has encroached and impinged on parts of his mind usually given over to more pleasing thoughts. In Villiers' eyes he has failed, he knows that. But whether Villiers has time and energy to expend on expediting threats might be another matter. Just now, Villiers is very likely comprehending how tenuous the role of a prime-minister-in-waiting can be.

No-one will have said anything to his face but there is bound to have been talk. There will be those who went to see Grace's painting and saw some face in the crowd they thought resembled his own. Others may have noted the presence of his friend, Goldolphin at his side as their figures attempt to board an overcrowded river-craft. They may have noticed who else was in their company. The likenesses on the prints were arguable; he has been assured by so-called friends that those in the original were not.

On such grounds he can understand why Villiers has done everything possible to distance himself from Mylnehurst Abbey and from fellow members of The Albion Club. What he cannot understand is why the man has severed all connections with himself, whom he accuses erroneously and quite inexplicably as being the *primum mobile* of the whole sorry business. Because of this distancing, it has proved impossible for Osiris to meet with him and explain why he has so far been unable to prevent *The Enquirer* continuing to print its lies and to entreat him not to set in motion the mechanism which will initiate his downfall. This novel and alarming state of impotency has driven him some way beyond distraction.

So it is that he almost welcomes the plain-sealed letter which arrives this morning, unsigned as always. *My dear Osiris*, he reads – as if they were still on terms! – *I am in receipt of your little picture. Whether or not this is an original portion of G's masterpiece or a well-executed copy is immaterial. The work is extremely fine and the faces clearly recognisable. Judging by the interest already shown, this picture and its brothers could be as damaging to us as the original painting. If you wish to secure your future, you will locate and send to me every other example seen at the saleroom by the shopkeeper. You will also enquire discreetly at the other auction houses and also among the London art dealers to discover if similar items have been offered for sale. There may exist one example which I am particularly anxious to hold in my hands. You will know it when you see it.*

Though keenly aware of the baneful threat watermarked in this message, Osiris is almost heartened. A channel of communication has been opened with Villiers. He no longer feels at the mercy of forces beyond his control; he can at least take action. Checking his appearance in the tall, gilt-framed mirror in which many young ladies and an occasional young man have readjusted their apparel before taking their leave (he must on all accounts visit his barber on Jermyn Street) he calls for Towse to pack his bag with expedition and have the carriage brought around to the front of Mylnehurst Abbey.

Sixty One

The auctioneer is in full flow, distracting Mouse from dark thoughts with practised eloquence and theatrical showmanship. At one moment he is as tearful as a Drury Lane player because a certain exotic item – of which he pronounces 'there is not its match West of Canton' – is to fall under his hammer for the paltry sum of four guineas. At the next Mouse sees him leaning into the crowd and sharing conspiratorial whispers about the personal life of the dowager whose recent passing has allowed her cabinets to be opened and her secrets to be exposed to the world.

Michel does not listen. She considers the pictures hanging one above the other on walls splendidly lit by the great glass lantern in the ceiling, ladies in fine dress, family pets with glistening coats, highly-groomed horses and ships of the line blazing away before listlessly returning her gaze to the crowd of mostly bewigged heads below. She weighs the likelihood of the murderous Osiris De'Ath or one of his agents standing somewhere in this room, and being, perhaps, a mere dagger's thrust away from her.

Until the items they are here to see come up for sale they have nothing to do but to listen to the loquacious auctioneer and pick out well-known faces in the great crowd. Mouse is uncomfortable. He has stood there almost a full hour and more than once has glanced longingly at the unsold sofas and chairs lining the walls. "A great pity we could not see the pictures on the viewing day," he laments,

"These lots were offered for auction only yesterday," Michel says. "But thanks to the frenzy got up by our friends at the *Globe,* the fragments were rushed straight into the next sale."

"You discovered the vendor, you say?"

"A Carey Street dealer who bought them at a sale much like this before anyone realised what they might be. He expects to turn a profit today."

"Remember, we are here to identify those bidders who are particularly interested in buying these lots," Mouse says. "Be sure you watch the crowd closely."

"You expect these pieces to feature more New Citizens?"

"I do. What seems to have survived the fire are the lower parts of the picture where, as you will know, most of these small figures were grouped."

Michel rises on her toes to survey the faces in the crowd. "I wonder if the dark figure himself is here today?"

Mouse glances about before saying, "Did you mark a likeness to De'Ath in that face?"

"I had no cause to closely examine the figure when Grace painted it," Michel says. "I only recall that the face was in deep shadow."

"Well, whether he is come or no, we are not here to arrest this creature. We cannot. Not until we have proof enough to hang him or at least to see him festering upon a prison hulk. If one of these fragments contains that figure, a close inspection could be everything to us"

"If..." Michel says.

"*If* is all we have," Mouse says, raising his eyes to a frame on the wall, where a rich young couple languish beneath a tree, before sighing loudly. "Dear me, but this would have been so much easier and our case that much stronger if Grace's journals had not burnt. He did not keep fair copies, I suppose?"

"I am sure he did," Michel says, "and equally sure they too would have burned."

Mouse removes his wig and runs his hand over newly-cropped hair before violently shaking the wig as if he might dislodge something nesting there. "We must proceed with all caution, Michel. Whoever went to such fatal lengths to see the picture destroyed is capable of taking any measure to prevent its continued existence."

Again, they scrutinise the crowd. Some of these countenances Michel knows already from the errands she ran here for Gretch. She has already seen Mr Powell the colourist, who has affected not to know her. Behind her she hears again the flat Midlands tones of the Staffordshire brewer painted by Mr Grace as he demands to know, "Has the world gone mad?"

A large painting of a moonlit, limestone gorge is carried away by porters. The auctioneer takes a sip from an ornate silver cup before proceeding.

"We arrive now," he says, "At the lots which I believe have brought a great many of you here today, though how many have come to make a purchase and how many merely to satisfy ravenous curiosity we will soon ascertain."

The noise in the room diminishes, the coughing stops and lorgnettes are raised as the porters, a man and a boy, approach the auctioneer's rostrum. The boy offers two small framed pictures for the inspection of buyers. The man holds aloft a larger picture. There is a moment's silence and then some whispering. Mouse cranes to obtain a closer view. "Are these indeed fragments of Grace's picture?" he asks Michel. "I seem to recall looking at similar scenes in the artist's studio. Do watch the bidders closely."

There is violent movement below him. He turns to Michel in time to see her start suddenly and begin to barge through the knot of dandified bucks before her. He follows her dark, hatless head as it bobs through the crowd, sees her thread her way towards the auctioneer's rostrum, oblivious to outraged cries of complaint and astonished looks. Mouse himself watches amazed as she snatches one of the paintings from the boy's grasp and inspects it closely. The auctioneer is thrown off balance. "This is outrageous..." he splutters.

Mouse tries hard to discern the exchange above the noise of people being scandalised.

"*These are my pictures*." Is that what she says? The din in the room is making hearing anything impossible. What she seems to be saying now makes no sense to him at all. "*I painted every one. You have no authority to sell them. These pictures are my property*."

Mouse cannot see what happens next, Michel is lost to sight behind taller heads but movements in the crowd allow him glimpses of her as she struggles to escape the clutches of saleroom staff who appear to be finding her removal more challenging than they anticipated. There is scuffling, a cry of pain and a loud exclamation. "She bit me!" Mouse hears. His eyes track the three men and the struggling girl to the door. He hears a man in a tricorn hat say he will fetch a Runner and the fellow seems about to do so when the imposing figure of a man who is built like a blacksmith blocks his way and forcibly takes charge of the termagant.

Only Mouse has been able to view the auction. The doors now barred to Adam and Michel, he returns to the sale-room where the uproar has caused disarray. While order is being restored, Mouse finds the opportunity to occupy a position close to the front and directly before pictures which are being held a little tighter by chastised porters. He wishes now that he had his stool but that is being employed by a young lady who is having smelling-salts administered. As he tries to improve a vantage framed by shiny elbows and dress coats, Mouse puzzles over his companion's unexpected behaviour – he cannot imagine what has come over her, thinks she has had a turn, perhaps. The restored auctioneer recaptures his attention when he raises laughter in the room with his talk of "another escaped Bedlamite."

The small picture held now above Mouse's bewigged head depicts a watery hell: he sees heads of desperate people bobbing in a frothing and fire-lit Thames, open mouths crying noiselessly for salvation while some drown and others are fought off by people packing boats already dangerously low in the water. Mouse looks as closely as he can but recognises no-one in the composition. This picture is the first to be offered for sale. Bidding is slow and the auctioneer has work to do before the room is once more in the palm of his hand and is ready to join the game.

"Two guineas?" the auctioneer snorts, "For such a jolly boating scene? Who will give me three?"

Mouse suspects that most of today's crowd has come to view a curiosity and not to buy a painting. Certainly not this one, he thinks as a Midlands voice pronounces the picture "A damnable monstrosity. Quite fitting that most on't original were destroyed by fire!"

"Twenty one shillings and sixpence," calls someone else.

"Really!" the auctioneer says but has the picture turned briefly towards himself. "Curious though it may be, this is undeniably a detail taken from Henry Grace's masterpiece thought to have been destroyed in the fire that razed his house in Leicester Fields."

"And no scorch marks?" says the man from the Midlands, "I call that remarkable!"

Unruffled, the auctioneer explains that sections were evidently cut away from the painting shortly before the larger part was consumed by fire. "And you must agree with me," he says, "that a piece of Grace's extraordinary, contentious and devilishly mysterious picture, any piece at all, cannot prove anything other than a certain and most lucrative investment."

But the picture sells at no great price to a dealer in curios Mouse has seen once or twice at Molly's.

Its brother in size depicts a band of drunken whores jeering at their frightened, half-dressed patrons who are spurning appeals to fight the flames with buckets and hooked poles in favour of flinging themselves from the river stairs. Mouse is stirred to see several faces from coffee houses and taverns he has frequented as the *City Gossip*. He is further encouraged to find likenesses of names which have come up in his searchings through the archives of Narcissus Pyke. One of these men is a functionary at the Court of St James, his companion a Member of Parliament for a rotten borough.

Mouse is not the only viewer to note the presence of the high and mighty in this picture – the chatterers Mouse hears behind him are raucously amused and the names of men so wickedly lampooned circulate quickly throughout the space. Mouse looks about him and notes that others are taking a quieter interest. Bidding for this item is much more lively, with hands raised and papers waved all about the room. The painting sells for twenty guineas to a bidder lost somewhere in the crowd.

The third and largest picture is held up for inspection. Mouse hopes that somewhere on its busy canvas are the figures he has come here to see. His gaze follows the routes of burning streets beyond St Pauls and passes over countless heads and wide-eyed, shiny-pink faces streaming towards the river, over rooftops, some aflame, towards the portion of the picture in which he expects to see a coach and before it the dark figure and the girl who is presumably dead.

He is unsure of the precise location of this little scene – Obadiah had reported it as being beyond St Paul's but quite where, he had neglected to specify. So mouse carefully tracks his eyes over every inch of the composition, wondering if he might have missed the grim tableau among so much violent confusion. But he is not mistaken, no such scene appears here. He has found nothing to connect Osiris De'Ath with murder.

"Perhaps," Mouse fumes, as they stand across the wide street from the auction house where people are now leaving, some with servants bearing their treasures, "If you had not contrived to get yourself ejected from these proceedings we might have identified interested bidders."

"Those pictures are my property," Michel asserts, hotly, "They are apprentice pieces."

"Yours? You painted them?"

"Did I not just tell you that? I wanted to grow my expertise with miniatures and small figures, so I made copies from the original, just the parts where I could employ fine brushes and lenses to perfect my abilities in this field."

"Then why were they on sale today?"

"Jamie Gretch sent them to the sale rooms along with anything else he could lay his hands on. They would have been sold weeks ago. It never entered my mind that the so-called fragments on sale today might be these same works."

"Well, I congratulate you on gulling such connoisseurs," Mouse says. His voice carries an unfamiliar, bitter tone.

"I am sorry. I truly am," Michel says, "I forget myself sometimes."

"I will not dispute that. Now, I would ask you to think carefully, Michel. Did you copy the part of the picture containing the dark figure? Is there another picture, somewhere?"

"No, no, please do not feed your hopes Mr Malone. I had no interest in that portion of the picture. I wanted only to copy faces and fine detail."

Mouse sighs, watches the painting of the rich young couple under a tree being loaded onto a sprung cart with a jumble of other acquisitions. "I did not think we could enjoy such fortune," he says. "That we might have plainly identified Osiris De'Ath was too much to ask from a fate that has not been kind to us of late."

"I painted other faces," Michel offers, "There is one other picture which shows countenances that anyone would know."

"Who did you paint?"

"When I sat down before Grace's picture I remarked immediately the faces of two eminent figures in the English establishment, one of whom is presently being considered as prime minister in waiting."

"Edward Villiers."

"And at his side a red-headed man I have seen walking with Mr Grace."

"Did he have a small scar upon his right cheek?"

"I remember that because it gave him a smile that was not true."

"That will have been Lord Godolphin, First Secretary to the Admiralty. The injury is supposed to have been sustained in a duel."

"I could not easily forget either physog," Michel says. "These were faces of well-fed entitlement that the artist had twisted horribly with fear and hatred. The men are pictured hauling frightened children from a ferry-boat in order to rob them of their places. Mr Grace must have been choked with poisoned humours that day."

"And these faces were prominent in your composition?"

"They were. The way Grace presented these men would have aroused a visceral revulsion in anyone who saw them. It was powerfully done and I felt compelled to make them the focus of my own composition. "

"But they are still recognisable?"

"They would be known instantly to colleagues and members of the House and to anyone who visits the print-shop windows, I should say. "

"Do you recall anything else of your composition, Michel?"

"Only this. There were men with them who sometimes had visited with Mr Grace."

"Other men? Michel, this picture will be crucial to our case." Mouses rocks from shoe to shoe, betraying suppressed excitement. "I tell you, the balance may yet tip in our favour. You know where that picture is now?"

"I regret that too was sent to auction."

"To this sale room? Tell me it is here."

Michel shakes her head.

"I am truly sorry to have raised your hopes. The fact is that Gretch had dealings with all the auction houses. It might have gone to any one of them. And whoever it went to will doubtless have sold it on by now."

She is surprised that Mouse is not immediately downcast. Instead, she notes a gleam in his eye.

"Then I must solicit the help of someone who perhaps can help me find it," Mouse says as he swallows his disappointment. "Find me a cabriolet, and with good fortune, I will see you at Grub Street before we turn the screws on tomorrow's edition."

Sixty Two

There usually is little to distinguish Grub Street on a Sunday from the same place on a Monday. Denizens keeping the Sabbath are usually those who have burned their lamp-oil late into the night, scratching away at any little thing for which a penny might be turned and also, those who caroused too late in the taverns. For many of these hacks and drones, Saturday night is a time to spend last pennies on gin and wine and to boast of intentions they will commit to paper just as soon as they return to their writing tables, but most will be at their places of work the next morning. Few of these scratchers and scribblers, dreamers and drones can afford the fourth commandment.

There are some curious-looking buildings on this narrow thoroughfare, such as the ramshackle townhouse which blocks light for workers at the Dipped Quill and leans drunkenly upon great oaken buttresses, around which roof-tiles stripped by last night's violent storm now lie smashed. The ground-floor apartment of this edifice is occupied by Marney's print shop – here, embryonic journalist Will Templeton watched with burning interest the comings and goings at *The Enquirer* across the way. Marney's prints periodicals, some of which are authored by a lean and harassed-looking man who is always behind with his rent on the rooms above and pens most of the content himself. He considers himself the sharpest satirical squib writer in the city, a view which must any day now be shared by habitués of the coffee-houses where he pushes his productions.

Above dwell two brothers, one a writer of short histories and fantastical books of travel, the other a producer of pamphlets, who will espouse any political or religious allegiance, dependent on which zealot or politician is discreetly funding his efforts. The attic at the top of the house has been taken by a pale and hungry-looking young man who tells anyone interested that a garret is the only proper place for a poet who aspires to greatness. He has not been seen by anyone for three weeks.

Further down the street between cheap lodging-houses and an oft-frequented bagnio are crumbling edifices providing poorly-furnished rooms for playwrights, legal scribes, compilers of dictionaries and a man who is writing a novel, he will tell you, but who appears to subsist on money he earns selling brass buttons. Some of these heads will perhaps have turned to witness the editor of *The Enquirer* breakfasting on a slice of pie as he makes his return from the home of Narcissus Pyke, where the heavy storm compelled him to shelter that night. He stops, frowns and picks at the pie's contents before deciding to take another bite.

"With all respect, Master," Will Templeton complains as he brushes meddling fingers away from the type he is composing. "You really must trust me with this. You forget I worked at Marney's for full two years before coming to you. You are discomposing the composer."

He attempts to resume his work but already, he knows when something is agitating his new employer and says, "What troubles you, sir?"

His master gives every sign of being in two minds about disclosing anything. He fiddles with a rule, picks up leaden characters, puts them back. At last, he erupts. "It is just this, Will. With great good fortune, we will soon have something for these presses that will be read by everyone and remembered long after our time. Something that will keep us all safe and see justice done. That is, if my quest is blessed with success. That is the frustrating thing. It is all in the lap of fortune."

Michel glances up from a proof she is correcting. "There is news?"

"I can reset now if you have a story," Will says.

Will is eager, Mouse thinks. He has already observed to Michel that the boy shows aptitude both in his printing and his writing and is is now an indispensable cog in their business machine.

"Not today, Will, I spoke hastily because I am hopeful. Hopes are all I have, in point of truth. Wait a while and we shall see." He looks over the reversed report of the signing of a treaty at Paris which will end the war with America. "But how is all here? Has Scoggins delivered that fresh paper? And did the boys get today's edition out on time?"

"There is this," Will says and holds up an official-looking document with a broken red seal. "I hope you do not mind, but it looked important."

"Another writ," Mouse says. "Well, if a newspaper is properly doing its job, it must expect such. Who is suing us this time?"

"Osiris De'Ath."

"What? De'Ath? Give that to me."

Mouse seizes the document and scuttles over to the windows where he holds it up to the light, Michel reading over his shoulder. He accords the writ that same fine attention with which Obadiah used to con his galley proofs. He does everything with it except turn it upside down to see if it makes any better sense that way up.

"But this is ridiculous, it is utterly ludicrous," he exclaims at last. "Why has he done this?"

"He is under attack. As we know, a writ is the usual resort for those calumnied in the press," Michel says.

"But his case cannot stand up, you know yourself how careful we have been with our choice of words. We have insinuated, yes, but we have spelt out nothing. He is wasting his time and throwing away a small fortune, with lawyers such as these at Lincoln's Inn. Those attorneys must be laughing down their sleeves."

"Why does he not see there is no hope of a successful prosecution?" Will says.

"I cannot imagine. He has no need of sending a warning shot over our bows, he has already given us a broadside. I cannot but think he has erred here."

"That would be most unlike De'Ath. Perhaps he has been ill-advised."

Mouse takes a bite of his pie.

Will says, "Could it not be that he is under strain and clutches at straws? Perhaps he has suffered a brainstorm of some sort."

Wiping the last morsel of pie from his lips, Mouse says, "I do not know. We will try to find out. But for now, I have other news. Michel, I have been with Mr Pyke and he has given me reason to hope."

"The archivist? You think he can help us find my picture? This is news indeed. You must tell me all."

But hearing a sudden scuffling and the door flung open, she looks up from her page to see that Mouse is now scurrying across the back court towards the jakes as she has never seen him hurry before.

Sixty Three

Osiris De'Ath has been making preparations he never envisaged himself making. Discreetly and through agents, he has been disposing of stock and liquidising other assets. Dusty documents have been presented at banks, secret caches opened. He has been making enquiries about the likely values and saleability of certain artworks and inventories have been drawn up of particularly valuable pieces of furniture.

Some items have already been sold, quietly and not through the public sale rooms. He has been disposing of his subterranean assets too, but these dealings have not been at all to his satisfaction. Had a buyer offered him the price at which he is now letting go his illicit liquor, he would have choked on his own brandy. Now, the carts come at night and the work is completed in silence, his servants keeping drawn their curtains and their minds on other things.

His right eyelid flutters as he treads the boards of his upper gallery, where empty spaces speak of pictures sold. He stops by an opened window and peers out over grounds where building work on a temple he planned by the lake has ceased and men no longer plant trees on the distant hillside. Closer to the house, a sinewy fox breaks cover and runs low towards a lakeside copse, pursued by neither hounds nor men.

He wonders if he has been precipitate and ponders the changes in himself. Where once his every move would have been calculated and sure-footed, now fingerposts point in every direction and sometimes he knows not which path to take.

He shakes off the mood and tells himself that these are temporary measures. He must be doing the right thing, he always has. He has assets now to set himself up in comfort anywhere, should circumstances demand it. And if – or rather, when – this squall blows itself out he will not find it difficult to put everything straight once again. He will have suffered financially, certainly, but the tables have taught him to be sanguine about taking a loss here and there.

While light remains in the sky he finds reason to hope but at night sleep will not come. Instead, he is plagued by visions of revenue men and unsold French brandy, of enormous loans suddenly recalled and credit withdrawn, of losing his magistracy, his standing, his name.

He sees that name spelt out in large newspaper print, sees those cursed papers on every man's lap in clubs and coffee houses, hears it misused and bandied about, lies told about him and dreadful doings laid at his door. The gossip that has circulated in these places of convivial conversation and also in the parks and the pleasure gardens of the capital, with nowhere else to go, has reached the ears of its subject.

That he might be imprisoned, marooned on a hulk or even worse are not eventualities he entertains. He may have done a little organising, set one or two balls in motion but it was other men who behaved so monstrously, he is a convenient scapegoat and one day he will clear his name and then they will hear from him, these fools.

Money matters connected with this realising of assets have taken him up to London on numerous occasions. During some of these jaunts up town he has of course run into people he knows, encounters which have had various outcomes. On St James' Street he almost collides with George Collins, who is rolling out of Boodles. Collins is a little the worse for drink and so eager to talk with him that Osiris has to brush his hands from his coat.

"I confess I am surprised to see you abroad with your name on everyone's lips," Collins slurs, a ruddy eye upon the windows of the club's new premises. "Let us walk around the corner, we should not be seen together."

"I have nothing to say to you," Osiris snaps.

"It is all coming out, is it not? The caverns? That newspaper knows it all, I am sure, and as soon as they can prove it, they will print. They will print and we will be damned. And what then? Take a glass with me at White's, there is no-one there at this time. We must talk about all of this."

"You may do as you wish. I have my own plans," Osiris says, once again detaching urgent fingers.

"You wonder what a pass we have come to when Edward Villiers is so confounded."

"Villiers? What do you know?"

"He is a troubled man. People are watching the wind before they throw in their lots with him. And if Villiers goes, we all go. I tell you, De'Ath, I see ruin for us all. Even those far gone with the disease will be prised from their bedchambers and pilloried. I really do not know what I will do. Perhaps I will retreat to a little place I have in Yorkshire and wait until this damnable business is all done with."

"Stand firm, man, all this is nonsense," Osiris tells him. "Tell the others to deny and deny. They can prove nothing. We only fall if some fool talks."

While he is being shaved and before the pomade is applied to his hair (these days, Osiris is one of those gentlemen who leads the fashion in going wigless) he hears again the frightened voice of Collins asking him what he himself will do? What indeed? He has considered throwing in his cards and fleeing to France, where his mother is no longer with her count but is living in surprising comfort at an address in the Paris suburbs, where there will always be a place for him, she writes. It will be somewhere to base himself while he finds a decent chateau in good repair. He might have a pleasing life there.

But Osiris does not see himself living in France, not while a certain last toothsome chance remains for him in England. That chance is bound up in the whims and fancies of a young man whom he met for the first time a short while ago, although he has of course been aware of his existence for some twenty one years.

Sixty Four

The ragtag community of Grub Street has remarked a significant increase in activity at the sign of the Dipped Quill. There is not an hour in the day when there are no candles in the windows, no silhouetted figures bent at tables. It is indeed a much busier place, now. A second printing press – an improved model – has more than doubled *The Enquirer*'s capacity to produce newspapers and it is difficult now to progress from one end of the building to the other without disturbing people at work or negotiating stocks of news-sheet or great obelisks of printed newspapers.

Michel has suggested decamping to larger premises, but there is nothing of the sort available on the street just now and to move elsewhere, Mouse counters, would mean losing the useful resources upon their doorstep. Presently, finding a skilled hack to pen an article or uncover a story is only a matter of stepping across the street. And then, of course, there is Obadiah. On this matter, he had yet to find resolution. Here he has spent his happiest hours, but here too is the place where that terrible, terrible thing was done. He has at least promised his friends and hirelings that he will give the matter thought.

In point of fact, he might be out scouting for more commodious premises today, for all those at this newspaper's offices know.

"Where is Mr Malone, today?" Michel says, wearily.

Adam Brewer hoists another bundle of newspapers onto his back and drops them heavily onto the cart waiting outside. Returning for another, he says, "These days, with him, who is to say?"

"He was out betimes again this morning," Will says. "No word about where he was bound. Took his coat and off he went. Five minutes after, he was back for his wig."

"This is the third time this week," Michel says. "Have you asked him what business he is about?"

"Of course I have," Will says. "I cannot put this paper together without knowing what he wants in it. But all he says is, he is on business. Important business, he says. On the trail of something, he says."

"What is the matter with him?" Adam says. "He forgets his meals. And he does not clean the house. That is not like him, not a bit of it. A fit of the melancholy, do you think?"

Will says, "Last night, he sent me with another message for this Narcissus Pyke cove. I tried to read it but it seemed to be written in code."

"He looks like he has something to say but cannot say it," Adam says, "Looks fit to burst with it, sometimes."

Michel breaks the silence that has fallen. "Perhaps he does not want to reveal himself in case what he is about comes to nothing. That would be like Mouse."

"It would," Will says, slowly, "but of course, with Mr Mouse it may be something else entirely."

"If Mouse is not available, we must organise ourselves," Michel says. "Will, you have sufficient news to fill this next edition?"

Will nods.

"Our leading story is one I should not like Mr Mouse watching me set anyway. They are hanging a highwayman at Tyburn and it may be the last time anyone is hanged there. Instead, there will be a gallows built outside of Newgate prison."

"And what more?

"I plan to talk to some Quakers who are to create a committee against the trading of slaves. They maintain that the practice is contrary to laws of God and the rights of men."

"Good. Find a sailor who has manned a slaver and let him tell you what he knows. You might try the taverns at Limehouse. And do we have something about the accursed business that has plagued us all for so long?"

"Of course. We allude to an "unnamed source" – that is you, Miss Michel – having knowledge of the picture sold some time ago at Christie's and whose present location is apparently unknown. I reckon I have described the people shown there as finely as you painted them. Of course, I have not named Edward Villiers and Lord Godolphin, but my words can fit no-one else."

"Let me see that, please," Michel says. "If De'Ath is turning to the law we must choose every word with consummate care."

When she has digested the piece Will has written, she nods her head and offers Mouse's protege a quick smile. "Good," she says. "You have hit the tone exactly and neither said too much nor too little. I think we will be upsetting a lot of little boats. It cannot be long before someone in this accursed sodality gives himself away."

Sixty Five

His presence in London requested, Osiris enters the great, stone-built house through a discreet door off the cobbled courtyard and is escorted along noisy passageways where servants scuttle, through an enormous chamber in which numerous plasterers and painters work atop high ladders and then into a quiet ante-room. After he has waited there long enough to gather dust, he is admitted into a larger room where a table laid for supper is situated beneath a wall hung with pictures, two of which he recognises immediately as works by his protege, Henry Grace, at the peak of his powers. A dandified fellow in a cloud of hair-powder wafts towards him and whispers protocols before wafting out again.

How unlike his last project is the Prince of Wales, Osiris thinks when the two men enjoy a private dinner together. This young man is better-learned and more experienced in every way than was Henry Grace at his age. He is a much better conversationalist and positively suppurates charm. It is obvious from his physique that he enjoys his food – Osiris has lost count of the courses served – and he talks with reasonable authority on the arts. He enjoys bedding women and spends his mountain of money like nobody is taking a tally, or so Osiris has heard. After he has discoursed at length about his grand plans for remodelling a palace on the Sussex coast, the Prince adjusts his leg on the stool where it rests and addresses his guest on another matter.

"We have heard something," the Prince says, "of the curious entertainments which you managed down in Albermarle's caverns."

Osiris is sharply aware that this is the moment that will make or undo him, the instant when he discovers whether the Prince has invited him there to offer him a similar but much more lavishly-remunerated position as master of revels at the Prince's own debauches – or is already cognisant of how he allowed the reckless behaviour of frightened men to ruin everything. Ah, but why then would he have been invited to sup with a prince?

"We would like to know," the Prince says, his eyes peering deep into Osiris's, "If all we have heard is quite correct."

Osiris puts down his fork and leaves off fiddling with the plate of food he has been too agitated to eat.

"It may save time if you tell me what you already know, your royal..."

"Call me Prinny. Everyone other fool does. Get on with it, man."

Until this moment he had not imagined how difficult it might be to explain quite what he has been about at Mylehurst Abbey.

"Your Royal Highness, it has sometimes fallen to my humble self," Osiris says after busy thought, "to sate the peculiar whims and desires of some very particular gentlemen. I think I can boast that whatever fancies my clients have envisioned, I have been pleased to supply."

The Prince takes a last mouthful of green goose, belches loudly, pushes back his chair and begins to pick at his yellow teeth.

"Tell us everything, omit nothing."

He tells the Prince all about the hungry twins, the Chinese girls who spoke no English, the Putney cripple, the daughter of the Indian Raja, the blind girl from Woolwich, the dwarfs and the blind albino boy, but says nothing about the despoiled children. Nor does he mention the disease which had then raged through their despoilers like an avenging demon.

"We find this all quite delicious," the Prince says, encouraging Osiris to venture that perhaps it is something run upon similar lines which the Prince would like him to organise at Carlton House, with the greatest possible discretion, of course? The Prince says nothing and slowly, it occurs to Osiris that he is being peered at in the way that an entomologist might view an unusual species of beetle. Almost immediately, he discovers another side to his genial host, who now adds, "If rumours are true, we are surprised that some of your activities have not had you hanged."

It is a moment when anything might happen, Osiris realises. He watches the Prince's expressionless countenance for an indication of which way the wind will blow. Perhaps the Prince will ring the little bell at his elbow and men will come in and take him away. How long this moment seems. He watches and then, when he thinks he detects some small relaxation among the facial muscles, he says, "Then might I ask why I am here? Is there some other service I might perform for your royal highness?"

The Price smiles widely, his joke over.

"There is. What we want from you is something quite particular."

"I am entirely at your service, your Royal Highness."

The Prince's gaze wanders about the room and alights upon a large and elaborately-framed painting which hangs above one of Mr Adam's fireplaces. He waves his toothpick at it.

"There is in this town a rather toothsome delicacy," he tells Osiris, “which we crave but have as yet been unable to procure for ourselves.”

Osiris looks. The painting is one of Grace's larger works and Osiris recalls aiding the artist with its composition. The scene will be familiar to anyone who frequents the theatre. Standing centre-stage by the bed is Othello, mighty, military, *in extremis* and embodied here by a bricklayer employed by a member of the Albion. The man's dark face is in shadow, an oblique beam of dust-moted light falling instead upon his intended victim: Desdemona, small, fragile and attired in a thin, white shift, through which the beam of window light clearly delineates the lithe shape of her young body and small breasts, meets his gaze with a surprise that is toppling into terror. The blue eyes which glisten brightly clearly convey her knowingness of what may happen to her. Osiris remembers watching Grace paint this scene and seeing him become increasingly frustrated with the young girl who seemed incapable of conveying anything remotely resembling terror. Osiris had been obliged to bend down and whisper something in her ear. “That is it,” Grace had said to her immediately afterwards, “You have it now.”

“You want this girl?”

“We should hardly need a pander such as yourself for that. We want Grace, man.”

“Grace? But he is dead, I...”

“My people dealt with Grace's agent, someone called Gretch, we believe, but we have been told that this is no longer possible.”

“No, your Royal Highness.”

“We also know that you were Grace's mentor for much of his work and that you too were involved in many of Grace's dealings in the world of art.”

"That is true. If your Royal Highness will kindly recall, I facilitated his acquisition of both this *Othello* and *Samson With Delilah*?"

The prince lifts himself a little from his stool and farts loudly. Now he unbuttons his coat and allows his eyes to roam around those parts of his *Othello* where details struggle to escape from the shadows before coming to rest upon the merciless glint in the general's eyes.

"Which brings us to the matters in hand."

"Your Royal Highness?"

"It is just this. We had been eagerly awaiting the completion of Henry Grace's painting of London burning, the picture every fool was talking about. We were to enjoy a private viewing the very week it burned. Grace's masterpiece was to crown our collection of his most significant works. We were very sorry indeed to hear of its destruction."

"Your Highness will have heard, I am sure..."

"That some parts of this picture survived the flames. Yes, we have heard that."

"I have been looking for these pictures and..."

"You have an interest in them, De'Ath?"

"I have been commissioned to locate and secure them."

"By the man who aspires to become our next prime minister, we think?"

"Your Highness is very well informed."

"And what does he promise you, should you succeed?"

Osiris walks out on a limb. "Nothing that I am sure your Royal Highness's largesse and protection would not better. I know where two of these portions are. It will not be difficult to get hold of them."

"Mr De'Ath, if you are as quick as we take you to be, you will know that we are interested only in one particular remnant. This picture features the true likenesses of men who may hold power in the country very soon, if things go their way."

"That is by no means certain," Osiris says. "Edward Villiers is in a parlous position just now. He may lack backing when it comes to the vote."

"We can see that he lacks nothing," the Prince says, "And once in power we think he may then be amenable to certain little requests we may have to make, while he knows that picture is in our safe keeping. Never mind what Villiers is offering you. Find this picture for us and you will find yourself in an altogether better position."

"A place at Court? Under your protection?"

"How dare you bother us with details, man! Find that picture."

"Your Royal Highness may consider it already done." Osiris says, disgusting himself with his new-found obsequiousness. The Prince empties his cup, dabs at his mouth and walks towards the door. "Prinny," he says. "You may call us Prinny."

Sixty Six

In a far less affluent part of the city, where piles of rags are hawked as second-best clothes and women with half-naked infants crumple gin-drunk in doorways, curious eyes mark an odd-looking individual making sure-footed progress towards some destination of his own knowing. It is quite a thing to be considered odd-looking on a street like this, where caged animals that pace and flutter or pine and droop go unremarked and anything of value has likely been stolen this very morning. The man appears not to notice the cripples and old soldiers who beg for alms, nor see the antics of fire-eaters and jugglers or hear the men of every hue who convene on corners and talk in tongues only they can comprehend.

The man is sixty, or seventy, or perhaps he is even older – or is much younger, really there is no telling. He has one of those faces which accretes the corrugations of passing years but through whose bright, pale-blue eyes – magnified by the pebble spectacles which clamp to his temples – can be decried the youthful self trapped inside. His straw-thin frame is sleeved in the costume of another age: what was once a knee-length, sky-blue coat with a dozen buttons he wears with a yellowing vest, knee-britches and filthy stockings over shoes whose buckles no longer match. Atop a head which may or may not be bald, he wears a grey and threadbare wig very much of the older style.

The fellow appears to be oblivious to defects in his uniform and with some audacity, carries himself as a gentleman. He walks quickly and unlike so many who lounge and laugh, or beg for pennies or insinuate their hands into other men's pockets, this fellow surely has honest purpose. He has a countenance rare in these streets, open and unguarded, but evidently his mind is preoccupied as his eyes fail to see a costermonger's cart being shoved out from an alleyway and he falls headlong into the street. The man regains his feet and dusts himself off as well he possibly can – there is no profit for street-sweepers here – and, seeming not to see or hear the gaggle of women who point and snort, he turns nimbly about a sharp corner and is soon lost among a maze of shadowy, smaller byways.

Narcissus Pyke stops before a shop and consults the list he has obtained from the auctioneer he knows of old. He scrutinises the decaying sign that hangs above the door and tries to make out lettering that the passage of time has long-since faded. Satisfied he has arrived at his destination, he peers into small, grimy bow-windows stuffed with examples of the taxidermist's art: a brace of squirrels clutching nuts, three prancing terriers, a curled spaniel which might be asleep by a fire and a bushy-brushed fox whose glassy eyes swivel to assure himself that he is not pursued. Behind this display he sees framed pictures, three indifferent portraits in oil so large they must rob the shop of light and a cluster of watercolours which Pyke judges the work of enthusiastic but unskilled amateurs. He presses his face to the window to descry the treasures inside.

A place such as this is a fabulous gold-mine to a man like Narcissus Pyke, who loves nothing better than a pandemonium of unsorted bric-a-brac from whose murky depths he so often has retrieved some dull-looking item which to him is a jewel. For Pyke is not only a collector of newspapers and the facts contained therein, but also of historic objects, of unusual items for which no-one has yet ascribed a value and in some cases even a use.

His rickety, four floored house in Spitalfiends is a monument to the collector, to the fruits of a lifetime's fossicking, hours and days spent rifling through ancient documents, rummaging in curio shops and scrabbling over dust-heaps in search of some unknowable thing that will crown his life's efforts. Today, he is putting his skills at the service of a kindred spirit and knowing what he now knows, its discovery interests him quite as much as it does his commissioner. He has spent long days upon its trail and if he does not find it here, he knows not where to look for it next.

He pushes hard to open a sticky door and steps down into a gloomy place where a single shaft of dust-moted light illuminates a small space on the floorboards and leaves in half-light the stacks of carelessly filled shelves, on which he discerns among other detritus, old cooking pots, trivets, flatirons, foxed mirrors, candlesticks, stair-rods and warming-pans. Also offered for sale, he notes, are chipped bed-pans, tied bundles of ancient books, folded rugs, several military swords and, quite possibly, the blunderbuss which is now levelled at his stomach. The thin man holding the gun is old, fifty five if he is a day, and though it is mid-afternoon, he is still draped in a green, decorated silk banyan. His querulous voice demands to know what does he want, coming here at this inconvenient time?

“This time? What o-clock is it?” Pyke enquires. If he is bothered by the wide-mouthed weapon which at any moment might be fired or perhaps go off on its own accord, he does not advertise it. Instead, he fumbles in his pockets and frowns. "Dear me, where is my pocket-watch? I had it in my hand not half-an-hour ago."

The man smiles joylessly and stacks the gun upon a shelf. "No-one but a fool fetches out his watch on these streets," he says. "Ask about and you will be able to buy it back."

"Such a world!" Pyke says and glances at his list before extending a bony hand. "I have the pleasure of Darius Blunt, I believe? Allow me to introduce myself."

The man takes a step towards him, as if to claim his space.

"I know who you are, Pyke, I seen you at the sales and at the flash-markets. You've robbed me of many a prize I had set my sights on. And what is it you would rob me of today? Speak up, my hearing is not the best."

"I will rob you of nothing," Pyke says, "I am come not for myself but for Mr Morris Malone of *The Enquirer.*"

"Not the fellow who was hung? The one who is turning London upside down looking for bits of a picture that was burned? Well, I can tell you now, I got none of those bits. Unless they come in lately and I ain't sorted them yet. I buy a lot of stuff, as you can see. "

"I want to look through your stock anyway," Pyke says.

"Why would I let you do that, you thieving magpie?"

Pyke slips a hand inside his coat and opens a small bag for Darius Blunt's inspection. "I will charge you two of those pretty coins for the honour, then?" Blunt says and dips bony fingers into the bag. Pyke watches him and notices for the first time the patch on the man's balding skull which is raw and blue. "You have been injured?" he says.

"That?" Blunt says, touching the place, "*They* did that."

"Who did what? What has happened?"

"I was robbed. Or rather, I might have been robbed had they taken something."

"What do you mean?"

"I will tell you. Some time before Monday dawn, Satan starts with his barking. Such a noise. There's someone in the house, he's saying, and will not be quieted until I have got up and taken a look. So I peer down the stairs and I see a light flickering upon a wall. Satan is right. There is someone there and they have a lantern. I have had people in here before and between us, Satan and I have always managed to see them off. And so I thought it would go this time."

"But this was different?"

"Satan's blood was up. I could not hold him back. He tears down the stairs and next, I hear a man scream and I hear Satan a-tussling and a-growling and sounding like his teeth was fully employed. I enter the room and see this fellow pressed hard against the wall by my dog who is up on his hind legs and like to have this fellow's throat out and might have done so had not this other villain, who I had not seen until then, taken a pistol from his coat and shot my Satan dead."

"But they took nothing?" Pyke says.

"I ain't finished yet. The fellow Satan was making a meal of is lying there yelping like a beaten bitch and I see this one who has shot my dog, the dog I have adored this seven year, and my blood boils. He looks no Goliath to me and so I reach for the brass candlestick I keep on yonder table, intending to crack open his skull with it. I am groping where the stick should be but now is not. And that is when I see a flash and feel such savage pain and remember no more."

"You were struck with the candlestick?"

"Aye, and when I recovered myself they were gone, both of them. Just my poor Satan, lying there with a hole through his heart."

"Do you know who these men were?"

"It was too dark to make out a face. But the way the one with the gun bore himself, I remember thinking, he is not from these parts. A gentleman, he was."

"I must ask you once again. Did they take anything? Did you note anything missing?"

The man laughs and waves his hand at the chaotic shelves. "Would you know if an item had been took from this lot?"

"But you have already said they took nothing."

"They took nothing of great value. I do not trade in such stuff. I feed the appetites of those who will never be able to afford nice things. But here and there, as chance will have it, I come across something which is indeed of value and if it is being offered at a digestible price, I will have it and pass it on to one of my more select customers. I had a certain number of such items and not one had been taken."

"They searched these shelves?"

"These shelves was all disturbed, nothing in its proper place. Yes, I would say they hunted hard before Satan heard them."

"You keep goods in other parts of this house?"

"I keep the better items with the stuff I have yet to sort and price in a room at the back. They had yet to try their luck in there. Well, well. First these vagabonds, now you. What is it the world is after?"

"I tell you, I cannot say. It may not exist. But where there is a possibility, I will go. And in that room is where I shall go first," Pyke says.

"You are welcome to do so," Blunt says, "But I warn you, do not try to gull me over the price. If it is valuable to you, it will be so to me, too. Come with me."

The noisome smell which Pyke had become aware of immediately upon entering the shop becomes very much more potent as he follows Blunt down a narrow passage and into the rear of the building where a work-bench is littered with small tools, lit candles and a pile of horse-hair. There is a fire in the grate on which a pot of glue simmers. Pyke turns and steps sharply back in fright as bared fangs and wild eyes greet him. For a moment, he sees a great beast upon a table preparing to pounce but then sees that the beast's ribcage is open and a quantity of horsehair and cotton cloth is escaping from a great rent.

"Satan cannot harm you now," Blunt says and indicates the far wall of the room. "The place you want is behind that door."

Pyke takes another two downward steps and enters a room poorly-illuminated by a barred street-level grill set high in the wall. The place is filled almost completely with sacks and old tea chests, some stacked neatly. A number of sacks are stuffed into the cupboards of old furniture and others apparently slung upon high shelves. Against one wall are stacked pictures of various sizes. Pyke opens out the pile and looks upon the likenesses of well-fed men with dogs, women in fine hats, scenes of Athens, Rome and Venice and at the back of the pile, obstructed by furniture and just beyond his reach are two or three more which he will not bother inspecting. He has not come here for pictures.

In another corner are bibles and hymnals, pamphlets and books – he sees a full set of Vitruvius's architectural writings and a finely-bound tome lettered *The Lives of the Artists* – and beneath them piled high and already smelling like they have been left too long in a damp place are other books. He picks his way through such obstacles with some difficulty, setting a figurine of Aphrodite teetering as he narrowly avoids treading upon children's toys and toppling stacks of dishes and towers of cups and saucers and all the other things that remain when a spirit leaves a house and there is no-one to claim the earthly chattels.

Pyke makes himself a space and after poking about in several dusty, hessian sacks, he empties one upon the floor, quickly decides that what he looks for is not among the pile and empties another. There is an urgency to his ferreting today, he does not wish to disappoint the man who has solicited his help. He remembers that man in lesser days, when he cleared away pots in the coffee houses, remembers the indignities he was made to suffer, recalls turning away in anguish when the man was made to dance upon a table. He remembers too how he would linger by Pyke's table, and how they would both enjoy exchanging views on some subject of shared interest before the pot-man was called away by imperious voices. Both men sensed a kinship.

Morris Malone and the older man established stronger bonds long before Mouse acquired the editorship of *The Enquirer* under such terrible circumstances. The kinship they shared was one of inquisitiveness, both men being the sorts who are unable to let a curious matter go until they have turned it inside out and understood it perfectly. Pyke relished making himself useful to his younger friend, becoming an avid supplier of tit-bits and overheard conversations for Mouse to commit to his green notebook and continued to supply useful gossip and nuggets of wisdom for his newspaper.

Recently, together and separately, they have followed a trail, Mouse going here, he going there and now Pyke's friend has supplied him with their most promising lead to date. He squints at the small window where the light is failing and prays that this does not prove one more blind alley. He is breaking a sweat as he works faster. He lights a candle from one in the lightless hallway and finds it a place upon a crowded table and on he goes. At last, he finishes – and despairs at failing to find his prize. But then he recalls a few sacks he dismissed early and empties all these out into one great pile. He chuckles and smiles broadly and would execute a little caper had he only the space. Though it does not glitter, what he picks up now is surely gold. He picks a watercolour at random, pays Blunt well over the odds for it and turns towards the door. As he leaves the shop, he encounters another man entering it and for some reason he cannot understand, feels doubly glad that his prize is concealed beneath his coat.

Sixty Seven

"Damn them, damn them all," Osiris De'Ath breathes as he brushes aside ostlers and passengers at the coaching inn door. Well, he has been receiving some knocks himself of late. Every day he feels a little more vulnerable and a little more threatened, both conditions made the more worrisome for being quite novel to him. Why the devil will nothing go his way? So he fumes as he cuts a way through a jostling mob of heavy-laden travellers who loudly remonstrate. Once in the sanctuary of the hired room, he drops into a chair by the fire, calls for the waiter and allows his man to remove his boots. He considers using one of those boots to kick Towse in the teeth, now that he has failed him on such important business.

Discovering after protracted effort that the picture he seeks was sold along with other items to a dealer in the Dials, he had sent Towse to purchase it. But as he hears it, the dealer took against something in Towse's manner and was adamant that he could not be expected to lay hands on whatever he wanted at the drop of a hat. With only the Prince's protection standing between himself and imminent disaster, Osiris had decided to accelerate matters and that plan, being too desperate, had failed, just as his resort to the law had failed. He hopes they have not killed the man but only because that might be one more complication.

He buys *The Enquirer* from a boy in the lobby and opens it with hands that should be steadier, wondering what dangerous, vitriolic nonsense he will find there this day – there always is something. What he saw in its pages only yesterday had uncapped a Vesuvian rage. His tormentors at this pestilent newspaper have all-but named him, Osiris De'Ath, as the weird figure in the picture which everyone would have forgotten by now, had not that meddling footman commissioned those prints. It is ridiculous, beyond crediting. How could that man possibly be him? He knows the value of gold too well to gift such stuff to carrion. But will others be so sure? In his experience, most fools will believe what is put in front of them. Some days he can almost hear the hounds at his back.

He tells Towse that he wants to be alone and pours himself a large brandy. He has full two hours to wait until his southbound coach departs.

The bitter irony of it all is that he is not the guilty man. He is a poet, a dilettante, a patron of the arts. He did not drive those girls to distraction or death. He knew nothing of these crimes until the first body had been found, which was about the time that the other silly girl had been confined to Bethlem Hospital. It had not even been his idea to put Ran Clayton in charge of disposing of the girls once they had been used and discarded by the members of the Albion Club. He thinks it was Collins, that soak he saw up in London, who first sent Clayton out in a coach with a girl and the vague instruction to get rid of her. How Ranelegh Clayton was ever voted into the Albion, Osiris cannot imagine.

Some of those girls, as he now understands it, had been turned out of the carriage at remote locations, where they would have been too bewildered to say accurately what had happened to them or where they had been. This was all to the good. Then one of them must have caught Clayton's eye and long-pent, dark thoughts had begun to bubble and burst. Whether he had meant to kill or whether circumstances had gotten beyond his control Osiris had not established, but certain it was that someone had mutilated one girl at least and that similar mutilations had been performed upon the body of the girl whose throat was cut at Limehouse.

Osiris did not doubt that Clayton was capable of such things. One thing was certain. This damnable newspaper would not drop the matter. He feels keenly the injustice of it all. He had done nothing, only obeyed the dictates of others. The unholy cure had been no idea of his; they had conjured that themselves. And now they are throwing him to the dogs. If things do not improve, he fears he will go mad. He sets down his glass, tips back his head and surrenders himself to sleep.

When he awakens it is to news of a very much better sort. There before him stands Towse, short of breath and looking very agitated. Under his arm and not entirely covered with a cloth is a painting. As chance will have it the portion of the painting that is revealed to him as his man stands there waiting like a dog for his reward is the twisted, terror-stricken visage of Edward Villiers. There being presently no-one else in the saloon, it is safe for Towse to display his prize. Osiris drinks it in. Before him is his freedom, his protection from persecution, his future.

"You have amazed me, Andrew," he says to the other man, who glows. "How did you get it?"

Towse's ruddy face lowers like Scottish weather. His eyes are unreadable.

“Is it not enough that I did?” he says.

His tone borders on impertinence. Osiris looks at him anew, marking as he does so the tiny flecks of red which have appeared on his valet's cheek and neck, about which he will say nothing.

Sixty Eight

"So, you are about this mysterious *business* of yours today?" Michel asks pointedly. Mouse expresses his surprise at seeing her here as they coalesce with the noisy crowds funnelling onto London Bridge. Her soft voice works hard to compete with the chatter of the transpontine throng, the street-sellers crying their wares and the cackle of swooping seagulls. Passing them now, two blousy young harlots hitch their skirts and trip along, laughing raucously. Michel tries to say something more, but now a boatman is bellowing warnings and cursing creatively as he broaches the currents beneath the bridge. She bends a little to make herself heard by Mouse.

"You will have to clarify that," Mouse shouts into her ear before they are briefly separated by a pear-shaped coster pushing an apple-laden barrow.

"The business you keep so close. The business that sends you out at all hours."

"Close? I hope it is not in my nature to be secretive. I have someone to see in Southwark, that is all." Mouse quickens his step so his small legs may match Michel's strides. "Anyway, you have disturbed my train of thought."

"What were you thinking of?" Michel shouts, above the shrieks of the young whores.

"It so happens that I was thinking of you, Michel."

"Me?"

"You."

"Have I done something to displease you?"

"Nothing of the sort. But it has occurred to me that I have been very selfish. I have torn you from the life you love."

A long moment passes before Michel responds.

"I lost that life the night Jamie Gretch burned alive and Adam Brewer offered me a roof," she says at last. "You have provided me with another life and I thank you for it." Where the shops on the bridge have been pulled down, Mouse stops, hoists himself upon a stone ledge and peers over the parapet. On the river far below, ferrymen are feathering their oars while a lighter freighted with coal ploughs slowly on, past the taverns and the great warehouses on the riverbanks.

"Look," he says, "Are you not stirred to paint a lively scene like this?"

"I have seen all I want of rivers and ferryboats," Michel says, flatly. "We must bring an end to what we are about before I can think of painting or doing anything else. I will speak plainly with you, Mouse. I am fearful. We are playing with fire and brimstone."

Mouse lifts and lightly squeezes her hand. "We may yet face trials, that is true. But let us take a moment to imagine a time when all this is only a memory. What then, Michel? What would you paint?"

Eyes ensnared by the swirling eddies and whirlpools created by the great stone piers, Michel thinks for a moment. "I would paint a counterbalance to the chaos and mayhem that Henry Grace saw in this world,' she says, before glancing upwards towards dome of St Pauls. "I would not want people to look at what I have done and see a city filled with terror and steeped in guilt."

"Good, Michel. People need hope in these days. They hunger for it. A picture like that would be well-received, I am sure of it. And who knows, it may make your fortune, once people know how much of *The New Fire of London* was really yours."

"No, this work must not be tainted by such concerns. I will paint this picture for all the people who have believed in us, for the victims and those who helped save you. I shall not even sign it. I shall paint it and have it hung somewhere it may do some good. And then I will retire to quieter things."

"You will not retire from painting?"

"I cannot do that. But my subjects will be essays in tranquillity, I think."

Mouse smiles and casts her a doubtful look.

"That does not sound like you."

Michel laughs. "You may be proved right. But we will see. I should like to try a seascape, although I have heard it is customary to first set one's eyes upon the sea. Well. It is getting late and one of us should return to Grub Street. I must turn back now. We cannot let a boy edit *The Enquirer*."

"No, but if ever we do, Will might be that boy," Mouse says. He drops down from his ledge and is resuming his walk to Southwark when he stops, turns and calls to Michel.

"I will forget my head, wig and all, one day," he says. "Talking of the sea has reminded me that I have news for you."

"Then tell me."

"I have heard something from a friend in Brighthelmstone."

"Brighthelmstone?"

"A little place on the South Coast – a little place which will quickly grow, I think, now that the Prince of Wales is to spend more time there. In fact, it is from a functionary of the Prince that I have this news."

"Which is?"

"Tell me, Michel, did the Prince's agents buy from Henry Grace?"

"Anyone with pretensions to taste bought from us at one time," Michel says. "As I recall, the Prince commissioned a portrait of the actress, Mary Robinson and purchased two of Mr Grace's finest history paintings, *Samson With Delilah* and *The Betrayal of Desdemona.* Mr Grace was given to understand that should he produce any more work of similar quality, he would find a ready market at Carlton House."

"Then I think I can trust my source. John Stebbing was a butler at Carlton House who supplied me with court news and gossip. He has now been transferred to the Prince's residence in Brighthelmstone. Stebbing writes that an important work by Henry Grace has lately been acquired for the Prince's collection. His description was inadequate and so I requested further details."

"And he described my painting, the one we search for?"

“He did indeed. The Prince has it now. But it is who sold it to him that should interest us.”

“Which was?”

“Osiris De'Ath.”

“De'Ath? But how could he find it when we could not?”

“Believe me, Michel, no-one is more galled by that question than me. I sometimes think we are not paying sufficient attention to the network that feeds us.”

“We are distracted, Mouse. Nothing is going to operate as it should until we have closed the book on the business we have in hand. So let us screw our courage to the sticking place and make a start. Here is what puzzles me. We have assumed that De'Ath wanted that picture as leverage against his enemies – it is no secret that there is a schism between himself and Edward Villiers – so why would an experienced gambler such as he part with his high card?”

“That has confounded me too,” Mouse says. “From what my sources tell me, De'Ath has recently been converting assets into cash, so he cannot be short of that commodity. I can only think that he has put his trust in the Prince to help him in some way.”

“Royal protection? Would the Prince offer that? With such a cloud as we have created hanging over him? Surely Prince George cannot afford to be seen with such a pariah?”

“Our Prince can afford to do what he likes, and spends much of his time and his father's money doing just that.”

“And where is De'Ath now? I pray he has not slipped away somewhere?”

"Stebbing tells me he remains at Brighthelmstone. Accommodated by the Prince at Grove House."

"I say again, why would the Prince do that?"

"The Prince has his reasons, Michel. And his peccadillos."

"This is no time for riddling."

"Then I will be plain," Mouse says. "Our Prince is fully intent upon enjoying himself to the utmost before kingship is thrust upon him. To say he is profligate somewhat understates the case."

"I have heard he overspends upon the arts and architecture," Michel says.

"And that is why he is here in Brighthelmstone now. As I understand it, he has grand plans to remodel a pavilion there in the style of a Maharajah's palace. It is quite extraordinary. But it is what else he spends his money on that concerns us today."

"Which is?"

"Gaming and high living, as you would expect of any gentleman of wealth. But mark this. Stebbing tells me there were gatherings at Carlton House of the Roman variety."

"Roman?"

"Perhaps it is enough to say that wine is taken and women enjoyed."

"Orgies, then?" Will says.

"And the Prince attends such things?"

"As an active participant, if what I hear is true," Mouse says. "There is one such entertainment imminent at his Brighthelmstone residence and by Stebbing's account, De'Ath has been given charge of it. He appears to be reprising the role he played the caves at Mylnehurst Abbey. The Prince may find Osiris De'Ath a very useful servant."

"While he remains at Grove House we cannot touch him. But he cannot stay there for ever."

"Nor it it intended that he does. There is talk of the Prince installing him is a small palazzo he has at Venice, where De'Ath will source and send back fine art for his place at Brighthelmstone and live himself in fine style, safe from persecution here."

"This is insufferable," Michele storms. "Where is the justice? After all this man has done? If not by his own hand then by those of his puppets?"

"Michel, calm yourself, I have thought about this."

"Then what are we to do?"

"I will tell you. I will first see my man in Southwark and then we will pack our bags. I shall instruct Will to look after the newspaper for a few days and see that he gives all prominence to a certain little item I have written for him. As for you, Michel, you are going to see the sea."

Michel watches until the dwarf is lost to sight in the crowds on the south side of the bridge. And then, for no good reason she can think of, she begins to cry.

Sixty Nine

Michel Angelo, artist, stands before the opened window and gazes towards a shimmering infinity. She has never before seen the ocean and she allows herself to be captivated by sunlight flickering upon a billion splinters of water whose fascinating tones change with every blink of the eye and gain much from the contrast provided by a bank of black clouds lowering in the West. One day she will capture this, she thinks, and automatically begins listing the colours she will combine to recreate what she now sees – white of silver, cobalt blue, malachite? But now at last her eye is caught by the small, familiar figure she has been watching for, who scuttles towards the house, pressing a threadbare wig to his head.

"What is there to eat? I went out without a morsel inside me," Mouse is gasping as he surmounts the last of four-pair of steep stairs to the Brighthelmstone rooms they have taken. He finds an elevating cushion and seats himself at the rough table where dishes lie uncleared, while Michel looks for the toasting fork.

"I have waited all morning for you," Michel says.

"I have been detained. Has a parcel arrived for me?" Mouse's eyes roam the room in search of such a thing.

"There has been no parcel," Michel says. "Who would send a parcel to Brighthelmstone?"

“Why, Narcissus Pyke, of course.”

“Of course?”

“Dear me, have I not told you of this? You do know I have been working with Pyke this past fortnight to track the thing we most need?”

“I know you have been disappearing, both here and in London,” Michel says, “but I do not recall you telling anyone why.”

“Do I have to account for my every movement?” Mouse says, “I hope not, for I should find that quite limiting. Why did you not ask me? Any one of you might have done that and cleared up the mystery immediately.”

“You have been so very short-tempered of late that no-one liked to do that.”

“Is that the way I have been with everybody? If that is case I am truly sorry. But I have been pulled this way and that, being as many times elated – thinking we have at last come upon that which we seek – as cast down that a promising lead has come to nothing. That sort of thing will put a man in a bad mood, I assure you.”

“Well, recover yourself now,” Michel says, putting before him a slice of buttered toast, “and tell me all. What is it that you have been about?”

Mouse bites into the toast, chews, swallows cold tea, takes another bite and then, brushing crumbs from his shirt, he says, “I have been on the trail of Henry Grace's journals, those parts I know nothing of.”

“His journals?” Michel frowns and does not hide her disappointment. “Then I regret you have been on a fool's errand. I told you, they would have burned with the house. And burned quicker than anything else.”

Mouse looks about the table, as if another slice of toast might be hidden behind teacups or the stack of various newspapers.

"No, no, take a moment to reflect," he says. "As you have had cause to remember, Gretch was at that time consigning everything he could to the salerooms in an effort to keep the establishment at Leicester Fields afloat. So to the salerooms I went. I wasted a lot of time going to the wrong house to begin with but then I met with a man at Sotheby's who recollected seeing some books of writings by the artist whose name has lately been on all lips. Christie's had first been offered them but had found them unsuitable. He let them go for sale as part of a job lot, not realising their worth."

"But he was useful, this man?" Michel asks.

"He was. We now know that the journals, along with some books and statuary and, I believe, your painting, Michel, were sold to a dealer of curios in Seven Dials. On the day that we left for the coast, Pyke was on his way there to secure them for us. I only pray that this dealer has not realised their importance."

"How will we know if your friend has succeeded?"

"If he has, he will forward the journals to us at this address."

"You deem writings to be more important than a picture?" Michel says, thoughtfully.

"In this case, yes, a hundred times yes. Do you not think that if Grace was as mired in guilt as it seems he was, he would have confessed his crimes to his diary?"

There is a moment's silence while Mouse removes his wig and runs his fingers through short, chestnut hair.

“You may be right,” Michel concedes. “But no such things have come here today.”

Mouse signs off a long and detailed letter of instructions which is addressed to Will Templeton at the sign of the Dipped Quill, Grub Street, London. Seeing him put down his quill, Michel asks how he has fared on this morning's enterprise?

“I went to the Prince's residence at Grove House,” Mouse says, “where I found out as much as I could from coachmen and cabmen who linger there. I was briefly able to see Stebbing, too.”

“And what did you learn?” Michel asks.

“Just this. The Prince has been summoned earlier than he expected to attend upon his father, the King on some business of finance. Stebbing tells me the Prince leaves for London tomorrow morning and he does not know when he might return. De'Ath is to stay at Grove House at least until the entertainment, which will happen soon after the Prince returns. So the plan I outlined to you in London will have to be actioned before he gets back.”

“We are going ahead with this madcap scheme?”

“If you are still willing. The time would seem to be right for it.”

“Why would you believe that?”

“From what I hear from Stebbing, our harrying has unsettled our quarry quite as much as we hoped it might – he may be receiving our latest thrust as we speak if Will and Adam have got the paper out on time. The uncertainty of his position has maddened him to the point where he spends much of the day closeted in his room.”

"Has he been seen outside of Grove House?"

"He will not go out without good purpose, Stebbing says. In his opinion, De'Ath is teetering on the edge of mental prostration and if given a push, our bird may take flight. So, I say we act now. If you are quite happy to do this thing, Michel? As I have told you, I was able to buy back the clothes you pawned and you will find these in my valise."

"You know I will not refuse. I cannot. But it is one thing to drive him from his refuge and arrest him and quite another to see him convicted on the paltry evidence we have amassed thus far."

"That is unfortunately true. And we cannot count on your painting helping to convict," Mouse says. "Stebbing suspects that the Prince may have reasons to withhold the picture and give his support to Villiers. The success of our design and our hope of obtaining justice for poor Obadiah rests entirely upon the retrieval of Grace's journals."

"But if Pyke fails? What will we do then? Watch this monster fly to Venice?"

"For goodness sake, let us not admit of that possibility, Michel. Rather, put your faith in God and good chance that Narcissus succeeds."

Seventy

A servant whose daily duty it is to light the candles of Grove House will have begun by lighting his own candle from another or even taking a taper from the fire in the kitchen and then ascending back stairs to kindle the bracketed torches set on either side of the doors, which guide visitors and moths at night or in a sea-fog.

He will then return inside where a footman will lower the candelabra on their chains that he may ignite the tiered wicks on each of three wheels. There are candles stowed in niches on the stairs, in wall-mounts along hallways and they stand erect in brass and silver sticks in windows and upon tables in every room he visits on his rounds. In this way, the candlelighter sees almost the whole of the house and many of its residents, too. He enjoys his work; here he might have brief converse with a fellow servant in a quiet corridor or even steal a kiss with an under-housemaid in some unfrequented passage. And when he is done, he will relay anything curious he has encountered on his travels to interested members of his confraternity at the kitchen dinner-table.

To discover something others have not is a thing greatly to be wished below stairs at Grove House. In this fashion, cooks, parlour-maids, kitchen and scullery-maids, footmen and coachmen have overheard private conversations, learned of adulterous liaisons, seen some shocking undergarments and along the way have discovered secrets of State. The lowliest staff have sometimes been privy to important news before the higher echelons of the Price's household and certainly before the news is known to the Prince himself. There is an element of rivalry and competition to the practise of gossip-gathering and information-harvesting.

This evening, Tom Peck the candlelighter thinks he has something to capture the attention of everyone present. He will as always await the departure of the butler, Mr Jackson and the housekeeper, Mrs Moreton to retire with Ramsay, the ladies-maid before sharing his spoils with his associates. He wishes devoutly that these three would eat their cheese and swallow their tea with a little more expedition.

"So I knocked and I waited at the door," Tom Peck tells the others this evening. "But was there an answer to my knock? I tell you, there was not."

"Was he asleep?"

"No, he was not."

"How could you know that?"

"Allow me to tell you. As you know, he has not left his room these last three days and yesterday would not let Suki make up his fire nor change his pot."

"He was not looking right when last I saw him," Suki says.

"So was it not my duty to see that nothing was amiss?"

"What did you do, Tom?" asks Flora, who is second parlourmaid.

"I applied my eye to the keyhole."

"You could lose your place for that," says Ford, a footman.

"And what did you see?" says Suki.

"Nothing, at first. Just his sheets all tangled upon the floor."

"Is that all you have to tell us?" asks Ford.

"Then I think I hear a noise, so I look again and I see his naked legs and I hear him talking, too."

"What was he doing?" demands Suki, "Who was he talking to?"

"That is the thing," Tom Peck says. "I see his legs walking up and down his room and I see only his legs."

"Then who was he talking to?"

"Nobody. He was enjoying a little converse with himself."

"He was talking with himself?" Suki says.

"First sign of you know what," says the footman with a smirk.

"It does not surprise me," says Flora, whose mouth is not quite empty of syllabub. "He behaved strangely when I went for his sheets, it being washday. There he was, hair all undone, in his nightshirt at four in the afternoon and using such dreadful language as you might hear in a low tavern. Or so I am told."

"He cursed you, Suki?"

"No, it was like he did not see me. He was cursing himself or his fortunes, I think, nothing he said made any sense to me. I do not know what a man like him is doing at Grove House, I am sure."

"I can answer that," says Mr Stebbing, as he sets down a tray of empty teacups he has carried downstairs, "although as I have told you too often before, I do not approve of gossip in this house."

"Please, Mr Stebbing, who is this man?"

"His name is De'Ath, if you please."

"Like Death?"

"And looking more the part every day," says the footman.

"Mind your tongue, Ford. That man is a guest of his Royal Highness and as such should be accorded our respect, no matter what."

"The Prince has had some rum visitors, but no-one like this," Flora says. "Last morning. I went in and, well, I do not like to say what he had done to his sheets."

"In this case," Stebbing says, "I feel justified in discussing this guest as the Prince appears to be entertaining second thoughts about him."

"Why did he come here in the first place?" asks Tom Peck.

"Why indeed," says Stebbing, ruminatively. "It seems we are to have a rout such as we had at Carlton House and this man is to take change of the affair. I will say nothing about these routs as they were not the sort of entertainments I would approve."

"You must tell us all, Mr Stebbing," Ford says.

"Do not tease us," Suki says.

"I will say no more, except that this man has some experience in arranging such things and is to assist in the preparations. Also, he has done the Prince some service – I believe the procurement of a painting was involved and the Prince was talking about sending him to Venice as his art agent. He was to lend him a palazzo he has there."

"It sounds like a suite in a certain London Tower would be more suited to this gentleman," says Ford.

"Was to? Then the Prince has changed his mind?" Tom Peck asks.

"That looks like the case but I cannot be sure," Stebbing says. "Certain information has reached Royal ears to the man's great discredit. Were this up to me, I would have him cast out on the instant. But it seems that unless we hear worse about this man, he will be kept on to see about this entertainment. What will happen to him after that I cannot imagine."

Osiris stoops and picks up the pages of newsprint which slipped from his hand. He sits down upon a small French chair in the closet which has been assigned for his accommodation while the Prince travels to London. It is his left eyelid which has started to flicker now. The footman who delivered him the newspaper must have seen his face plummet as he glanced at the front page of *The Enquirer*. He looks at it again and still he cannot believe what he reads. Yet here it is, set in Caslon font on newsprint he can feel between his fingers, scorching his stuttering eyes.

Henry Grace, he reads for a third time, *the painter presumed by all to have perished in the fire that consumed his house at Leicester Fields is apparently risen from the dead and has been seen by reliable witnesses outside lawyers' chambers at Lincoln's Inn Fields and also at Westminster Hall. Our sources were not the only eyes to be astounded by the sightings at these places. Where Mr Grace has been concealing himself since the fire, The Enquirer will be at pains to discover. We suggest he may gave been taken abroad to some congenial place of recuperation because he is reported as looking much recovered, although he continues to present to the world a curious spectacle in his Venetian festival mask.*

This cannot possibly be right. It is a mistake, false news, a terrible joke. People make mistakes, they see things that are not there. On Monday, or Tuesday, possibly, he thought he had seen a little girl who was abused in his caves and found dead soon afterwards. Confounded, untrusting of his senses, he had followed the girl down narrow passages and through kitchens and scanned every surprised face without seeing her own. He had been mistaken, just as these fools have been.

How like the damned *Enquirer* to print something that is so evidently untrue. Of course it is untrue. How can it possibly be true when he himself had administered the overdose of laudanum that finally saw Henry Grace off? He had held his hand and felt the weak pulse fade and disappear and then had slipped away without mentioning that the master of the house was no more. It was an act of mercy, nothing more, no matter how convenient the man's passing might be to certain people. This outrageous story is untrue, how could he have entertained it for a moment? It is some mischief concocted by those hellish people at *The Enquirer*. He comforts himself with this thought until he takes up a copy of *The Messenger* and reads an almost identical report.

He had not spent much thought on his last encounter with Henry Grace. In days following, he had been pleased that a cause of perturbation had been erased, pleased that his standing with men on the cusp of power was repaired, pleased even that he had been able to perform this small act of grace for his old friend. The friend himself he did not think of, perhaps he tried not to. But Henry Grace, he soon discovered, was not someone you might easily ignore.

At night, the younger Henry would creep unbidden into his mind and rebellious thoughts would usher him back to times long gone. He remembered clearly how it had been. Henry was the fool, the dupe, Osiris led. There was always that ordering to their relationship. In this way they had travelled Europe together, Paris, Milan, Rome, Venice and then, Naples. Henry was a buffoon with talent he did not know was his, someone to be tutored, enlightened and exploited. He was a fool but he was a fool who had always listened to him, someone who would go anywhere with him and it seemed, do anything for him.

At night he still saw his face, before the lesions had come. The sensations that beset him on such nights were new to him and he did not welcome them. It was impossible. Could it be that he himself was plagued with guilt, no matter that he had done absolutely nothing wrong?

He shakes himself free of such thinking and addresses the immediate crisis. Henry Grace alive, recovered, abroad. It is unthinkable. What might he recall of Osiris' last visit with him? Will he remember Osiris De'Ath lifting his head and pouring the tincture of opium down his throat even though he gagged and tried so hard to close his mouth and avert his face? What might Henry tell people? And who would he tell? *The Enquirer* would not be long in tracking him down to demand a full explanation of the masterpiece that was burned. What else might Henry Grace tell them? He needs to be gone and that soon. When will the Prince return and let him embark for Venice?

For the first time in his existence, Osiris feels stranded, beleaguered, helpless. A life lived on his own terms, neither wanting nor trusting anybody has left him with no friend to help him, no confidante to advise him. He feels naked and will need royal protection before he feels clothed again.

He closes his eyes and strives for a few moments of respite from vengeful pursuers and men who should be dead. The carriages that have been trundling past his window have momentarily stopped, the street hawkers are quiet for once. He feels himself slipping towards the safe haven of sleep. And then he is ripped from its embrace by the sound of his own name shouted from the street. The shouting propels him from his chair to the long windows. He does not see him at first, sees only the line of carriages and the children playing with hoops in the street, but now the leading carriage moves away and standing upon the cobbles, and staring directly at him, quite impossibly, is Henry Grace.

Seventy One

Looking up from my candlelit page I say, "It was true, then. There was a maid at Leicester Fields who said the master killed someone."

Just after sunset, a carrier had stopped outside our apartments and a maid of all work had hurried up the stairs carrying a tinplate box. Mouse had laid out the notebooks upon the table like they were treasures from an ancient tomb, but hours later his head is resting heavily upon an inky hand as he turns over one more leaf of Henry Grace's journal. Adam has fallen asleep in a chair, where he snores loudly.

"Killed someone? That is what Grace believed and that is what put him in thrall to De'Ath. You told me yourself there is evidence of this belief in his paintings. Who knows, perhaps it inspired his *Othello*."

"Belief, you say? He confesses to his crime in his own handwriting."

Mouse puts down the magnifying glass which has been aiding his tired eyes, leafs through a small, bound volume and quickly finds the page he wants.

"Miss Angelo, you are too quick to condemn. Look at this paragraph, here. Henry Grace does not remember pushing Francesca from the window." Mouse turns over several more closely-written pages. "No corpse was found and nor can I find any mention of Grace recalling the act at some later date. In any case, Osiris De'Ath made sure they left the republic before the facts of the matter could be established. I expect this was some ploy of De'Ath's to strengthen his hold on a man whose talents he needed to bankroll his profligate life. He had been wringing money from Grace since their first meeting in Calais."

We read on and become by turns appalled, sickened and angered by the actions of men who would save their own lives or reputations by sacrificing innocents. And then Mouse reads out something which shakes my very foundations. From a later journal, he tells me that the Foundling Hospital was a favourite fishing ground for the Albion Club, certain weak and venal officials being susceptible to bribes. I close my eyes, but the horror will not be be shut out. "Georgie," I breathe as I am revisited by the dark, silent figure who came in the night, seeing again the little foundling's bruises and her hopeless face. At this moment, De'Ath should count himself fortunate that he is not within a dagger's strike of me.

Some moments pass before I can compose myself and give any meaning to Mouse's words. Oh, Georgie, I am thinking.

"To return to the matter of whether or not Grace killed someone in Venice," he is saying, "it does not much matter, except to the girl herself, of course. Not for our purposes. What I do think is that on top of the guilt he burdened himself with in Venice, was piled the culpability he felt for the atrocities at Mylnehurst and that this created a quite intolerable burden. Grace could find no way of alleviating his guilt. His only weapon was his brush. Painting himself and every other guilty party into that picture was an act of contrition, one he no doubt hoped would weigh in his favour when the disease that was slowly destroying him took its final toll."

I have to speak up. "It was a cowardly way, if what he had painted was not intended to be seen until after his own death. Those men deserved to be severely punished."

“I mean to see that they are. I have been speaking with a friendly Lincoln's Inn lawyer whose acquaintance I have had at Molly's. Mr Robertson has agreed to examine everything we propose to print about them. In this way we shall always be this side of the law, if only just. Our readers will be properly horrified to learn what these men have done and we shall not make it hard for them to identify those responsible.”

“What will come of them?” I ask. “They deserve worse than public vilification.”

“Michel, *The Enquirer* will not rest until every surviving members of this evil coterie has suffered for his sins. Parliamentary seats will be lost, dreams shattered. We will create such a storm that the government itself may be brought down. My lawyer friend will assist parents of the violated children to bring actions against those responsible, and I hope that somewhere in this process we may discover the identity of the fiend personally responsible for killing at least two of those poor little girls.”

“You do not think that man is De'Ath?”

“De'Ath would have been more consistent and altogether less messy. These crimes are the crude work of someone satisfying base and animal needs. Someone who was perhaps De'Ath's instrument, we cannot know. Whoever it is, I should very much like to see the law take its ultimate course with him and with De'Ath.”

“Even that,” I say, after a moment's hesitation. “I would wish it for them all.”

Seventy Two

Henry Grace stands in the middle of the street while angry cabmen shout and urge him to get out of their way. The fashionable people promenading outside the Prince's residence pretend not to see him but also to be ignored is the half-dressed man with wild hair who stands at an opened window of the Prince's house, shaking like a Bedlam lunatic. He cranes from the balcony of the upper room, putting himself in imminent danger of crashing onto the flags below as he calls out to the man stopping traffic in the street. The madman on the balcony thinks this cannot be, the other man cannot be there, he killed that man himself.

Dark thoughts flutter like bats about a belfry: has Grace returned to sport with him, to drive him insane? His jangled mind tries to consider what else might a vengeful man do. He will betray him somehow, Osiris is certain of that. He shouts again, tells Grace to stay where he is, he will come down to him. In shirtsleeves and bare feet, he throws himself down the grand staircase and surprises the footmen attending the doors by quitting the house in this outrageous state of undress.

The footmen watch with heightening interest as he hurls himself at the gates, flies into the street, searching up and down for they know not what, running uselessly this way and that until he tires himself out and then, returning with his shirt soaked in sweat, drags himself back up the staircase. The footmen look at each other and raise their eyebrows. They will have a banquet for the kitchen dinner-table today.

That night, he knows no rest. He dwells on his present plight where once he would have dwelled on more useful things; dupes he might exploit, money he might acquire, power that could be his. He beats on his bolster as he tells himself he has played the wrong cards. He should never have associated himself with these men who now disown him, he should not have thought to please them with silly games underground and the Devil knows, he should surely have seen the folly of allowing them to sacrifice children in a delusional quest to be cured of a disease that they had brought upon themselves.

Dawn has long broken and still he has not slept. He cannot sleep. He gets up and opens the bag he has brought with him. At the bottom of the bag, he finds what he is looking for, an opium pipe much like the one used by Henry in Paris all those years ago, whose bowl he now busily scrapes out. He locates the opium paste and affixes a small pellet of the stuff to a needle, which he holds over the flame of his bedside candle.

When the consistency of the paste is elastic, he rolls it into a ball again and places this into the bowl. He sucks hungrily on his pipe, seeking refuge from the terrors that presently riot through his troubled mind and then rests his heavy head upon a pillow and allows the kindly miasma to do its work. A moment of precious peace and then –

"Why did you kill me?"

Materialising from a vaporous blue cloud, the familiar features of the young Henry Grace. The addict sits up.

"I have not killed you," he says, "You are alive, the newspapers report it."

"I am abroad," he hears, "but I am not alive. Who could survive a dosing of laudanum such as you gave to me?"

“You were in great pain, Henry. I could not see you suffer. Would you not have done as much for me?”

“You lied to me. You stole from me. You told me I had murdered.”

“No. I did not say that.”

“They are coming for you, Osiris. We are coming for you. You will be fed to the wolves, it is all over for you. Even your caves are closed to you now.”

“No, you are quite wrong,” he says and sitting up, he tries to shake his head free of the narcotic fumes. There is a place, there always has been. He will not wait to be let down by the Prince and false promises of a palace in Venice. He will after all return to Lady Jane. That is the answer, it was there along! He will be safe with his mother, they will not follow him to France, all may yet be well if he makes haste. He will take a carriage to Newhaven, where he has heard the Antelope is presently anchored, bound for Dieppe. As Brighthelmstone rouses itself, Osiris starts to dress and to pack his bag.

The streets have not yet filled with their carriages and carts, peddlers and beggars and with care he should be be able to get away from this place without undue attention. He peers often from this window, fearing he does not know what, perhaps a body of Runners come to clap him in heavy chains. The Prince has gone up to London and thankfully, the rain-lashed cobbles outside the house are clear of their fashionable strollers and he cannot see anyone who might present a danger to him. Osiris lets go a long-pent breath. His way is clear, he has only to throw himself into a hackney carriage and he will be for Newhaven and France. He is not to know that his most feared antagonists are already below, mounting the steps to the doors of Grove House.

It is beginning to rain hard and the wind that has been whistling about fishermen's sheds and blasting through tight alleyways has picked up again. Boats bob furiously at their moorings and the sea looks an inhospitable place today. Beyond the Prince's grand residence, a foul kennel festers and spills into the street much like the one that runs down Grub Street. Mouse plucks at something on my sleeve as we stand protected from the weather by the portico of Grove House.

He has done his best to help me to dress, the old material now requiring some repairs and a hot iron if I am to closely counterfeit Henry Grace as I did at Bath, but I have wished that poor old Jamie Gretch had been there to assist. Just now, a long lock of unruly hair has descended from beneath my wig and Mouse is stuffing it back like horsehair into a chair as the footmen are opening the doors to our knock.

Stebbing has assured Mouse that news of Henry Grace's resurrection is all the talk above and below stairs and my appearance there will be more than sufficient to distract the staff while Mouse locates De'Ath in his first-floor room and somehow persuades him from the building. In light of the damning information we communicated here last evening, we have full permission to do as we will, on the strict understanding that the connection between Grove House and its remarkable guest is severed with all possible discretion. Everything depends on our quarry being successfully driven from the Royal residence, when he may be taken up and delivered to justice, but Adam has not yet returned from running an errand and I have asked Mouse how he can accomplish our aim without Adam's imposing presence?

Mouse sets straight his old wig and says, "If Adam does not return in time, I will tell De'Ath precisely what will happen when London opens its newspapers today. I will tell him from that moment on he will be fox, not hunter, and there will be a great many hounds. I will tell him that

Adam is already fetching the Runners. He will understand that the game is up. In this case, I think he will have no other recourse but to fly towards whatever bolt-hole he may have prepared."

And so, it is only Mouse and I who face the opening doors of the Prince's residence. And now that the footman holding the door peers through the eye-holes of my mask and seems to find in there not a middle-aged and pox-ravaged painter but an anxious young girl, I am sure we are undone.

My heart beats like Adam's hammer when I see that all the Prince's household has turned out for me. At Bath, with Grace's own valet to attend me, I had every confidence in my appearance. Now, I fear the suit no longer fits, that my hair has escaped again – and surely there is something mis-shaping my pocket? I feel Mouse's hand on my back, gently propelling me across the threshold. Doors are opening and faces are appearing all down the long passageways, while others have appeared atop the staircase, which we now ascend, followed by flunkeys and footmen. Several times I hear my name whispered, or rather, that of my late master.

It is all becoming too much, the noise, the attention, the fear of discovery, this suffocating mask. I am thinking I cannot keep up the pretence one moment longer when I hear the man I take to be Stebbing ordering the servants back to their work, now that they have all gawked. He steps closer to inspect my dress and meeting my eyes I have cause to wonder if he is not faintly amused? If he is, he says nothing, but politely ushers me through a pair of imposing doors and into a long chamber, a picture gallery, I see, where thankfully he bows his head and leaves me to myself.

One of several long mirrors framed in gold reflects a strange figure wearing an embroidered blue coat and a white and gold Venetian festival mask. People would have turned out to see me without all this talk of resurrection. My thoughts are with Mouse. Did he even hear me when I told him that De'Ath has a pistol? I long to quit this room and go to Mouse's aid, but I cannot. Instead, I listen to the loud ticking of the long clock at the end of the gallery and wait. I inspect my appearance in the mirror and put right my wig, which is a little aslant. I lift the mask to cool my face and replace it quickly when I hear voices behind the doors. I smile when I discover that the thing misshaping my pocket is a pair of dressmaker's scissors, left there by a thoughtless Mouse as he helped me with my garb.

The sounds of a working house permeate the empty room, the faint clatter of pans from the kitchen somewhere below, the familiar rattle of a poker in a grate, a voice raised and now, above me, the discernible fall of wooden heels on bare boards. Beyond high windows, bowing trees are being stripped of their leaves while rivulets of rainwater fill gutters and the foul kennel slops its filth upon new-laid paving-stones. I beguile the time with the paintings on the walls but my eyes pass listlessly over works by Jan Steen, Teniers the Younger, George Stubbs, Tom Gainsborough.

A self-portrait by Rembrandt is snagging my interest when above the yowling of the wind outside, I hear heavy steps descending wooden stairs. I look about me, at four high, oak-clad walls. There is no second door, no stairs, but still I hear the clack and clump of shoes, louder with every step. Before I can gather my thoughts, there is a sharp 'click' of a locksmith's catch; a concealed door has just opened in the oak panelling behind me. I turn about, expecting to see a servant bearing a chamber-pot – and my heart misses a beat.

The door swings wider, and wider still and then some wreckage of a man misses his step and all but falls into the room. The bag he clutches drops to the parquet floor as he sees me. With clothes dishevelled, hair uncombed and a madly flickering eyelid, he appears wilder even than I saw him just a day past. Blood drains from my cheeks as panic rises; my breath comes fast and hot behind my mask. It hits me with the force of a cyclone that this thing standing before me, regarding me uncertainly, has every reason to wish Henry Grace's apprentice dead.

There is no-one else in this room. If murdering me is his intention, then now would be his chance. I have already led Osiris De'Ath a merry dance up the street before this house, but I was then in a commanding position. At this moment, De'Ath has the upper hand and I do not know what he might do next. The pistol I saw in his house may lie in his bag, a knife in his pocket; the tiny black pupils reveal nothing. He might so easily slide a blade between my ribs before disappearing once again up that hidden stairway.

My strongest impulse is to run, to fly down the room to the door, haul it open and scream out for help. But then, as De'Ath takes his bearings, eyes marking windows and exits, I am afforded a moment of unexpected clarity and see him for what he really is. Before me stands the creature who dragged Georgie from her bed and fed her to human jackals, who ordered other innocents despoiled and much worse. Here stands the beast responsible for Obadiah's murder, the monster who burned alive Jamie Gretch. I cannot run.

Instead, I look into unsteady eyes, no longer fearful for myself. My courage, I concede, is bolstered by the pair of scissors my hand tightens about, deep in my pocket. If he threatens me, I will use them before he can reach for his bag and whatever it contains. At this moment he appears as much shocked to see me as I am to see him. It will be most effective, I judge, if I strike him in the eye and I am choosing which one to blind when De'Ath takes a step backwards, his pallid features falling into an unseemly, beseeching expression as he starts to speak.

"I have told you this already," he says, as if we were resuming a conversation, "why are you not satisfied?"

I cannot reply, for fear of giving the game away. Piqued by my silence, he becomes more agitated.

"Listen to me now, I will tell you all. The truth of the matter is this. I poisoned you, yes, but only to end your suffering. Damnation, man, have you not shot a sick dog? I acted out of mercy, nothing more." He awaits an answer which does not come. A new, simpering tone repels me as he adds, "We were such friends, Henry, you and I. Surely you see it was nothing other than an act of love?"

I remain silent, motionless, watching carefully his smallest move, ready to strike if I need to and at the same time, I am trying to make sense of the awful thing he is saying. De'Ath's eyes, which have been crazily wandering the walls, fix now upon a striking portrait of Lady Macbeth, painted by my late master. The lady stands upon a mossy battlement, her resolute face at odds with that of her fearful husband. Both figures are bathed in an oblique and unearthly light.

Macbeth is pressing against her breast the bloody dagger, mutely imploring her to take the instrument that has lately murdered the king. There is an ungodly gleam in her eyes as she soothes his troubled brow and on his countenance I recognise the same abject look that I saw on my master's face, that day in the painting room with De'Ath, who now looses a short, hard laugh.

"You would not have painted that without me," De'Ath says. "I created you. I showed you all that life can offer, I gave you the experience you sorely lacked. Without that, where would you be? Painting pretty pictures in the park, that is where." Sweeping a ringed hand across the great work above him, he says, "This portrait is mine before it is yours, Henry. You say I stole from you, but I took only what was mine. I earned every shilling."

The anger I have felt rising seeks a vent. Barely conscious of what I am doing, I take a step towards him. He retreats, warns me to keep away. "And this is how I am repaid," he says. "You cannot do this, Henry. These visitations must cease."

He breaks my gaze but turning his head he encounters my strange masked image reflected in one mirror and then another and searches in vain for the concealed door which a spring has now closed. I am left in no doubt. He fears me, or rather, he fears this simulacrum of Henry Grace. His madly flickering eye steals back to me and he beholds me as he might a ghost.

"In the Devil's name, what do you want with me?" His tone now is desperate, perhaps despairing as black eyes seek answers through the holes in my mask. "Are you living or dead?" he implores. "Speak, curse you!"

Clamorous rage boils, overpowers. I can do nothing but yield to a maelstrom of fury. I struggle to free unwieldy scissors from a deep pocket, with every intention of using them with lethal effect. I see not De'Ath but poor Georgie and the little girls he threw to hungry dogs in holes in the ground. He deserves every deep cut I will give him including the thrust that will kill him. I care nothing for what will become of me in consequence.

But, perhaps, higher powers do. Before I can loose my violence I become aware of loud footsteps clacking on polished floorboards. It is a moment before I realise what is happening and I struggle to let go the scissors and my deadly resolution. When I have regained some control of my senses, I break my gaze with De'Ath and recognise the butler, Stebbing, accompanied by two tall footmen. At the same moment, Mouse, now with Adam, emerges from the hidden doorway.

De'Ath is confounded. Outnumbered, he wears the look of cornered animal. This is my moment. I tear off the mask and relish the effect. Now it is De'Ath himself who wears a grotesque visage, as sudden realisation battles with rage and bafflement. Before this worm can articulate whatever imprecation is on his lips, he is firmly addressed by Mr Stebbing.

"So, here you are, sir," the butler says in measured tones, "We thought we had lost you."

De'Ath musters what little composure he can and demands to know what in Hell's name they mean by this intrusion?

"I have had my orders from the Prince, sir," Stebbing says. "His Royal Highness has requested that you be removed from these premises following his departure for London, no more to be seen at Grove House, on peril of…"

De'ath looks about with loathing, at Mouse, at Adam, at me and perhaps sees the others who have come into the room to investigate the disturbance. He makes his decision.

"Save your blasted lip, I am going, anyway," he fumes. He picks up his bag and turns towards the doors but Stebbing pulls a copy of *The Messenger* from his coat.

"A moment, if you please," he says."There is something about you in this newspaper that the Prince does not like. And in the light of what he has read, His Royal Highness feels strongly that any further association with you here or in any other place would be very much to the detriment of the Royal House. Read it, if you will."

We watch as De'Ath snatches the newspaper and scans its front page. I know what his eyes are passing over, having helped Mouse with the composition of the piece Mouse requested his friend Latham to run as prominently as he dares. This is the news which finally exposes and names Osiris De'Ath as the monstrous puppet-master pulling the strings of those who would maim or murder innocent children. Nothing in this report is leavened or omitted, the crimes committed in that hellish place underground are described in nauseating detail, the names of those who committed them are spelled out, the bomb is exploded.

I think, how like Mouse to pass his moment of glory to his friend at *The Messenger*. De'Ath reads no-more than he can stomach. Stebbing signals to the footmen, who clasp his arms like Tower warders and escort him from the room. The doors close behind them but De-Ath can be heard raving madly as he is apparently manhandled down the stairs. I must see where he goes and rush to the window where I witness De'Ath

cast unceremoniously from the doors. There is whispering in the room as he picks himself up and retrieves his bag from the bushes where the footmen have thrown it. He turns and appears to direct some awful curse towards the house, or perhaps it is to the sky and the Gods who have decreed his ignominious downfall, but whatever he cries is carried off on the wind, towards France.

The show is not ended. Walking away from the house, he struggles to make any headway against driving rain and the punishing Westerly wind, which now blows him from his feet. Footmen and housemaids have joined others crowding the windows, pointing, laughing, some jeering as if the butler, Stebbing was not present. All attention lies with events beyond the windows, where Osiris De'Ath, once never less than superbly turned-out, appears now like a soaked and sorry scarecrow.

And even now, his humiliation is not over. De'Ath slips backwards on muddy ground and attempting to regain his footing, he can do little to prevent himself from sliding towards and then toppling into the verminous kennel.

The spectators in the gallery room erupt like a bear-pit crowd and Stebbing does nothing to restore order, any possibility of his desired discretion has long since disappeared. He too watches closely as De'Ath struggles to regain his feet. His hair matted with filth, his clothing sodden and ruined, he picks up his bag and sets off again, his shambling gait taking him in a seawards direction. This degrading scene is a fitting precursor for the terrible punishment which awaits him, I am thinking, when I realise with a start that we are missing our chance. We could not arrest the man on Royal premises, but it is looking like we have lost our chance now that he is beyond them. In a panic, I look about me for Mouse and Adam to help me follow and apprehend our prey, when on the street below I spy a hulking great fellow and a dwarf in dogged pursuit.

Seventy Three

"I have news of De'Ath," Mouse says, hanging up his wet coat and fussily storing his old, leather portmanteau under a chair by the old printing press. He sits to unfasten and remove his muddy boots.

"I will say nothing of how we should already know all the news about him, had you and Adam not lost him in the lanes of Brighthelmstone," I say.

Mouse has found me helping Adam to learn his letters. The blacksmith wants to become a newspaperman just like Mouse and I have not the heart to tell him that this will take more than mere enthusiasm. He should stay with blacksmithing, I think, but he has set his heart on becoming more useful to the man he says saved him. I suppose he might make Mouse a useful printer; he is fascinated by the different leaden characters I show him and tells me that given a small furnace, he could fashion such things with ease.

Mouse waits for us to finish, restlessly pulling away at the wig he will not let me spend money on replacing. When I can see no more hairs removed I ask the question he has been waiting for.

"Well," I say, "And how was your visit to Newhaven?"

"It was worth the discomfort of the coach," Mouse says. "I visited the harbour-master's office and found there a record of a passage to France purchased in De'Ath's name."

"If he has escaped to France, then there is no justice in this world," I say. The tinder of my anger catches a spark.

"Wait, Michel, there is more. The harbour-master warned De'Ath that the *Antelope* would not be taking on passengers in conditions like that. He said to him that if the seas got up any higher, the captain would surely weigh anchor and go in search of a calmer haven. Not long after that he received a dumbfounding report of a man putting to sea in a skiff and pulling in the direction of the *Antelope*. He did not at first believe it. No-one but a suicide would go out in a small boat in weather like that."

"This was De'Ath?"

"He was convinced of it. The harbour-master took his telescope to some high point and followed the progress of the boat as the man pulled against the high seas, appearing and disappearing as he rode the great waves. As the harbour-master watched him struggle with his oars, he saw the *Antelope* preparing to sail away under a heavily-reefed mainsail. Still the little boat battled on, the man said, in extreme danger of being upturned or smashed at any moment."

"Did he gain the *Antelope?*" I ask, "I must know that."

"Rain and waves were obscuring his vision but by the time the harbour-master had secured his instrument to obtain a sharper view, the craft was being thrown about like a piece of flotsam and at this distance the harbour-master could no longer tell if the tiny skiff was still manned. He said that that anyone going into the water in such seas would have drowned, beyond a doubt."

"But if the boat had closed with the *Antelope*, might the survivor have got himself aboard the ship?"

"The harbour-master could not tell me. By this time, the embattled craft had disappeared into the lea of the ship and seeing it no more, he presumed it sunk. There is only the very smallest possibility that De'Ath was sighted by the lookout and miraculously brought aboard. I think it much more likely that he was washed into the sea. The *Antelope* has sailed, so we cannot interview its captain. Now that the storm has abated, they are searching for De'Ath's boat but nothing has yet been found. The skiff may have been washed miles down the coast or have broken up on shoals."

"What of the body?" Adam asks.

"They are peering into every inlet and all along the shoreline but as I now understand it, those lost at sea can take their time to wash up, if ever they are going to do so. No, I think we must assume that Osiris De'Ath will no longer trouble this world."

"Which is a better place for his going," Adam says.

"If we cannot pursue him, then he has cheated us again, I say. "And that is a pill I find very hard to swallow. But, tell me, what of the others?"

"Mr Robertson will see that prosecutions are brought against every man involved. It will take time, these people have good lawyers themselves but I think the truth will out if we persevere. In the meantime, their indictments will be sufficient to ruin many reputations and threaten parliamentary seats. Edward Villiers is no longer being considered as a future prime minister and Lord Goldolphin has fled abroad. I would be surprised if the government itself lasts the year."

"That is all very well," I say, "But none of this weighs evenly with what happened to those little girls."

"It certainly does not," Mouse says. "Two, possibly three, were murdered. One lost her sanity. They all lost their self-respect, their marriage prospects and their trust in men. They have been ruined. London's children must be better protected. God knows, they should fare so much better than this."

Some years have passed before I go with Mouse and my new friend to a place where London children are in fact faring very well. Mr Gilpin is pleased to welcome us into his study at the Foundling Hospital, where globes and optical instruments share floor-space with framed sketches, a violin and a display of skulls from small animals.

Once it became known – as *The Enquirer* ensured it would – that some of the Hospital's charges had been borrowed from the wards like books from a library, questions were asked in the House and the incoming government, keen to distance itself from the administration that had recently collapsed in disarray, had ordered the appointment of a new Hospital board. Mouse had been happy to use his newspaper to campaign for Mr Gilpin, on my recommendation. Mr Gilpin – who had been dismissed after his teaching methods were deemed too progressive – was more than ready to return and reform the hospital. He is a talented educator.

Mr Gilpin has given us a tour of the institution as it is under his governorship. Much of the main house remains unchanged, although everything seems cleaner, brighter. The paintings I spent so many hours deciphering still hang in the places I expect them to be and Mr Handel's instrument remains in the chapel, where it is played by the most talented of the Hospitallers. The kitchen is being scrubbed down as we pass through it but a smell of wholesome baking lingers. As I was nearing the end of my term there, food had become scarce, portions smaller and we were always hungry, so I am unsurprised when Mr Gilpin tells me that certain officers in authority had been defrauding the Hospital. In the ward where I slept, I pause by the small crib that once was my bed and say a silent prayer for the little girl who was sometimes my bedfellow.

"And tell me," Mr Gilpin says, "Are you happy?"

I glance at Cicily who sits at my side and see my smile reflected in her eyes. I nod.

Mr Gilpin, who is searching about his desk for his spectacles, seems not to have noticed. "I expect you have had suits from numerous young men," he says.

Cicily presses my hand as I tell him I have had only one proposal and that from a young, hard-working man who would be happier with someone else, which I told him as gently as I could.

"And you still paint?"

"I suppose I do, but I am finding that there is more in this world than colour," I tell him. I have in mind the sweetest cottage in Hampstead village, where children are warned to avoid the crabby spinster who inhabits it.

I ask him if the Hospital's collection still attracts the fashionable on Sundays.

"It does, although these days there is one painting they come to see above all others, as you must surely have heard. But I guess that is why you here?"

"I came to see the place which made me an artist," I say, which is only partly a lie. "But now that I am here, I should very much like to see the painting in its new home. And I should also like to show it to my good friend, Mr Malone."

As we traverse the courtyard towards the space where my painting hangs, Mouse is talking to Mr Gilpin about the care of children and of the laws that need enacting for their protection. In the past years, Mouse himself has changed little despite his newspaper having become something of a national institution. There are now many imitators run by people who see a chance to make easy money but the largest part of London's readership remains loyal to *The Enquirer*. Readers, he says, have an appetite for the truth. Despite having re-sited the newspaper in larger premises that happen to be convenient for patrons of the Cheshire Cheese tavern, Mouse still visits Molly's in the evenings, where the students of this penny university very often afford him a seat at the top of their table and where he is served with obsequious deference by the pot-man, who I believe is called Dick Clik.

If Mouse is proud of his newspaper, he is prouder still of a slim volume he has lately published, this being the poems of his friend and mentor, Obadiah Bone. It has not sold many copies and its only reviews have appeared in *The Enquirer*, but it is a project that has afforded him much quiet satisfaction.

He and my former mentor are now discussing paintings and art, and Mouse is telling Mr Gilpin of how our fancies will often find people whose faces we think we recognise in their compositions. I walk ahead, knowing what he will say next. He will tell Mr Gilpin that he recently had occasion to see a painting depicting the horrors following the recent turmoil in France and wearing the sans culottes of a revolutionary soldier who stands beneath the guillotine, he swears he sees a man he once knew as Osiris De'Ath.

Mr Gilpin leads us into a high-ceilinged room which is empty of anything except for the large work hung centrally on the wall facing visitors entering the space. High-set, north-facing windows offer an even illumination. I hear Mouse gasp as I look closely at the work I have spent these last years creating and think it worth my efforts. I have taken the bones of Henry Grace's idea and recreated his vision as seen by someone who still has hope for themselves and for others.

In my *Metropolis*, the viewer sees first the cross surmounting the dome of St Paul's Cathedral as a bird wheeling high above might see it. Then, through a swirling mass of chimney smoke, he sees the parks and the tenter grounds, the church spires and abbey towers, the market gardens and the brick and timber yards, the Inns of Court, the demesnes of great houses, the empty streets of the newly-built crescents. He sees wharfs and warehouses lining a shining river on which ferries ply and ships lie at anchor two, three and four deep and he watches as huddled traffic traverses London Bridge.

Coming closer, he sees the hospitals and the prisons, the main thoroughfares and the myriad small streets with their shops and taverns, their alleys and courts. Closer still and he might see the overbuilt and populous poor districts of Alsatia, Seven Dials, Bermondsey and St Giles in the Fields and their burgeoning burial grounds.

The places Henry Grace set afire I have rebuilt and repopulated and the tiny figures in my painting, each one of which I paint with the care and precision of a miniaturist, are no more guilty than is any man. All have their secrets but they do not inhabit a city so steeped in sin that it deserves to burn, as Henry Grace believed. For every man who lounges by a gin house door, there is another pushing a cart to market, briskly sweeping a road or laying tiles on the roof of another new dwelling. Every one of my tiny figures can choose for himself whether he takes the road to perdition or the one that leads to redemption. I am their artist, not their judge.

The End

Bibliography

Among the many books and other sources I consulted for *In Leicester Fields* were:

The Pleasures of the Imagination, John Brewer, Harper Collins
The Secret History of Georgian London, Dan Cruickshank, Windmill
A Polite and Commercial People, England 1727-1783, Paul Langford, Oxford
Eighteenth Century London Life, Rosamond Bayne-Powell, John Murray 1937
The Grand Tour, Christopher Hibbert, Thames Methuen
Hogarth, Jenny Uglow, Faber
Dr Johnson's London, Liza Picard, Phoenix Press
Prince of Pleasure, Saul David, Little, Brown and Company
What Jane Austen Ate and Charles Dickens Knew, Daniel Pool, Robinson
Dining With the Georgians, A Delicious History, Emma Kay, Amberley
The Newgate Calendar, Various, Wordsworth.
The Glory of Venice, Royal Academy of Arts, 1994

www.ingramcontent.com/pod-product-compliance
Ingram Content Group UK Ltd.
Pitfield, Milton Keynes, MK11 3LW, UK
UKHW040114240226
468345UK00007B/32

9 781919 218427